THE LA[illegible] .

She was a [illegible] en, the lords of [illegible] its against them and she won. It had [illegible] ned before and it is sure never to happen again, but she did win. She was not even of human extraction. She was cat-derived, though human in outward shape, which explains the C in front of her name. Her father's name was C'mackintosh and her name C'mell. She won her tricks against the lawful and assembled Lords of the Instrumentality.

It all happened at Earthport, greatest of buildings, smallest of cities, standing twenty-five kilometers high at the western edge of the Smaller Sea of Earth.

Ever since mankind had gone through the Rediscovery of Man, bringing back governments, money, newspapers, national languages, sickness and occasional death, there had been the problem of the underpeople—people who were not human, but merely humanly shaped from the stock of Earth animals. They could speak, sing, read, write, work, love and die; but they were not covered by human law, which gave them a legal status close to animals or robots.

It was evident that humanity, having settled all of its own basic problems, was not quite ready to let Earth animals, no matter how much they might be changed, assume a full equality with man. . . .

—*from "The Ballad of Lost C'mell"*
by Cordwainer Smith

CATS IN SPACE

And Other Places

Edited by
BILL FAWCETT

BAEN BOOKS

CATS IN SPACE

This is a work of fiction. All the characters and events portrayed in this book are fictional, and any resemblance to real people or incidents is purely coincidental.

A Baen Books Original

Baen Publishing Enterprises
P.O. Box 1403
Riverdale, N.Y. 10471

ISBN: 0-671-72118-6

Cover art by Dean Morrissey

First printing, May 1992

Distributed by
SIMON & SCHUSTER
1230 Avenue of the Americas
New York, N.Y. 10020

Printed in the United States of America

CONTENTS

Cats

Alien Cats

ACKNOWLEDGMENTS

The Game of Rat and Dragon by Cordwainer Smith, copyright © 1955 by Galaxy Publishing Corp, for *Galaxy Science Fiction.* Reprinted by permission of the author and the author's agents, Scott Meredith Literary Agency, Inc., 845 Third Avenue, New York, New York 10022.

Mouse by Fredric Brown, reprinted from *Thrilling Wonder Stories,* copyright 1949, by Standard Magazines Inc. Reprinted by permission of the author and the author's agents, Scott Meredith Literary Agency, Inc., 845 Third Avenue, New York, New York 10022.

Ship of Shadows by Fritz Leiber, copyright © 1969 Mercury Press, Inc. Reprinted by permission of the author and the author's agent, Richard Curtis Associates.

Schrödinger's Cat by Ursula Le Guin, copyright © 1974, 1982 Ursula K. Le Guin. From *Universe 5*, (Random House). Reprinted by permission of the author and the author's agent, Virginia Kidd.

Tales of a Starship's Cat by Judith R. Conly, copyright 1991 Judith R. Conly

Who's There? by Arthur C. Clarke, copyright © 1958 by United Newspapers Magazine Corporation. Reprinted by permission of the author.

Bullhead by David Drake, copyright © 1991 David Drake

Ordeal in Space by Robert A. Heinlein, copyright 1948. Reprinted by permission of the author's estate and the author's agent, Spectrum Literary Agency.

CATS

The Game of Rat and Dragon

Cordwainer Smith

1. The Table

Pinlighting is a hell of a way to earn a living. Underhill was furious as he closed the door behind himself. It didn't make much sense to wear a uniform and look like a soldier if people didn't appreciate what you did.

He sat down in his chair, laid his head back in the headrest, and pulled the helmet down over his forehead.

As he waited for the pin-set to warm up, he remembered the girl in the outer corridor. She had looked at it, then looked at him scornfully.

"Meow." That was all she had said. Yet it had cut him like a knife.

What did she think he was—a fool, a loafer, a uniformed nonentity? Didn't she know that for every half-hour of pinlighting, he got a minimum of two months' recuperation in the hospital?

By now the set was warm. He felt the squares of space around him, sensed himself at the middle of an immense grid, a cubic grid, full of nothing. Out in that nothingness, he could sense the hollow aching horror of space itself and could feel the terrible anxiety which his mind encountered whenever it met the faintest trace of inert dust.

As he relaxed, the comforting solidity of the Sun, the clockwork of the familiar planets and the moon rang in on him. Our own solar system was as charming and as simple as an ancient cuckoo clock filled with familiar ticking and with reassuring noises. The odd little moons of Mars swung around their planet like frantic mice, yet their regularity was itself an assurance that all was well. Far above the plane of the ecliptic, he could feel half a ton of dust more or less drifting outside the lanes of human travel.

Here there was nothing to fight, nothing to challenge the mind, to tear the living soul out of a body with its roots dripping in effluvium as tangible as blood.

Nothing ever moved in on the solar system. He could wear the pin-set forever and be nothing more than a sort of telepathic astronomer, a man who could feel the hot, warm protection of the sun throbbing and burning against his living mind.

Woodley came in.

"Same old ticking world," said Underhill. "Nothing to report. No wonder they didn't develop the pin-set until they began to planoform. Down here with the hot sun around us, it feels so good and so quiet. You can feel everything spinning and turning. It's nice and sharp and compact. It's sort of like sitting around home."

Woodley grunted. He was not much given to flights of fantasy.

Undeterred, Underhill went on. "It must have been pretty good to have been an ancient man. I wonder why they burned up their world with war. They didn't have to planoform. They didn't have to go out to earn their livings among the stars. They didn't have to dodge the rats or play the game. They couldn't have invented pin-lighting because they didn't have any need of it, did they, Woodley?"

Woodley grunted, "Uh-huh." Woodley was twenty-six years old and due to retire in one more year. He already had a farm picked out. He had gotten through ten years of hard work pinlighting with the best of them. He had kept his sanity by not thinking very much about his job, meeting the strains of the task whenever he had to meet them and thinking nothing more about his duties until the next emergency arose.

Woodley never made a point of getting popular among the partners. None of the partners liked him very much. Some of them even resented him. He was suspected of thinking ugly thoughts of the partners on occasion, but since none of the partners ever thought a complaint in articulate form, the other pinlighters and the chiefs of the Instrumentality left him alone.

Underhill was still full of the wonder of their job. Happily he babbled on. "What does happen to us when we planoform? Do you think it's sort of like dying? Did you ever see anybody who had his soul pulled out?"

"Pulling souls is just a way of talking about it," said Woodley. "After all these years, nobody knows whether we have souls or not."

"But I saw one once. I saw what Dogwood looked like when he came apart. There was something funny. It looked wet and sort of sticky as if it were bleeding and it went out of him—and you know what they did to Dogwood? They took him away, up in that part of the hospital where you and I never go—way up at the top part where the others are, where the others always have to go if they are alive after the rats of the up-and-out have gotten them."

Woodley sat down and lit an ancient pipe. He was burning something called tobacco in it. It was a dirty sort of habit, but it made him look very dashing and adventurous.

"Look here, youngster. You don't have to worry about that stuff. Pinlighting is getting better all the time. The partners are getting better. I've seen them pinlight two rats forty-six million miles apart in one and a half milliseconds. As long as people had to try to work the pinsets themselves, there was always the chance that with a minimum of four-hundred milliseconds for the human mind to set a pinlight, we wouldn't light the rats up fast enough to protect our planoforming ships. The partners have changed all that. Once they get going, they're faster than rats. And they always will be. I know it's not easy, letting a partner share your mind—"

"It's not easy for them, either," said Underhill.

"Don't worry about them. They're not human. Let them take care of themselves. I've seen more pinlighters go crazy from monkeying around with partners than I have ever seen caught by the rats. How many of them do you actually know of that got grabbed by rats?"

Underhill looked down at his fingers, which shone green and purple in the vivid light thrown by the tuned-in pin-set, and counted ships. The thumb for the *Andromeda*, lost with crew and passengers, the index finger and the middle finger for *Release Ships 43* and *56*, found with their pin-sets burned out and every man, woman, and child on board dead or insane. The ring finger, the little finger, and the thumb of the other hand were the first three battleships to be lost to the rats—lost as people realized that there was something out there *underneath space itself* which was alive, capricious, and malevolent.

Planoforming was sort of funny. It felt like—

Like nothing much.

Like the twinge of a mild electric shock.

Like the ache of a sore tooth bitten on for the first time.

Like a slightly painful flash of light against the eyes.

Yet in that time, a forty-thousand-ton ship lifting free above Earth disappeared somehow or other into two dimensions and appeared half a light-year or fifty light-years off.

At one moment, he would be sitting in the Fighting Room, the pin-set ready and the familiar solar system ticking around inside his head. For a second or a year (he could never tell how long it really was, subjectively), the funny little flash went through him and then he was loose in the up-and-out, the terrible open spaces between the stars, where the stars themselves felt like pimples on his telepathic mind and the planets were too far away to be sensed or read.

Somewhere in this outer space, a gruesome death awaited, death and horror of a kind which man had never encountered until he reached out for interstellar space itself. Apparently the light of the suns kept the Dragons away.

Dragons. That was what people called them. To ordinary people, there was nothing, nothing except the shiver of planoforming and the hammer blow of sudden death or the dark spastic note of lunacy descending into their minds.

But to the telepaths, they were dragons.

In the fraction of a second between the telepaths' awareness of a hostile something out in the black, hollow nothingness of space and the impact of a ferocious, ruinous psychic blow against all living things within the ship, the telepaths had sensed entities something like the dragons of ancient human lore, beasts more clever than beasts, demons more tangible than demons, hungry vortices of aliveness and hate compounded by unknown means out of the thin, tenuous matter between the stars.

It took a surviving ship to bring back the news—a ship in which, by sheer chance, a telepath had a light-beam ready, turning it out at the innocent dust so that, within the panorama of his mind, the dragon dissolved into nothing at all and the other passengers, themselves non-telepathic, went about their way not realizing that their own immediate deaths had been averted.

From then on, it was easy—almost.

Planoforming ships always carried telepaths. Telepaths had their sensitiveness enlarged to an immense range by the pin-sets, which were telepathic amplifiers adapted to the mammal mind. The pin-sets in turn were electronically geared into small dirigible light bombs. Light did it.

Light broke up the dragons, allowed the ships to reform three-dimensionally, skip, skip, skip, as they moved from star to star.

The odds suddenly moved down from a hundred to one against mankind to sixty to forty in mankind's favor.

This was not enough. The telepaths were trained to

become ultrasensitive, trained to become aware of the dragons in less than a millisecond.

But it was found that the dragons could move a million miles in just under two milliseconds and that this was not enough for the human mind to activate the light beams.

Attempts had been made to sheath the ships in light at all times.

This defense wore out.

As mankind learned about the dragons, so too, apparently, the dragons learned about mankind. Somehow they flattened their own bulk and came in on extremely flat trajectories very quickly.

Intense light was needed, light of sunlike intensity. This could be provided only by the light bombs. Pinlighting came into existence.

Pinlighting consisted of the detonation of ultra-vivid miniature photonuclear bombs, which converted a few ounces of magnesium isotope into pure visible radiance.

The odds kept coming down in mankind's favor, yet ships were being lost.

It became so bad that people didn't even want to find the ships because the rescuers knew what they would see. It was sad to bring back to Earth three hundred bodies ready for burial and two hundred or three hundred lunatics, damaged beyond repair, to be wakened, and fed, and cleaned, and put to sleep, wakened and fed again until their lives were ended.

Telepaths tried to reach into the minds of the psychotics who had been damaged by the dragons, but they found nothing there beyond vivid spouting columns of fiery terror bursting from the primordial id itself, the volcanic source of life.

Then came the partners.

Man and partner could do together what man could not do alone. Men had the intellect. Partners had the speed.

The partners rode their tiny craft, no larger than footballs, outside the spaceships. They planoformed with the ships. They rode beside them in their six-pound craft ready to attack.

The tiny ships of the partners were swift. Each carried a dozen pinlights, bombs no bigger than thimbles.

The pinlighters threw the partners—quite literally threw—by means of mind-to-firing relays directly at the dragons.

What seemed to be dragons to the human mind appeared in the form of gigantic rats in the minds of the partners.

Out in the pitiless nothingness of space, the partners' minds responded to an instinct as old as life. The partners attacked, striking with a speed faster than man's, going from attack to attack until the rats or themselves were destroyed. Almost all the time it was the partners who won.

With the safety of the interstellar skip, skip, skip of the ships, commerce increased immensely, the population of all the colonies went up, and the demand for trained partners increased.

Underhill and Woodley were a part of the third generation of pinlighters and yet, to them, it seemed as though their craft had endured forever.

Gearing space into minds by means of the pin-set, adding the partners to those minds, keying up the minds for the tension of a fight on which all depended—this was more than human synapses could stand for long. Underhill needed his two months' rest after half an hour of fighting. Woodley needed his retirement after ten years of service. They were young. They were good. But they had limitations.

So much depended on the choice of partners, so much on the sheer luck of who drew whom.

2. The Shuffle

Father Moontree and the little girl named West entered the room. They were the other two pinlighters. The human complement of the Fighting Room was now complete.

Father Moontree was a red-faced man of forty-five who had lived the peaceful life of a farmer until he reached his fortieth year. Only then, belatedly, did the authorities find he was telepathic and agree to let him late in life enter upon the career of pinlighter. He did well at it, but he was fantastically old for this kind of business.

Father Moontree looked at the glum Woodley and the musing Underhill. "How're the youngsters today? Ready for a good fight?"

"Father always wants a fight," giggled the little girl named West. She was such a little little girl. Her giggle was high and childish. She looked like the last person in the world one would expect to find in the rough, sharp dueling of pinlighting.

Underhill had been amused one time when he found one of the most sluggish of the partners coming away happy from contact with the mind of the girl named West.

Usually the partners didn't care much about the human minds with which they were paired for the journey. The partners seemed to take the attitude that human minds were complex and fouled up beyond belief, anyhow. No partner ever questioned the superiority of the human mind, though very few of the partners were much impressed by that superiority.

The partners liked people. They were willing to fight with them. They were even willing to die for them. But when a partner liked an individual the way, for example, that Captain Wow or the Lady May liked Underhill, the liking had nothing to do with intellect. It was a matter of temperament, of feel.

Underhill knew perfectly well that Captain Wow regarded his, Underhill's, brains as silly. What Captain Wow liked was Underhill's friendly emotional structure, the cheerfulness and glint of wicked amusement that shot through Underhill's unconscious thought patterns, and the gaiety with which Underhill faced danger. The words, the history books, the ideas, the science—Underhill could sense all that in his own mind, reflected back from Captain Wow's mind, as so much rubbish.

Miss West looked at Underhill. "I bet you've put stickum on the stones."

"I did not!"

Underhill felt his ears grow red with embarrassment. During his novitiate, he had tried to cheat in the lottery because he got particularly fond of a special partner, a lovely young mother named Murr. It was so much easier to operate with Murr and she was so affectionate toward him that he forgot pinlighting was hard work and that he was not instructed to have a good time with his partner. They were both designed and prepared to go into deadly battle together.

One cheating had been enough. They had found him out and he had been laughed at for years.

Father Moontree picked up the imitation-leather cup and shook the stone dice which assigned them their partners for the trip. By senior rights he took first draw.

He grimaced. He had drawn a greedy old character, a tough old male whose mind was full of slobbering thoughts of food, veritable oceans full of half-spoiled fish. Father Moontree had once said that he burped cod liver oil for weeks after drawing that particular glutton, so strongly had the telepathic image of fish impressed itself upon his mind. Yet the glutton was a glutton for danger as well as for fish. He had killed sixty-three dragons, more than any other partner in the service, and was quite literally worth his weight in gold.

The little girl West came next. She drew Captain Wow. When she saw who it was, she smiled.

"I *like* him," she said. "He's such fun to fight with. He feels so nice and cuddly in my mind."

"Cuddly, hell," said Woodley. "I've been in his mind, too. It's the most leering mind in this ship, bar none."

"Nasty man," said the little girl. She said it declaratively, without reproach.

Underhill, looking at her, shivered.

He didn't see how she could take Captain Wow so calmly. Captain Wow's mind *did* leer. When Captain

Wow got excited in the middle of a battle, confused images of dragons, deadly rats, luscious beds, the smell of fish, and the shock of space all scrambled together in his mind as he and Captain Wow, their consciousnesses linked together through the pin-set, became a fantastic composite of human being and Persian cat.

That's the trouble with working with cats, thought Underhill. It's a pity that nothing else anywhere will serve as partner. Cats were all right once you got in touch with them telepathically. They were smart enough to meet the needs of flight, but their motives and desires were certainly different from those of humans.

They were companionable enough as long as you thought tangible images at them, but their minds just closed up and went to sleep when you recited Shakespeare or Colegrove, or if you tried to tell them what space was.

It was sort of funny realizing that the partners who were so grim and mature out here in space were the same cute little animals that people had used as pets for thousands of years back on Earth. He had embarrassed himself more than once while on the ground saluting perfectly ordinary non-telepathic cats because he had forgotten for the moment that they were not partners.

He picked up the cup and shook out his stone dice.

He was lucky—he drew the Lady May.

The Lady May was the most thoughtful partner he had ever met. In her, the finely bred pedigree mind of a Persian cat had reached one of its highest peaks of development. She was more complex than any human woman, but the complexity was all one of emotions, memory, hope, and discriminated experience—experience sorted through without benefit of words.

When he had first come into contact with her mind, he was astonished at its clarity. With her he remembered her kittenhood. He remembered every mating experience she had ever had. He saw in a half-recognizable gallery all the other pinlighters with whom she had been paired for the fight. And he saw himself radiant, cheerful, and desirable.

He even thought he caught the edge of a longing—

A very flattering and yearning thought: *What a pity he is not a cat.*

Woodley picked up the last stone. He drew what he deserved—a sullen, scarred old tomcat with none of the verve of Captain Wow. Woodley's partner was the most animal of all the cats on the ship, a low, brutish type with a dull mind. Even telepathy had not refined his character. His ears were half chewed off from the first fights in which he had engaged. He was a serviceable fighter, nothing more.

Woodley grunted.

Underhill glanced at him oddly. Didn't Woodley ever do anything but grunt?

Father Moontree looked at the other three. "You might as well get your partners now. I'll let the Go-captain know we're ready to go into the up-and-out."

3. The Deal

Underhill spun the combination lock on the Lady May's cage. He woke her gently and took her into his arms. She humped her back luxuriously, stretched her claws, started to purr, thought better of it, and licked him on the wrist instead. He did not have the pin-set on, so their minds were closed to each other, but in the angle of her mustache and in the movement of her ears, he caught some sense of the gratification she experienced in finding him as her partner.

He talked to her in human speech, even though speech meant nothing to a cat when the pin-set was not on.

"It's a damn shame, sending a sweet little thing like you whirling around in the coldness of nothing to hunt for rats that are bigger and deadlier than all of us put together. You didn't ask for this kind of fight, did you?"

For answer, she licked his hand, purred, tickled his cheek with her long fluffy tail, turned around and faced him, golden eyes shining.

For a moment, they stared at each other, man squatting, cat standing erect on her hind legs, front claws digging into his knee. Human eyes and cat eyes looked across an immensity which no words could meet, but which affection spanned in a single glance.

"Time to get in," he said.

She walked docilely to her spheroid carrier. She climbed in. He saw to it that her miniature pin-set rested firmly and comfortably against the base of her brain. He made sure that her claws were padded so that she could not tear herself in the excitement of battle.

Softly he said to her, "Ready?"

For answer, she preened her back as much as her harness would permit and purred softly within the confines of the frame that held her.

He slapped down the lid and watched the sealant ooze around the seam. For a few hours, she was welded into her projectile until a workman with a short cutting arc would remove her after she had done her duty.

He picked up the entire projectile and slipped it into the ejection tube. He closed the door of the tube, spun the lock, seated himself in his chair, and put his own pin-set on.

Once again he flung the switch.

He sat in a small room, *small, small, warm, warm,* the bodies of the other three people moving close around him, the tangible light in the ceiling bright and heavy against his closed eyelids.

As the pin-set warmed, the room fell away. The other people ceased to be people and became small glowing heaps of fire, embers, dark red fire, with the consciousness of life burning like old red coals in a country fireplace.

As the pin-set warmed a little more, he felt Earth just below him, felt the ship slipping away, felt the turning Moon as it swung on the far side of the world, felt the planets and the hot, clear goodness of the sun which kept the dragons so far from mankind's native ground.

Finally, he reached complete awareness.

He was telepathically alive to a range of millions of miles. He felt the dust which he had noticed earlier high above the ecliptic. With a thrill of warmth and tenderness, he felt the consciousness of the Lady May pouring over into his own. Her consciousness was as gentle and clear and yet sharp to the taste of his mind as if it were scented oil. It felt relaxing and reassuring. He could sense her welcome of him. It was scarcely a thought, just a raw emotion of greeting.

At last they were one again.

In a tiny remote corner of his mind, as tiny as the smallest toy he had ever seen in his childhood, he was still aware of the room and the ship, and of Father Moontree picking up a telephone and speaking to a Go-captain in charge of the ship.

His telepathic mind caught the idea long before his ears could frame the words. The actual sound followed the idea the way that thunder on an ocean beach follows the lightning inward from far out over the seas.

"The Fighting Room is ready. Clear to planoform, sir."

4. The Play

Underhill was always a little exasperated the way that Lady May experienced things before he did.

He was braced for the quick vinegar thrill of planoforming, but he caught her report of it before his own nerves could register what happened.

Earth had fallen so far away that he groped for several milliseconds before he found the Sun in the upper rear right-hand corner of his telepathic mind.

That was a good jump, he thought. *This way we'll get there in four or five skips.*

A few hundred miles outside the ship, the Lady May thought back at him. "O warm, O generous, O gigantic man! O brave, O friendly, O tender and huge partner! O wonderful with you, with you so good, good, good, warm, warm, now to fight, now to go, good with you . . ."

He knew that she was not thinking words, that his mind took the clear amiable babble of her cat intellect and translated it into images which his own thinking could record and understand.

Neither one of them was absorbed in the game of

mutual greetings. He reached out far beyond her range of perception to see if there was anything near the ship. It was funny how it was possible to do two things at once. He could scan space with his pin-set mind and yet at the same time catch a vagrant thought of hers, a lovely, affectionate thought about a son who had had a golden face and a chest covered with soft, incredibly downy white fur.

While he was still searching, he caught the warning from her.

We jump again!

And so they had. The ship had moved to a second planoform. The stars were different. The sun was immeasurably far behind. Even the nearest stars were barely in contact. This was good dragon country, this open, nasty, hollow kind of space. He reached farther, faster, sensing and looking for danger, ready to fling the Lady May at danger wherever he found it.

Terror blazed up in his mind, so sharp, so clear, that it came through as a physical wrench.

The little girl named West had found something—something immense, long, black, sharp, greedy, horrific. She flung Captain Wow at it.

Underhill tried to keep his own mind clear. "Watch out!" he shouted telepathically at the others, trying to move the Lady May around.

At one corner of the battle, he felt the lustful rage of Captain Wow as the big Persian tomcat detonated light while he approached the streak of dust which threatened the ship and the people within.

The light scored near misses.

The dust flattened itself, changing from the shape of a sting ray into the shape of a spear.

Not three milliseconds had elapsed.

Father Moontree was talking human words and was saying in a voice that moved like cold molasses out of a heavy jar, "C-a-p-t-a-i-n." Underhill knew that the sentence was going to be "Captain, move fast!"

The battle would be fought and finished before Father Moontree got through talking.

Now, fractions of a millisecond later, the Lady May was directly in line.

Here was where the skill and speed of the partners came in. She could react faster than he. She could see the threat as an immense rat coming directly at her.

She could fire the light-bombs with a discrimination which he might miss.

He was connected with her mind, but he could not follow it.

His consciousness absorbed the tearing wound inflicted by the alien enemy. It was like no wound on Earth—raw, crazy pain which started like a burn at his navel. He began to writhe in his chair.

Actually he had not yet had time to move a muscle when the Lady May struck back at their enemy.

Five evenly spaced photonuclear bombs blazed out across a hundred-thousand miles.

The pain in his mind and body vanished.

He felt a moment of fierce, terrible, feral elation running through the mind of the Lady May as she finished her kill. It was always disappointing to the cats to find out that their enemies disappeared at the moment of destruction.

Then he felt her hurt, the pain and the fear that swept over both of them as the battle, quicker than the movement of an eyelid, had come and gone. In the same instant there came the sharp and acid twinge of planoform.

Once more the ship went skip.

He could hear Woodley thinking at him. "You don't have to bother much. This old son-of-a-gun and I will take over for a while."

Twice again the twinge, the skip.

He had no idea where he was until the lights of the Caledonia space port shone below.

With a weariness that lay almost beyond the limits of thought, he threw his mind back into rapport with the pin-set, fixing the Lady May's projectile gently and neatly in its launching tube.

She was half dead with fatigue, but he could feel the beat of her heart, could listen to her panting, and he grasped the grateful edge of a "Thanks" reaching from her mind to his.

5. The Score

They put him in the hospital at Caledonia.

The doctor was friendly but firm. "You actually got touched by that dragon. That's as close a shave as I've ever seen. It's all so quick that it'll be a long time before we know what happened scientifically, but I suppose you'd be ready for the insane asylum now if the contact had lasted several tenths of a millisecond longer. What kind of cat did you have out in front of you?"

Underhill felt the words coming out of him slowly. Words were such a lot of trouble compared with the speed and the joy of thinking, fast and sharp and clear, mind to mind! But words were all that could reach ordinary people like this doctor.

His mouth moved heavily as he articulated words. "Don't call our partners cats. The right thing to call them is partners. They fight for us in a team. You ought to know we call them partners, not cats. How is mine?"

"I don't know," said the doctor contritely. "We'll find out for you. Meanwhile, old man, you take it easy. There's nothing but rest than can help you. Can you make yourself sleep, or would you like us to give you some kind of sedative?"

"I can sleep," said Underhill. "I just want to know about the Lady May."

The nurse joined in. She was a little antagonistic. "Don't you want to know about the other people?"

"They're okay," said Underhill. "I knew that before I came in here."

He stretched his arms and sighed and grinned at them. He could see they were relaxing and were beginning to treat him as a person instead of a patient.

"I'm all right," he said. "Just let me know when I can go see my partner."

A new thought struck him. He looked wildly at the

doctor. "They didn't send her off with the ship, did they?"

"I'll find out right away," said the doctor. He gave Underhill a reassuring squeeze of the shoulder and left the room.

The nurse took a napkin off a goblet of chilled fruit juice.

Underhill tried to smile at her. There seemed to be something wrong with the girl. He wished she would go away. First she had started to be friendly and now she was distant again. *It's a nuisance being telepathic,* he thought. *You keep trying to reach even when you are not making contact.*

Suddenly she swung around on him.

"You pinlighters! You and your damn cats!"

Just as she stamped out, he burst into her mind. He saw himself a radiant hero, clad in his smooth suede uniform, the pin-set crown shining like ancient royal jewels around his head. He saw his own face, handsome and masculine, shining out of her mind. He saw himself very far away and he saw himself as she hated him.

She hated him in the secrecy of her own mind. She hated him because he was—she thought—proud and strange and rich, better and more beautiful than people like her.

He cut off the sight of her mind and, as he buried his face in the pillow, he caught an image of the Lady May.

"She *is* a cat," he thought. "That's all she is—a *cat!*"

But that was not how his mind saw her—quick beyond all dreams of speed, sharp, clever, unbelievably graceful, beautiful, wordless and undemanding.

Where would he ever find a woman who could compare with her?

Mouse

Fredric Brown

Bill Wheeler was, as it happened, looking out of the window of his bachelor apartment on the fifth floor on the corner of 83rd Street and Central Park West when the spaceship from Somewhere landed.

It floated gently down out of the sky and came to rest in Central Park on the open grass between the Simon Bolivar Monument and the walk, barely a hundred yards from Bill Wheeler's window.

Bill Wheeler's hand paused in stroking the soft fur of the Siamese cat lying on the windowsill and he said wonderingly, "What's that, Beautiful?" but the Siamese cat didn't answer. She stopped purring, though, when Bill stopped stroking her. She must have felt something different in Bill—possibly from the sudden rigidness in his fingers or possibly because cats are prescient and feel changes of mood. Anyway she rolled over on her back and said "Miaouw," quite plaintively. But Bill, for once, didn't answer her. He was too engrossed in the incredible thing across the street in the park.

It was cigar-shaped, about seven feet long and two feet in diameter at the thickest point. As far as size was concerned, it might have been a large toy model dirigible, but it never occurred to Bill—even at his first glimpse of it when it was about fifty feet in the air, just opposite his window—that it might be a toy or a model. There was something about it, even at the most casual look, that said *alien*. You couldn't put your finger on what it was. Anyway, alien or terrestrial, it had no visible means of support. No wings, propellers, rocket tubes or anything else—and it was made of metal and obviously heavier than air.

But it floated down like a feather to a point just about a foot above the grass. It stopped there and suddenly, out of one end of it (both ends were so nearly alike that you couldn't say it was the front or back) came a flash of fire that was almost blinding. There was a hissing sound with the flash and the cat under Bill Wheeler's hand turned over and was on her feet in a single lithe movement, looking out of the window. She spat once, softly, and the hairs on her back and the back of her neck stood straight up, as did her tail, which was now a full two inches thick.

Bill didn't touch her; if you know cats you don't when they're like that. But he said, "Quiet, Beautiful. It's all right. It's only a spaceship from Mars, to conquer Earth. It isn't a mouse."

He was right on the first count, in a way. He was wrong on the second, in a way. But let's not get ahead of ourselves like that.

After the single blast from its exhaust tube or whatever it was the spaceship dropped the last twelve inches and lay inert on the grass. It didn't move. There was now a fan-shaped area of blackened earth radiating from one end of it, for a distance of about thirty feet.

And then nothing happened except that people came running from several directions. Cops came running, too, three of them, and kept people from going too close to the alien object. Too close, according to the cops' idea, seemed to be closer than about ten feet. Which, Bill Wheeler thought, was silly. If the thing was going to explode or anything, it would probably kill everyone for blocks around.

But it didn't explode. It just lay there, and nothing happened. Nothing except that flash that had startled both Bill and the cat. And the cat looked bored now, and lay back down on the windowsill, her hackles down.

Bill stroked her sleek fawn-colored fur again, absent-mindedly. He said, "This is a day, Beautiful. That thing out there is from *outside*, or I'm a spider's nephew. I'm going down and take a look at it."

He took the elevator down. He got as far as the front door, tried to open it, and couldn't. All he could see through the glass was the backs of people, jammed tight against the door. Standing on tiptoes and stretching his neck to see over the nearest ones, he could see a solid phalanx of heads stretching from here to there.

He got back in the elevator. The operator said, "Sounds like excitement out front. Parade going by or something?"

"Something," Bill said. "Spaceship just landed in Central Park, from Mars or somewhere. You hear the welcoming committee out there."

"The hell," said the operator. "What's it doing?"

"Nothing."

The operator grinned. "You're a great kidder, Mr. Wheeler. How's that cat you got?"

"Fine," said Bill. "How's yours?"

"Getting crankier. Threw a book at me when I got home last night with a few under my belt and lectured me half the night because I'd spent three and a half bucks. You got the best kind."

"I think so," Bill said.

By the time he got back to the window, there was really a crowd down there. Central Park West was solid with people for half a block each way and the park was solid with them for a long way back. The only open area was a circle around the spaceship, now expanded to about twenty feet in radius, and with a lot of cops keeping it open instead of only three.

Bill Wheeler gently moved the Siamese over to one side of the windowsill and sat down. He said, "We got a box seat, Beautiful. I should have had more sense than to go down there."

The cops below were having a tough time. But reinforcements were coming, truckloads of them. They fought their way into the circle and then helped enlarge it. Somebody had obviously decided that the larger that circle was the fewer people were going to be killed. A few khaki uniforms had infiltrated the circle, too.

"Brass," Bill told the cat. "High brass. I can't make out insignia from here, but that one boy's at least a three-star; you can tell by the way he walks."

They got the circle pushed back to the sidewalk, finally. There was a lot of brass inside by then. And half a dozen men, some in uniform, some not, were starting, very carefully, to work on the ship. Photographs first, and then measurements, and then one man with a big suitcase of paraphernalia was carefully scratching at the metal and making tests of some kind.

"A metallurgist, Beautiful," Bill Wheeler explained to the Siamese, who wasn't watching at all. "And I'll bet you ten pounds of liver to one miaouw he finds that's an alloy that's brand new to him. And that it's got some stuff in it he can't identify.

"You really ought to be looking out, Beautiful, instead of lying there like a dope. This is a *day*, Beautiful. This may be the beginning of the end—or of something new. I wish they'd hurry up and get it open."

Army trucks were coming into the circle now. Half a dozen big planes were circling overhead, making a lot of noise. Bill looked up at them quizzically.

"Bombers, I'll bet, with pay loads. Don't know what they have in mind unless to bomb the park, people and all, if little green men come out of that thing with ray guns and start killing everybody. Then the bombers could finish off whoever's left."

But no little green men came out of the cylinder. The men working on it couldn't, apparently, find an opening in it. They'd rolled it over now and exposed the under side, but the under side was the same as the top. For all they could tell, the under side *was* the top.

And then Bill Wheeler swore. The army trucks were being unloaded, and sections of a big tent were coming out of them, and men in khaki were driving stakes and unrolling canvas.

"They *would* do something like that, Beautiful," Bill complained bitterly. "Be bad enough if they hauled it off, but to leave it there to work on and still to block off our view—"

The tent went up. Bill Wheeler watched the top of the tent, but nothing happened to the top of the tent and whatever went on inside he couldn't see. Trucks came and went, high brass and civvies came and went.

And after a while the phone rang. Bill gave a last affectionate rumple to the cat's fur and went to answer it.

"Bill Wheeler?" the receiver asked. "This is General Kelly speaking. Your name has been given to me as a competent research biologist. Tops in your field. Is that correct?"

"Well," Bill said. "I'm a research biologist. It would be hardly modest for me to say I'm tops in my field. What's up?"

"A spaceship has just landed in Central Park."

"You don't say," said Bill.

"I'm calling from the field of operations; we've run phones in here, and we're gathering specialists. We would like you and some other biologists to examine something that was found inside the—uh—spaceship. Grimm of Harvard was in town and will be here and Winslow of New York University is already here. It's opposite Eighty-third Street. How long would it take you to get here?"

"About ten seconds, if I had a parachute. I've been watching you out of my window." He gave the address and the apartment number. "If you can spare a couple of strong boys in imposing uniforms to get me through the crowd, it'll be quicker than if I try it myself. Okay?"

"Right. Send 'em right over. Sit tight."

"Good," said Bill. "*What* did you find inside the cylinder?"

There was a second's hesitation. Then the voice said, "Wait till you get here."

"I've got instruments," Bill said. "Dissecting equipment. Chemicals. Reagents. I want to know what to bring. Is it a little green man?"

"No," said the voice. After a second's hesitation again, it said, "It seems to be a mouse. A dead mouse."

"Thanks," said Bill. He put down the receiver and walked back to the window. He looked at the Siamese cat accusingly. "Beautiful," he demanded, "was somebody ribbing me, or—"

There was a puzzled frown on his face as he watched the scene across the street. Two policemen came hurrying out of the tent and headed directly for the entrance of his apartment building. They began to work their way through the crowd.

"Fan me with a blowtorch, Beautiful," Bill said. "It's the McCoy." He went to the closet and grabbed a valise, hurried to a cabinet and began to stuff instruments and bottles into the valise. He was ready by the time there was a knock on the door.

He said, "Hold the fort, Beautiful. Got to see a man about a mouse." He joined the policemen waiting outside his door and was escorted through the crowd and into the circle of the elect and into the tent.

There was a crowd around the spot where the cylinder lay. Bill peered over shoulders and saw that the cylinder was neatly split in half. The inside was hollow and padded with something that looked like fine leather, but softer. A man kneeling at one end of it was talking.

"—not a trace of any activating mechanism, any mechanism at *all*, in fact. Not a wire, not a grain or a drop of any fuel. Just a hollow cylinder, padded inside. Gentlemen, it *couldn't* have traveled by its own power in any conceivable way. But it came here, and from outside. Gravesend says the material is definitely extra-terrestrial. Gentlemen, I'm stumped."

Another voice said, "I've an idea, Major." It was the voice of the man over whose shoulder Bill Wheeler was leaning and Bill recognized the voice and the man with a start. It was the President of the United States. Bill quit leaning on him.

"I'm no scientist," the President said. "And this is just a possibility. Remember the one blast, out of that single exhaust hole? That might have been the destruction, the dissipation of whatever the mechanism or the propellant was. Whoever, whatever, sent or guided this contraption might not have wanted us to find out what made it run. It was constructed, in that case, so that, upon landing, the mechanism destroyed itself utterly. Colonel Roberts, you examined that scorched area of ground. Anything that might bear out that theory?"

"Definitely, sir," said another voice. "Traces of metal and silica and some carbon, as though it had been vaporized by terrific heat and then condensed and uniformly spread. You can't find a chunk of it to pick up, but the instruments indicate it. Another thing—"

Bill was conscious of someone speaking to him. "You're Bill Wheeler, aren't you?"

Bill turned. "Professor Winslow!" he said. "I've seen your picture, sir, and I've read your papers in the Journal. I'm proud to meet you and to—"

"Cut the malarkey," said Professor Winslow, "and take a gander at this." He grabbed Bill Wheeler by the arm and led him to a table in one corner of the tent.

"Looks for all the world like a dead mouse," he said, but it isn't. Not quite. I haven't cut it yet; waited for you and Grimm. But I've taken temperature tests and had hairs under the mike and studied musculature. It's—well, look for yourself."

Bill Wheeler looked. It looked like a mouse all right, a very small mouse, until you looked closely. Then you saw little differences, if you were a biologist.

Grimm got there and—delicately, reverently—they cut in. The differences stopped being little ones and became big ones. The bones didn't seem to be made of bone, for one thing, and they were bright yellow instead of white. The digestive system wasn't too far off the beam, and there was a circulatory system and a white milky fluid in it, but there wasn't any heart. There were, instead, nodes at regular intervals along the larger tubes.

"Way stations," Grimm said. "No central pump. You might call it a lot of little hearts instead of one big one. Efficient, I'd say. Creature built like this couldn't have heart trouble. Here, let me put some of that white fluid on a slide."

Someone was leaning over Bill's shoulder, putting uncomfortable weight on him. He turned his head to tell the man to get the hell away and saw it was the President of the United States. "Out of this world?" the President asked quietly.

"And how," said Bill. A second later he added, "Sir," and the President chuckled. He asked, "Would you say it's been dead long or that it died about the time of arrival?"

Winslow answered that one. "It's purely a guess, Mr. President, because we don't know the chemical make-up of the thing, or what its normal temperature is. But a rectal thermometer reading twenty minutes ago, when I got here, was ninety-five three and one minute ago it was ninety point six. At that rate of heat loss, it couldn't have been dead long."

"Would you say it was an intelligent creature?"

"I wouldn't say for sure, Sir. It's too alien. But I'd guess—definitely no. No more so than its terrestrial counterpart, a mouse. Brain size and convolutions are quite similar."

"You don't think it could, conceivably, have designed that ship?"

"I'd bet a million to one against it, Sir."

It had been mid-afternoon when the spaceship had landed; it was almost midnight when Bill Wheeler started home. Not from across the street, but from the lab at New York U., where the dissection and microscopic examinations had continued.

He walked home in a daze, but he remembered guiltily that the Siamese hadn't been fed, and hurried as much as he could for the last block.

She looked at him reproachfully and said "Miaouw,

miaouw, miaouw, miaouw—" so fast he couldn't get a word in edgewise until she was eating some liver out of the icebox.

"Sorry, Beautiful," he said then. "Sorry, too, I couldn't bring you that mouse, but they wouldn't have let me if I'd asked, and I didn't ask because it would probably have given you indigestion."

He was still so excited that he couldn't sleep that night. When it got early enough he hurried out for the morning papers to see if there had been any new discoveries or developments.

There hadn't been. There was less in the papers than he knew already. But it was a big story and the papers played it big.

He spent most of three days at the New York U. lab, helping with further tests and examinations until there just weren't any new ones to try and darn little left to try them on. Then the government took over what was left and Bill Wheeler was on the outside again.

For three more days he stayed home, tuned in on all news reports on the radio and video and subscribed to every newspaper published in English in New York City. But the story gradually died down. Nothing further happened; no further discoveries were made and if any new ideas developed, they weren't given out for public consumption.

It was on the sixth day that an even bigger story broke—the assassination of the President of the United States. People forgot the spaceship.

Two days later the prime minister of Great Britain was killed by a Spaniard and the day after that a minor employe of the Politburo in Moscow ran amuck and shot a very important official.

A lot of windows broke in New York City the next day when a goodly portion of a county in Pennsylvania went up fast and came down slowly. No one within several hundred miles needed to be told that there was—or had been—a dump of A-bombs there. It was in sparsely populated country and not many people were killed, only a few thousand.

That was the afternoon, too, that the president of the stock exchange cut his throat and the crash started. Nobody paid too much attention to the riot at Lake Success the next day because of the unidentified submarine fleet that suddenly sank practically all the shipping in New Orleans harbor.

It was the evening of that day that Bill Wheeler was pacing up and down the front room of his apartment. Occasionally he stopped at the window to pet the Siamese named Beautiful and to look out across Central Park, bright under lights and cordoned off by armed sentries, where they were pouring concrete for the anti-aircraft gun emplacements.

He looked haggard.

He said, "Beautiful, we saw the start of it, right from this window. Maybe I'm crazy, but I still think that spaceship started it. God knows how. Maybe I should have fed you that mouse. Things couldn't have gone to pot so *suddenly* without help from somebody or something."

He shook his head slowly. "Let's dope it out, Beautiful. Let's say something came in on that ship besides a dead mouse. What could it have been? What could it have done and be doing?

"Let's say that the mouse was a laboratory animal, a guinea pig. It was sent in the ship and it survived the journey but died when it got here. Why? I've got a screwy hunch, Beautiful."

He sat down in a chair and leaned back, staring up at the ceiling. He said, "Suppose the superior intelligence—from Somewhere—that made that ship came in with it. Suppose it wasn't the mouse—let's call it a mouse. Then, since the mouse was the only physical thing in the spaceship, the being, the invader, wasn't physical. It was an entity that could live apart from whatever body it had back where it came from. But let's say it could live in *any* body and it left its own in a safe place back home and rode here in one that was expendable, that it could abandon on arrival. That would explain the mouse and the fact that it died at the time the ship landed.

"Then the *being*, at that instant, just jumped into the body of someone here—probably one of the first people to run toward the ship when it landed. It's living in somebody's body—in a hotel on Broadway or a flophouse on the Bowery or anywhere—pretending to be a human being. That make sense, Beautiful?"

He got up and started to pace again.

"And having the ability to control other minds, it sets about to make the world—the Earth—safe for Martians or Venusians or whatever they are. It sees—after a few days of study—that the world is on the brink of destroying itself and needs only a push. So it could give that push.

"It could get inside a nut and make him assassinate the President, and get caught at it. It could make a Russian shoot his Number 1. It could make a Spaniard shoot the prime minister of England. It could start a bloody riot in the U.N., and make an army man, there to guard it, explode an A-bomb dump. It could—hell, Beautiful, it could push this world into a final war within a week. It practically *has* done it."

He walked over to the window and stroked the cat's sleek fur while he frowned down at the gun emplacements going up under the bright floodlights.

"And he's done it and even if my guess is right I couldn't stop him because I couldn't find him. And nobody would believe me, now. He'll make the world safe for Martians. When the war is over, a lot of little ships like that—or big ones—can land here and take over what's left ten times as easy as they could now."

He lighted a cigarette with hands that shook a little. He said, "The more I think of it, the more—"

He sat down in the chair again. He said, "Beautiful, I've got to *try*. Screwy as that idea is, I've got to give it to the authorities, whether they believe it or not. That Major I met was an intelligent guy. So is General Keely. I—"

He started to walk to the phone and then sat down again. "I'll call both of them, but let's work it out just a little finer first. See if I can make any intelligent suggestions how they could go about finding the—the *being*—"

He groaned. "Beautiful, it's impossible. It wouldn't even have to be a human being. It could be an animal, anything. It could be you. He'd probably take over whatever nearby type of mind was nearest his own. If he was remotely feline, you'd have been the nearest cat."

He sat up and stared at her. He said, "I'm going crazy, Beautiful. I'm remembering how you jumped and twisted just after that spaceship blew up its mechanism and went inert. And, listen, Beautiful, you've been sleeping twice as much as usual lately. Has your mind been out—

"Say, *that* would be why I couldn't wake you up yesterday to feed you. Beautiful, cats always wake up easily. *Cats* do."

Looking dazed, Bill Wheeler got up out of the chair. He said, "Cat, *am* I crazy, or—"

The Siamese cat looked at him languidly through sleepy eyes. Distinctly it said, "*Forget it.*"

And halfway between sitting and rising, Bill Wheeler looked even more dazed for a second. He shook his head as though to clear it.

He said, "What was I talking about, Beautiful? I'm getting punchy from not enough sleep."

He walked over to the window and stared out, gloomily, rubbing the cat's fur until it purred.

He said, "Hungry, Beautiful? Want some liver?"

The cat jumped down from the windowsill and rubbed itself against his leg affectionately.

It said, "Miaouw."

Ship of Shadows

Fritz Leiber

"Issiot! Ffool! Lushsh!" hissed the cat and bit Spar somewhere.

The fourfold sting balanced the gut-wretchedness of his looming hangover, so that Spar's mind floated as free as his body in the blackness of Windrush, in which shone only a couple of running lights dim as churning dreamglow and infinitely distant as the Bridge or the Stern.

The vision came of a ship with all sails set creaming through blue, wind-ruffled sea against a blue sky. The last two nouns were not obscene now. He could hear the whistle of the salty wind through shrouds and stays, its drumming against the taut sails, and the creak of the three masts and all the rest of the ship's wood.

What was wood? From somewhere came the answer: plastic alive-o.

And what force flattened the water and kept it from breaking up into great globules and the ship from spinning away, keel over masts, in the wind?

Instead of being blurred and rounded like reality, the vision was sharp-edged and bright—the sort Spar never told, for fear of being accused of second sight and so of witchcraft.

Windrush was a ship too, was often called the Ship. But it was a strange sort of ship, in which the sailors lived forever in the shrouds inside cabins of all shapes made of translucent sails welded together.

The only other things the two ships shared were the wind and the unending creaking. As the vision faded, Spar began to hear the winds of Windrush softly moaning through the long passageways, while he felt the creaking in the vibrant shroud to which he was clipped wrist and ankle to keep him from floating around in the Bat Rack.

Sleepday's dreams had begun good, with Spar having Crown's three girls at once. But Sleepday night he had been half-waked by the distant grinding of Hold Three's big chewer. Then werewolves and vampires had attacked him, solid shadows diving in from all six sides, while witches and their families tittered in the black shadowy background. Somehow he had been protected by the cat, familiar of a slim witch whose bared teeth had been an ivory blur in the larger silver blur of her wild hair. Spar pressed his rubbery gums together. The cat had been the last of the supernatural creatures to fade. Then had come the beautiful vision of the ship.

His hangover hit him suddenly and mercilessly. Sweat shook off him until he must be surrounded by a cloud of it. Without warning his gut reversed. His free hand found a floating waste tube in time to press its small trumpet to his face. He could hear his acrid vomit gurgling away, urged by a light suction.

His gut reversed again, quick as the flap of a safety hatch when a gale blows up in the corridors. He thrust the waste tube inside the leg of his short, loose slopsuit and caught the dark stuff, almost as watery and quite as explosive as his vomit. Then he had the burning urge to make water.

Afterward, feeling blessedly weak, Spar curled up in the equally blessed dark and prepared to snooze until Keeper woke him.

"Ssot!" hissed the cat. "Sleep no more! Ssee! Ssee shsharply!"

In his left shoulder, through the worn fabric of his

slopsuit, Spar could feel four sets of prickles, like the touch of small thorn clusters in the Gardens of Apollo or Diana. He froze.

"Sspar," the cat hissed more softly, quitting to prickle. "I wishsh you all besst. Mosst ashshuredly."

Spar warily reached his right hand across his chest, touched short fur softer than Suzy's, and stroked gingerly.

The cat hissed very softly, almost purring. "Ssturdy Sspar! Ssee ffar! Ssee fforever! Fforessee! Afftssee!"

Spar felt a surge of irritation at this constant talk of seeing—bad manners in the cat!— He decided that this was no witch cat left over from his dream, but a stray which had wormed its way through a wind tube into the Bat Rack, setting off his dream. There were quite a few animal strays in these days of the witch panic and the depopulation of the Ship, or at least of Hold Three.

Dawn struck the Bow then, for the violet fore-corner of the Bat Rack began to glow. The running lights were drowned in a growing white blaze. Within twenty heartbeats Windrush was bright as it ever would be on Workday or any other morning.

Out along Spar's arm moved the cat, a black blur to his squinting eyes. In teeth Spar could not see, it held a smaller gray blur. Spar touched the latter. It was even shorter furred, but cold.

As if irked, the cat took off from his bare forearm with a strong push of hind legs. It landed expertly on the next shroud, a wavery line of gray that vanished in either direction before reaching a wall.

Spar unclipped himself, curled his toes around his own pencil-thin shroud, and squinted at the cat.

The cat stared back with eyes that were green blurs which almost coalesced in the black blur of its outsize head.

Spar asked, "Your child? Dead?"

The cat loosed its gray burden, which floated beside its head.

"Chchild!" All the former scorn and more were back in the sibilant voice. "It izz a rat I sslew her, issiot!"

Spar's lips puckered in a smile. "I like you, cat. I will call you Kim."

"Kim-shlim!" the cat spat. "I'll call you Lushsh! Or ssot!"

The creaking increased, as it always did after dayspring and noon. Shrouds twanged. Walls crackled.

Spar swiftly swiveled his head. Though reality was by its nature a blur, he could unerringly spot movement.

Keeper was slowly floating straight at him. On the round of his russet body was mounted the great, pale round of his face, its bright pink target-center drawing attention from the tiny, wide-set, brown blurs of his eyes. One of his fat arms ended in the bright gleam of pliofilm, the other in the dark gleam of steel. Far beyond him was the dark red aft corner of the Bat Rack, with the great gleaming torus, or doughnut, of the bar midway between.

"Lazy, pampered he-slut," Keeper greeted. "All Sleepday you snored while I stood guard, and now I bring your morning pouch of moonmist to your sleeping shroud.

"A bad night, Spar," he went on, his voice growing sententious. "Werewolves, vampires, and witches loose in the corridors. But I stood them off, not to mention rats and mice. I heard through the tubes that the vamps got Girlie and Sweetheart, the silly sluts! Vigilance, Spar! Now suck your moonmist and start sweeping. The place stinks."

He stretched out the pliofilm-gleaming hand.

His mind hissing with Kim's contemptuous words, Spar said, "I don't think I'll drink this morning, Keeper. Corn gruel and moonbrew only. No, water."

"What, Spar?" Keeper demanded. "I don't believe I can allow that. We don't want you having convulsions in front of the customers. Earth strangle me!—what's that?"

Spar instantly launched himself at Keeper's steel-gleaming hand. Behind him his shroud twanged. With one hand he twisted a cold, thick barrel. With the other he pried a plump finger from a trigger.

"He's not a witch cat, only a stray," he said as they tumbled over and kept slowly rotating.

"Unhand me, underling!" Keeper blustered. "I'll have you in irons. I'll tell Crown."

"Shooting weapons are as much against the law as knives or needles," Spar countered boldly, though he already was feeling dizzy and sick. "It's you should fear the brig." He recognized beneath the bullying voice the awe Keeper always had of his ability to move swiftly and surely, though half-blind.

They bounced to rest against a swarm of shrouds. "Loose me, I say," Keeper demanded, struggling weakly. "Crown gave me this pistol. And I have a permit for it from the Bridge." The last at least, Spar guessed, was a lie. Keeper continued, "Besides, it's only a line-shooting gun reworked for heavy, elastic ball. Not enough to rupture a wall, yet sufficient to knock out drunks—or knock in the head of a witch cat!"

"Not a witch cat, Keeper," Spar repeated, although he was having to swallow hard to keep from spewing. "Only a well-behaved stray, who has already proved his use to us by killing one of the rats that have been stealing our food. His name is Kim. He'll be a good worker."

The distant blur of Kim lengthened and showed thin blurs of legs and tail, as if he were standing out rampant from his line. "Asset izz I," he boasted. "Ssanitary. Uzze wasste tubes. Sslay ratss, micece! Sspy out witchchess, vampss ffor you!"

"He speaks!" Keeper gasped. "Witchcraft!"

"Crown has a dog who talks," Spar answered with finality. "A talking animal's no proof of anything."

All this while he had kept firm hold of barrel and finger. Now he felt through their grappled bodies a change in Keeper, as though inside his blubber the master of the Bat Rack were transforming from stocky muscle and bone into a very thick, sweet syrup that could conform to and flow around anything.

"Sorry, Spar," he whispered unctuously. "It was a bad night and Kim startled me. He's black like a witch cat. An easy mistake on my part. We'll try him out as catcher. He must earn his keep! Now take your drink."

The pliant double pouch filling Spar's palm felt like

the philosopher's stone. He lifted it toward his lips, but at the same time his toes unwittingly found a shroud, and he dove swiftly toward the shing torus, which had a hole big enough to accommodate four barmen at a pinch.

Spar collapsed against the opposite inside of the hole. With a straining of its shrouds, the torus absorbed his impact. He had the pouch to his lips, its cap unscrewed, but had not squeezed. He shut his eyes and with a tiny sob blindly thrust the pouch back into the moonmist cage.

Working chiefly by touch, he took a pouch of corn gruel from the hot closet, snitching at the same time a pouch of coffee and thrusting it into an inside pocket. Then he took a pouch of water, opened it, shoved in five salt tablets, closed it, and shook and squeezed it vigorously.

Keeper, having drifted behind him, said into his ear, "So you drink anyhow. Moonmist not good enough, you make yourself a cocktail. I should dock it from your scrip. But all drunks are liars, or become so."

Unable to ignore the taunt, Spar explained, "No, only salt water to harden my gums."

"Poor Spar, what'll you ever need hard gums for? Planning to share rats with your new friend? Don't let me catch you roasting them in my grill! I should dock you for the salt. To sweeping, Spar!" Then, turning his head toward the violet fore-corner and speaking loudly: "And you! Catch mice!"

Kim had already found the small chewer tube and thrust the dead rat into it, gripping tube with foreclaws and pushing rat with aft. At the touch of the rat's cadaver against the solid wrist of the tube, a grinding began there which would continue until the rat was macerated and slowly swallowed away toward the great cloaca which fed the Gardens of Diana.

Three times Spar manfully swished salt water against his gums and spat into a waste tube, vomiting a little after the first gargle. Then, facing away from the Keeper as he gently squeezed the pouches, he forced into his throat the coffee—dearer than moonmist, the drink distilled from moonbrew—and some of the corn gruel.

He apologetically offered the rest to Kim, who shook his head. "Jusst had a mousse."

Hastily Spar made his way to the green starboard corner. Outside the hatch he heard some drunks calling with weary and mournful anger, "Unzip!"

Grasping the heads of two long waste tubes, Spar began to sweep the air, working out from the green corner in a spiral, quite like an orb spider building her web.

From the torus, where he was idly polishing its thin titanium, Keeper upped the suction on the two tubes, so that reaction sped Spar in his spiral. He need use his body only to steer course and to avoid shrouds in such a way that his tubes didn't tangle.

Soon Keeper glanced at his wrist and called, "Spar, can't you keep track of the time? Open up!" He threw a ring of keys which Spar caught, though he could see only the last half of their flight. As soon as he was well headed toward the green door, Keeper called again and pointed aft and aloft. Spar obediently unlocked and unzipped the dark and also the blue hatch, though there was no one at either, before opening the green. In each case he avoided the hatch's gummy margin and the sticky emergency hatch hinged close beside.

In tumbled three brewos, old customers, snatching at shrouds and pushing off from each other's bodies in their haste to reach the torus, and meanwhile cursing Spar.

"Sky strangle you!"

"Earth bury you!"

"Seas sear you!"

"Language, boys!" Keeper reproved. "Though I'll agree my helper's stupidity and sloth tempt a man to talk foul."

Spar threw the keys back. The brewos lined up elbow to elbow around the torus, three grayish blobs with heads pointing toward the blue corner.

Keeper faced them. "Below, below!" he ordered indignantly. "You think you're gents?"

"But you're serving no one aloft yet."

"There's only us three."

"No matter," Keeper replied. "Propriety, suckers! Unless you mean to buy the pouch, invert."

With low grumbles the brewos reversed their bodies so that their heads pointed toward the black corner.

Himself not bothering to invert, Keeper tossed them a slim and twisty faint red blur with three branches. Each grabbed a branch and stuck it in his face.

The pudge of his fat hand on glint of valve, Keeper said, "Let's see your scrip first."

With angry mumbles each unwadded something too small for Spar to see clearly, and handed it over. Keeper studied each item before feeding it to the cashbox. Then he decreed, "Six seconds of moonbrew. Suck fast," and looked at his wrist and moved the other hand.

One of the brewos seemed to be strangling, but he blew out through his nose and kept sucking bravely.

Keeper closed the valve.

Instantly one brewo splutteringly accused, "You cut us off too soon. That wasn't six."

The treacle back in his voice, Keeper explained. "I'm squirting it to you four and two. Don't want you to drown. Ready again?"

The brewos greedily took their second squirt and then, at times wistfully sucking their tubes for remnant drops, began to shoot the breeze. In his distant circling, Spar's keen ears heard most of it.

"A dirty Sleepday, Keeper."

"No, a good one, brewo—for a drunken sucker to get his blood sucked by a lust-tickling vamp."

"I was dossed safe at Pete's, you fat ghoul."

"Pete's safe? That's news!"

"Dirty Atoms to you! But vamps did get Girlie and Sweetheart. Right in the starboard main drag, if you can believe it. By Cobalt Ninety, Windrush is getting lonely! Third Hold, anyhow. You can swim a whole passageway by day without meeting a soul."

"How do you know that about the girls?" the second brewo demanded. "Maybe they've gone to another hold to change their luck."

"Their luck's run out. Suzy saw them snatched."

"Not Suzy," Keeper corrected, now playing umpire. "But Mable did. A proper fate for drunken sluts."

"You've got no heart, Keeper."

"True enough. That's why the vamps pass me by. But speaking serious, boys, the werethings and witches are running too free in Three. I was awake all Sleepday guarding. I'm sending a complaint to the Bridge."

"You're kidding."

"You wouldn't."

Keeper solemnly nodded his head and crossed his left chest. The brewos were impressed.

Spar spiraled back toward the green corner, sweeping farther from the wall. On his way he overtook the black blob of Kim, who was circling the periphery himself, industriously leaping from shroud to shroud and occasionally making dashes along them.

A fair-skinned, plump shape twice circled by blue—bra and culottes—swam in through the green hatch.

"Morning, Spar," a soft voice greeted. "How's it going?"

"Fair and foul," Spar replied. The golden cloud of blonde hair floating loose touched his face. "I'm quitting moonmist, Suzy."

"Don't be too hard on yourself, Spar. Work a day, loaf a day, play a day, sleep a day—that way it's best."

"I know. Workday, Loafday, Playday, Sleepday. Ten days make a terranth, twelve terranths make a sunth, twelve sunths make a starth, and so on, to the end of time. With corrections, some tell me. I wish I knew what all those names mean."

"You're too serious. You should— Oh, a kitten! How darling!"

"Kitten-shmitten!" the big-headed black blur hissed as it leaped past them. "Izz cat. Izz Kim."

"Kim's our new catcher," Spar explained. "He's serious too."

"Quit wasting time on old Toothless Eyeless, Suzy," Keeper called, "and come all the way in."

As Suzy complied with a sigh, taking the easy route of

the ratlines, her soft taper fingers brushed Spar's crumpled cheek. "Dear Spar . . ." she murmured. As her feet passed his face, there was a jingle of her charm-anklet—all goldwashed hearts, Spar knew.

"Hear about Girlie and Sweetheart?" a brewo greeted ghoulishly. "How'd you like your carotid or outside iliac sliced, your—?"

"Shut up, sucker!" Suzy wearily cut him off. "Gimme a drink, Keeper."

"Your tab's long, Suzy. How you going to pay?"

"Don't play games, Keeper, please. Not in the morning, anyhow. You know all the answers, especially to that one. For now, a pouch of moonbrew, dark. And a little quiet."

"Pouches are for ladies, Suzy. I'll serve you aloft. You got to meet your marks, but—"

There was a shrill snarl which swiftly mounted to a scream of rage. Just inside the aft hatch, a pale figure in vermilion culottes and bra—no, wider than that, jacket or short coat—was struggling madly, somersaulting and kicking.

Entering carelessly, like too swiftly, the slim girl had got parts of herself and her clothes stuck to the hatch's inside margin and the emergency hatch.

Breaking loose by frantic main force while Spar dove toward her and the brewos shouted advice, she streaked toward the torus, jerking at the ratlines, black hair streaming behind her.

Coming up with a *bong* of hip against titanium, she grabbed together her vermilion—yes, clutch coat—with one hand and thrust the other across the rocking bar.

Drifting in close behind, Spar heard her say, "Double pouch of moonmist, Keeper. Make it fast."

"The best of mornings to you, Rixende," Keeper greeted. "I would gladly serve you goldwater, except, well—" The fat arms spread. "—Crown doesn't like his girls coming to the Bat Rack by themselves. Last time he gave me strict orders to—"

"What the smoke! It's on Crown's account I came here, to find something he lost. Meanwhile, moonmist.

Double!" She pounded on the bar until reaction started her aloft, and she pulled back into place with Spar's unthanked help.

"Softly, softly, lady," Keeper gentled, the tiny brown blurs of his eyes vanishing with his grinning. "What if Crown comes in while you're squeezing?"

"He won't!" Rixende denied vehemently, though glancing past Spar quickly—black blur, blue of pale face, black blur again. "He's got a new girl. I don't mean Phanette or Doucette, but a girl you've never seen. Name of Almodie. He'll be busy with the skinny bitch all morning. And now uncage that double moonmist, you dirty devil!"

"Softly, Rixie. All in good time. What is it Crown lost?"

"A little black bag. About so big." She extended her slender hand, fingers merged. "He lost it here last Playday night, or had it lifted."

"Hear that, Spar?" Keeper said.

"No little black bags," Spar said very quickly. "But you did leave your big orange one here last night, Rixende. I'll get it." He swung inside the torus.

"Oh, damn both bags. Gimme that double!" the black-haired girl demanded frantically. "Earth Mother!"

Even the brewos gasped. Touching hands to the sides of his head, Keeper begged: "No big obscenities, please. They sound worse from a dainty girl, gentle Rixende."

"Earth Mother, I said! Now cut the fancy, Keeper, and give, before I scratch your face off and rummage your cages!"

"Very well, very well. At once, at once. But how will you pay? Crown told me he'd get my license revoked if I ever put you on his tab again. Have you scrip? Or . . . coins?"

"Use your eyes! Or you think this coat's got inside pockets." She spread it wide, flashing her upper body, then clutched it tight again. "Earth Mother! Earth Mother! Earth Mother!" The brewos babbled scandalized. Suzy snorted mildly in boredom.

With one fat hand-blob, Keeper touched Rixende's wrist where a yellow blur circled it closely. "You've got gold," he said in hushed tones, his eyes vanishing again, this time in greed.

"You know damn well they're welded on. My anklets too."

"But these?" His hand went to a golden blur close beside her head.

"Welded too. Crown had my ears pierced."

"But . . ."

"Oh, you atom-dirty devil! I get you, all right. Well, then, *all right*!" The last words ended in a scream more of anger than pain as she grabbed a gold blur and jerked. Blood swiftly blobbed out. She thrust forward her fisted hand. "Now *give*! Gold for a double moonmist."

Keeper breathed hard but said nothing as he scrabbled in the moonmist cage, as if knowing he had gone too far. The brewos were silent too. Suzy sounded completely unimpressed as she said, "*And* my dark." Spar found a fresh dry sponge and expertly caught up the floating scarlet blobs with it before pressing it to Rixende's torn ear.

Keeper studied the heavy gold pendant, which he held close to his face. Rixende milked the double pouch pressed to her lips and her eyes vanished as she sucked blissfully. Spar guided Rixende's free hand to the sponge, and she automatically took over the task of holding it to her ear. Suzy gave a hopeless sigh, then reached her whole plump body across the bar, dipped her hand into a cool cage, and helped herself to a double of dark.

A long, wiry, very dark brown figure in skintight dark violent jumpers mottled with silver arrowed in from the dark red hatch at a speed half again as great as Spar ever dared and without brushing a single shroud by accident or intent. Midway the newcomer did a half somersault as he passed Spar; his long, narrow bare feet hit the titanium next to Rixende. He accordioned up so expertly that the torus hardly swayed.

One very dark brown arm snaked around her. The other plucked the pouch from her mouth, and there was a snap as he spun the cap shut.

A lazy musical voice inquired, "What'd we tell you

would happen, baby, if you ever again took a drink on your own?"

The Bat Rack held very still. Keeper was backed against the opposite side of the hole, one hand behind him. Spar had his arm in his lost-and-found nook behind the moonbrew and moonmist cages and kept it there. He felt fearsweat beading on him. Suzy kept her dark close to her face.

A brewo burst into violent coughing, choked it to a wheezing end, and gasped subserviently. "Excuse me, coroner. Salutations."

Keeper chimed dully, "Morning . . . Crown."

Crown gently pulled the clutch coat off Rixende's far shoulder and began to stroke her. "Why, you're all gooseflesh, honey, and rigid as a corpse. What frightened you? Smooth down, skin. Ease up, muscles. Relax, Rix, and we'll give you a squirt."

His hand found the sponge, stopped, investigated, found the wet part, then went toward the middle of his face. He sniffed.

"Well, boys, at least we know none of you are vamps," he observed softly. "Else we'd found you sucking at her ear."

Rixende said very rapidly in a monotone, "I didn't come for a drink, I swear to you. I came to get that little bag you lost. Then I was tempted. I didn't know I would be. I tried to resist, but Keeper led me on. I—"

"Shut up," Crown said quietly. "We were just wondering how you paid him. Now we know. How were you planning to buy your third double? Cut off a hand or a foot? Keeper . . . show me your other hand. We said show it. That's right. Now unfist."

Crown plucked the pendant from Keeper's opened handblob. His yellow-brown eye-blurs on Keeper all the while, he wagged the precious bauble back and forth, then tossed it slowly aloft.

As the golden blur moved toward the open blue hatch at unchanging pace, Keeper opened and shut his mouth twice, then babbled, "I didn't tempt her, Crown, honest.

I didn't. I didn't know she was going to hurt her ear. I tried to stop her, but—"

"We're not interested," Crown said. "Put the double on our tab." His face never leaving Keeper's, he extended his arm aloft and pinched the pendant just before it straightlined out of reach.

"Why's this home of jollity so dead?" Snaking a long leg across the bar as easily as an arm, Crown pinched Spar's ear between his big and smaller toes, pulled him close and turned him round. "How're you coming along with the saline, baby? Gums hardening? Only one way to test it." Gripping Spar's jaw and lip with his other toes, he thrust the big one into Spar's mouth. "Come on, bite me, baby."

Spar bit. It was the only way not to vomit. Crown chuckled. Spar bit hard. Energy flooded his shaking frame. His face grew hot and his forehead throbbed under its drenching of fearsweat. He was sure he was hurting Crown, but the Coroner of Hold Three only kept up his low, delighted chuckle and when Spar gasped, withdrew his foot.

"My, my, you're getting strong, baby. We almost felt that. Have a drink on us."

Spar ducked his stupidly wide-open mouth away from the thin jet of moonmist. The jet struck him in his eye and stung so that he had to knot his fists and clamp his aching gums together to keep from crying out.

"Why's the place so dead, I ask again? No applause for baby and now baby's gone temperance on us. Can't you give us just one tiny laugh?" Crown faced each in turn. "What's the matter? Cat got your tongues?"

"Cat? We have a cat, a new cat, came just last night, working as catcher," Keeper suddenly babbled. "It can talk a little. Not as well as Hellhound, but it talks. It's very funny. It caught a rat."

"What'd you do with the rat's body, Keeper?"

"Fed it to the chewer. That is, Spar did. Or the cat."

"You mean to tell us that you disposed of a corpse without notifying us? Oh, don't go pale on us, Keeper. That's nothing. Why, we could accuse you of harboring a witch cat. You say he came last night, and that was a wicked night for witches. Now don't go green on us too. We were only putting you on. We were only looking for a small laugh.

"Spar! Call your cat! Make him say something funny."

Before Spar could call, or even decide whether he'd call Kim or not, the black blur appeared on a shroud near Crown, green eye-blurs fixed on the yellow-brown ones.

"So you're the joker, eh? Well . . . joke."

Kim increased in size. Spar realized it was his fur standing on end.

"Go ahead. Joke . . . like they tell us you can. Keeper, you wouldn't be kidding us about this cat being able to talk?

"Spar! Make your cat joke!

"Don't bother. We believe he's got his own tongue too. That the matter, Blackie?" He reached out his hand. Kim lashed at it and sprang away. Crown only gave another of his low chuckles.

Rixende began to shake uncontrollably. Crown examined her solicitously yet leisurely, using his outstretched hand to turn her head toward him, so that any blood that might have been coming from it from the cat's slash would have gone into the sponge.

"Spar swore the cat could talk," Keeper babbled. "I'll—"

"Quiet," Crown said. He put the pouch to Rixende's lips, squeezed until her shaking subsided and it was empty, then flicked the crumpled pliofilm toward Spar.

"And now about that little black bag, Keeper," Crown said flatly.

"Spar!"

The latter dipped into his lost-and-found nook, saying quickly, "No little black bags, coroner, but we did find this one the lady Rixende forgot last Playday night," and he turned back holding out something big, round, gleamingly orange, and closed with drawstrings.

Crown took and swung it slowly in a circle. For Spar, who couldn't see the strings, it was like magic. "Bit too big, and a mite the wrong shade. We're certain we lost the little black bag here, or had it lifted. You making that Bat Rack a tent for dips, Keeper?"

"Spar—?"

"We're asking *you*, Keeper."

Shoving Spar aside, Keeper groped frantically in the nook, pulling aside the cages of moonmist and moonbrew pouches. He produced many small objects. Spar could distinguish the largest—an electric hand-fan and a bright red footglove. They hung around Keeper in a jumble.

Keeper was panting and had scrabbled his hands for a full minute in the nook without bringing out anything more, when Crown said, his voice lazy again, "That's enough. The little black bag was of no importance to us in any case."

Keeper emerged with a face doubly blurred, surrounded by a haze of sweat. He pointed an arm at the orange bag.

"It might be inside that one!"

Crown opened the bag, began to search through it, changed his mind, and gave the whole bag a flick. Its remarkably numerous contents came out and moved slowly aloft at equal speeds, like an army on the march in irregular order. Crown scanned them as they went past.

"No, not here." He pushed the bag toward Keeper. "Return Rix's stuff to it and have it ready for us the next time we dive in—"

Putting his arm around Rixende, so that it was his hand that held the sponge to her ear, he turned and kicked off powerfully for the aft hatch. After he had been out of sight for several seconds, there was a general sigh; the three brewos put out new scripwads to pay for another squirt. Suzy asked for a second double dark, which Spar handed her quickly, while Keeper shook off his daze and ordered Spar, "Gather up all the floating trash, especially Rixie's, and get that back in her purse. On the jump, lubber!" Then he used the electric hand-fan to cool and dry himself.

It was a mean task Keeper had set Spar, but Kim came

to help, darting after objects too small for Spar to see. Once he had them, in his hands, Spar could readily finger or sniff which was which.

When his impotent rage at Crown had faded, Spar's thoughts went back to Sleepday night. Had his vision of vamps and werewolves been dream only?—now that he knew the werethings had been abroad in force. If only he had better eyes to distinguish illusion from reality! Kim's "Ssee! Ssee shsharply!" hissed in his memory. What would it be like to see sharply? Everything brighter? Or closer?

After a weary time the scattered objects were gathered and he went back to sweeping and Kim to his mouse hunt. As Workday morning progressed, the Bat Rack gradually grew less bright, though so gradually it was hard to tell.

A few more customers came in, but all for quick drinks, which Keeper served them glumly; Suzy judged none of them worth cottoning up to.

As time slowly passed, Keeper grew steadily more fretfully angry, as Spar had known he would after groveling before Crown. He tried to throw out the three brewos, but they produced more crumpled scrip, which closest scrutiny couldn't prove counterfeit. In revenge he short-squinted them and there were arguments. He called Spar off his sweeping to ask him nervously, "That cat of yours—he scratched Crown, didn't he? We'll have to get rid of him; Crown said he might be a witch cat, remember?" Spar made no answer. Keeper set him renewing the glue of the emergency hatches, claiming that Rixende's tearing free from the aft one had shown it must be drying out. He gobbled appetizers and drank moonmist with tomato juice. He sprayed the Bat Rack with some abominable synthetic scent. He started counting the boxed scrip and coins but gave up the job with a slam of self-locking drawer almost before he'd begun. His grimace fixed on Suzy.

"Spar!" he called. "Take over! And over-squirt the brewos on your peril!"

Then he locked the cash box, and giving Suzy a

meaningful jerk of his head toward the scarlet starboard hatch, he pulled himself toward it. With an unhappy shrug toward Spar, she wearily followed.

As soon as the pair were gone, Spar gave the brewos an eight-second squirt, waving back their scrip, and placed two small serving cages—of fritos and yeast balls—before them. They grunted their thanks and fell to. The light changed from healthy bright to corpse white. There was a faint, distant roar, followed some seconds later by a brief crescendo of creakings. The new light made Spar uneasy. He served two more suck-and-dives and sold a pouch of moonmist at double purser's prices. He started to eat an appetizer, but just then Kim swam in to proudly show him a mouse. He conquered his nausea, but began to dread the onset of real withdrawal symptoms.

A potbellied figure clad in sober black dragged itself along the ratlines from the green hatch. On the aloft side of the bar there appeared a visage in which the blur of white hair and beard hid leather-brown flesh, though accentuating the blurs of gray eyes.

"Doc!" Spar greeted, his misery and unease gone, and instantly handed out a chill pouch of three-star moonbrew. Yet all he could think to say in his excitement was the banal, "A bad Sleepday night, eh, Doc? Vamps and—"

"—And other doltish superstitions, which was every sunth, but never wane," an amiable, cynical old voice cut in. "Yet, I suppose I shouldn't rob you of your illusions, Spar, even the terrifying ones. You've little enough to live by, as it is. And there *is* viciousness astir in Windrush. Ah, that smacks good against my tonsils."

Then Spar remembered the important thing. Reaching deep inside his slopsuit, he brought out, in such a way as to hide it from the brewos below, a small flat narrow black bag.

"Here, Doc," he whispered, "you lost it last Playday. I kept it safe for you."

"Dammit, I'd lose my jumpers, if I ever took them off," Doc commented, hushing his voice when Spar put finger to lips. "I suppose I started mixing moonmist with my moonbrew—again?"

"You did, Doc. But you didn't lose your bag. Crown or one of his girls lifted it, or snagged it when it sat loose beside you. And then I . . . I, Doc, lifted it from Crown's hip pocket. Yes, and kept that secret when Rixende and Crown came in demanding it this morning."

"Spar, my boy, I am deeply in your debt," Doc said. "More than you can know. Another three-star, please. Ah, nectar. Spar, ask any reward of me, and if it lies merely within the realm of the first transfinite infinity, I will grant it."

To his own surprise, Spar began to shake—with excitement. Pulling himself forward halfway across the bar, he whispered hoarsely, "Give me good eyes, Doc!" adding impulsively, "and teeth!"

After what seemed a long while, Doc said in a dreamy, sorrowful voice, "In the Old Days, that would have been easy. They'd perfected eye transplants. They could regenerate cranial nerves, and sometimes restore scanning power to an injured cerebrum. While transplanting tooth buds from a stillborn was intern's play. But now . . . Oh, I might be able to do what you ask in an uncomfortable, antique, inorganic fashion, but . . ." He broke off on a note that spoke of the misery of life and the uselessness of all effort.

"The Old Days," one brewo said from the corner of his mouth to the brewo next to him. "Witch talk!"

"Witch-smitch!" the second brewo replied in like fashion. "The flesh mechanic's only senile. He dreams all four days, not just Sleepday."

The third brewo whistled against the evil eye a tune like the wind.

Spar tugged at the long-armed sleeve of Doc's black jumper. "Doc, you promised. I want to see sharp, bite sharp!"

Doc laid his shrunken hand commiseratingly on Spar's forearm. "Spar," he said softly, "seeing sharply would only make you very unhappy. Believe me, I *know*. Life's easier to bear when things are blurred, just as it's best when thoughts are blurred by brew or mist. And while there are people in Windrush who yearn to bite sharply, you are not their kind. Another three-star, if you please."

"I quit moonmist this morning, Doc," Spar said somewhat proudly as he handed over the fresh pouch.

Doc answered with a sad smile, "Many quit moonmist every Workday morning and change their minds when Playday comes around."

"Not me, Doc! Besides," Spar argued, "Keeper and Crown and his girls and even Suzy all see sharply, and they aren't unhappy."

"I'll tell you a secret, Spar," Doc replied. "Keeper and Crown and the girls are all zombies. Yes, even Crown with his cunning and power. To them Windrush is the universe."

"It isn't, Doc?"

Ignoring the interruption, Doc continued, "But you wouldn't be like that, Spar. You'd want to know more. And that would make you far unhappier than you are."

"I don't care, Doc," Spar said. He repeated accusingly, "You promised."

The gray blurs of Doc's eyes almost vanished as he frowned in thought. Then he said, "How would this be, Spar? I know moonmist brings pains and sufferings as well as easings and joys. But suppose that every Workday morning and Loafday noon I should bring you a tiny pill that would give you all the good effects of moonmist and none of the bad. I've one in this bag. Try it now and see. And every Playday night I would bring you without fail another sort of pill that would make you sleep soundly with never a nightmare. Much better than eyes and teeth. Think it over."

As Spar considered that, Kim drifted up. He eyed Doc with his close-set green blurs. "Resspectfful greetingsss, ssir," he hissed. "Name izz Kim."

Doc answered, "The same to you, sir. May mice be ever abundant." He softly stroked the cat, beginning with Kim's chin and chest. The dreaminess returned to his voice. "In the Old Days, all cats talked, not just a few sports. The entire feline tribe. And many dogs, too—

pardon me, Kim. While as for dolphins and whales and apes . . ."

Spar said eagerly, "Answer me one question, Doc. If your pills give happiness without hangover, why do you always drink moonbrew yourself and sometimes spike it with moonmist?"

"Because for me—" Doc began and then broke off with a grin. "You trapped me, Spar. I never thought you used your mind. Very well, on your own mind be it. Come to my office this Loafday—you know the way? Good!—and we'll see what we can do about your eyes and teeth. And now a double pouch for the corridor."

He paid in bright coins, thrust the big squinchy three-star in a big pocket, and said, "See you, Spar. So long, Kim," and tugged himself toward the green hatch, zigzagging.

"Ffarewell, ssir," Kim hissed after him.

Spar held out the small black bag. "You forgot it again, Doc."

As Doc returned with a weary curse and pocketed it, the scarlet hatch unzipped and Keeper swam out. He looked in a good humor now and whistled the tune of "I'll Marry the Man on the Bridge" as he began to study certain rounds on scrip-till and moonbrew valves, but when Doc was gone he asked Spar suspiciously, "What was that you handed the old geezer?"

"His purse," Spar replied easily. "He forgot it just now." He shook his loosely fisted hand and it chinked. "Doc paid in coins, Keeper." Keeper took them eagerly. "Back to sweeping, Spar."

As Spar dove toward the scarlet hatch to take up larboard tubes, Suzy emerged and passed him with face averted. She sidled up to the bar and unsmilingly snatched the pouch of moonmist Keeper offered her with mock courtliness.

Spar felt a brief rage on her behalf, but it was hard for him to keep his mind on anything but his coming appointment with Doc. When Workday night fell swiftly as a hurled knife, he was hardly aware of it and felt none of his customary unease. Keeper turned on full all the lights in the Bat Rack. They shone brightly while beyond the translucent walls there was a milky churning.

Business picked up a little. Suzy made off with the first likely mark. Keeper called Spar to take over the torus, while he himself got a much-erased sheet of paper and, holding it to a clipboard held against his bent knees, wrote on it laboriously, as if he were thinking out each word, perhaps each letter, often wetting his pencil in his mouth. He became so absorbed in his difficult task that without realizing he drifted off toward the black below hatch, rotating over and over. The paper got dirtier and dirtier with his scrawlings and smudgings, new erasures, saliva and sweat.

The short night passed more swiftly than Spar dared hope, so that the sudden glare of Loafday dawn startled him. Most of the customers made off to take their siestas.

Spar wondered what excuse to give Keeper for leaving the Bat Rack, but the problem was solved for him. Keeper folded the grimy sheet, and sealed it with hot tape. "Take this to the Bridge, loafer, to the Exec. Wait." He took the repacked orange bag from its nook and pulled on the cords to make sure they were drawn tight. "On your way deliver this at Crown's Hole. With all courtesy and subservience, Spar! Now, on the jump!"

Spar slid the sealed message into his only pocket with working zipper and drew that tight. Then he dove slowly toward the aft hatch, where he almost collided with Kim. Recalling Keeper's talk of getting rid of the cat, he caught hold of him around the slim furry chest under the forelegs and gently thrust him inside his slopsuit, whispering, "You'll take a trip with me, little Kim." The cat set his claws in the thin material and steadied himself.

For Spar, the corridor was a narrow cylinder ending in mist either way and decorated by lengthwise blurs of green and red. He guided himself chiefly by touch and memory, this time remembering that he must pull himself against the light wind hand-over-hand along the centerline. After curving past the larger cylinders of the fore-and-aft gangways, the corridor straightened. Twice he worked his way around centrally slung fans whirring so softly that he recognized them chiefly by the increase in breeze before passing them and the slight suction after.

Soon he began to smell soil and green stuff growing. With a shiver he passed a black round that was the elastic-curtained door to Hold Three's big chewer. He met no one—odd even for Loafday. Finally he saw the green of the Gardens of Apollo and beyond it a huge black screen, in which hovered toward the aft side a small, smoky-orange circle that always filled Spar with inexplicable sadness and fear. He wondered in how many black screens that doleful circle was portrayed, especially in the starboard end of Windrush. He had seen it in several.

So close to the gardens that he could make out wavering green shoots and the silhouette of a floating farmer, the corridor right-angled below. Two dozen pulls along the line and he floated by an open hatch, which both memory for distance and the strong scent of musky, mixed perfumes told him was the entry to Crown's Hole. Peering in, he could see the intermelting and silver spirals of the decor of the great globular room. Directly opposite the hatch was another large black screen with the red-mottled dun disk placed similarly off-center.

From under Spar's chin, Kim hissed very softly, but urgently, "Sstop! Ssilencce, on your liffe!" The cat had poked his head out of the slopsuit's neck. His ears tickled Spar's throat. Spar was getting used to Kim's melodrama, and in any case the warning was hardly needed. He had just seen the half-dozen floating naked bodies and would have held still if only from embarrassment. Not that Spar could see genitals any more than ears at the distance. But he could see that save for hair, each body was of one texture: one very dark brown and the other five—or was it four? no, five—fair. He didn't recognize the two with platinum and golden hair, who also happened to be the two palest. He wondered which was Crown's new girl, name of Almodie. He was relieved that none of the bodies were touching.

There was the glint of metal by the golden-haired girl,

and he could just discern the red blur of a slender, five-forked tube which went from the metal to the five other faces. It seemed strange that even with a girl to play bartender, Crown should have moonbrew served in such plebeian fashion in his patatial Hole. Of course the tube might carry moonwine, or even moonmist.

Or was Crown planning to open a rival bar to the Bat Rack? A poor time, these days, and a worse location, he mused as he tried to think of what to do with the orange bag.

"Sslink off!" Kim urged still more softly.

Spar's fingers found a snap-ring by the hatch. With the faintest of clicks he secured it around the draw-cords of the pouch and then pulled back the way he had come.

But faint as the click had been, there was a response from Crown's Hole—a very deep, long growl.

Spar pulled faster at the centerline. As he rounded the corner leading inboard, he looked back.

Jutting out from Crown's hatch was a big, prick-eared head narrower than a man's and darker even than Crown's.

The growl was repeated.

It was ridiculous he should be so frightened of Hellhound, Spar told himself as he jerked himself and his passenger along. Why, Crown sometimes even brought the big dog to the Bat Rack.

Perhaps it was that Hellhound never growled in the Bat Rack, only talked in a hundred or so monosyllables.

Besides, the dog couldn't pull himself along the centerline at any speed. He lacked sharp claws. Though he might be able to bound forward, caroming from one side of the corridor to another.

This time the center-slit black curtains of the big chewer made Spar veer violently. He was a fine one—going to get new eyes today and frightened as a child!

"Why did you try to scare me back there, Kim?" he asked angrily.

"I ssaw shsheer evil, issiot!"

"You saw five folk sucking moonbrew. And a harmless dog. This time you're the fool, Kim; you're the idiot!"

Kim shut up, drawing in his head, and refused to say another word. Spar remembered about the vanity and touchiness of all cats. But by now he had other worries. What if the orange bag were stolen by a passerby before Crown noticed it? And if Crown did find it, wouldn't he know Spar, forever Keeper's errandboy, had been peeping? That all this should happen on the most important day of his life! His verbal victory over Kim was small consolation.

Also, although the platinum-haired girl had interested him most of the two strange ones, something began to bother him about the girl who'd been playing bartender, the one with golden hair like Suzy's, but much slimmer and paler—he had the feeling he'd seen her before. And something about her had frightened him.

When he reached the central gangways, he was tempted to go to Doc's office before the Bridge. But he wanted to be able to relax at Doc's and take as much time as needed, knowing all errands were done.

Reluctantly he entered the windy violet gangway and dove at a fore angle for the first empty space on the central gang-line, so that his palms were only burned a little before he had firm hold of it and was being sped fore at about the same speed as the wind. Keeper was a miser, not to buy him handgloves, let alone footgloves!—but he had to pay sharp attention to passing the shroud-slung roller bearings that kept the thick, moving line centered in the big corridor. It was an easy trick to catch hold of the line ahead of the bearing and then get one's hand out of the way, but it demanded watchfulness.

There were few figures traveling on the line and fewer still being blown along the corridor. He overtook a doubled-up one tumbling over and over and crying out in an old cracked voice, "Jacob's Ladder, Tree of Life, Marriage Lines . . ."

He passed the squeeze in the gangway marking the division between the Third and Second Holds without being stopped by the guard there and then he almost missed the big blue corridor leading aloft. Again he slightly burned his palms making the transfer from one moving gang-line to another. His fretfulness increased.

"Sspar, you issiot—!" Kim began.

"Ssh!—we're in officers' territory," Spar cut him off, glad to have that excuse for once more putting down the impudent cat. And true enough, the blue spaces of Windrush always did fill him with awe and dread.

Almost too soon to suit him, he found himself swinging from the gang-line to a stationary monkey jungle of tubular metal just below the deck of the Bridge. He worked his way to the aloft-most bars and floated there, waiting to be spoken to.

Much metal, in many strange shapes, gleamed in the Bridge, and there were irregularly pulsing rainbow surfaces, the closest of which sometimes seemed ranks and files of tiny lights going on and off—red, green, all colors. Aloft of everything was an endless velvet-black expanse very faintly blotched by churning, milky glintings.

Among the metal objects and the rainbows, floated figures all clad in the midnight blue of officers. They sometimes gestured to each other, but never spoke a word. To Spar, each of their movements was freighted with profound significance. These were the gods of Windrush, who guided everything, if there were gods at all. He felt reduced to importance to a mouse, which would be chased off chittering if it once broke silence.

After a particularly tense flurry of gestures, there came a brief distant roar and a familiar creaking and crackling. Spar was amazed, yet at the same time realized he should have known that the Captain, the Navigator, and the rest were responsible for the familiar diurnal phenomena.

It also marked Loafday noon. Spar began to fret. His errands were taking too long. He began to lift his hand tentatively toward each passing figure in midnight blue. None took the least note of him.

Finally he whispered, "Kim—?"

The cat did not reply. He could hear a purring that might be a snore. He gently shook the cat. "Kim, let's talk."

"Shshut off! I ssleep! Ssh!" Kim resettled himself and

his claws and recommenced his purring snore—whether natural or feigned, Spar could not tell. He felt very despondent.

The lunths crept by. He grew desperate and weary. He must not miss his appointment with Doc! He was nerving himself to move farther aloft and speak, when a pleasant, young voice said, "Hello, grandpa, what's on your mind?"

Spar realized that he had been raising his hand automatically and that a person as dark-skinned as Crown, but clad in midnight blue, had at last taken notice. He unzipped the note and handed it over. "For the Exec."

"That's my department." A trilled crackle—fingernail slitting the note? A larger crackle—note being opened. A brief wait. Then, "Who's Keeper?"

"Owner of the Bat Rack, sir. I work there."

"Bat Rack?"

"A moonbrew mansion. Once called the Happy Torus, I've been told. In the Old Days, Wine Mess Three, Doc told me."

"Hmm. Well, what's all this mean, gramps? And what's your name?"

Spar stared miserably at the dark-mottled gray square. "I can't read, sir. Name's Spar."

"Hmm. Seen any . . . er . . . supernatural beings in the Bat Rack?"

"Only in my dreams, sir."

"Mmm. Well, we'll have a look in. If you recognize me, don't let on. I'm Ensign Drake, by the way. Who's your passenger, grandpa?"

"Only my cat, Ensign," Spar breathed in alarm.

"Well, take the black shaft down." Spar began to move across the monkey jungle in the direction pointed out by the blue arm-blur.

"And next time remember animals aren't allowed on the Bridge."

As Spar traveled below, his warm relief that Ensign Drake had seemed quite human and compassionate was mixed with anxiety as to whether he still had time to visit Doc. He almost missed the shift to the gang-line grinding aft in the dark red maindrag. The corpse-light brightening into the false dawn of later afternoon bothered him. Once more he passed the tumbling bent figure, this time croaking, "Trinity, Trellis, Wheat Ear . . ."

He was fighting down the urge to give up his visit to Doc and pull home to the Bat Rack, when he noticed he had passed the second squeeze and was in Hold Four with the passageway to Doc's coming up. He dove off, checked himself on a shroud and began the hand-drag to Doc's office, as far larboard as Crown's Hole was starboard.

He passed two figures clumsy on the line, their breaths malty in anticipation of Playday. Spar worried that Doc might have closed his office. He smelled soil and greenery again, from the Gardens of Diana.

The hatch was shut, but when Spar pressed the bulb, it unzipped after three honks, and the white-haloed gray-eyed face peered out.

"I'd just about given up on you, Spar."

"I'm sorry, Doc. I had to—"

"No matter. Come in, come in. Hello, Kim—take a look around if you want."

Kim crawled out, pushed off from Spar's chest, and soon was engaged in a typical cat's tour of inspection.

And there was a great deal to inspect, as even Spar could see. Every shroud in Doc's office seemed to have objects clipped along its entire length. There were blobs large and small, gleaming and dull, light and dark, translucent and solid. They were silhouetted against a wall of the corpse-light Spar feared, but had no time to think of now. At one end was a band of even brighter light.

"Careful, Kim!" Spar called to the cat as he landed against a shroud and began to paw his way from blob to blob.

"He's all right," Doc said. "Let's have a look at you, Spar. Keep your eyes open."

Doc's hands held Spar's head. The gray eyes and leathery face came so close they were one blur.

"Keep them open, I said. Yes, I know you have to blink them, that's all right. Just as I thought. The lenses are dissolved. You've suffered the side-effect which one in ten do who are infected with the Lethean rickettsia."

"Styx ricks, Doc?"

"That's right, though the mob's got hold of the wrong river in the Underworld. But we've all had it. We've all drunk the water of Lethe. Though sometimes when we grow very old we begin to remember the beginning. Don't squirm."

"Hey, Doc, is it because I've had the Styx ricks I can't remember anything back before the Bat Rack?"

"It could be. How long have you been at the Rack?"

"I don't know, Doc. Forever."

"Before I found the place, anyhow. When the Rum-dum closed here in Four. But that's only a starth ago."

"But I'm awful old, Doc. Why don't I start remembering?"

"You're not old, Spar. You're just bald and toothless and etched by moonmist and your muscles have shriveled. Yes, and your mind has shriveled too. Now open your mouth."

One of Doc's hands went to the back of Spar's neck. The other probed. "Your gums are tough, anyhow. That'll make it easier."

Spar wanted to tell about the salt water, but when Doc finally took his hand out of Spar's mouth, it was to say, "Now open wide as you can."

Doc pushed into his mouth something big as a hand-bag and hot. "Now bite down hard."

Spar felt as if he had bitten fire. He tried to open his mouth, but hands on his head and jaw held it closed. Involuntarily he kicked and clawed air. His eyes filled with tears.

"Stop writhing! Breathe through your nose. It's not that hot. Not hot enough to blister, anyhow."

Spar doubted that, but after a bit decided it wasn't quite hot enough to bake his brain through the roof of his mouth. Besides, he didn't want to show Doc his cowardice. He held still. He blinked several times and the general blur became the blurs of Doc's face and the cluttered room silhouetted by the corpse-glare. He tried to smile, but his lips were already stretched wider than their muscles could ever have done. That hurt too; he realized now that the heat was abating a little.

Doc was grinning for him. "Well, you would ask an old drunkard to use techniques he'd only read about. To make it up to you, I'll give you teeth sharp enough to sever shrouds. Kim, please get away from that bag."

The black blur of the cat was pushing off from a black blur twice his length. Spar mumbled disapprovingly at Kim through his nose and made motions. The larger blur was shaped like Doc's little bag, but bigger than a hundred of them. It must be massive too, for in reaction to Kim's push it had bent the shroud to which it was attached and—the point—the shroud was very slow in straightening.

"That bag contains my treasure, Spar," Doc explained, and when Spar lifted his eyebrows twice to signal another question, went on, "No, not coin and gold and jewels, but a second transfinite infinitude—sleep and dreams and nightmares for every soul in a thousand Windrushes." He glanced at his wrist. "Time enough now. Open your mouth." Spar obeyed, though it cost him new pain.

Doc withdrew what Spar had bitten on, wrapped in it gleam, and clipped it to the nearest shroud. Then he looked in Spar's mouth again.

"I guess I did make it a bit too hot," he said. He found a small pouch, set it to Spar's lips, and squeezed it. A mist filled Spar's mouth and all pain vanished.

Doc tucked the pouch in Spar's pocket. "If the pain returns, use it again."

But before Spar could thank Doc, the latter had pressed a tube to his eye. "Look, Spar, what do you see?"

Spar cried out, he couldn't help it, and jerked his eye away.

"What's wrong, Spar?"

"Doc, you gave me a dream," Spar said hoarsely. "You won't tell anyone, will you? And it tickled."

"What was the dream like?" Doc asked eagerly.

"Just a picture, Doc. The picture of a goat with the tail of a fish. Doc, I saw the fish's"—his mind groped—

"scales! Everything had . . . edges! Doc, is *that* what they mean when they talk about seeing sharply?"

"Of course, Spar. This is good. It means there's no cerebral or retinal damage. I'll have no trouble making up field glasses—that is, if there's nothing seriously wrong with my antique pair. So you still see things sharp-edged in dreams—that's natural enough. But why were you afraid of me telling?"

"Afraid of being accused of witchcraft, Doc. I thought seeing things like that was clairvoyance. The tube tickled my eye a little."

"Isotopes and insanity! It's supposed to tickle. Let's try the other eye."

Again Spar wanted to cry out, but he restrained himself, and this time he had no impulse to jerk his eye away, although there was again the faint tickling. The picture was that of a slim girl. He could tell she was female because of her general shape. But he could see her edges. He could see . . . details. For instance, her eyes weren't mist-bounded colored ovals. They had points at both ends, which were china-white . . . triangles. And the pale violet round between the triangles had a tiny black round at its center.

She had silvery hair, yet she looked young, he thought, though it was hard to judge such matters when you could see edges. She made him think of the platinum-haired girl he'd glimpsed in Crown's Hole.

She wore a long, gleaming white dress, which left her shoulders bare, but either art or some unknown force had drawn her hair and her dress toward her feet. In her dress it made . . . folds.

"What's her name, Doc? Almodie?"

"No. Virgo. The Virgin. You can see her edges?"

"Yes, Doc. Sharp. I get it!—like a knife. And the goatfish?"

"Capricorn," Doc answered, removing the tube from Spar's eye.

"Doc, I know Capricorn and Virgo are the names of lunths, terranths, sunths, and starths, but I never knew they had pictures. I never knew they *were* anything."

"You— Of course, you've never seen watches, or stars, let alone the constellations of the zodiac."

Spar was about to ask what all *those* were, but then he saw that the corpse-light was all gone, although the ribbon of brighter light had grown very wide.

"At least in this stretch of your memory," Doc added. "I should have your new eyes and teeth ready next Loafday. Come earlier if you can manage. I may see you before that at the Bat Rack, Playday Night or earlier."

"Great, Doc, but now I've got to haul. Come on, Kim! Sometimes business heavies up Loafday night, Doc, like it was Playday night come at the wrong end. Jump in, Kim."

"Sure you can make it back to the Bat Rack all right, Spar? It'll be dark before you get there."

"Course I can, Doc."

But when night fell, like a heavy hood jerked down over his head, halfway down the first passageway, he would have gone back to ask Doc, to guide him, except he feared Kim's contempt, even though the cat still wasn't talking. He pulled ahead rapidly, though the few running lights hardly let him see the centerline.

The fore gangway was even worse—completely empty and its lights dim and flickering. Seeing by blurs bothered him now that he knew what seeing sharp was like. He was beginning to sweat and shake and cramp from his withdrawal from alcohol, and his thoughts were a tumult. He wondered if *any* of the weird things that had happened since meeting Kim were real or dream. Kim's refusal—or inability?—to talk any more was disquieting. He began seeing the misty rims of blurs that vanished when he looked straight toward them. He remembered Keeper and the brewos talking about vamps and witches.

Then, instead of waiting for the Bat Rack's green hatch, he dove off into the passageway leading to the aft one. This passageway had no lights at all. Out of it he thought he could hear Hellhound growling, but couldn't be sure because the big chewer was grinding. He was scrabbing with panic when he entered the Bat Rack through the dark red hatch, remembering barely in time to avoid the new glue.

The place was jumping with light and excitement and dancing figures, and Keeper at once began to shout abuse at him. He dove into the torus and began taking orders and serving automatically, working entirely by touch and voice, because withdrawal now had his vision swimming—a spinning blur of blurs.

After a while they got better, but his nerves got worse. Only the unceasing work kept him going—and shut out Keeper's abuse—but he was getting too tired to work at all. As Playday dawned, with the crowd around the torus getting thicker all the while, he snatched a pouch of moonmist and set it to his lips.

Claws dug his chest. "Issiot! Ssot! Sslave of ffear!"

Spar almost went into convulsions, but put back the moonmist. Kim came out of the slopsuit and pushed off contemptuously, circled the bar and talked to various of the drinkers, soon became a conversation piece. Keeper started to boast about him and quit serving. Spar worked on and on and on through sobriety more nightmarish than any drunk he could recall. And far, far longer.

Suzy came in with a mark and touched Spar's hand when he served her dark to her. It helped.

He thought he recognized a voice from below. It came from a kinky-haired, slop-suited brewo he didn't know. But then he heard the man again and thought he was Ensign Drake. There were several brewos he didn't recognize.

The place started really jumping. Keeper upped the music. Singly or in pairs, somersaulting dancers bounded back and forth between shrouds. Others toed a shroud and shimmied. A girl in black did splits on one. A girl in white dove through the torus. Keeper put it on her boyfriend's check. Brewos tried to sing.

Spar heard Kim recite:

"Izz a cat.
"Kilzz a rat.
"Greetss each guy,
"Thin or ffat.

"Ssay dolls, hi!"

Playday night fell. The pace got hotter. Doc didn't come. But Crown did. Dancers parted and a whole section of drinkers made way aloft for him and his girls and Hellhound, so that they had a third of the torus to themselves, with no one below in that third either. To Spar's surprise they all took coffee except the dog, who when asked by Crown, responded, "Bloody Mary," drawing out the words in such deep tones that they were little more than a low "Bluh-Muh" growl.

"Iss that sspeech, I assk you?" Kim commented from the other side of the torus. Drunks around him choked down chuckles.

Spar served the pouched coffee piping hot with felt holders and mixed Hellhound's drink in a self-squeezing syringe with sipping tube. He was very groggy and for the moment more afraid for Kim than himself. The face blurs tended to swim, but he could distinguish Rixende by her black hair, Phanette and Doucette by their matching red-blonde hair and oddly red-mottled fair skins, while Almodie *was* the platinum-haired pale one, yet she looked horribly right between the dark brown, purple-vested blur to one side of her and the black, narrower, prick-eared silhouette to the other.

Spar heard Crown whisper to her, "Ask Keeper to show you the talking cat." The whisper was very low and Spar wouldn't have heard it except that Crown's voice had a strange excited vibrancy Spar had never known in it before.

"But won't they fight then?—I mean Hellhound," she answered in a voice that sent silvery tendrils around Spar's heart. He yearned to see her face through Doc's tube. She would look like Virgo, only more beautiful. Yet, Crown's girl, she could be no virgin. It was a strange and horrible world. Her eyes *were* violet. But he was sick of blurs. Almodie sounded very frightened, yet she continued, "Please don't, Crown." Spar's heart was captured.

"But that's the whole idea, baby. And nobody don't's us. We thought we'd schooled you to that. We'd teach you another lesson here, except tonight we smell high fuzz—lots of it. Keeper!—our new lady wishes to hear your cat talk. Bring it over."

"I really don't . . ." Almodie began and went no further.

Kim came floating across the torus while Keeper was shouting in the opposite direction. The cat checked himself against a slender shroud and looked straight at Crown. "Yess?"

"Keeper, shut that junk off." The music died abruptly. Voices rose, then died abruptly too. "Well, cat, talk."

"Shshall ssing insstead," Kim announced and began an eerie caterwauling that had a pattern but was not Spar's idea of music.

"It's an abstraction," Almodie breathed delightedly. "Listen, Crown, that was a diminished seventh."

"A demented third, I'd say," Phanette commented from the other side.

Crown signed them to be quiet.

Kim finished with a high trill. He slowly looked around at his baffled audience and then began to groom his shoulder.

Crown gripped a ridge of the torus with his left hand and said evenly, "Since you will not talk to us, will you talk to our dog?"

Kim stared at Hellhound sucking his Bloody Mary. His eyes widened, their pupils slitted, his lips writhed back from needle-like fangs.

He hissed, "Schschweinhund!"

Hellhound launched himself, hind paws against the palm of Crown's left hand, which threw him forward toward the left, where Kim was dodging. But the cat switched directions, rebounding hindward from the next shroud. The dog's white-jagged jaws snapped sideways a foot from their mark as his great-chested black body hurtled past.

Hellhound landed with four paws in the middle of a fat drunk, who puffed out his wind barely before his swallow, but the dog took off instantly on reverse course. Kim bounced back and forth between shrouds. This time hair flew when jaws snapped, but also a rigidly spread paw slashed.

Crown grabbed Hellhound by his studded collar, restraining him from another dive. He touched the dog below the eye and smelled his fingers. "That'll be enough, boy," he said. "Can't go around killing musical geniuses." His hand dropped from his nose to below the torus and came up loosely fisted. "Well, cat, you've talked with our dog. Have you a word for us?"

"Yess!" Kim drifted to the shroud nearest Crown's face. Spar pushed off to grab him back, while Almodie gazed at Crown's fist and edged a hand toward it.

Kim loudly hissed, "Hellzz sspawn! Ffiend!"

Both Spar and Almodie were too late. From between two of Crown's fisted fingers a needle-stream jetted and struck Kim in his open mouth.

After what seemed to Spar a long time, his hand interrupted the stream. Its back burned acutely.

Kim seemed to collapse into himself, then launched himself away from Crown, toward the dark, open-jawed.

Crown said, "That's mace, an antique weapon like Greek fire, but well-known to our folk. The perfect answer to a witch cat."

Spar sprang at Crown, grappled his chest, tried to butt his jaw. They moved away from the torus at half the speed with which Spar had sprung.

Crown got his head aside. Spar closed his gums on Crown's throat. There was a *snick*. Spar felt wind on his bare back. Then a cold triangle pressed his flesh over his kidneys. Spar opened his jaws and floated limp. Crown chuckled.

A blue fuzz-glare, held by a brewo, made everything in the Bat Rack look more corpse-like than larboard light. A voice commanded, "Okay, folks, break it up. Go home. We're closing the place."

Sleepday dawned, drowning the fuzz-glare. The cold triangle left Spar's back. There was another *snick*. Saying, "Bye-bye, baby," Crown pushed off through the white glare toward four women's faces and one dog's. Phanette's and

Doucette's faintly red-mottled ones were close beside Hellhound's, as if they might be holding his collar.

Spar sobbed and began to hunt Kim. After a while Suzy came to help him. The Bat Rack emptied. Spar and Suzy cornered Kim. Spar grasped the cat around the chest. Kim's forelegs embraced his wrist, claws pricking. Spar got out the pouch Doc had given him and shoved its mouth between Kim's jaws. The claws dug deep. Taking no note of that, Spar gently sprayed. Gradually the claws came out and Kim relaxed. Spar hugged him gently. Suzy bound up Spar's wounded wrist.

Keeper came up followed by two brewos, one of them Ensign Drake, who said, "My partner and I will watch today by the aft and starboard hatches." Beyond them the Bat Rack was empty.

Spar said, "Crown has a knife." Drake nodded.

Suzy touched Spar's hand and said, "Keeper, I want to stay here tonight. I'm scared."

Keeper said, "I can offer you a shroud."

Drake and his mate dove slowly toward their posts.

Suzy squeezed Spar's hand. He said, rather heavily, "I can offer you my shroud, Suzy."

Keeper laughed and, after looking toward the Bridge men, whispered, "I can offer you mine, which, unlike Spar, I own. And moonmist. Otherwise, the passageways."

Suzy sighed, paused, then went off with him.

Spar miserably made his way to the fore-corner. Had Suzy expected him to fight Keeper? The sad thing was that he no longer wanted her, except as a friend. He loved Crown's new girl. Which was sad too.

He was very tired. Even the thought of new eyes tomorrow didn't interest him. He clipped his ankle to a shroud and tied a rag over his eyes. He gently clasped Kim, who had not spoken. He was asleep at once.

He dreamed of Almodie. She looked like Virgo, even to the white dress. She held Kim, who looked sleek as polished black leather. She was coming toward him, smiling. She kept coming without getting closer.

Much later—he thought—he woke in the drip of withdrawal. He sweat and shook, but that was minor. His nerves were jumping. Any moment, he was sure, they would twitch all his muscles into a stabbing spasm of sinew-snapping agony. His thoughts were moving so fast he could hardly begin to understand one in ten. It was like speeding through a curving, ill-lit passageway ten times faster than the main drag. If he touched a wall, he would forget even what little Spar knew, forget he was Spar. All around him black shrouds whipped in perpetual sine curves.

Kim was no longer by him. He tore the rag from his eyes. It was dark as before. Sleepday night. But his body stopped speeding and his thoughts slowed. His nerves still crackled, and he still saw the black snakes whipping, but he knew them for illusion. He even made out the dim glows of three running lights.

Then he saw two figures floating toward him. He could barely make out their eye-blurs, green in the smaller, violet in the other, whose face was spreadingly haloed by silvery glints. She was pale and whiteness floated around her. And, instead of a smile, he could see the white horizontal blur of bared teeth. Kim's teeth too were bared.

Suddenly he remembered the golden-haired girl who he'd thought was playing bartender in Crown's Hole. She was Suzy's one-time friend Sweetheart, snatched last Sleepday by vamps.

He screamed, which in Spar was a hoarse, retching bellow, and scrabbled at his clipped ankle.

The figures vanished. Below, he thought.

Lights came on. Someone dove and shook Spar's shoulder. "What happened, gramps?"

Spar gibbered while he thought what to tell Drake. He loved Almodie and Kim. He said, "Had a nightmare. Vamps attacked me."

"Description?"

"An old lady and a . . . a . . . little dog."

The other officer dove in. "The black hatch is open."

Drake said, "Keeper told us that was always locked. Follow through, Fenner." As the other dove below,

"You're sure this was a nightmare, gramps. A *little* dog? And an *old* woman?"

Spar said, "Yes," and Drake dove after his comrade, out through the black hatch.

Workday dawned. Spar felt sick and confused, but he set about his usual routine. He tried to talk to Kim, but the cat was as silent as yesterday afternoon. Keeper bullied and found many tasks—the place was a mess from Playday. Suzy got away quickly. She didn't want to talk about Sweetheart or anything else. Drake and Fenner didn't come back.

Spar swept and Kim patrolled, out of touch. In the afternoon Crown came in and talked with Keeper while Spar and Kim were out of earshot. They mightn't have been there for all notice Crown took of them.

Spar wondered about what he had seen last night. It might really have been a dream, he decided. He was no longer impressed by his memory-identification of Sweetheart. Stupid of him to have thought that Almodie and Kim, dream or reality, were vamps. Doc had said vamps were superstitions. But he didn't think much. He still had withdrawal symptoms, only less violent.

When Loafday dawned, Keeper gave Spar permission to leave the Bat Rack without his usual prying questions. Spar looked around for Kim, but couldn't see his black blob. Besides, he didn't really want to take the cat.

He went straight to Doc's office. The passageways weren't as lonely as last Loafday. For a third time he passed the bent figure croaking, "Seagull, Kestrel, Cathedral . . ."

Doc's hatch was unzipped, but Doc wasn't there. Spar waited a long while, uneasy in the corpse-light. It wasn't like Doc to leave his office unzipped and unattended. And he hadn't turned up at the Bat Rack last night, as he'd half promised.

Finally Spar began to look around. One of the first things he noticed was that the big black bag, which Doc had said contained his treasure, was missing.

Then he noticed the gleaming pliofilm bag in which Doc had put the mold of Spar's gums, now held something different. He unclipped it from its shroud. There were two items in it.

He cut a finger on the first, which was half circle, half pink and half gleaming. He felt out its shape more cautiously then, ignoring the tiny red blobs welling from his finger. It had an irregular depression in its pink top and bottom. He put it in his mouth. His gums mated with the depressions. He opened his mouth, then closed it, careful to keep his tongue back. There was a *snick* and a dull *click*. He had teeth!

His hands were shaking, not just from withdrawal, as he felt the second item.

It was two thick rounds joined by a short bar and with a thicker long bar ending in a semicircle going back from each.

He thrust a finger into one of the rounds. It tickled, just as the tube had tickled his eyes, only more intensely, almost painfully.

Hands shaking worse than ever, he fitted the contraption to his face. The semi-circles went around his ears, the rounds circled his eyes, not closely enough to tickle.

He could see sharply! *Everything* had edges, even his spread-fingered hands and the . . . clot of blood on one finger. He cried out—a low, wondering wail—and scanned the office. At first the scores and dozens of sharp-edged objects, each as distinct as the pictures of Capricorn and Virgo had been, were too much for him. He closed his eyes.

When his breathing was a little evener and his shaking less, he opened them cautiously and began to inspect the objects clipped to the shrouds. Each one was a wonder. He didn't know the purpose of half of them. Some of them with which he was familiar by use or blurred sight startled him greatly in their appearance—a comb, a brush, a book with pages (that infinitude of ranked black marks), a wrist watch (the tiny pictures around the circular margin of Capricorn and Virgo, and of the Bull and the Fishes, and so on, and the narrow bars radiating from the center and swinging swiftly or slowly or not at all—and pointing to the signs of the zodiac.

Before he knew it, he was at the corpse-glow wall. He faced it with a new courage, though it forced from his lips another wondering wail.

The corpse-glow didn't come from everywhere, though it took up the central quarter of his field of vision. His fingers touched taut, transparent pliofilm. What he saw beyond—a great way beyond, he began to think—was utter blackness with a great many tiny . . . points of bright light in it. Points were even harder to believe in than edges, he had to believe what he saw.

But centrally, looking much bigger than all the blackness, was a vast corpse-white round pocked with faint circles and scored by bright lines and mottled with slightly darker areas.

It didn't look as if it were wired for electricity, and it certainly didn't look afire. After a while Spar got the weird idea that its light was reflected from something much brighter *behind* Windrush.

It was infinitely strange to think of so much *space* around Windrush. Like thinking of a reality containing reality.

And if Windrush were between the hypothetical brighter light and the pocked white round, its shadow ought to be on the latter. Unless Windrush were almost infinitely small. Really these speculations were utterly too fantastic to deal with.

Yet could anything be too fantastic? Werewolves, witches, points, edges, size and space beyond any but the most insane belief.

When he had first looked at the corpse-white object, it had been round. And he had heard and felt the creakings of Loafday noon, without being conscious of it at the time. But now the round had its fore edge evenly sliced off, so that it was lopsided. Spar wondered if the hypothetical incandescence behind Windrush were moving, or the white round. Such thoughts, especially the last, were dizzying almost beyond endurance.

He made for the open door, wondering if he should zip it behind him, decided not to. The passageway was another amazement, going off and off and off, and narrowing as it went. Its walls bore . . . arrows, the red pointing to larboard, the way from which he'd come, the green pointing starboard, the way he was going. The arrows were what he'd always seen as dash-shaped blurs. As he pulled himself along the strangely definite dragline, the passageway stayed the same diameter, all the way up to the violet main drag.

He wanted to jerk himself as fast as the green arrows to the starboard end of Windrush to verify the hypothetical incandescence and see the details of the orange-dun round that always depressed him.

But he decided he ought first to report Doc's disappearance to the Bridge. He might find Drake there. And report the loss of Doc's treasure too, he reminded himself.

Passing faces fascinated him. Such a welter of noses and ears! He overtook the croaking, bent shape. It was that of an old woman whose nose almost met her chin. She was doing something twitchy with her fingers to two narrow sticks and a roll of slender, fuzzy line. He impulsively dove off the dragline and caught hold of her, whirling them around.

"What are you doing, grandma?" he asked.

She puffed with anger. "Knitting," she answered indignantly.

"What are the words you keep saying?"

"Names of knitting patterns," she replied, jerking loose from him and blowing on. "Sand Dunes, Lightning, Soldiers Marching . . ."

He started to swim for the dragline, then saw he was already at the blue shaft leading aloft. He grabbed hold of its speeding centerline, not minding the burn, and speeded to the Bridge.

When he got there, he saw there was a multitude of stars aloft. The oblong rainbows were all banks of multicolored lights winking on and off. But the silent officers—they looked very old, their faces stared as if they were sleep-swimming, their gestured orders were mechanical. He wondered if they knew where Windrush was going—or anything at all, beyond the Bridge of Windrush.

A dark, young officer with tightly curly hair floated to him. It wasn't until he spoke that Spar knew he was Ensign Drake.

"Hello, gramps. Say, you look younger. What are those things around your eyes?"

"Field glasses. They help me see sharp."

"But field glasses have tubes. They're a sort of binocular telescope."

Spar shrugged and told about the disappearance of Doc and his big, black treasure bag.

"But you say he drank a lot and he told you his treasures were dreams? Sounds like he was wacky and wandered off to do his drinking somewhere else."

"But Doc was a regular drinker. He always came to the Bat Rack."

"Well, I'll do what I can. Say, I've been pulled off the Bat Rack investigation. I think that character Crown got at someone higher up. The old ones are easy to get at—not so much greed as going by custom, taking the easiest course. Fenner and I never did find the old woman and the little dog, or any female and animal . . . or anything."

Spar told about Crown's earlier attempt to steal Doc's little black bag.

"So you think the two cases might be connected. Well, as I say, I'll do what I can."

Spar went back to the Bat Rack. It was very strange to see Keeper's face in detail. It looked old and its pink target center was a big red nose crisscrossed by veins. His brown eyes were not so much curious as avid. He asked about the things around Spar's eyes. Spar decided it wouldn't be wise to tell Keeper about seeing sharply.

"They're a new kind of costume jewelry, Keeper. Blasted Earth, I don't have any hair on my head, ought to have something."

"Language, Spar! It's like a drunk to spend precious scrip on such a grotesque bauble."

Spar neither reminded Keeper that all the scrip he'd earned at the Bat Rack amounted to no more than a wad as big as his thumb-joint, nor that he'd quit drinking. Nor did he tell him about his teeth, but kept them hidden behind his lips.

Kim was nowhere in sight. Keeper shrugged. "Gone off somewhere. You know the ways of strays, Spar."

Yes, thought Spar, *this one's stayed put too long.*

He kept being amazed that he could see *all* of the Bat Rack sharply. It was a hexagon criscrossed by shrouds and made up of two pyramids put together square base to square base. The apexes of the pyramids were the violet fore and dark red aft corners. The four other corners were the starboard green, the black below, the larboard scarlet, and the blue aloft, if you named them from aft in the way the hands of a watch move.

Suzy drifted in early Playday. Spar was shocked by her blowsy appearance and bloodshot eyes. But he was touched by her signs of affection and he felt the strong friendship between them. Twice when Keeper wasn't looking he switched her nearly empty pouch of dark for a full one. She told him that, yes, she'd once known Sweetheart and that, yes, she'd heard people say Mable had seen Sweetheart snatched by vamps.

Business was slow for Playday. There were no strange brewos. Hoping against fearful, gut-level certainty, Spar kept waiting for Doc to come in zigzagging along the ratlines and comment on the new gadgets he'd given Spar and spout about the Old Days and his strange philosophy.

Playday night Crown came in with his girls, all except Almodie. Doucette said she'd had a headache and stayed at the Hole. Once again, all of them ordered coffee, though to Spar all of them seemed high.

Spar covertly studied their faces. Though nervous and alive, they all had something in their stares akin to those he'd seen in most of the officers on the Bridge. Doc had said they were all zombies. It was interesting to find out that Phanette's and Doucette's red-mottled appearance was due to . . . freckles, tiny reddish star-clusters on their white skins.

"Where's that famous talking cat?" Crown asked Spar.

Spar shrugged. Keeper said, "Strayed. For which I'm

glad. Don't want a little feline who makes fights like last night."

Keeping his yellow-brown irised eyes on Spar, Crown said, "We believe it was that fight last Playday gave Almodie her headache, so she didn't want to come back tonight. We'll tell her you got rid of the witch cat."

"I'd have got rid of the beast if Spar hadn't," Keeper put in. "So you think it was a witch cat, coroner?"

"We're certain. What's that stuff on Spar's face?"

"A new sort of cheap eye jewelry, coroner, such as attracts drunks."

Spar got the feeling that this conversation had been prearranged, that there was a new agreement between Crown and Keeper. But he just shrugged again. Suzy was looking angry, but she said nothing.

Yet she stayed behind again after the Bat Rack closed. Keeper put no claim on her, though he leered knowingly before disappearing with a yawn and a stretch through the scarlet hatch. Spar checked that all six hatches were locked and shut off the lights, though that made no difference in the morning glare, before returning to Suzy, who had gone to his sleeping shroud.

Suzy asked, "You didn't get rid of Kim?"

Spar answered, "No, he just strayed, as Keeper said at first. I don't know where Kim is."

Suzy smiled and put her arms around him. "I think your new eye-things are beautiful," she said.

Spar said, "Suzy, did you know that Windrush isn't the Universe? That it's a ship going through space around a white round marked with circles, a round much bigger than all Windrush?"

Suzy replied, "I know Windrush is sometimes called the Ship. I've seen that round—in pictures. Forget all wild thoughts, Spar, and lose yourself in me."

Spar did so, chiefly from friendship. He forgot to clip his ankle to the shroud. Suzy's body didn't attract him. He was thinking of Almodie.

When it was over, Suzy slept. Spar put the rag around his eyes and tried to do the same. He was troubled by withdrawal symptoms only a little less bad than last

Sleepday's. Because of that little, he didn't go to the torus for a pouch of moonmist. But then there was a sharp jab in his back, as if a muscle had spasmed there, and the symptoms got much worse. He convulsed, once, twice, then just as the agony became unbearable, blanked out.

Spar woke, his head throbbing, to discover that he was not only clipped, but lashed to his shroud, his wrists stretched in one direction, his ankles in the other, his hands and his feet both numb. His nose rubbed the shroud.

Light made his eyelids red. He opened them a little at a time and saw Hellhound poised with bent hind legs against the next shroud. He could see Hellhound's great stabbing teeth very clearly. If he had opened his eyes a little more swiftly, Hellhound would have dove at his throat.

He rubbed his sharp metal teeth together. At least he had more than gums to meet an attack on his face.

Beyond Hellhound he saw black and transparent spirals. He realized he was in Crown's Hole. Evidently the last jab in his back had been the injection of a drug.

But Crown had not taken away his eye jewelry, nor noted his teeth. He had thought of Spar as old Eyeless Toothless.

Between Hellhound and the spirals, he saw Doc lashed to a shroud and his big black bag clipped next to him. Doc was gagged. Evidently he had tried to cry out. Spar decided not to. Doc's gray eyes were open and Spar thought Doc was looking at him.

Very slowly Spar moved his numb fingers on top of the knot lashing his wrists to the shroud and slowly contracted all his muscles and pulled. The knot slid down the shroud a millimeter. So long as he did something slowly enough, Hellhound could not see it. He repeated his action at intervals.

Even more slowly he swung his face to the left. He saw nothing more than that the hatch to the corridor was zipped shut, and that beyond the dog and Doc, between the black spirals, was an empty and unfurnished cabin whose whole starboard side was stars. The hatch to that cabin was open, with its black-striped emergency hatch wavering beside it.

With equal slowness he swung his face to the right, past Doc and past Hellhound, who was eagerly watching him for signs of life or waking. He had pulled down the knot on his wrists two centimeters.

The first thing he saw was a transparent oblong. In it were more stars and, by its aft edge, the smoky orange round. At last he could see the latter more clearly. The smoke was on top, the orange underneath and irregularly placed. The whole was about as big as Spar's palm could have covered, if he had been able to stretch out his arm to full length. As he watched, he saw a bright flash in one of the orange areas. The flash was short, then it turned to a tiny black round pushing out through the smoke. More than ever, Spar felt sadness.

Below the transparency, Spar saw a horrible tableau. Suzy was strapped to a bright metal rack guyed by shrouds. She was very pale and her eyes were closed. From the side of her neck went a red sipping-tube which forked into five branches. Four of the branches went into the red mouths of Crown, Rixende, Phanette, and Doucette. The fifth was shut by a small metal clip, and beyond it Almodie floated cowering, hands over her eyes.

Crown said softly, "We want it all. Strip her, Rixie."

Rixende clipped shut the end of her tube and swam to Suzy. Spar expected her to remove the blue culottes and bra, but instead she simply began to massage one of Suzy's legs, pressing always from ankle toward waist, driving her remaining blood nearer her neck.

Crown removed his sipping tube from his lips long enough to say, "Ahh, good to the last drop." Then he had mouthed the blood that had spurted out in the interval and had the tube in place again.

Phanette and Doucette convulsed with soundless giggles.

Almodie peered between her parted fingers, out of her mass of platinum hair, then scissored them shut again.

After a while Crown said, "That's all we'll get. Phan and Doucie, feed her to the big chewer. If you meet anyone in the passageway, pretend she's drunk. Afterward we'll get Doc to dose us high, and give him a little brew if he behaves, then we'll drink Spar."

Spar had his wrist knot more than halfway to his teeth. Hellhound kept watching eagerly for movement, unable to see movement that slow. Slaver made tiny gray globes beside his fangs.

Phanette and Doucette opened the hatch and steered Suzy's dead body through it.

Embracing Rixende, Crown said expansively toward Doc, "Well, isn't it the right thing, old man? Nature bloody in tooth and claw, a wise one said. They've poisoned everything there." He pointed toward the smoky orange round sliding out of sight. "They're still fighting, but they'll soon all be dead. So death should be the rule too for this gimcrack, so-called survival ship. Remember they are aboard her. When we've drunk the blood of everyone aboard Windrush, including their blood, we'll drink our own, if our own isn't theirs."

Spar thought, *Crown thinks too much in they's.* The knot was close to his teeth. He heard the big chewer start to grind.

In the empty next cabin, Spar saw Drake and Fenner, clad once more as brewos, swimming toward the open hatch.

But Crown saw them too. "Get 'em, Hellhound," he directed, pointing. "It's our command."

The big black dog bulleted from his shroud through the open hatch. Drake pointed something at him. The dog went limp.

Chuckling softly, Crown took by one tip a swastika with curved, gleaming, razor-sharp blades and sent it spinning off. It curved past Spar and Doc, went through the open hatch, missed Drake and Fenner—and Hellhound—and struck the wall of stars.

There was a rush of wind, then the emergency hatch smacked shut. Spar saw Drake, Fenner, and Hellhound, wavery through the transparent pliofilm, spew blood, bloat, burst bloodily open. The empty cabin they had been in disappeared. Windrush had a new wall and Crown's Hole was distorted.

Far beyond, growing ever tinier, the swastika spun toward the stars.

Phanette and Doucette came back. "We fed in Suzy. Someone was coming, so we beat it." The big chewer stopped grinding.

Spar bit cleanly through his wrist lashings and immediately doubled over to bite his ankles loose.

Crown dove at him. Pausing to draw knives, the four girls did the same.

Phanette, Doucette, and Rixende went limp. Spar had the impression that small black balls had glanced from their skulls.

There wasn't time to bite his feet loose, so he straightened. Crown hit his chest as Almodie bit his feet.

Crown and Spar giant-swung around the shroud. Then Almodie had cut Spar's ankles loose. As they spun off along the tangent, Spar tried to knee Crown in the groin, but Crown twisted and evaded the blow as they moved toward the inboard wall.

There was the *snick* of Crown's knife unfolding. Spar saw the dark wrist and grabbed it. He butted at Crown's jaw. Crown evaded. Spar set his teeth in Crown's neck and bit.

Blood covered Spar's face, spurted over it. He spat out a hunk of flesh. Crown convulsed. Spar fought off the knife. Crown went limp. That the pressure in a man should work against him.

Spar shook the blood from his face. Through its beads, he saw Keeper and Kim side by side. Almodie was clutching his ankles. Phanette, Doucette, Rixende floated.

Keeper said proudly, "I shot them with my gun for drunks. I knocked them out. Now I'll cut their throats, if you wish."

Spar said, "No more throat-cutting. No more blood." Shaking off Almodie's hands, he took off for Doc, picking up Doucette's floating knife by the way.

He slashed Doc's lashings and cut the gag from his face.

Meanwhile Kim hissed, "Sstole and ssecreted Keeper's sscrip from the boxx. Ashshured him you sstole it, Sspar. You and Ssuzzy. Sso he came. Keeper izz a shshlemiel."

Keeper said, "I saw Suzy's foot going into the big chewer. I knew it by its anklet of hearts. After that I had the courage to kill Crown or anyone. I loved Suzy."

Doc cleared his throat and croaked, "Moonmist." Spar found a triple pouch and Doc sucked it all. Doc said, "Crown spoke the truth. Windrush is a plastic survival ship from Earth. Earth"—he motioned toward the dull orange round disappearing aft in the window—"poisoned herself with smog pollution and nuclear war. She spent gold for war, plastic for surival. Best forgotten. Windrush went mad. Understandably. Even with the Lethean rickettsia, or Styx ricks, as you call it. Thought Windrush was the cosmos. Crown kidnapped me to get my drugs, kept me alive to know the doses."

Spar looked at Keeper. "Clean up here," he ordered. "Feed Crown to the big chewer."

Almodie pulled herself from Spar's ankles to his waist. "There was a second survival ship. Circumluna. When Windrush went mad, my father and mother—and you—were sent here to investigate and cure. But my father died and you got Styx ricks. My mother died just before I was given to Crown. She sent you Kim."

Kim hissed, "My fforebear ccame from Ccircumluna to Windrushsh, too. Great-grandmother. Taught me the ffiguress for Windrushsh . . . Radiuss from moon-ccenter, two thoussand five hundred miless. Period, ssixx hourss—sso, the sshort dayss. A terranth izz the time it takess Earth to move through a cconsstellation, and sso on."

Doc said, "So, Spar, you're the only one who remembers without cynicism. You'll have to take over. It's all yours, Spar."

Spar had to agree.

Schrödinger's Cat

Ursula K. Le Guin

As things appear to be coming to some sort of climax, I have withdrawn to this place. It is cooler here, and nothing moves fast.

On the way here I met a married couple who were coming apart. She had pretty well gone to pieces, but he seemed, at first glance, quite hearty. While he was telling me that he had no hormones of any kind, she pulled herself together, and by supporting her head in the crook of her right knee and hopping on the toes of the right foot, approached us shouting, "Well, what's *wrong* with a person trying to express themselves?" The left leg, the arms and the trunk, which had remained lying in the heap, twitched and jerked in sympathy.

"Great legs," the husband pointed out, looking at the slim ankle. "My wife has great legs."

A cat has arrived, interrupting my narrative. It is a striped yellow tom with white chest and paws. He has long whiskers and yellow eyes. I never noticed before that cats had whiskers above their eyes; is that normal? There is no way to tell. As he had gone to sleep on my knee, I shall proceed.

Where?

Nowhere, evidently. Yet the impulse to narrate remains. Many things are not worth doing, but almost anything is worth telling. In any case, I have a severe congenital case of Ethica laboris puritanica, or Adam's Disease. It is incurable except by total decephalization. I even like to dream when asleep, and to try and recall my dreams: it assures me that I haven't wasted seven or eight hours just lying there. Now here I am, lying, here. Hard at it.

Well, the couple I was telling you about finally broke up. The pieces of him trotted around bouncing and cheeping, like little chicks, but she was finally reduced to nothing but a mass of nerves; rather like fine chicken-wire, in fact, but hopelessly tangled.

So I came on, placing one foot carefully in front of the other, and grieving. This grief is with me still. I fear it is part of me, like foot or loin or eye, or may even be myself: for I seem to have no other self, nothing further, nothing that lies outside the borders of grief.

Yet I don't know what I grieve for: my wife? my husband? my children, or myself? I can't remember. Most dreams are forgotten, try as one will to remember. Yet later music strikes the note and the harmonic rings along the mandolin-strings of the mind, and we find tears in our eyes. Some note keeps playing that makes me want to cry; but what for? I am not certain.

The yellow cat, who may have belonged to the couple that broke up, is dreaming. His paws twitch now and then, and once he makes a small, suppressed remark with his mouth shut. I wonder what a cat dreams of, and to whom he was speaking just then. Cats seldom waste words. They are quiet beasts. They keep their counsel, they reflect. They reflect all day, and at night their eyes reflect. Overbred Siamese cats may be as noisy as little dogs, and then people say, "They're talking," but the noise is further from speech than is the deep silence of the hound or the tabby. All this cat can say is meow, but maybe in his silences he will suggest to me what it is that I have lost, what I am grieving for. I have a feeling that he knows. That's why he came here. Cats look out for Number One.

It was getting awfully hot. I mean, you could touch less and less. The stove-burners, for instance; now, I know that stove-burners always used to get hot, that was their final cause, they existed in order to get hot. But they began to get hot without having been turned on. Electric units or gas rings, there they'd be when you came into the kitchen for breakfast, all four of them glaring away, the air above them shaking like clear jelly with the heat waves. It did no good to turn them off, because they weren't on in the first place. Besides, the knobs and dials were also hot, uncomfortable to the touch.

Some people tried hard to cool them off. The favorite technique was to turn them on. It worked sometimes, but you could not count on it. Others investigated the phenomenon, tried to get at the root of it, the cause. They were probably the most frightened ones, but man is most human at his most frightened. In the face of the hot stove-burners they acted with exemplary coolness. They studied, they observed. They were like the fellow in Michelangelo's "Last Judgment" who has clapped his hands over his face in horror as the devils drag him down to Hell—but only over one eye. The other eye is busy looking. It's all he can do, but he does it. He observes. Indeed, one wonders if Hell would exist if he did not look at it. However, neither he nor the people I am talking about had enough time left to do much about it. And then finally of course there were the people who did not try to do or think anything about it at all.

When hot water came out of the cold-water taps one morning, however, even people who had blamed it all on the Democrats began to feel a more profound unease. Before long, forks and pencils and wrenches were too hot to handle without gloves; and cars were really terrible. It was like opening the door of an oven going full blast, to open the door of your car. And by then, other people almost scorched your fingers off. A kiss was like a branding iron. Your child's hair flowed along your hand like fire.

Here, as I said, it is cooler; and, as a matter of fact, this animal is cool. A real cool cat. No wonder it's pleasant to pet his fur. Also he moves slowly, at least for the most part, which is all the slowness one can reasonably expect of a cat. He hasn't that frenetic quality most creatures acquired—all they did was ZAP and gone. They lacked presence. I suppose birds always tended to be that way, but even the hummingbird used to halt for a second in the very center of his metabolic frenzy, and hang, still as a hub, present, above the fuchsias—then gone again, but you knew something was there besides the blurring brightness. But it got so that even robins and pigeons, the heavy impudent birds, were a blur; and as for swallows, they cracked the sound barrier. You knew of swallows only by the small, curved sonic booms that looped about the eaves of old houses in the evening.

Worms shot like subway trains through the dirt of gardens, among the writhing roots of roses.

You could scarcely lay a hand on children, by then: too fast to catch, too hot to hold. They grew up before your eyes.

But then, maybe that's always been true.

I was interrupted by the cat, who woke and said meow once, then jumped down from my lap and leaned against my legs diligently. This is a cat who knows how to get fed. He also knows how to jump. There was a lazy fluidity to his leap, as if gravity affected him less than it does other creatures. As a matter of fact there were some localized cases, just before I left, of the failure of gravity; but this quality in the cat's leap was something quite else. I am not yet in such a state of confusion that I can be alarmed by grace. Indeed, I found it reassuring. While I was opening a can of sardines, a person arrived.

Hearing the knock, I thought it might be the mailman. I miss mail very much, so I hurried to the door and said, "Is it the mail?" A voice replied, "Yah!" I opened the door. He came in, almost pushing me aside in his haste.

He dumped down an enormous knapsack he had been carrying, straightened up, massaged his shoulders, and said, "Wow!"

"How did you get here?"

He stared at me and repeated, "How?"

At this, my thoughts concerning human and animal speech recurred to me, and I decided that this was probably not a man, but a small dog. (Large dogs seldom go yah, wow, how, unless it is appropriate to do so.)

"Come on, fella," I coaxed him. "Come, come on, that's a boy, good doggie!" I opened a can of pork and beans for him at once, for he looked half-starved. He ate voraciously, gulping and lapping. When it was gone he said, "Wow!" several times. I was just about to scratch him behind the ears when he stiffened, his hackles bristling, and growled deep in his throat. He had noticed the cat.

The cat had noticed him some time before, without interest, and was now sitting on a copy of *The Well-Tempered Clavichord* washing sardine oil off its whiskers.

"Wow!" the dog, whom I had thought of calling Rover, barked. "Wow! Do you know what that is? *That's Schrödinger's cat!*"

"No, it's not; not any more; it's my cat," I said, unreasonably offended.

"Oh, well, Schrödinger's dead, of course, but it's his cat. I've seen hundreds of pictures of it. Erwin Schrödinger, the great physicist, you know. Oh, wow! To think of finding it here!"

The cat looked coldly at him for a moment, and began to wash its left shoulder with negligent energy. An almost religious expression had come into Rover's face. "It was meant," he said in a low, impressive tone. "Yah. It was *meant*. It can't be a mere coincidence. It's too improbable. Me, with the box; you, with the cat; to meet—here—now." He looked up at me, his eyes shining with happy fervor. "Isn't it wonderful?" he said. "I'll get the box set up right away." And he started to tear open his huge knapsack.

While the cat washed its front paws, Rover unpacked.

While the cat washed its tail and belly, regions hard to reach gracefully, Rover put together what he had unpacked, a complex task. When he and the cat finished their operations simultaneously and looked at me, I was impressed. They had come out even, to the very second. Indeed it seemed that something more than chance was involved. I hoped it was not myself.

"What's that?" I asked, pointing to a protuberance on the outside of the box. I did not ask what the box was, as it was quite clearly a box.

"The gun," Rover said with excited pride.

"The gun?"

"To shoot the cat."

"To shoot the cat?"

"Or to *not shoot* the cat. Depending on the photon."

"The photon?"

"Yah! It's Schrödinger's great *Gedankenexperiment*. You see, there's a little emitter here. At Zero Time, five seconds after the lid of the box is closed, it will emit one photon. The photon will strike a half-silvered mirror. The quantum mechanical probability of the photon passes through the mirror is exactly one-half, isn't it? So! If the photon passes through, the trigger will be activated and the gun will fire. If the photon is deflected, the trigger will not be activated and the gun will not fire. Now, you put the cat in. The cat is in the box. You close the lid. You go away! You stay away! What happens?" Rover's eyes were bright.

"The cat gets hungry?"

"The cat gets shot—or not shot," he said, seizing my arm, though not, fortunately, in his teeth. "But the gun is silent, perfectly silent. The box is soundproof. There is no way to know whether or not the cat has been shot until you lift the lid of the box. There is NO way! Do you see how central this is to the whole of quantum theory? Before Zero Time the whole system, on the quantum level or on our level, is nice and simple. But after Zero Time the whole system can be represented only by a linear combination of two waves. We cannot predict the behavior of the photon, and thus, once it has behaved, we cannot predict the state of the system it has determined. We cannot predict it! God plays dice with the world! So it is beautifully demonstrated that if you desire certainty, any certainty, you must create it yourself!"

"How?"

"By lifting the lid of the box, of course," Rover said, looking at me with sudden disappointment, perhaps a touch of suspicion, like a Baptist who finds he has been talking church matters not to another baptist as he thought, but to a Methodist, or even, God forbid, an Episcopalian. "To find out whether the cat is dead or not."

"Do you mean," I said carefully, "that until you lift the lid of the box, the cat has neither been shot nor not been shot?"

"Yah!" Rover said, radiant with relief, welcoming me back to the fold. "Or maybe, you know, both."

"But why does opening the box and looking reduce the system back to one probability, either live cat or dead cat? Why don't we get included in the system when we lift the lid of the box?"

There was a pause. "How?" Rover barked distrustfully.

"Well, we would involve ourselves in the system, you see, the superposition of two waves. There's no reason why it should only exist *inside* an open box, is there? So when we came to look, there we would be, you and I, both looking at a live cat, and both looking at a dead cat. You see?"

A dark cloud lowered on Rover's eyes and brow. He barked twice in a subdued, harsh voice, and walked away. With his back turned to me he said in a firm, sad tone, "You must not complicate the issue. It is complicated enough."

"Are you sure?"

He nodded. Turning, he spoke pleadingly. "Listen. It's all we have—the box. Truly it is. The box. And the cat. And they're here. The box, the cat, at last. Put the cat in the box. Will you? Will you let me put the cat in the box?"

"No," I said, shocked.

"Please. Please. Just for a minute. Just for half a minute! Please let me put the cat in the box!"

"Why?"

"I can't stand this terrible uncertainty," he said, and burst into tears.

I stood some while indecisive. Though I felt sorry for the poor son of a bitch, I was about to tell him, gently, No, when a curious thing happened. The cat walked over to the box, sniffed around it, lifted his tail and sprayed a corner to mark his territory, and then lightly, with that marvelous fluid ease, leapt into it. His yellow tail just flicked the edge of the lid as he jumped, and it closed, falling into place with a soft, decisive click.

"The cat is in the box," I said.

"The cat is in the box," Rover repeated in a whisper, falling to his knees. "Oh, wow. Oh, wow. Oh, wow."

There was silence then: deep silence. We both gazed, I afoot, Rover kneeling, at the box. No sound. Nothing happened. Nothing would happen. Nothing would ever happen, until we lifted the lid of the box.

"Like Pandora," I said in a weak whisper. I could not quite recall Pandora's legend. She had let all the plagues and evils out of the box, of course, but there had been something else, too. After all the devils were let loose, something quite different, quite unexpected, had been left. What had it been? Hope? A dead cat? I could not remember.

Impatience welled up in me. I turned on Rover, glaring. He returned the look with expressive brown eyes. You can't tell me dogs haven't got souls.

"Just exactly what are you trying to prove?" I demanded.

"That the cat will be dead, or not dead," he murmured submissively. "Certainty. All I want is certainty. To know for *sure* that God *does* play dice with the world."

I looked at him for a while with fascinated incredulity. "Whether he does, or doesn't," I said, "do you think he's going to leave you a note about it in the box?" I went to the box, and with a rather dramatic gesture, flung the lid back. Rover staggered up from his knees, gasping, to look. The cat was, of course, not there.

Rover neither barked, nor fainted, nor cursed, nor wept. He really took it very well.

"Where is the cat?" he asked at last.

"Where is the box?"

"Here."

"Where's here?"

"Here is now."

"We used to think so," I said, "but really we should use larger boxes."

He gazed about him in mute bewilderment, and did not flinch even when the roof of the house was lifted off just like the lid of a box, letting in the unconscionable, inordinate light of the stars. He had just time to breathe. "Oh, wow!"

I have identified the note that keeps sounding. I checked it on the mandolin before the glue melted. It is the note A, the one that drove Robert Schumann mad. It is a beautiful, clear tone, much clearer now that the stars are visible. I shall miss the cat. I wonder if he found what it was we lost?

Tales of a Starship's Cat
Judith R. Conly

Adoption

Your kit-large paws, deprived of fur,
rouse me from sib-side stalking dreams.
Your laughter mocks my miniature growl
until your nose, my first-won prey,
receives my thread-fine parallel brand.
Your arms, silver-shielded in claw-rejecting cloth,
parade me proudly to my new domain,
and, amid your shipmates' cheers and glee,
enthrone me, triumphant, in the captain's chair.

Patrol

As our travels cross air-enclosed, sun-tied seasons,
my rounds span humans' hour-bound cycles.
I trace the sleep-quiet corridor from quarters
and leap down ladders ill-designed for feline feet,
until I reach the reassuring engines' lair
and confirm their great maternal purr.

My trail past forbidden places then leads
to the cavern stacked with the curious containers
that inconveniently change at planetfall.
True to my duty, I examine each bulky box and bundle,
signing them with my seal of approval,
and explore every obscure crevice and corner,
to capture and execute any unpredicted passengers.
Finally, wearing fresh-groomed contentment,
I return to awakening crew-filled decks
where, satisfied of the galley's security,
I collect my morning's edible salary,
and report to sleep-sluggish, coffee-clutching comrades
all the details of our home's nightside status.

Weightlessness

My yowl rebounds from former floor,
and, fur puffed toward no-direction-down,
my tail flails, wild propeller in a pirouetting room,
accelerating its frantic random dance.
The light assaults my night-adjusted eyes
as I master my recalcitrant tangle of limbs
and thrash my way across wide mocking space,
to cling with suddenly insufficient claws
to the fabric-shored island of an arbitrary wall.

Partnership

The years spread stars across our path,
and we pad delicately from world to stepstone world.
While you, compelled by human curiosity,
explore the strange-scented reaches of every grimy port,
I stand stiff-legged sentry at our steel border,
until, long past the setting of each alien sun,
you drag in your feet and your dubious cargo
to pass through my meticulous inspection.
At last, late in our unvarying portable night,

with long-withheld repast delivered and enjoyed,
I deem my countless duties well discharged
and stretch my work-weary body on our shared bunk
and purr contentment into the security of your side.

scrabbling with panic when he entered the flat [illegible]

Who's There?

Arthur C. Clarke

When Satellite Control called me, I was writing up the day's progress report in the Observation Bubble—the glass-domed office that juts out from the axis of the Space Station like the hubcap of a wheel. It was not really a good place to work, for the view was too overwhelming. Only a few yards away I could see the construction teams performing their slow-motion ballet as they put the station together like a giant jigsaw puzzle. And beyond them, twenty thousand miles below, was the blue-green glory of the full Earth, floating against the ravelled star clouds of the Milky Way.

"Station Supervisor here," I answered. "What's the trouble?"

"Our radar's showing a small echo two miles away, almost stationary, about five degrees west of Sirius. Can you give us a visual report on it?"

Anything matching our orbit so precisely could hardly be a meteor; it would have to be something we'd dropped—perhaps an inadequately secured piece of equipment that had drifted away from the station. So I assumed: but when I pulled out my binoculars and searched the sky around Orion, I soon found my mistake.

Though this space traveller was man-made, it had nothing to do with us.

"I've found it," I told Control. "It's someone's test satellite—cone-shaped, four antennae, and what looks like a lens system in its base. Probably U.S. Air Force, early nineteen-sixties, judging by the design. I know they lost track of several when their transmitters failed. There were quite a few attempts to hit this orbit before they finally made it."

After a brief search through the files, Control was able to confirm my guess. It took a little longer to find out that Washington wasn't in the least bit interested in our discovery of a twenty-year-old stray satellite, and would be just as happy if we lost it again.

"Well, we can't do *that*," said Control. "Even if nobody wants it, the thing's a menace to navigation. Someone had better go out and haul it aboard."

That someone, I realized, would have to be me. I dared not detach a man from the closely knit construction teams, for we were already behind schedule—and a single day's delay on this job cost a million dollars. All the radio and TV networks on Earth were waiting impatiently for the moment when they could route their programs through us, and thus provide the first truly global service, spanning the world from Pole to Pole.

"I'll go out and get it," I answered, snapping an elastic band over my papers so that the air currents from the ventilators wouldn't set them wandering around the room. Though I tried to sound as if I was doing everyone a great favor, I was secretly not at all displeased. It had been at least two weeks since I'd been outside; I was getting a little tired of stores schedules, maintenance reports, and all the glamorous ingredients of a Space Station Supervisor's life.

The only member of the staff I passed on my way to the air lock was Tommy, our recently acquired cat. Pets mean a great deal to men thousand of miles from Earth, but there are not many animals that can adapt themselves to a weightless environment. Tommy mewed plaintively at me as I clambered into my spacesuit, but I was in too much of a hurry to play with him.

At this point, perhaps I should remind you that the suits we use on the station are completely different from the flexible affairs men wear when they want to walk around on the moon. Ours are really baby spaceships, just big enough to hold one man. They are stubby cylinders about seven feet long, fitted with low-powered propulsion jets, and a pair of accordian-like sleeves at the upper end for the operator's arms. Normally, however, you keep your hands drawn inside the suit, working the manual controls in front of your chest.

As soon as I'd settled down inside my very exclusive spacecraft, I switched on power and checked the gauges on the tiny instrument panel. There's a magic word, "FORB," that you'll often hear spacemen mutter as they climb into their suits; it reminds them to test fuel, oxygen, radio batteries. All my needles were well in the safety zone, so I lowered the transparent hemisphere over my head and sealed myself in. For a short trip like this, I did not bother to check the suit's internal lockers, which were used to carry food and special equipment for extended missions.

As the conveyor belt decanted me into the air lock, I felt like an Indian papoose being carried along on its mother's back. Then the pumps brought the pressure down to zero, the outer door opened, and the last traces of air swept me out into the stars, turning me very slowly head over heels.

The station was only a dozen feet away, yet I was now an independent planet—a little world of my own. I was sealed up in a tiny, mobile cylinder, with a superb view of the entire universe, but I had practically no freedom of movement inside the suit. The padded seat and safety belts prevented me from turning around, though I could reach all the controls and lockers with my hands or feet.

In space, the great enemy is the sun, which can blast you to blindness in seconds. Very cautiously, I opened up the dark filters on the "night" side of my suit, and turned my head to look out at the stars. At the same time, I switched on the helmet's external sunshade to automatic, so that whichever way the suit gyrated, my eyes would be shielded from that intolerable glare.

Presently, I found my target—a bright fleck of silver whose metallic glint distinguished it clearly from the surrounding stars. I stamped on the jet-control pedal and felt the mild surge of acceleration as the low-powered rockets set me moving away from the station. After ten seconds of steady thrust, I estimated that my speed was great enough and cut off the drive. It would take me five minutes to coast the rest of the way, and not much longer to return with my salvage.

And it was at that moment, as I launched myself out into the abyss, that I knew something was horribly wrong.

It is never completely silent inside a spacesuit; you can always hear the gentle hiss of oxygen, the faint whirr of fans and motors, the susurration of your own breathing—even, if you listen carefully enough, the rhythmic thump that is the pounding of your heart. These sounds reverberate through the suit, unable to escape into the surrounding void; they are the unnoticed background of life in space, for you are aware of them only when they change.

They had changed now; to them had been added a sound which I could not identify. It was an intermittent, muffled thudding, sometimes accompanied by a scraping noise, as of metal upon metal.

I froze instantly, holding my breath and trying to locate the alien sound with my ears. The meters on the control board gave no clues; all the needles were rock-steady on their scales, and there were none of the flickering red lights that would warn of impending disaster. That was some comfort, but not much. I had long ago learned to trust my instincts in such matters; their alarm signals were flashing now, telling me to return to the station before it was too late. . . .

Even now, I do not like to recall those next few minutes, as panic slowly flooded into my mind, like a rising tide, overwhelming the dams of reason and logic which every man must erect against the mystery of the universe.

I knew then what it was like to face insanity; no other explanation fitted the facts.

For it was no longer possible to pretend that the noise disturbing me was that of some faulty mechanism. Though I was in utter isolation, far from any other human being or, indeed, any material object, I was not alone. The soundless void was bringing to my ears the faint but unmistakable stirrings of life.

In that first, heart-freezing moment, it seemed that something was trying to get into my suit—something invisible, seeking shelter from the cruel and pitiless vacuum of space. I whirled madly in my harness, scanning the entire sphere of vision around me except for the blazing, forbidden cone towards the sun. There was nothing there, of course. There could not be—yet that purposeful scrabbling was clearer than ever.

Despite the nonsense that has been written about us, it is not true that spacemen are superstitious. But can you blame me if, as I came to the end of logic's resources, I suddenly remembered how Bernie Summers had died, no farther from the station than I was at this very moment?

It was one of those "impossible" accidents; it always is. Three things had gone wrong at once. Bernie's oxygen regulator had run wild and sent the pressure soaring; the safety valve had failed to blow—and a faulty joint had given way instead. In a fraction of a second, his suit was open to space.

I had never known Bernie, but suddenly his fate became of overwhelming importance to me—for a horrible idea had come into my mind. One does not talk about these things, but a damaged spacesuit is too valuable to be thrown away, even if it has killed its wearer. It is repaired, renumbered—and issued to someone else. . . .

What happens to the soul of a man who dies between the stars, far from his native world? Are you still here, Bernie, clinging to the last object that linked you to your lost and distant home?

As I fought the nightmares that were swirling around me—for now it seemed that the scratchings and soft fumblings were coming from all directions—there was one last hope to which I clung. For the sake of my sanity, I had to prove that this wasn't Bernie's suit—that the metal walls so closely wrapped around me had never been another man's coffin.

It took me several tries before I could press the right button and switch my transmitter to the emergency wavelength. "Station!" I gasped. "I'm in trouble! Get records to check my suit history and—"

I never finished; they say my yell wrecked the microphone. But what man alone in the absolute isolation of a spacesuit would *not* have yelled when something patted him softly on the back of the neck?

I must have lunged forward, despite the safety harness, and smashed against the upper edge of the control panel. When the rescue squad reached me a few minutes later, I was still unconscious, with an angry bruise across my forehead.

And so I was the last person in the whole satellite relay system to know what had happened. When I came to my senses an hour later, all our medical staff was gathered around my bed, but it was quite a while before the doctors bothered to look at me. They were much too busy playing with the three cute little kittens our badly misnamed Tommy had been rearing in the seclusion of my spacesuit's Number Five Storage Locker.

Bullhead

David Drake

"That don't half stink," grumbled the mule as Old Nathan came out of the shed with the saddle over his left arm and a bucket of bait in his right hand.

"Nobody asked you t' like it," the cunning man replied sharply. "Nor me neither, ifen it comes t' thet. It brings catfish like it's manna from hivven, and I *do* like a bit of smoked catfish fer supper."

"Waal, then," said the mule, "you go off t' yer fish and I'll mommick up some more oats while yer gone. Then we're both hap—"

The beast's big head turned toward the cabin and its ears cocked forward. "Whut's thet coming?" it demanded.

Old Nathan set the bucket down and hung the saddle over a fence rail. He'd been raised in a time when the Tennessee Territory was wilderness and the few folk you met liable to be wilder yet—the Whites worse than the Indians.

But that was long decades ago. He'd gotten out of the habit of *always* keeping his rifle close by and loaded. But a time like this, when somebody crept up so you didn't hear his horse on the trail—

Then you remembered that your rifle was in the cabin,

fifty feet away, and that a man of seventy didn't move so quick as the boy of eighteen who'd aimed that same rifle at King's Mountain.

"Halloo the house?" called the visitor, and Old Nathan's world slipped back to this time of settlement and civilization. The voice was a woman's, not that of an ambusher who'd hitched his horse to a sapling back along the trail so as to shoot the cunning man unawares.

"We're out the back!" Old Nathan called. "Come through the cabin, or I'll come in t' ye."

It wasn't that he had enemies, exactly; but there were plenty folks around afraid of what the cunning man did—or what they thought he did. Fear had pulled as many triggers as hatred over the years, he guessed.

"T'morry's a good time t' traipse down t' the river," the mule said complacently as it thrust its head over the snake-rail fence to chop a tuft of grass just within its stretch. "Or never a'tall, that's better yet."

"We're goin' t' check my trot line t'day, sooner er later!" Old Nathan said over his shoulder. "Depend on it!"

Both doors of the one-room cabin were open. Old Nathan liked the ventilation, though the morning was cool. His visitor came out onto the back porch where the water barrel stood and said, "Oh, I didn't mean t' take ye away from business. You jest go ahead 'n I'll be on my way."

Her name was Ellie. Ellie Ransden, he reckoned, since she'd been living these three years past with Bully Ransden, though it wasn't certain they'd had a preacher marry them. Lot of folks figured these old half-lettered stump-hole preachers hereabouts, they weren't much call to come between a couple of young people and God no-ways.

Though she still must lack a year of twenty, Ellie Ransden had a woman's full breasts and hips. Her hair, black as thunder, was her glory. It was piled now on top of her head with pins and combs, but if she shook it out, it would be long enough to fall to the ground.

The combs were the only bit of fancy about the

woman. She wore a gingham dress and went barefoot, with calluses to show that was usual for her till the snow fell. Bully Ransden wasn't a lazy man, but he had a hard way about him that put folk off, and he'd started from less than nothing. . . .

If there was a prettier woman in the county than Ellie Ransden, Old Nathan hadn't met her.

"Set yerse'f," Old Nathan grunted, nodding her back into the cabin. "I'll warm some grounds."

"Hit don't signify," Ellie said. She looked up toward a corner of the porch overhang where two sparrows argued about which had stolen the thistle seed from the other. "I jest figgered I'd drop by t' be neighborly, but if you've got affairs . . . ?"

"The fish'll wait," said the cunning man, dipping a gourd of water from the barrel. He'd drunk the coffee in the pot nigh down to the grounds already. "I was jest talkin' t' my mule."

Ellie's explanation of what she was doing here was a lie for at least several reasons. First, Bully Ransden was no friend to the cunning man. Second, the two cabins, Old Nathan's and Ransden's back some miles on the main road, were close enough to be neighbors in parts as ill-settled as these—but in the three years past, Ellie hadn't felt the need to come down this way.

The last reason was the swollen redness at the corners of the young woman's eyes. *Mis'ry was what brought folks most times t' see the cunning man, t' see Old Nathan the Witch. Mis'ry and anger. . . .*

Old Nathan poured water into the iron coffeepot on the table of his one-room cabin. Some of last night's coffee grounds, the beans bought green and roasted in the fireplace, floated on the inch of liquid remaining. They'd have enough strength left for another heating.

"Lots of folks, they talk t' their animals," he added defensively as he hung the refilled pot on the swinging bar and pivoted it back over the fire. *Not so many thet hear what the beasts answer back, but* thet *was nobody's affair save his own.*

"Cullen ain't a bad man, ye know," Ellie Ransden said

in a falsely idle voice as she examined one of the cabin's pair of glazed sash-windows.

Old Nathan set a knot of pitchy lightwood in the coals to heat the fire up quickly. She was likely the only soul in the country called Bully Ransden by his baptized name. "Thet's for them t' say as knows him better 'n I do," he said aloud. "Or care t' know him."

"He was raised hard, thet's all," Ellie said to the rectangles of window glass. "I reckon—"

She turned around and her voice rose in challenge, though she probably didn't realize what was happening. "—thet you're afeerd t' cross him, same as airy soul hereabouts?"

Old Nathan snorted. "I cain't remember the time I met a man who skeerd me," he said. "Seeins as I've got this old, I don't figger I'll meet one hereafter neither."

He smiled, amused at the way he'd reacted to the girl's—the woman's—obvious ploy. "Set," he offered, gesturing her to the rocking chair.

Ellie moved toward the chair, then angled off in a flutter of gingham like a butterfly unwilling to light for nervousness. She stood near the fireplace, staring in the direction of the five cups of blue-rimmed porcelain on the fireboard above the hearth. Her hands twisted together instinctively as if she were attempting to strangle a snake.

"Reckon you heerd about thet *Modom* Taliaferro down t' Oak Hill," she said.

Old Nathan seated himself in the rocker. There was the straight chair beside the table if Ellie wanted it. Now that he'd heard the problem, he didn't guess she was going to settle.

"Might uv heard the name," the cunning man agreed. "Lady from New Orleens, bought 'Siah Chesson's house from his brother back in March after thet dead limb hit 'Siah."

Oak Hill, the nearest settlement, wasn't much, but its dozen dwellings were mostly of saw-cut boards. There was a store, a tavern, and several artisans who supplemented their trade with farm plots behind the houses.

Not a place where a wealthy, pretty lady from New Orleans was likely to be found; but it might be that Madame Francine Taliaferro didn't *choose* to be found by some of those looking for her.

Ellie turned and glared at Old Nathan. "She's a whore!" she blazed, deliberately holding his eyes.

Pitch popped loudly in the hearth. Old Nathan rubbed his beard. "I ain't heard," he said mildly, "thet the lady's sellin' merchandise of *any* sort."

"Then she's a witch," Ellie said, as firm as a tree-trunk bent the last finger's breadth before it snaps.

"Thet's a hard word," the cunning man replied. "Not one t' spread where it mayn't suit."

He had no desire to hurt his visitor, but he wasn't the man to tell a lie willingly; and he wasn't sure that right now, a comforting lie wouldn't be the worse hurt.

"Myse'f," the cunning man continued, "I don't reckon she's any such a thing. I reckon she's a purty woman with money and big-city ways, and thet's all."

Ellie threw her hands to her face. "She's old!" the girl blubbered as she turned her back. "She mus' be thutty!"

Old Nathan got up from the rocker with the caution of age. "Yes ma'm," he agreed dryly. "I reckon thet's rightly so."

He looked at the fire to avoid staring at the back of the woman, shaking with sobs. "I reckon the coffee's biled," he said. "I like a cup t' steady myse'f in the mornings."

Ellie tugged a kerchief from her sleeve. She wiped her eyes, then blew her nose violently before she turned again.

"Why look et the time!" she said brightly. "Why, I need t' be runnin' off right now. Hit's my day t' bake light-bread fer Cullen, ye know."

Ellie's false, fierce smile was so broad that it squeezed another tear from the corner of her eye. She brushed the drop away with a knuckle, as though it had been a gnat about to bite.

"He's powerful picky about his vittles, my Cull is," she went on. "He all'us praises my cookin', though."

Ellie might have intended to say more, but her eyes scrunched down and her upper lip began to quiver with the start of another sob. She turned and scampered out the front door in a flurry of check-patterned skirt. "Thankee fer yer time!" she called as she ran up the trail.

Old Nathan sighed. He swung the bar off the fire, but he didn't feel any need for coffee himself just now. He looked out the door toward the empty trail.

And after a time, he walked to the pasture to resume saddling the mule.

The catfish was so large that its tail and barbel-fringed head both poked over the top of the oak-split saddle basket. "It ain't so easy, y'know," the mule complained as it hunched up the slope where the track from the river joined the main road, "when the load's unbalanced like that."

Old Nathan sniffed. "Ifen ye like," he said, "I'll put a ten-pound rock in t'other side t' give ye balance."

The mule lurched up onto the road. "Hey, watch it, ye old fool!" shouted a horseman, reining up from a canter. Yellow grit sprayed from beneath the horse's hooves.

Old Nathan cursed beneath his breath and dragged the mule's head around. *There was no call fer a body t' be ridin' so blame fast where a road was all twists 'n tree roots—*

But there was no call fer a blamed old fool t' drive his mule acrost thet road, without he looked first t' see what might be a'comin'.

"You damned old hazard!" the horseman shouted. His horse blew and stepped high in place, lifting its hooves as the dust settled. "I ought t' stand you on yer haid 'n drive you right straight int' the dirt like a tint-peg!"

"No, ye hadn't out t' do thet, Bully Ransden," the cunning man replied. "And ye hadn't ought t' try, neither."

He muttered beneath his breath, then waved his left hand down through the air in an arc. A trail of colored light followed his fingertips, greens and blues and yellows, flickering and then gone. Only the gloom of late afternoon among the overhanging branches made such pale colors visible.

"But I'll tell ye I'm sorry I rid out in front of ye," Old Nathan added. "Thet ye do hev a right to."

He was breathing heavily with the effort of casting the lights. He could have fought Bully Ransden and not be any more exhausted—but he would have lost the fight. The display, trivial though it was in fact, set the younger man back in his saddle.

"Howdy, mule," said Ransden's horse. "How're things goin' down yer ways?"

"I guess ye think I'm skeered of yer tricks!" Ransden said. He patted the neck of his horse with his right hand, though just now the animal was calmer than the rider.

" 'Bout like common, I reckon," the mule replied. "Work, work, work, an' fer whut?"

"If yer not," Old Nathan replied in a cold bluster, "thin yer a fool, Ransden. And thet's as may be."

He raised his left hand again, though he had no intention of doing anything with it.

Now that Old Nathan had time to look, his eyes narrowed at the younger man's appearance. Ransden carried a fishing pole in his left hand. The ten-foot length of cane was an awkward burden for a horseman hereabouts—where even the main road was a pair of ruts, and branches met overhead most places.

Despite the pole, Bully Ransden wasn't dressed for fishing. He wore a green velvet frock coat some sizes too small for his broad shoulders, and black storebought trousers as well. His shirt alone was homespun, but clean and new. The garment was open well down the front so that the hair on Ransden's chest curled out in a vee against the gray-white fabric.

"Right now," the mule continued morosely, "we been off loadin' fish. Whutiver good was a fish t' airy soul, I ask ye?"

"Waal," Ransden said, "I take yer 'pology. See thet ye watch yerse'f the nixt time."

"I'm headed inter the sittlement," said the horse in satisfaction. "I allus git me a feed uv oats there, I do."

"Goin' into the settlement, thin?" Old Nathan asked, as if it were no more than idle talk between two men who'd met on the road.

The cunning man and Bully Ransden had too much history between them to be no more than that, though. Each man was unique in the county—known by everyone and respected, but feared as well.

Old Nathan's art set him apart from others. Bully Ransden had beaten his brutal father out of the cabin when he was eleven. Since that time, fists and knotted muscles had been the Bully's instant reply to any slight or gibe directed at the poverty from which he had barely raised himself—or the fact he was the son of a man hated and despised by all in a land where few angels had settled.

Old Nathan's mouth quirked in a smile. He and Ransden were stiff-necked men, as well, who both claimed they didn't care what others thought so long as they weren't interfered with. There was some truth to the claim as well. . . .

"I reckon I might head down thet way," Ransden said, as though there was ought else in the direction he was heading. "Might git me some supper t' Shorty's er somewhere."

He took notice of the mule's saddle baskets and added, "Say, old man—thet's a fine catfish ye hev there."

"Thet's right," Old Nathan agreed. "I figger t' fry me a steak t'night 'n smoke the rest."

"Hmph," the mule snorted, looking sidelong up at the cunning man. "Wish thut some of us iver got oats t' eat."

"I might buy thet fish offen ye," Ransden said. "I've got a notion t' take some fish back fer supper t'morry. How much 'ud ye take fer him?"

"Hain't interested in sellin'," Old Nathan said, his eyes narrowing again. "Didn't figger airy soul as knew Shorty 'ud et his food—or drink the pizen he calls whiskey. I'd uv figgered ye'd stay t' home t'night. Hain't nothin' so good as slab uv hot bread slathered with butter."

Bully Ransden flushed, and the tendons of his bull

neck stood out like cords. "You been messin' about my Ellie, old man?" he asked.

The words were almost unintelligible. Emotion choked Ransden's voice the way ice did streams during the spring freshets.

Old Nathan was careful not to raise his hand. A threat that might forestall violence at a lower emotional temperature would precipitate it with the younger man in his current state. *Nothing* would stop Bully Ransden now if he chose to attack; nothing but a bullet in the brain, and that might not stop him soon enough to save his would-be victim.

"I know," the cunning man said calmly, "what I know. D'ye doubt *thet*, Bully Ransden?"

The horse stretched out his neck to browse leaves from a sweet-gum sapling which had sprouted at the edge of the road. Ransden jerked his mount back reflexively, but the movement took the danger out of a situation cocked and primed to explode.

Ransden looked away. "Aw, hit's no use t' talk to an old fool like you," he muttered. "I'll pick up a mess uv bullheads down t' the sittlement. Gee-up, horse!"

He spurred his mount needlessly hard. As the horse sprang down the road with a startled complaint, Ransden shouted over his shoulder, "I'm a grown man! Hit's no affair of yourn where I spend my time—nor Ellie's affair neither!"

Old Nathan watched the young man go. He was still staring down the road some moments after Ransden had disappeared. The mule said in a disgusted voice, "I wouldn't mind t' get back to a pail of oats, old man."

"Git along, thin," the cunning man said. "Fust time I ever knowed ye t' be willing t' do airy durn thing."

But his heart wasn't in the retort.

The cat came in, licking his muzzle both with relish and for the purpose of cleanliness. "Found the fish guts in the mulch pile," he said. "Found the head too. Thankee."

"Thought ye might like hit," said Old Nathan as he

knelt, adding sticks of green hickory to his fire. "Ifen ye didn't, the corn will next Spring."

The big catfish, cleaned and split open, lay on the smokeshelf just below the throat of the fireplace. Most folk, they had separate smokehouses—vented or chinked tight, that was a matter of taste. Even so, the fireplace smokeshelf was useful for bits of meat that weren't worth stoking up a smoker meant for whole hogs and deer carcases.

As for Old Nathan—he wasn't going to smoke and eat a hog any more than he was going to smoke and eat a human being . . . though there were plenty hogs he'd met whose personalities would improve once their throats were slit.

Same was true of the humans, often enough.

Smoke sprouted from the underside of the hickory billet and hissed up in a sheet. Trapped water cracked its way to the surface with a sound like that of a percussion cap firing.

"Don't reckon there's an uglier sight in the world 'n a catfish head," said the cat as he complacently groomed his right forepaw. He spread the toes and extended the white, hooked claws, each of them needle sharp. "A passel uv good meat to it, though."

"Don't matter what a thing looks like," Old Nathan said, "so long's it tastes right." He sneezed violently, backed away from his fire, and sneezed again.

"Thought I might go off fer a bit," he added to no one in particular.

The cat chuckled and began to work on the other paw. "Chasin' after thet bit uv cunt come by here this mornin', are ye? Give it up, ole man. *You're* no good t' the splittails."

"Ye think thet's all there is, thin?" the cunning man demanded. "Ifen I don't give her thet one help, there's no he'p thet matters a'tall?"

"Thet's right," the cat said simply. He began licking his genitals with his hind legs spread wide apart. His belly fur was white, while the rest of his body was yellow to tigerishly orange.

Old Nathan sighed. "I used t' think thet way myse'f," he admitted as he carried his tin wash basin out to the back porch. *Bout time t' fill the durn water barrel from the creek; but thet 'ud wait. . . .*

"Used t' think?" the tomcat repeated. "Used t' *know*, ye mean. Afore ye got yer knackers shot away."

"I knowed a girl a sight like Ellie Ransden back thin . . ." Old Nathan muttered.

The reflection in the water barrel was brown, the underside of the shakes covering the porch. Old Nathan bent to dip a basinful with the gourd scoop. He saw his own face, craggy and hard. His beard was still black, though he wouldn't see seventy again.

Then, though he hadn't wished it—*he thought*—and he hadn't said the words—*aloud*—there was a woman's face, young and full-lipped and framed in hair as long and black as the years since last he'd seen her, the eve of marching off with Colonel Sevier to what ended at King's Mountain. . . .

"Jes' turn 'n let me see ye move, Slowly," Old Nathan whispered to his memories. "There's nairy a thing so purty in all the world."

The reflection shattered. The grip of the cunning man's right hand had snapped the neck of the gourd. The hollowed body fell into the barrel.

Old Nathan straightened, wiping his eyes and forehead with the back of his hand. He tossed the gourd neck off the porch. "Niver knew why her folks, they named her thet, Slowly," he muttered. "Ifen it was them 'n not a name she'd picked herse'f."

The cat hopped up onto the cane seat of the rocking chair. He poised there for a moment, allowing the rockers to return to balance before he settled himself.

"I'll tell ye a thing, though, cat," the cunning man said forcefully. "Afore King's Mountain, I couldn't no more talk t' you an' t' other animals thin I could talk t' this hearth rock."

The tomcat curled his full tail over his face, then flicked it barely aside.

"Afore ye got yer knackers blowed off, ye mean?" the

cat said. The discussion wasn't of great concern to him, but he demanded precise language nonetheless.

"Aye," Old Nathan said, glaring at the animal. "Thet's what I mean."

The cat snorted into his tail fur. "Thin you made a durned bad bargain, old man," he said.

Old Nathan tore his eyes away from the cat. The tin basin was still in his left hand. He sighed and hung it up unused.

"Aye," he muttered. "I reckon I did, cat."

He went out to saddle the mule again.

Ransden's cabin had a single door, in the front. It was open, but there was no sign of life within.

Old Nathan dismounted and wrapped the reins around the porch rail.

"Goin' t' water me?" the mule snorted.

"In my own sweet time, I reckon," the cunning man snapped back.

"Cull?" Ellie Ransden called from the cabin. "Cullen?" she repeated as she swept to the door. Her eyes were swollen and tear-blurred; they told her only that the figure at the front of her cabin wasn't *her* man. She ducked back inside—and reappeared behind a long flintlock rifle much like the one which hung on pegs over Old Nathan's fireboard.

"Howdy," said the cunning man. "Didn't mean t' startle ye, Miz Ransden."

Old Nathan spoke as calmly as though it were an everyday thing for him to look down the small end of a rifle. It wasn't. It hadn't been for many years, and that was a thing he didn't regret in the least about the passing of the old days.

"Oh!" she said, coloring in embarrassment. "Oh, do please come in. I got coffee, ifen hit ain't biled dry by now."

She lifted the rifle's muzzle before she lowered the hammer. The trigger dogs made a muted double click in releasing the mainspring's tension.

Ellie bustled quickly inside, fully a housewife again.

"Oh, law!" she chirped as she set the rifle back on its pegs. "Here the fust time we git visitors in I don't know, and everything's all sixes 'n sevens!"

The cabin was neat as a pin, all but the bed where the eagle-patterned quilt was disarrayed. It didn't take art to see that Ellie had flung herself there crying, then jumped up in the hope her man had come home.

Bully Ransden must have knocked the furniture together himself. Not fancy, but it was all solid work, pinned with trenails rather than iron. There were two chairs, a table, and the bed. Three chests held clothes and acted as additional seats—though from what Ellie had blurted, the couple had few visitors, which was no surprise with Bully Ransden's reputation.

The windows in each end wall had shutters but no glazing. Curtains, made from sacking and embroidered with bright pink roses, set off their frames.

The rich odor of fresh bread filled the tiny room.

"Oh, law, what *hev* I done?" Ellie moaned as she looked at the fireplace.

The dutch oven sat on coals raked to the front of the hearth. They'd burned down, and the hotter coals pilled onto the cast iron lid were now a mass of fluffy white ash. Ellie grabbed fireplace tongs and lifted the lid away.

"Oh, hit's *ruint*!" the girl said.

Old Nathan reached into the oven and cracked the bread loose from the surface of the cast iron. The load had contracted slightly as it cooled. It felt light, more like biscuit than bread, and the crust was a brown as deep as a walnut plank.

"Don't look ruint t' me," he said as he lifted the loaf to one of the two pewter plates sitting ready on the table. "Looks right good. I'd admire t' try a piece."

Ellie Ransden picked up a knife with a well-worn blade. Unexpectedly, she crumpled into sobs. The knife dropped. It stuck in the cabin floor between the woman's bare feet, unnoticed as she bawled into her hands.

Old Nathan stepped around the table and touched Ellie's shoulders to back her away. Judging from how the light played, the butcher knife had an edge that would slice to the bone if she kicked it. The way the gal carried on, she might not notice the cut—and she might not care if she did.

"I'm *ugly*!" Ellie cried as she wrapped her arms around Old Nathan. "I cain't blame him, I've got t' be an old frumpy thing 'n he don't love me no more!"

For the moment, she didn't know who she held, just that he was warm and solid. She could talk at the cunning man, whether he listened or not.

"Tain't thet," Old Nathan muttered, feeling awkward as a hog on ice. One of the high-backed tortoiseshell combs that held and ornamented Ellie's hair tickled his beard. "Hit's jest the newness. Not thet he don't love ye. . . ."

He spoke the words because they were handy; but as he heard them come out, he guessed they were pretty much the truth. *"Cullen ain't a bad man,"* the girl had said, back to the cunning man's cabin. *No worse 'n most men*, the cunning man thought, *and thet's a* durned *poor lot.*

"Don't reckon there's a purtier girl in the county," Old Nathan said aloud. "Likely there's not in the whole blame state."

Ellie squeezed him firmly, this time a conscious action, and stepped back. She reached into her sleeve for her handkerchief, then saw it crumpled on the quilt where she'd been lying. She snatched up the spare of linen, turned aside, and blew her nose firmly.

"You're a right good man," Ellie mumbled before she looked around again.

She raised her chin and said, pretending that her face was not flushed and tear-streaked, "Ifen it ain't me, hit's thet *bitch* down t' the sittlement. Fer a month hit's been Francine this 'n Francine that an' him spendin' the ev'nins out an' thin—"

Ellie's upper lip trembled as she tumbled out her recent history. The cunning man bent to tug the butcher knife from the floor and hide his face from the woman's.

"She witched him, sir!" Ellie burst out. "I heerd what

you said up t' yer cabin, but I tell ye, she *witched* my Cull. He ain't *like* this!"

Old Nathan rose. He set the knife down, precisely parallel to the edge of the table, and met the woman's eyes. "Yer Cull ain't the fust man t' go where his pecker led," he said, harshly to be able to get the words out of his own throat. "Tain't witch'ry, hit's jest human nature. An' don't be carryin' on, 'cause he'll be back—sure as the leaves turn."

Ellie wrung her hands together. The handkerchief was a tiny ball in one of them. "Oh, d' ye think he will, sir?" she whispered. "Oh, sir, could ye give me a charm t' bring him back? I'd be iver so grateful. . . ."

She looked down at her hands. Her lips pressed tightly together while silent tears dripped again from her eyes.

Old Nathan broke eye contact. He shook his head slightly and said, "No, I won't do thet."

"But ye could?" Ellie said sharply. The complex of emotions flowing across her face hardened into anger and determination. The woman who was wife to Bully Ransden could either be soft as bread dough or as strong and supple as a hickory pole. There was nothing in between—

And there was nothing soft about Ellie Ransden.

"I reckon ye think I couldn't pay ye," she said. "Waal, ye reckon wrong. There's my combs—"

She tossed her head; the three combs of translucent tortoiseshell, decorative but necessary as well to hold a mass of hair like Ellie's, quivered as they caught the light.

"Rance Holden, he'd buy thim back fer stock, I reckon. Mebbe thet *Modom* Francine—" the viciousness Ellie concentrated in the words would have suited a mother wren watching a blacksnake near her chicks "—'ud want thim fer *her* hair. And there's my Pappy's watch, too, thet Cullen wears now. Hit'll fetch somethin', I reckon, the case, hit's true gold."

She swallowed, chin regally high—but looking so young and vulnerable that Old Nathan wished the world were a different place than he knew it was and always would be.

"So, Mister Cunning Man," Ellie said. "I reckon I kin raise ten silver dollars. Thet's good pay fer some li'l old charm what won't take you nothin' t' make."

"I don't need yer money," Old Nathan said gruffly. "Hain't thet. I'm tellin' ye, hit's wrong t' twist folks around thet way. Ifen ye got yer Cullen back like thet, he wouldn't like what it was ye hed. An' I *ain't* about t' do thet thing!"

"Thin you better go on off," Ellie said. "I'm no sort uv comp'ny t'day."

She flung herself onto the bed, burying her face in the quilt. She was sobbing.

Old Nathan bit his lower lip as he stepped out of the cabin. *Hit warn't the world I made, hit's jest the one I live in.*

"Leastways when ye go fishin'," the mule grumbled from the porch rail, "thur's leaves t' browse."

Wouldn't hurt him t' go see Madame Taliaferro with his own eyes, he reckoned.

Inside the cabin the girl cried, "Oh why cain't I jes' *die*, I'm so miser'ble!"

For as little good as he'd done, Old Nathan guessed he might better have stayed to home and saved himself and his mule a ride back in the dark.

The sky was pale from the recently set sun, but the road was in shadows. They would be deeper yet by the time the cunning man reached the head of the track to his cabin. The mule muttered a curse every time it clipped a hoof in a rut, but it didn't decide to balk.

The bats began their everlasting refrain, "Dilly, dilly, come and be killed," as they quartered the air above the road. *Thet peepin' nonsense was enough t' drive a feller t' distraction—er worse!*

Just as well the mule kept walking. This night, Old Nathan was in a mood to speak phrases that would blast the bones right out of the durned old beast.

Somebody was coming down the road from Oak Hill, singing merrily. It took a moment to catch actual phrases of the song, "*. . . went a-courtin', he did ride . . .*" and a moment further to identify the voice as Bully Ransden's.

"*. . . an' pistol by his side, uh-huh!*"

Ransden came around the next bend in the trail, carrying not the bottle Old Nathan expected in his free hand but rather a stringer of bullheads. He'd left the long cane pole behind somewhere during the events of the evening.

"Hullo, mule," Ransden's horse whinnied. "Reckon I ate better'n *you* did t'night."

"Hmph," grunted the mule. "Leastways my master ain't half-shaved an' going t' ride me slap inter a ditch 'fore long."

"Howdy, feller," Bully Ransden caroled. "Ain't it a fine ev'nin?"

Ransden wasn't drunk, maybe, but he sure-hell didn't sound like the man he'd been since he grew up—which was about age eleven, when he beat his father out of the cabin with an ax handle.

"Better fer some thin others, I reckon," Old Nathan replied. He clucked the mule to the side, giving the horseman the room he looked like he might need.

Ransden's manner changed as soon as he heard the cunning man's voice. "So hit's you, is it, old man?" he said.

He tugged hard on his reins, twisting his mount across the road in front of Old Nathan. "Hey, easy on!" the horse complained. "No call fer thet!"

"D'ye figger t' spy on me, feller?" Ransden demanded, turned crossways in his saddle. He shrugged his shoulders, straining the velvet jacket dangerously. "Or—"

Bully Ransden didn't carry a gun, but there was a long knife in his belt. Not that he'd need it. Ransden was young and strong enough to break a fence rail with his bare hands, come to that. He'd do the same with Old Nathan, for all that the cunning man had won his share of fights in his youth—

And later. It was a hard land still, though statehood had come thirty years past.

"I'm ridin' on home, Cullen Ransden," Old Nathan said. "Reckon ye'd do well t' do the same."

"By God," said Ransden. "By *God*! Where you been to, old man? Hev you been sniffin' round my Ellie? By God, if she's been—"

The words echoed in Old Nathan's mind, where he heard them an instant before they were spoken.

The power that poured into the cunning man was nothing that he had summoned. It wore him like a cloak, responding to the threat Bully Ransden was about to voice.

"—slippin' around on me, I'll wring the bitch's—"

Old Nathan raised both hands. Thunder crashed in the clear sky, then rumbled away in diminishing chords.

The power was nothing to do with the cunning man, but he shaped it as a potter shapes clay on his wheel. He spread his fingers. The tree trunks and roadway glowed with a light as faint as foxfire. It was just enough to throw each rut and bark ridge into relief, as though they were reflecting the pale sky.

"Great God Almighty!" muttered Bully Ransden. His mouth fell open. The string of small fish in his left hand trembled slightly.

"Ye'll do *what* to thet pore little gal, Bully Ransden?" the cunning man asked in a harsh, cracked voice.

Ransden touched his lips with his tongue. He tossed his head as if to clear it. "Reckon I misspoke," he said; not loud but clearly, and he met Old Nathan's eyes as he said the words.

"Brag's a good dog, Ransden," Old Nathan said. "But Hold-fast is better."

He lowered his arms. The vague light and the last trembling of thunder had already vanished.

The mule turned and stared back at its rider with one bulging eye. "Whut in tar-*nation* was that?" it asked.

Bully Ransden clucked to his horse. He pressed with the side, not the spur, of his right boot to swing the beast back in line with the road. "Don't you think I'm afeerd t' meet you, old man," he called; a little louder than necessary, and at a slightly higher pitch than intended.

Ransden *was* afraid; but that wouldn't keep him from facing the cunning man, needs must—

As surely as Old Nathan would have faced the Bully's fist and hobnailed boots some moments earlier.

The rushing, all-mastering power was gone now, leaving Old Nathan shaken and as weak as a man wracked with a three-days flux. "Jest go yer way, Ransden," he muttered, "and I'll go mine. I don't wish fer any truck with you."

He heeled the mule's haunches and added, "Git on with ye, thin, mule."

The mule didn't budge. "I don't want no part uv these doins," it protested. "Felt like hit was a dad-blame thunderbolt sittin' astride me, hit did."

Ransden walked his nervous horse abreast of the cunning man. "I don't know why I got riled nohow," he said, partly for challenge but mostly just in the brutal banter natural to the Bully's personality. "Hain't as though you're a man, now, is it?"

He spurred his horse off down the darkened trail, laughing merrily.

Old Nathan trembled, gripping the saddle horn with both hands. "Git on, mule," he muttered. "I hain't got the strength t' fight with ye."

Faintly down the road drifted the words, *"Froggie wint a-courtin', he did ride . . ."*

Bright midday sun dappled the white-painted boards of the Isiah Chesson house. It was a big place for this end of the country, with two rooms below and a loft. In addition, there was a stable and servants' quarters at the back of the lot. How big it seemed to Madame Francine Taliaferro, late of New Orleans, was another matter.

"Whoa-up mule," Old Nathan muttered as he peered at the dwelling. It sat a musket shot down the road and around a bend from the next house of the Oak Hill settlement. The front door was closed, and there was no sign of life behind the curtains added to the windows since the new tenant moved in.

Likely just as well. The cunning man wanted to observe Madame Taliaferro, but barging up to her door and knocking didn't seem a useful way to make her introduction.

Still . . .

In front of the house was a well-manicured lawn. A pair of gray squirrels, plump and clothed in fur grown sleekly full at the approach of Fall, hopped across the lawn—and over the low board fence which had protected Chesson's sauce garden, now grown up in vines.

"Hoy, squirrel!" Old Nathan called. "Is the lady what lives here t' home?"

The nearer squirrel hopped up on his hind legs, looking in all directions. "What's thet? What's thet I heard?" he chirped.

"Yer wastin' yer time," the mule said. "Hain't a squirrel been born yet whut's got brain enough t' tell whether hit's rainin'."

"He's talkin' t' ye," the other squirrel said as she continued to snuffle across the short grass of the lawn. "He says, is the lady home t' the house?"

The male squirrel blinked. "Huh?" he said to his mate. "What would I be doin' in a house?" He resumed a tail-high patrol which seemed to ignore the occasional hickory nuts lying in the grass.

"Told ye so," the mule commented.

Old Nathan scowled. Boards laid edgewise set off a path from the front door to the road. A pile of dog droppings marked the gravel.

"Squirrel," the cunning man said. "Is there a little dog t' home, now?"

"What?" the male squirrel demanded. "Whur is it? Thet nasty little monster's come back!"

"Now, don't yet git yerse'f all stirred up!" his mate said. "Hit's all right, hit's gone off down the road already."

"Thankee, squirrels," Old Nathan said. "Git on, mule."

"Ifen thet dog's not here, thin whyiver did he say it was?" the male squirrel complained loudly.

"We could uv done thet a'ready, ye know," the mule said as he ambled on toward the main part of town. "Er we could uv stayed t' home."

"Thet's right," Old Nathan said grimly. "We could."

He *knew* he was on a fool's errand, because only a durned fool would think Francine Taliaferro might be using some charm or other on the Ransden boy. He didn't need a mule to tell him.

Rance Holden's store was the center of Oak Hill, unless you preferred to measure from Shorty Hitchcock's tavern across the one dirt street. Holden's building was gable-end to the road. The store filled the larger square room, while Rance and his wife lived in the low rectangular space beneath the eaves overhanging to the left.

The family's space had been tight when the Holdens had children at home. The five boys and the girl who survived were all moved off on their own by now.

"Don't you tie me t' the rail thur," the mule said. "Somebody 'll spit t'baccy at me sure."

"Thin they'll answer t' me," the cunning man said. "But seeins as there's nobody on the porch, I don't figger ye need worry."

Four horses, one with a side-saddle, were hitched to the rail. Usually there were several men sitting on the board porch among barrels of bulk merchandise, chewing tobacco and whittling; but today they were all inside. That was good evidence that Madame Francine Taliaferro was inside as well. . . .

The interior of Holden's store was twelve foot by twelve foot. Not spacious by any standard, it was now packed with seven adults—

And a pug dog who tried to fill as much space as the humans.

"Hey, you old bastard!" the dog snapped as the cunning man stepped through the open door. "I'm going to bite you till you bleed, and there's nothing you can do about it!"

"Howdy Miz Holden, Rance," Old Nathan said. "Thompson—" a nod to the saddler, a cadaverous man with a full beard but no hair above the level of his ears "—Bart—" another nod, this time to the settlement's miller, Bart Alpers—

"I'm *going* to bite you!" the little dog yapped as it

lunged forward and dodged back. "I'll do just that, and you don't dare to stop me!"

Nods, murmured *howdies/yer keepin' well* from the folk who crowded the store.

"—'n Mister M'Donald," the cunning man said with a nod for the third white man, a husky, hard-handed man who'd made a good thing of a tract ten miles out from the settlement. M'Donald looked even sillier in an ill-fitting blue tailcoat than Bully Ransden had done in his finery the evening before.

Madame Taliaferro's black servant, on the other hand, wore his swallowtail coat, ruffed shirt, and orange breeches with an air of authority. He stood behind his mistress, with his eyes focused on infinity and his hands crossed behind his back.

"Now, Cesar," the woman who was the center of the store's attention murmured to her dog. She looked at Old Nathan with an unexpected degree of appraisal. "Baby be good for ma-ma."

"*Said* I'm going to bite you!" insisted the dog. "Here goes!"

Old Nathan whispered inaudible words with his teeth in a tight smile. The little dog *did* jump forward to bite his pants legs, sure as the Devil was loose in the world.

The dog froze.

"Mum," Old Nathan said as he reached down and scooped the dog up in his hand. The beast's mouth was open. Sudden terror filled its nasty little eyes.

Francine Taliaferro had lustrous dark hair—not a patch on Ellie's, but groomed in a fashion the younger woman's could never be. Her face was pouty-pretty, heavily powdered and rouged, and the skirt of her blue organdy dress flared out in a fashion that made everyone else in the store stand around like the numbers on a clock dial with her the hub.

But that's what it would have been anyway; only perhaps with the others pressing in yet closer.

Old Nathan handed the stiffened dog to Madame Taliaferro. "Hain't the cutest li'l thing?" the cunning man said.

The woman's red lips opened in shock, but by reflex her gloved hands accepted the petrified animal that was thrust toward her. As soon as Old Nathan's fingers no longer touched the animal's fur, the dog resumed where it had stopped. Its teeth snapped into its mistress's white shoulder.

Three of the men shouted. Madame Taliaferro screamed in outrage and flung Cesar up into the roof shakes. The dog bounced down into a shelf of yard goods, then ran out the door. It was yapping unintelligibly.

Old Nathan smiled. "Jest cute as a button."

There was no more magic in this woman than there was truth in a politician's heart. If Ellie had a complaint, it was against whatever fate had led a woman—a *lady*—so sophisticated to Oak Hill.

And complaint agin Bully Ransden, fer bein' a durned fool; but folks were, men 'n women both. . . .

"By God!" M'Donald snarled. "I oughter break ye in two fer thet!"

He lurched toward the cunning man but collided with Alpers, who cried, "I won't let ye fall!" as he tried to grab the woman. Rance Holden tried to crawl out from behind the counter while his wife glared, and Thompson blathered as though somebody had just fallen into a mill saw.

"Everyone stop this at once!" Madame Taliaferro cried with her right index finger held upright. Her voice was as clear and piercing as a well-turned bell.

Everyone *did* stop. All eyes turned toward the woman; which was no doubt as things normally were in Madame Taliaferro's presence.

"I'll fetch yer dog," blurted Bart Alpers.

"Non!" Taliaferro said. "Cesar must have had a little cramp. He will stay outside till he is better."

"Warn't no cramp, Francine, honey," M'Donald growled. "Hit war this sonuvabitch here what done it!" He pushed Alpers aside.

"What d'ye reckon happint t' Cesar, M'Donald?" Old Nathan said. The farmer was younger by thirty years and strong, but he hadn't the personality to make a threat frightening even when he spoke the flat truth."D'ye want t' touch me 'n larn?"

M'Donald stumbled backward from the bluff—for it was all bluff, what Old Nathan had done to the dog had wrung him out bad as lifting a quarter of beef. But the words had this much truth in them: those who struck the cunning man would pay for the blow, in one way or another; and pay in coin they could ill afford.

"I don't believe we've been introduced," said the woman. She held out her hand. The appraisal was back in her eyes. "I'm Francine Taliaferro, but do call me Francine. I'm—*en vacance* in your charming community."

"*He* ain't no good t' ye," M'Donald muttered bitterly, his face turned to a display of buttons on a piece of card.

The cunning man took Taliaferro's hand, though he wasn't rightly sure what she expected him to do with it. There were things he knew, plenty of things and important ones; but right just now, he understood why other men reacted as they did to Francine Taliaferro.

"M' name's Nathan. I live down the road a piece, Columbia ways."

Even a man with a woman like Ellie waiting at home for him.

"I reckon *this* gen'lman come here t' do business, Rance," said Mrs. Holden to her husband in a poisonous tone of voice. "Don't ye reckon ye ought t' he'p him?"

"I'll he'p him, Maude," Holden muttered, trying—and he knew he would fail—to interrupt the rest of the diatribe. He was a large, soft man, and his hair had been white for years. "Now, how kin—"

"Ye *are* a storekeeper, ain't ye?" Mrs. Holden shrilled. "Not some spavined ole fool thinks spring has come again!"

Holden rested his hands on the counter. His eyes were downcast. One of the other men chuckled. "Now, Nathan," the storekeeper resumed. "Reckon you're here fer more coffee?"

The cunning man opened his mouth to say he'd take a peck of coffee and another of baking soda. He didn't need either just now, but he'd use them both and they'd serve as an excuse for him to have come into Oak Hill.

"Ye've got an iv'ry comb," he said. The words he spoke weren't the ones he'd had in mind at all. "Reckon I'll hev thet and call us quits fer me clearin' the rats outen yer barn last fall."

Everyone in the store except Holden himself stared at Old Nathan. The storekeeper winced and, with his eyes still on his hands, said, "I reckon thet comb, hit must hev been sold. I'd like t' he'p ye."

"Whoiver bought thet thing!" cried the storekeeper's wife in amazement. She turned to the niche on the wall behind the counter, where items of special value were flanked to either side by racks of yard goods. The two crystal goblets remained, but they had been moved inward to cover the space where the ornate ivory comb once stood.

Mrs. Holden's eyes narrowed. "Rance Holden, you go look through all the drawers this minute. Nobody bought thet comb and you know it!"

"Waal, mebbe hit was stole," Holden muttered. He half-heartedly pulled out one of the drawers behind the counter and poked with his fingers at the hairpins and brooches within.

The cunning man smiled grimly. "Reckon I kin he'p ye," he said.

He reached over the counter and took one of the pins, ivory like the comb for which he was searching. The pin's blunt end was flattened and drilled into a filigree for decoration. He held the design between the tips of his index fingers, pressing just hard enough to keep the pin pointed out horizontally.

"What is this that you are doing, then?" Francine Taliaferro asked in puzzlement.

The other folk in the store knew Old Nathan. Their faces were set in gradations between fear and interest, depending on the varied fashions in which they viewed the cunning man's arts.

Old Nathan swept the pin over the counter. Midway it dipped, then rose again.

"Check the drawers there," the cunning man directed. He moved the hairpin back until it pointed straight down. "Reckon hit's in the bottom one."

"Why, whut would that iv'ry pin be doin' down there with the women's shoes?" Mrs. Holden demanded.

"Look, I tell ye, I'll pay ye cash fer what ye did with the rats," the storekeeper said desperately. "How much 'ud ye take? Jest name—"

He was standing in front of the drawer Old Nathan had indicated. His wife jerked it open violently, banging it against Holden's instep twice and a third time until he hopped away, wincing.

Mrs. Holden straightened, holding a packet wrapped with tissue paper and blue ribbon. It was of a size to contain the comb.

She started to undo the ribbon. Her face was red with fury.

Old Nathan put his hand out. "Reckon I'll take it the way i'tis," he said.

"How d'ye guess the comb happint t' be all purtied up 'n hid like thet, Rance?" Bart Alpers said loudly. "Look to me like hit were a present fer som'body, if ye could git her alone."

Francine Taliaferro raised her chin. "I know nothing of this," she said coldly.

Rance Holden took the packet from his wife's hands and gave it to Old Nathan. "I figger this makes us quits fer the rats," he said in a dull voice. He was slumped like a man who'd been fed his breakfast at the small end of a rifle.

"Thankee," Old Nathan said. "I reckon thet does."

The shouting behind him started before the cunning man had unhitched his mule. The timbre of Mrs. Holden's voice was as sharp and cutting as that of Francine Taliaferro's lapdog.

Taking the comb didn't make a lick of sense, except that it showed the world what a blamed fool God had made of Rance Holden.

Old Nathan rode along, muttering to himself. It would

have been awkward to carry the packet in his hand, but once he'd set the fancy bit of frippery down into a saddle basket, that didn't seem right either.

Might best that he sank the durn thing in the branch, because there wasn't ought he could do with the comb that wouldn't make him out to be a worse fool than Rance. . . .

The mule was following its head onto the cabin trail. Suddenly its ears cocked forward and its leading foot hesitated a step. Through the woods came, "*Froggie wint a-courtin', he did ride. . . .*"

"Hey, thur!" called the mule.

"Oh, hit's you come back, is it?" Bully Ransden's horse whinnied in reply. "I just been down yer way."

Horse and mule came nose to nose around a bend fringed by dogwood and alders. The riders watched one another: Old Nathan stiff and ready for trouble, but the younger man as cheerful as a cat with a mouse for a toy.

"Glad t' see ye, Nathan old feller," Bully Ransden said.

He kneed his mount forward to bring himself alongside the cunning man, left knee to left knee. The two men were much of a height, but the horse stood taller than the mule and increased the impression of Ransden's far greater bulk. "I jest dropped by in a neighborly way," he continued, "t' warn ye there's been prowlers up t' my place. Ye might want t' stick close about yer own."

He grinned. His teeth were square and evenly set. They had taken the nose off a drover who'd wrongly thought he was a tougher man than Bully Ransden.

This afternoon Ransden wore canvas breeches and a loose-hanging shirt of gray homespun. The garment's cut had the effect of emphasizing Bully's muscular build, whereas the undersized frock coat had merely made him look constrained.

"I thankee," Old Nathan said stiffly. He wished Bully Ransden would stop glancing toward the saddle basket, where he might notice the ribbon-tied packet. "Reckon I kin deal with sech folk as sneak by whin I'm gone."

He *wished* he were forty years younger, and even then he'd be a lucky man to avoid being crippled in a rough and tumble with Bully Ransden. This was one cat-quick, had shoulders like an ox . . . and once the fight started, Bully Ransden didn't quit so long as the other fellow still could move.

Ransden's horse eyed Old Nathan, then said to the mule, "Yer feller ain't goin' t' do whativer hit was he did last night, is he? I cain't much say I liked thet."

"Didn't much like hit myse'f," the mule agreed morosely. "He ain't a bad old feller most ways, though."

"Like I said," Ransden grinned. "Jest a neighborly warnin'. Y' see, I been leavin' my rifle-gun t' home most times whin I'm out 'n about . . . but I don't figger t' do thet fer a while. I reckon if I ketch someb'dy hangin' round my cabin, I'll shoot him same's I would a dog chasin' my hens."

Old Nathan looked up to meet the younger man's eyes. "Mebbe," he said deliberately, "you're goin' t' stay home 'n till yer own plot fer a time?"

"Oh, land!" whickered the horse, reacting to the sudden tension. "Now it'll come sure!"

For a moment, Old Nathan thought the same thing . . . and thought the result was going to be very bad. Sometimes you couldn't help being afraid, but that was a reason itself to act as fear warned you not to.

Ransden shook his head violently, as if he were a horse trying to brush away a gadfly. His hair was shoulder length and the color of sourwood honey. The locks tossed in a shimmering dance.

Suddenly, unexpectedly, the mood changed. Bully Ransden began to laugh. "Ye know," he said goodhumoredly, "ifen you were a man, I might take unkindly t' words like thet. Seeins as yer a poor womanly critter, though, I don't reckon I will."

He kicked his horse a step onward, then reined up again as if to prove his mastery. The animal nickered in complaint.

"Another li'l warning, old man," Ransden called playfully over his shoulder. "Ye hadn't ought t' smoke meat on too hot uv a fire. You might shrink hit right up."

Ransden spurred his mount forward, jerking the left

rein at the same time. The horse's flank jolted solidly against the mule's hindquarters, knocking the lighter animal against an oak sapling.

"Hey thur, you!" the mule brayed angrily.

"*Sword 'n pistol* by *his side!*" Bully Ransden caroled as he trotted his horse down the trail.

"Waal," said the mule as he resumed his measured pace toward the cabin. "I'm glad *that's* ended."

"D'ye think it is, mule?" the cunning man asked softly. "From the way the Bully was talkin', I reckon he jest managed t' start it fer real."

The two cows were placidly chewing their cud in the railed paddock behind the cabin. "Thar's been another feller come by here," the red heifer offered between rhythmic, sideways strokes of her jaws.

"Wouldn't milk us, though," the black heifer added. " 'Bout time somebody does, ifen ye ask me."

"Don't recall askin' ye *any* blame thing," Old Nathan muttered.

He dismounted and uncinched the saddle. "Don't 'spect ye noticed what the feller might be doin' whilst he was here, did ye?" he asked as if idly.

"Ye goin' t' strip us now?" the black demanded. "My udder's full as full, it is."

"He wint down t' the crik," the red offered. "Carried a fish down t' the crik."

Old Nathan dropped two gate bars and led the mule into the enclosure with the cows. His face was set.

"Criks is whur fish belong," the black heifer said. "Only I wish they didn't nibble at my teats whin I'm standing thur, cooling myse'f."

"This fish don't nibble airy soul," the red heifer explained in a superior tone. "This fish were dead 'n dry."

Old Nathan removed the mule's bridle and patted the beast on the haunch. "Git some hay," he said. "I'll give ye a handful uv oats presently. I reckon afore long you 'n me goin' t' take another ride, though."

"Why*ever* do a durn fool thing like that?" the mule complained. "Ye kin ride a cow the next time. I'm plumb tuckered out."

" 'Bout *time*," the black heifer repeated with emphasis, "thet you milk us!"

The cunning man paused, halfway to his back porch, and turned. "I'll be with ye presently," he said. "I ain't in a mood t' be pushed, so I'd advise ye as a friend thet y'all not push me."

The cows heard the tone and looked away, as though they were studying the movements of a late-season butterfly across the paddock. The mule muttered, "Waal, I reckon I wouldn't mind a bit uv a walk, come t' thet."

The cat sauntered through the front door of the cabin as Old Nathan entered by the back. "Howdy, old man," the cat said. "I wouldn't turn down a bite of somp'in if it was goin'."

"I'll hev ye a cup uv milk if ye'll wait fer it," the cunning man said as he knelt to look at the smoke shelf of his fireplace. The greenwood fire had burnt well down, but there was no longer any reason to build it higher.

The large catfish was gone, as Old Nathan had expected. In its place was a bullhead less than six inches long; one of those Ransden had bought in town the day before, though he could scarcely have thought that Ellie believed he'd spent the evening fishing.

"What's thet?" the cat asked curiously.

Old Nathan removed the bullhead from the shelf, "Somethin' a feller left me," he said.

The bullhead hadn't been a prepossessing creature even before it spent a day out of water. Now its smooth skin had begun to shrivel and its eyes were sunken in; the eight barbels lay like a knot of desiccated worms.

"He took the fish was there and tossed hit in the branch, I reckon," he added in a dreamy voice, holding the bullhead and thinking of a time to come shortly. "He warn't a thief, he jest wanted t' make his point with me."

"Hain't been cleaned 'n it's gittin' *good* 'n ripe," the cat noted, licking his lips. "Don't figger you want it, but you better believe *I* do."

"Sorry, cat," the cunning man said absently. He set the bullhead on the fireboard to wait while he got together the other traps he would need. Ellie Ransden would have a hand mirror, so he needn't take his own. . . .

"Need t' milk the durn cows, too," he muttered aloud.

The cat stretched up the wall beside the hearth. He was not really threatening to snatch the bullhead, but he wasn't far away in case the cunning man walked out of the cabin and left the fish behind. "Whativer do *you* figger t' do with thet ole thing?" he complained.

"Feller used hit t' make a point with me," Old Nathan repeated. His voice was distant and very hard. "I reckon I might hev a point t' make myse'f."

"Hallo the house!" Old Nathan called as he dismounted in front of Ransden's cabin.

He'd covered more miles on muleback recently than his muscles approved. Just now he didn't feel stiff, because his blood was heated with what he planned to do—and what was likely to come of it.

He'd pay for that in the morning, he supposed; and he supposed he'd be alive in the morning to pay. He'd do what he came for regardless.

The cabin door banged open. Ellie Ransden wore a loose dress she'd sewn long ago of English cloth, blue in so far as the sun and repeated washings had left it color. Her eyes were puffy from crying, but the expression of her face was compounded of concern and horror.

"Oh, sir, Mister Nathan, ye *mustn't* come by here!" she gasped. "Cullen, he'll shoot ye sure! I niver *seen* him so mad as whin he asked hed you been by. An' my Cull . . ."

The words *"my Cull"* rang beneath the surface of the girl's mind. Her face crumpled. Her hands pawed out blindly. One touched a porch support. She gripped it and collapsed against the cedar pole, blubbering her heart out.

Old Nathan stepped up onto the porch and put his arms around her. Decent folk didn't leave an animal in pain, and that's what this girl was now, something alive that hurt like to die. . . .

The mule snorted and began to sidle away. There hadn't been time to loop his reins over the porch railing.

Old Nathan pointed an index finger at the beast. "Ifen you stray," he snarled, "hit's best thet ye find yerse'f another hide. I'll hev *thet* off ye, sure as the Divil's in Hell."

"Fine master you are," the mule grumbled in a subdued voice.

Though the words had not been directed at Ellie, Old Nathan's tone returned the girl to present circumstances as effectively as a bucket of cold water could have done. She stepped back and straightened.

"Oh, law," she murmured, dabbing her face with her dress's full sleeves. "But Mister Nathan, ye mustn't stay. I won't hev ye kilt over me, nor—"

She eyed him quickly, noting the absence of an obvious weapon but finding that less reassuring then she would have wished. "Nor aught t' happen to my Cull neither. He—" she started to lose control over her voice and finished in a tremolo "—ain't a bad man!"

"Huh," the cunning man said. He turned to fetch his traps from the mule's panniers. He was about as embarrassed as Ellie, and he guessed he had as much reason.

"I ain't goin' t' hurt Bully Ransden," he said, then added what was more than half a lie, "And better men thin him hev thought they'd fix *my* flint."

Ellie Ransden tossed her head. "Waal," she said, "I reckon ye know yer own business, sir. Won't ye come in and set a spell? I don't mind sayin' I'm glad fer the comp'ny."

Her face hardened into an expression that Old Nathan might have noticed on occasion if he looked into mirrors more often. "I've coffee, an' there's a jug uv good wildcat . . . but ifen ye want fancy French wines all the way from New Or-leens, I guess ye'll hev t' go elsewheres."

With most of his supplies in one hand and the fish wrapped in a scrap of bark in his left, Old Nathan followed the woman into her cabin. "I'd take some coffee now," he said. "And mebbe when we've finished, I'd sip a mite of whiskey."

Ellie Ransden took the coffee pot a step toward the bucket in the corner, half full with well water. Without looking at the cunning man, she said, "Thin you might do me up a charm after all?"

"I will not," Old Nathan said flatly. "But fer what I will do, ye'll hev to he'p."

He set his gear on the table. The bark unwrapped. The bullhead's scaleless skin was black, and the fish had a noticeable odor.

Ellie filled the pot and dropped in an additional pinch of beans, roasted and cracked rather than ground. "Reckon I'll he'p, thin," she said bitterly. "All I been doin', keepin' house 'n fixin' vittles, thet don't count fer nothing the way some people figgers."

"I'll need thet oil lamp," the cunning man said, "but don't light it. And a plug t' fit the chimley end; reckon a cob'll suit thet fine. *And* a pair of Bully Ransden's britches. Best they be a pair thet ain't been washed since he wore thim."

"Reckon I kin find thet for ye," the woman said. She hung the coffee over the fire, then lifted a pair of canvas trousers folded on top of a chest with a homespun shirt. They were the garments Bully Ransden wore when Old Nathan met him earlier in the day. "Cull allus changes 'fore he goes off in the ev'nin' nowadays. Even whin he pretends he's fishin'."

She swallowed a tear. "An' don't he look a sight in the jacket he had off Neen Tobler fer doin' his plowing last spring? Like a durned ole greenbelly *fly*, thet's how he looks!"

"Reckon ye got a mirror," Old Nathan said as he unfolded the trousers on the table beside the items he had brought from his own cabin. "If ye'll fetch it out, thin we can watch; but hit don't signify ifen ye don't."

"I've a hand glass fine as iver ye'll see," Ellie Ransden said with cold pride. She stepped toward a chest, then stopped and met the cunning man's eyes. "You won't hurt him, will ye?" she asked. "I—"

She covered her face with her hands. "I druther," she whispered, "thet she hev him thin thet he be hurt."

"Won't hurt him none," Old Nathan said. "I jest figger

t' teach the Bully a lesson he's been beggin' t' larn, thet's all."

The young woman was on the verge of tears again. "Fetch the mirror," Old Nathan said gruffly. That gave her an excuse to turn away and compose herself as he proceeded with the preparations.

The words that the cunning man murmured under his breath were no more the spell than soaking yeast in water made a cake; but, like the other, these words were necessary preliminaries.

By its nature, the bullhead's wrinkling corpse brought the flies he needed. The pair that paused momentarily to copulate may have been brought to the act by nature alone or nature aided by art. The cause didn't matter so long as the necessary event occurred.

Old Nathan swept his right hand forward, skimming above the bullhead to grasp the mating pair unharmed within the hollow of his fingers. He looked sidelong to see whether the girl had noticed the quickness and coordination of his movement: he was like an old man, right enough, but that didn't mean he was ready for the knacker's yard. . . .

He realized what he was doing and compressed his lips over a sneer of self-loathing. Durned old *fool*!

The flies blurred within the cunning man's fingers like a pair of gossamer hearts beating. He positioned his fist over the lamp chimney, then released his captives carefully within the glass. For a moment he continued to keep the top end of the chimney covered with his palm; then Ellie slid a corncob under the cunning man's hand to close the opening.

The flies buzzed for some seconds within the thin glass before they resumed their courtship.

The woman's eyes narrowed as she saw what Old Nathan was doing with the bullhead, but she did not comment. He arranged the other items to suit his need before he looked up.

"I'll be sayin' some words, now," he said. "Hit wouldn't do ye airy good t' hear thim, and hit might serve ye ill ifen ye said thim after me, mebbe by chance."

Ellie Ransden's mouth tightened at the reminder of the forces being brought to bear on the man she loved. "I reckon you know best," she said. "I'll stand off till ye call me."

She stepped toward the cabin's only door, then paused and looked again at Old Nathan. "These words you're a-speakin'—ye found thim writ in books?"

He shook his head. "They're things I know," he explained, "the way I know . . ."

His voice trailed off. He'd been about to say, "—yer red hen's pleased as pleased with the worm she jest grubbed up from the leaves," but that wasn't something he rightly wanted to speak, even to this girl.

"Anyhow, I just know hit," he finished lamely.

Ellie nodded and walked out onto the porch of her cabin. "I'll water yer mule," she called. "Reckon he could use thet."

The beast wheezed its enthusiastic agreement.

Old Nathan sang and gestured his way through the next stage of the preliminaries. His voice cracked and he couldn't hold a key, but that didn't seem to matter.

The cunning man wasn't sure what *did* matter. When he worked, it was as if he walked into a familiar room in the dead dark of night. Occasionally he would stumble, but not badly; and he would always feel his way to the goal that he would not see.

He laid the bullhead inside the crotch of Ransden's trousers.

In between snatches of verse—not English, and not any language to which he could have put a name—Old Nathan whistled. He thought of boys whistling as they passed through a churchyard; chuckled bitterly; and resumed whistling, snatches from *Mossy Groves* that a fiddler would have had trouble recognizing.

"How would ye like, my Mossy Groves,
T' spend one night with me?"

Most of the life had by now crackled out of the extra stick of lightwood Ellie had tossed on the fire. Beyond the cabin walls, the night was drawing in.

The pair of trousers shifted on the table, though the air was still.

A familiar task; but, like bear hunting, familiarity didn't remove all the danger. This wasn't for Ellie, for some slip of a girl who loved a fool of a man. This was because Bully Ransden had issued a challenge, and because Old Nathan knew the worst that could happen to a man was to let fear cow him into a living death—

And maybe it *was* a bit for Ellie.

"The ver' first blow the king gave him,
Moss' Groves, he struck no more. . . ."

Life had risks. Old Nathan murmured his spells.

He was breathing hard when he stepped back, but he knew he'd been successful. Though the lines of congruence were invisible, they stretched their complex web among the objects on the table and across the forest to the house on the outskirts of Oak Hill. The lines were as real and stronger than the hard steel of a knife edge. The rest was up to Bully Ransden. . . .

Old Nathan began to chuckle.

Ellie stood beside him. She had moved back to the doorway when the murmur of the cunning man's voice ceased, but she didn't venture to speak.

Old Nathan grinned at her. "Reckon I'd take a swig uv yer popskull, now," he said. His throat was dry as a summer cornfield.

"Hit's done, thin?" the girl asked in a distant tone. She hefted a brown-glazed jug out from the corner by the bed and handed it to the cunning man, then turned again to toss another pine knot on the fire. The coffee pot, forgotten, still hung from the pivot bar.

Old Nathan pulled the stopper from the jug and swigged the whiskey. It was a harsh, artless rum, though it had kick enough for two. Bully Ransden's taste in liquor was similar to Madame Taliaferro's taste in the men of these parts. . . .

"My part's done," the cunning man said. He shot the

stopper home again. "Fer the rest, I reckon we'll jest watch."

He set the jug down against the wall. "Pick up the mirror," he explained. "That's what we'll look in."

Gingerly, Ellie raised the mirror from the table where it lay among the other paraphernalia. The frame and handle were curly maple finished with beeswax, locally fitted through of the highest craftsmanship. The bevel-edged four-inch glass was old and European in provenance. Lights glinted like jewels on its flawless surface.

Ellie gasped. The lights were not reflections from the cabin's hearth. They shone through the curtained windows of Francine Taliaferro's house.

"Won't hurt ye," Old Nathan said. "Hain't airy thing in all this thet could hurt *you*."

When he saw the sudden fear in her eyes, he added gruffly, "Not yer man neither. I done told ye thet!"

Ellie brought the mirror close to her face to get a better view of the miniature image. When she realized that she was blocking the cunning man's view, she colored and held the glass out to him.

Old Nathan shook his head with a grim smile. "You watch," he said. "I reckon ye earned thet from settin' up alone the past while."

Bully Ransden's horse stood in the paddock beside the Taliaferro house. Madame Taliaferro's black servant, now wearing loose garments instead of his livery, held the animal by a halter and curried it with smooth, flowing strokes.

"He's singin'," the woman said in wonder. She looked over at the cunning man. "I kin hear thet nigger a-singin'!"

"Reckon ye might," Old Nathan agreed.

Ellie pressed her face close to the mirror's surface again. Her expression hardened. Lamplight within the Chesson house threw bars of shadow across the curtains as a breeze caressed them.

"She's laughin'," Ellie whispered. "She's laughin', an' she's callin' him on."

"Hain't nothin' ye didn't know about," Old Nathan said. "Jest watch an' wait."

The cunning man's face was as stark as the killer he had been; one time and another, in one fashion or other. It was a hard world, and he was not the man to smooth its corners away with lies.

The screams were so loud that the mule heard them outside and snorted in surprise. Francine Taliaferro's voice cut the night like a glass-edged saw, but Bully Ransden's tenor bellows were louder yet.

The servant dropped his curry comb and ran for the house. Before he reached it, the front door burst open. Bully Ransden lurched out onto the porch, pulling his breeches up with both hands.

The black tried to stop him or perhaps just failed to get out of the way in time. Ransden knocked the servant over the porch rail with a sideways swipe of one powerful arm.

"What's hap'nin?" Ellie cried. Firelight gleamed on her fear-widened eyes. "What is hit?"

Old Nathan lifted the lamp chimney and shook it, spilling the flies unharmed from their glass prison. Mating complete for their lifetimes, they buzzed from the cabin on separate paths.

The trousers on the table quivered again. The tip of a barbel peeked from the waistband.

"Hain't airy thing hap'nin' now," the cunning man said. "I figgered thet's how you'd choose hit t' be."

Bully Ransden leaped into the paddock and mounted his horse bareback. He kicked at the gate bars, knocking them from their supports.

Madame Taliaferro appeared at the door, breathing in great gasps. The peignoir she wore was so diaphanous that with the lamplight behind her she appeared to be clothed in fog. She stared in horror at Bully Ransden.

Riding with nothing but his knees and a rope halter, Ransden jumped his horse over the remaining gate bars and galloped out of the mirror's field. Taliaferro and her black servant watched him go.

"I'll be off, now," Old Nathan said. There was nothing

of what he'd brought to Ransden's cabin that he needed to take back. "I don't choose t' meet Bully on the road, though I reckon he'll hev things on his mind besides tryin' conclusions with me."

He was shivering so violently that his tongue and lips had difficulty forming the words.

"But what's the matter with Cull?" Ellie Ransden begged.

"Hain't *nothin'* the matter!" Old Nathan gasped.

He put a hand on the doorframe to steady himself, then stepped out into the night. Had it been an ague, he could have dosed himself, but the cunning man was shaking in reaction to the powers he had summoned and channeled . . . successfully, though at a price.

Ellie followed him out of the cabin. She gripped Old Nathan's arm as he fumbled in one of the mule's panniers. "Sir," she said fiercely, "I've a right to know."

"Here," the cunning man said, thrusting a tissue-wrapped package into her hands. "Yer Cull, hit niver was he didn't love ye. This is sompin' he put back t' hev Rance Holden wrap up purty-like. I told Rance I'd bring it out t' ye."

The girl's fingers tugged reflexively at the ribbon, but she paused with the packet only half untied. The moon was still beneath the trees, so there was no illumination except the faint glow of firelight from the cabin's doorway. She caressed the lines of the ivory comb through the tissue.

"I reckon," Ellie said deliberately, "Cullen fergot 'cause of all the fishin' he's been after this past while." She tilted up her face and kissed Old Nathan's bearded cheek, then stepped away.

The cunning man mounted his mule and cast the reins loose from the rail. He was no longer shivering.

"Yer Cull, he give me a bullhead this forenoon," he said.

"We goin' home t' get some rest, naow?" the mule asked.

"Git up, mule," Old Nathan said, turning the beast's head. To Ellie he went on, "T'night, I give thet fish back t' him; an fer a while, I put hit where he didn't figger t' find sech a thing."

As the mule clopped down the road at a comfortable pace, Old Nathan called over his shoulder, "Sure *hell* thet warn't whut Francine Taliaferro figgered t' see there!"

Ordeal in Space

Robert A. Heinlein

Maybe we should never have ventured out into space. Our race has but two basic, innate fears; noise and the fear of falling. Those terrible heights— Why should any man in his right mind let himself be placed where he could fall . . . and fall . . . and fall— But all Spacemen are crazy. Everybody knows that.

The medicos had been very kind, he supposed. "You're lucky. You want to remember that, old fellow. You're still young and your retired pay relieves you of all worry about your future. You've got both arms and legs and are in fine shape."

"Fine shape!" His voice was unintentionally contemptuous.

"No, I mean it," the chief psychiatrist had persisted gently. "The little quirk you have does you no harm at all—except that you can't go out into space again. I can't honestly call acrophobia a neurosis; fear of falling is normal and sane. You've just got it a little more strongly than most—but that is not abnormal, in view of what you have been through."

The reminder set him to shaking again. He closed his eyes and saw the stars wheeling below him again. He was falling . . . falling endlessly. The psychiatrist's voice came through to him and pulled him back. "Steady, old man! Look around you."

"Sorry."

"Not at all. Now tell me, what do you plan to do?"

"I don't know. Get a job, I suppose."

"The Company will give you a job, you know."

He shook his head. "I don't want to hang around a spaceport." Wear a little button in his shirt to show that he was once a man, be addressed by a courtesy title of captain, claim the privileges of the pilots' lounge on the basis of what he used to be, hear the shop talk die down whenever he approached a group, wonder what they were saying behind his back—no, thank you!

"I think you're wise. Best to make a clean break, for a while at least, until you are feeling better."

"You think I'll get over it?"

The psychiatrist pursed his lips. "Possible. It's functional, you know. No trauma."

"But you don't think so?"

"I didn't say that. I honestly don't know. We still know very little about what makes a man tick."

"I see. Well, I might as well be leaving."

The psychiatrist stood up and shoved out his hand. "Holler if you want anything. And come back to see us in any case."

"Thanks."

"You're going to be all right. I know it."

But the psychiatrist shook his head as his patient walked out. The man did not walk like a spaceman; the easy, animal self-confidence was gone.

Only a small part of Great New York was roofed over in those days; he stayed underground until he was in that section, then sought out a passageway lined with bachelor rooms. He stuck a coin in the slot of the first one which displayed a lighted "vacant" sign, chucked his jump bag inside, and left. The monitor at the intersection gave him the address of the nearest placement office. He went there, seated himself at an interview desk, stamped in his finger prints, and started filling out forms. It gave him a curious back-to-the-beginning feeling; he had not looked for a job since pre-cadet days.

He left filling in his name to the last and hesitated even then. He had had more than his bellyful of publicity; he did not want to be recognized; he certainly did not want to be throbbed over—and most of all he did not want anyone telling him he was a hero. Presently he printed in the name "William Saunders" and dropped the forms in the slot.

He was well into his third cigarette and getting ready to strike another when the screen in front of him at last lighted up. He found himself staring at a nice-looking brunette. "Mr. Saunders," the image said, "will you come inside, please? Door seventeen."

The brunette in person was there to offer him a seat and a cigarette. "Make yourself comfortable, Mr. Saunders. I'm Miss Joyce. I'd like to talk with you about your application."

He settled himself and waited, without speaking.

When she saw that he did not intend to speak, she added, "Now take this name 'William Saunders' which you have given us—we know who you are, of course, from your prints."

"I suppose so."

"Of course I know what everybody knows about you, but your action in calling yourself 'William Saunders,' Mr.—"

"Saunders."

"—Mr. Saunders, caused me to query the files." She held up a microfilm spool, turned so that he might read his own name on it. "I know quite a lot about you now—more than the public knows and more than you saw fit to put into your application. It's a good record, Mr. Saunders."

"Thank you."

"But I can't use it in placing you in a job. I can't ever refer to it if you insist on designating yourself as 'Saunders.'"

"The name is Saunders." His voice was flat, rather than emphatic.

"Don't be hasty, Mr. Saunders. There are many positions in which the factor of prestige can be used quite legitimately to obtain for a client a much higher beginning rate of pay than—"

"I'm not interested."

She looked at him and decided not to insist. "As you wish. If you will go to reception room B, you can start your classification and skill tests."

"Thank you."

"*If* you should change your mind later, Mr. Saunders, we will be glad to reopen the case. Through that door, please."

Three days later found him at work for a small firm specializing in custom-built communication systems. His job was calibrating electronic equipment. It was soothing work, demanding enough to occupy his mind, yet easy for a man of his training and experience. At the end of his three months' probation he was promoted out of the helper category.

He was building himself a well-insulated rut, working, sleeping, eating, spending an occasional evening at the public library or working out at the YMCA—and never, under any circumstances, going out under the open sky nor up to any height, not even a theater balcony.

He tried to keep his past life shut out of his mind, but his memory of it was still fresh; he would find himself day-dreaming—the star-sharp, frozen sky of Mars, or the roaring night life of Venusburg. He would see again the swollen, ruddy bulk of Jupiter hanging over the port on Ganymede, its oblate bloated shape impossibly huge and crowding the sky.

Or he might, for a time, feel again the sweet quiet of the long watches on the lonely reaches between the planets. But such reveries were dangerous; they cut close to the edge of his new peace of mind. It was easy to slide over and find himself clinging for life to his last handhold on the steel sides of the *Valkyrie*, fingers numb and failing, and nothing below him but the bottomless well of space.

Then he would come back to Earth, shaking uncontrollably and gripping his chair or the workbench.

The first time it had happened at work he had found one of his benchmates, Joe Tully, staring at him curiously. "What's the trouble, Bill?" he had asked. "Hangover?"

"Nothing," he had managed to say. "Just a chill."

"You had better take a pill. Come on—let's go to lunch."

Tully led the way to the elevator; they crowded in. Most of the employees—even the women—preferred to go down via the drop chute, but Tully always used the elevator. "Saunders," of course, never used the drop chute; this had eased them into the habit of lunching together. He knew that the chute was safe, that, even if the power should fail, safety nets would snap across at each floor level—but he could not force himself to step off the edge.

Tully said publicly that a drop-chute landing hurt his arches, but he confided privately to Saunders that he did not trust automatic machinery. Saunders nodded understandingly but said nothing. It warmed him toward Tully. He began feeling friendly and not on the defensive with another human being for the first time since the start of his new life. He began to want to tell Tully the truth about himself. If he could be sure that Joe would not insist on treating him as a hero—not that he really objected to the role of hero. As a kid, hanging around spaceports, trying to wangle chances to go inside the ships, cutting classes to watch takeoffs, he had dreamed of being a "hero" someday, a hero of the spaceways, returning in triumph from some incredible and dangerous piece of exploration. But he was troubled by the fact that he still had the same picture of what a hero should look like and how he should behave; it did not include shying away from open windows, being fearful of walking across an open square, and growing too upset to speak at the mere thought of boundless depths of space.

Tully invited him home for dinner. He wanted to go, but fended off the invitation while he inquired where Tully lived. The Shelton Homes, Tully told him, naming one of those great, boxlike warrens that used to disfigure the Jersey flats. "It's a long way to come back," Saunders said doubtfully, while turning over in his mind ways to get there without exposing himself to the things he feared.

"You won't have to come back," Tully assured him. 'We've got a spare room. Come on. My old lady does her own cooking—that's why I keep her."

"Well, all right," he conceded. "Thanks, Joe." The La Guardia Tube would take him within a quarter of a mile; if he could not find a covered way he would take a ground cab and close the shades.

Tully met him in the hall and apologized in a whisper. "Meant to have a young lady for you, Bill. Instead we've got my brother-in-law. He's a louse. Sorry."

"Forget it, Joe. I'm glad to be here." He was indeed. The discovery that Bill's flat was on the thirty-fifth floor had dismayed him at first, but he was delighted to find that he had no feeling of height. The lights were on, the windows occulted, the floor under him was rock solid; he felt warm and safe. Mrs. Tully turned out in fact to be a good cook, to his surprise—he had the bachelor's usual distrust of amateur cooking. He let himself go to the pleasure of feeling at home and safe and wanted; he managed not even to hear most of the aggressive and opinionated remarks of Joe's in-law.

After dinner he relaxed in an easy chair, glass of beer in hand, and watched the video screen. It was a musical comedy; he laughed more heartily than he had in months. Presently the comedy gave way to a religious program, the National Cathedral Choir; he let it be, listening with one ear and giving some attention to the conversation with the other.

The choir was more than halfway through *Prayer for*

Travelers before he became fully aware of what they were singing:

"—hear us when we pray to Thee
For those in peril on the sea.

"Almighty Ruler of the all
Whose power extends to great and small,
Who guides the stars with steadfast law,
Whose least creation fills with awe;
Oh, grant Thy mercy and Thy grace
To those who venture into space."

He wanted to switch it off, but he had to hear it out, he could not stop listening to it, though it hurt him in his heart with the unbearable homesickness of the hopelessly exiled. Even as a cadet this one hymn could fill his eyes with tears; now he kept his face turned away from the others to try to hide from them the drops wetting his cheeks.

When the choir's "amen" let him do so he switched quickly to some other—any other—program and remained bent over the instrument, pretending to fiddle with it, while he composed his features. Then he turned back to the company, outwardly serene, though it seemed to him that anyone could see the hard, aching knot in his middle.

The brother-in-law was still sounding off.

"We ought to annex 'em," he was saying. "That's what we ought to do. Three-Planets Treaty—what a lot of ruddy rot! What right have they got to tell us what we can and can't do on Mars?"

"Well, Ed," Tully said mildly, "it's their planet, isn't it? They were there first."

Ed brushed it aside. "Did we ask the Indians whether or not they wanted us in North America? Nobody has any right to hang on to something he doesn't know how to use. With proper exploitation—"

"You been speculating, Ed?"

"Huh? It wouldn't be speculation if the government

wasn't made up of a bunch of weak-spined old women. 'Rights of Natives,' indeed. What rights do a bunch of degenerates have?"

Saunders found himself contrasting Ed Schultz with Knath Sooth, the only Martian he himself had ever known well. Gentle Knath, who had been old before Ed was born, and yet was rated as young among his own kind. Knath. . . . why, Knath could sit for hours with a friend or trusted acquaintance, saying nothing, needing to say nothing. "Growing together" they called it—his entire race had so grown together that they had needed no government, until the Earthman came.

Saunders had once asked his friend why he exerted himself so little, was satisfied with so little. More than an hour passed and Saunders was beginning to regret his inquisitiveness when Knath replied, "My fathers have labored and I am weary."

Saunders sat up and faced the brother-in-law. "They are not degenerate."

"Huh? I suppose *you* are an expert!"

"The Martians aren't degenerate, they're just tired," Saunders persisted.

Tully grinned. His brother-in-law saw it and became surly. "What gives you the right to an opinion? Have you ever been to Mars?"

Saunders realized suddenly that he had let his censors down. "Have you?" he answered cautiously.

"That's beside the point. The best minds all agree—" Bill let him go on and did not contradict him again. It was a relief when Tully suggested that, since they all had to be up early, maybe it was about time to think about beginning to get ready to go to bed.

He said goodnight to Mrs. Tully and thanked her for a wonderful dinner, then followed Tully into the guest room. "Only way to get rid of that family curse we're saddled with, Bill," he apologized. "Stay up as long as you like." Tully stepped to the window and opened it. "You'll sleep well here. We're up high enough to get honest-to-goodness fresh air." He stuck his head out and took a couple of big breaths. "Nothing like the real article," he continued as he withdrew from the window. "I'm a country boy at heart. What's the matter, Bill?"

"Nothing. Nothing at all."

"I thought you looked a little pale. Well, sleep tight. I've already set your bed for seven; that'll give us plenty of time."

"Thanks, Joe. Goodnight." As soon as Tully was out of the room he braced himself, then went over and closed the window. Sweating, he turned away and switched the ventilation back on. That done, he sank down on the edge of the bed.

He sat there for a long time, striking one cigarette after another. He knew too well that the peace of mind he thought he had regained was unreal. There was nothing left to him but shame and a long, long hurt. To have reached the point where he had to knuckle under to a tenth-rate knothead like Ed Schultz—it would have been better if he had never come out of the *Valkyrie* business.

Presently he took five grains of "Fly-Rite" from his pouch, swallowed it, and went to bed. He got up almost at once, forced himself to open the window a trifle, then compromised by changing the setting of the bed so that it would not turn out the lights after he got to sleep.

He had been asleep and dreaming for an indefinitely long time. He was back in space again—indeed, he had never been away from it. He was happy, with the full happiness of a man who has awakened to find it was only a bad dream.

The crying disturbed his serenity. At first it made him only vaguely uneasy, then he began to feel in some way responsible—he must do something about it. The transition to falling had only dream logic behind it, but it was real to him. He was grasping, his hands were slipping, had slipped—and there was nothing under him but the black emptiness of space—

He was awake and gasping, on Joe Tully's guestroom bed; the lights burned bright around him.

But the crying persisted.

He shook his head, then listened. It was real all right.

Now he had it identified—a cat, a kitten by the sound of it.

He sat up. Even if he had not had the spaceman's traditional fondness for cats, he would have investigated. However, he liked cats for themselves, quite aside from their neat shipboard habits, their ready adaptability to changing accelerations, and their usefulness in keeping the ship free of those other creatures that go wherever man goes. So he got up at once and looked for this one.

A quick look showed him that the kitten was not in the room, and his ear led him to the correct spot; the sound came in through the slightly opened window. He shied off, stopped, and tried to collect his thoughts.

He told himself that it was unnecessary to do anything more; if the sound came in through his window, then it must be because it came out of some nearby window. But he knew that he was lying to himself; the sound was close by. In some impossible way the cat was just outside his window, thirty-five stories above the street.

He sat down and tried to strike a cigarette, but the tube broke in his fingers. He let the fragments fall to the floor, got up and took six nervous steps toward the window, as if he were being jerked along. He sank down to his knees, grasped the window and threw it wide open, then clung to the windowsill, his eyes shut tight.

After a time the sill seemed to steady a bit. He opened his eyes, gasped, and shut them again. Finally he opened them again, being very careful not to look out at the stars, not to look down at the street. He had half expected to find the cat on a balcony outside his room—it seemed the only reasonable explanation. But there was no balcony, no place at all where a cat could reasonably be.

However, the mewing was louder than ever. It seemed to come from directly under him. Slowly he forced his head out, still clinging to the sill, and made himself look down. Under him, about four feet lower than the edge of the window, a narrow ledge ran around the side of the building. Seated on it was a woebegone ratty-looking kitten. It stared up at him and meowed again.

It was barely possible that, by clinging to the sill with

one hand and making a long arm with the other, he could reach it without actually going out the window, he thought—if he could bring himself to do it. He considered calling Tully, then thought better of it. Tully was shorter than he was, had less reach. And the kitten had to be rescued now, before the fluff-brained idiot jumped or fell.

He tried for it. He shoved his shoulders out, clung with his left arm and reached down with his right. Then he opened his eyes and saw that he was a foot or ten inches away from the kitten still. It sniffed curiously in the direction of his hand.

He stretched till his bones cracked. The kitten promptly skittered away from his clutching fingers, stopping a good six feet down the ledge. There it settled down and commenced washing its face.

He inched back inside and collapsed, sobbing, on the floor underneath the window. "I can't do it," he whispered. "I can't do it. Not again—"

The Rocket Ship *Valkyrie* was two hundred and forty-nine days out from Earth-Luna Space Terminal and approaching Mars Terminal on Deimos, outer Martian satellite. William Cole, Chief Communications Officer and relief pilot, was sleeping sweetly when his assistant shook him. "Hey! Bill! Wake up—we're in a jam."

"Huh? Wazzat?" But he was already reaching for his socks. "What's the trouble, Tom?"

Fifteen minutes later he knew that his junior officer had not exaggerated; he was reporting the facts to the Old Man—the primary piloting radar was out of whack. Tom Sandburg had discovered it during a routine check, made as soon as Mars was inside the maximum range of the radar pilot. The captain had shrugged. "Fix it, Mister—and be quick about it. We need it."

Bill Cole shook his head. "There's nothing wrong with it, Captain—inside. She acts as if the antenna were gone completely."

"That's impossible. We haven't even had a meteor alarm."

"Might be anything, Captain. Might be metal fatigue and it just fell off. But we've got to replace that antenna. Stop the spin on the ship and I'll go out and fix it. I can jury-rig a replacement while she loses her spin."

The *Valkyrie* was a luxury ship, of her day. She was assembled long before anyone had any idea of how to produce an artificial gravity field. Nevertheless she had pseudogravity for the comfort of her passengers. She spun endlessly around her main axis, like a shell from a rifled gun; the resulting angular acceleration—miscalled "centrifugal force"—kept her passengers firm in their beds, or steady on their feet. The spin was started as soon as her rockets stopped blasting at the beginning of a trip and was stopped only when it was necessary to maneuver into a landing. It was accomplished, not by magic, but by reaction against the contrary spin of a flywheel located on her centerline.

The captain looked annoyed. "I've started to take the spin off, but I can't wait that long. Jury-rig the astrogational radar for piloting."

Cole started to explain why the astrogational radar could not be adapted to short-range work, then decided not to try. "It can't be done, sir. It's a technical impossibility."

"When I was your age I could jury-rig anything! Well, find me an answer, Mister. I can't take this ship down blind. Not even for the Harriman Medal."

Bill Cole hesitated for a moment before replying, "I'll have to go out while she's still got spin on her, Captain, and make the replacement. There isn't any other way to do it."

The captain looked away from him, his jaw muscles flexed. "Get the replacement ready. Hurry up about it."

Cole found the captain already at the airlock when he arrived with the gear he needed for the repair. To his surprise the Old Man was suited up. "Explain to me what I'm to do," he ordered Bill.

"You're not going out, sir?" The captain simply nodded.

Bill took a look at his captain's waist line, or where his waist line used to be. Why, the Old Man must be thirty-five it he were a day! "I'm afraid I can't explain too clearly. I had expected to make the repair myself."

"I've never asked a man to do a job I wouldn't do myself. Explain it to me."

"Excuse me, sir—but can you chin yourself with one hand?"

"What's that got to do with it?"

"Well, we've got forty-eight passengers, sir, and—"

"Shut up!"

Sandburg and he, both in space suits, helped the Old Man down the hole after the inner door of the lock was closed and the air exhausted. The space beyond the lock was a vast, starflecked emptiness. With spin still on the ship, every direction outward was "down," down for millions of uncounted miles. They put a safety line on him, of course—nevertheless it gave him a sinking feeling to see the captain's head disappear in the bottomless, black hole.

The line paid out steadily for several feet, then stopped. When it had been stopped for several minutes, Bill leaned over and touched his helmet against Sandburg's. "Hang on to my feet. I'm going to take a look."

He hung his head down out the lock and looked around. The captain was stopped, hanging by both hands, nowhere near the antenna fixture. He scrambled back up and reversed himself. "I'm going out."

It was no great trick, he found, to hang by his hands and swing himself along to where the captain was stalled. The *Valkyrie* was space-to-space ship, not like the sleek-sided jobs we see around earthports; she was covered with handholds for the convenience of repairmen at the terminals. Once he reached him, it was possible, by grasping the same steel rung that the captain clung to, to aid him in swinging back to the last one he had quitted. Five minutes later Sandburg was pulling the Old man up through the hole and Bill was scrambling after him.

He began at once to unbuckle the repair gear from the captain's suit and transfer it to his own. He lowered himself back down the hole and was on his way before the older man had recovered enough to object, if he still intended to.

Swinging out to where the antenna must be replaced was not too hard, though he had all eternity under his toes. The suit impeded him a little—the gloves were clumsy—but he was used to spacesuits. He was a little winded from helping the captain, but he could not stop to think about that. The increased spin bothered him somewhat; the airlock was nearer the axis of spin than was the antenna—he felt heavier as he moved out.

Getting the replacement antenna shipped was another matter. It was neither large nor heavy, but he found it impossible to fasten it into place. He needed one hand to cling by, one to hold the antenna, and one to handle the wrench. That left him shy one hand, no matter how he tried it.

Finally, he jerked his safety line to signal Sandburg for more slack. Then he unshackled it from his waist, working with one hand, passed the end twice through a handhold and knotted it; he left about six feet of it hanging free. The shackle on the free end he fastened to another handhold. The result was a loop, a bright, an improvised bosun's chair, which would support his weight while he man-handled the antenna into place. The job went fairly quickly then.

He was almost through. There remained one bolt to fasten on the far side, away from where he swung. The antenna was already secured at two points and its circuit connection made. He decided he could manage it with one hand. He left his perch and swung over, monkey fashion.

The wrench slipped as he finished tightening the bolt; it slipped from his grasp, fell free. He watched it go, out and out and out, down and down and down, until it was so small he could no longer see it. It made him dizzy to watch it, bright in the sunlight against the deep black of space. He had been too busy to look down, up to now.

He shivered. "Good thing I was through with it," he said. "It would be a long walk to fetch it." He started to make his way back.

He found that he could not.

He had swung past the antenna to reach his present position, using a grip on his safety-line swing to give him a few inches more reach. Now the loop of line hung quietly, just out of reach. There was no way to reverse the process.

He hung by both hands and told himself not to get panicky—he must think his way out. Around the other side? No, the steel skin of the *Valkyrie* was smooth there—no handhold for more than six feet. Even if he were not tired—and he had to admit that he was, tired and getting a little cold—even if he were fresh, it was an impossible swing for anyone not a chimpanzee.

He looked down—and regretted it.

There was nothing below him but stars, down and down, endlessly. Stars, swinging past as the ship spun with him, emptiness of all time and blackness and cold.

He found himself trying to hoist himself bodily onto the single narrow rung he clung to, trying to reach it with his toes. It was a futile, strength-wasting excess. He quieted his panic sufficiently to stop it, then hung limp.

It was easier if he kept his eyes closed. But after a while he always had to open them and look. The Big Dipper would swing past and then, presently, Orion. He tried to compute the passing minutes in terms of the number of rotations the ship made, but his mind would not work clearly, and, after a while, he would have to shut his eyes.

His hands were becoming stiff—and cold. He tried to rest them by hanging by one hand at a time. He let go with his left hand, felt pins-and-needles course through it, and beat it against his side. Presently it seemed time to spell his right hand.

He could no longer reach up to the rung with his left hand. He did not have the power left in him to make the extra pull; he was fully extended and could not shorten himself enough to get his left hand up.

He could no longer feel his right hand at all.

He could see it slip. It was slipping—

The sudden release in tension let him know that he was falling . . . falling. The ship dropped away from him.

He came to with the captain bending over him. "Just keep quiet, Bill."

"Where—"

"Take it easy. The patrol from Deimos was already close by when you let go. They tracked you on the 'scope, matched orbits with you, and picked you up. First time in history, I guess. Now keep quiet. You're a sick man—you hung there more than two hours, Bill."

The meowing started up again, louder than ever. He got up on his knees and looked out over the windowsill. The kitten was still away to the left on the ledge. He thrust his head cautiously out a little further, remembering not to look at anything but the kitten and the ledge. "Here, kitty!" he called. "Here, kit-kit-kitty! Here, kitty, come kitty!"

The kitten stopped washing and managed to look puzzled.

"Come, kitty," he repeated softly. He let go of the windowsill with his right hand and gestured toward it invitingly. The kitten approached about three inches, then sat down. "Here, kitty," he pleaded and stretched his arm as far as possible.

The fluff ball promptly backed away again.

He withdrew his arm and thought about it. This was getting nowhere, he decided. If he were to slide over the edge and stand on the ledge, he could hang on with one arm and be perfectly safe. He knew that, he knew it would be safe—he needn't look down!

He drew himself back inside, reversed himself, and, with great caution, gripping the sill with both arms, let his legs slide down the face of the building. He focused his eyes carefully on the corner of the bed.

The ledge seemed to have been moved. He could not find it, and was beginning to be sure that he had reached past it, when he touched it with one toe—then he had both feet firmly planted on it. It seemed about six inches wide. He took a deep breath.

Letting go with his right arm, he turned and faced the kitten. It seemed interested in the procedure but not disposed to investigate more closely. If he were to creep along the ledge, holding on with his left hand, he could just about reach it from the corner of the window—

He moved his feet one at a time, baby fashion, rather than pass one past the other. By bending his knees a trifle, and leaning, he could just manage to reach it. The kitten sniffed his groping fingers, then leaped backward. One tiny paw missed the edge; it scrambled and regained its footing. "You little idiot!" he said indignantly, "do you want to bash your brains out?

"If any," he added. The situation looked hopeless now; the baby cat was too far away to be reached from his anchorage at the window, no matter how he stretched. He called "Kitty, kitty" rather hopelessly, then stopped to consider the matter.

He could give it up.

He could prepare himself to wait all night in the hope that the kitten would decide to come closer. Or he could go get it.

The ledge was wide enough to take his weight. If he made himself small, flat to the wall, no weight rested on his left arm. He moved slowly forward, retaining the grip on the window as long as possible, inching so gradually that he hardly seemed to move. When the window frame was finally out of reach, when his left hand was flat to smooth wall, he made the mistake of looking down, down, past the sheer wall at the glowing pavement far below.

He pulled his eyes back and fastened them on a spot on the wall, level with his eyes and only a few feet away. He was still there!

And so was the kitten. Slowly he separated his feet, moving his right foot forward, and bent his knees. He stretched his right hand along the wall, until it was over and a little beyond the kitten.

He brought it down in a sudden swipe, as if to swat a fly. He found himself with a handful of scratching, biting fur.

He held perfectly still then, and made no attempt to check the minor outrages the kitten was giving him. Arms still outstretched, body flat to the wall, he started his return. He could not see where he was going and could not turn his head without losing some little of his margin of balance. It seemed a long way back, longer than he had come, when at last the fingertips of his left hand slipped into the window opening.

He backed up the rest of the way in a matter of seconds, slid both arms over the sill, then got his right knee over. He rested himself on the sill and took a deep breath. "Man!" he said aloud. "That was a tight squeeze. You're a menace to traffic, little cat."

He glanced down at the pavement. It was certainly a long way down—looked hard, too.

He looked up at the stars. Mighty nice they looked and mighty bright. He braced himself in the window frame, back against one side, foot pushed against the other, and looked at them. The kitten settled down in the cradle of his stomach and began to buzz. He stroked it absent-mindedly and reached for a cigarette. He would go out to the port and take his physical and his psycho tomorrow, he decided. He scratched the kitten's ears. "Little fluffhead," he said, "how would you like to take a long, long ride with me?"

Space-Time for Springers

Fritz Leiber

Gummitch was a superkitten, as he knew very well, with an I.Q. of about 160. Of course, he didn't talk. But everybody knows that I.Q. tests based on language ability are very one-sided. Besides, he would talk as soon as they started setting a place for him at table and pouring him coffee. Ashurbanipal and Cleopatra ate horsemeat from pans on the floor and they didn't talk. Baby dined in his crib on milk from a bottle and he didn't talk. Sissy sat at table but they didn't pour her coffee and she didn't talk—not one word. Father and Mother (whom Gummitch had nicknamed Old Horsemeat and Kitty-Come-Here) sat at table and poured each other coffee and they *did* talk. Q. E. D.

Meanwhile, he would get by very well on thought projection and intuitive understanding of all human speech—not even to mention cat patois, which almost any civilized animal could play by ear. The dramatic monologues and Socratic dialogues, the quiz and panel show appearances, the felidological expedition to darkest Africa (where he would uncover the real truth behind lions and tigers), the exploration of the outer planets—all these could wait. The same went for the books for which he was ceaselessly accumulating material: *The Encyclopedia of Odors, Anthropofeline Psychology, Invisible Signs and Secret Wonders, Space-Time for Springers, Slit Eyes Look at Life*, et cetera. For the present it was enough to live existence to the hilt and soak up knowledge, missing no experience proper to his age level—to rush about with tail aflame.

So to all outward appearances Gummitch was just a vividly normal kitten, as shown by the succession of nicknames he bore along the magic path that led from blue-eyed infancy toward puberty: Little One, Squawker, Portly, Bumble (for purring not clumsiness), Old Starved-to-Death, Fierso, Lover-boy (affection not sex), Spook and Catnik. Of these only the last perhaps requires further explanation: the Russians had just sent Muttnik up after Sputnik, so that when one evening Gummitch streaked three times across the firmament of the living room floor in the same direction, past the fixed stars of the humans and the comparatively slow-moving heavenly bodies of the two older cats, and Kitty-Come-Here quoted the line from Keats:

Then felt I like some watcher of the skies
When a new planet swims into his ken;

it was inevitable that Old Horsemeat would say, "Ah—Catnik!"

The new name lasted all of three days, to be replaced by Gummitch, which showed signs of becoming permanent.

The little cat was on the verge of truly growing up, at least so Gummitch overheard Old Horsemeat comment to Kitty-Come-Here. A few short weeks, Old Horsemeat said, and Gummitch's fiery flesh would harden, his slim neck thicken, the electricity vanish from everything but his fur, and all his delightful kittenish qualities rapidly give way to the earth-bound singlemindedness of a tom. They'd be lucky, Old Horsemeat concluded, if he didn't turn completely surly like Ashurbanipal.

Gummitch listened to these predictions with gay unconcern and with secret amusement from his vantage point of superior knowledge, in the same spirit that he accepted so many phases of his outwardly conventional existence: the murderous side-long looks he got from Ashurbanipal and Cleopatra as he devoured his own horsemeat from his own little tin pan, because they sometimes were given canned catfood but he never; the stark idiocy of Baby, who didn't know the difference between a live cat and a stuffed teddy bear and who tried to cover up his ignorance by making goo-goo noises and poking indiscriminately at all eyes; the far more serious—because cleverly hidden—maliciousness of Sissy, who had to be watched out for warily—especially when you were alone—and whose retarded—even warped—development, Gummitch knew, was Old Horsemeat and Kitty-Come-Here's deepest, most secret, worry (more of Sissy and her evil ways soon); the limited intellect of Kitty-Come-Here, who despite the amounts of coffee she drank was quite as featherbrained as kittens are supposed to be and who firmly believed, for example, that kittens operated in the same space-time as other beings—that to get from *here* to *there* they had to cross the space *between*—and similar fallacies; the mental stodginess of even Old Horsemeat, who although he understood quite a bit of the secret doctrine and talked intelligently to Gummitch when they were alone, nevertheless suffered from the limitations of his status—a rather nice old god but a maddeningly slow-witted one.

But Gummitch could easily forgive all this massed inadequacy and downright brutishness in his felino-human household, because he was aware that he alone knew the real truth about himself and about other kittens and babies as well, the truth which was hidden from weaker minds, the truth that was as intrinsically incredible as the germ theory of disease or the origin of the whole great universe in the explosion of a single atom.

As a baby kitten Gummitch had believed that Old Horsemeat's two hands were hairless kittens permanently attached to the ends of Old Horsemeat's arms but having an independent life of their own. How he had hated and loved those two five-legged sallow monsters, his first playmates, comforters and battle-opponents!

Well, even that fantastic discarded notion was but a trifling fancy compared to the real truth about himself!

The forehead of Zeus split open to give birth to Minerva. Gummitch had been born from the waist-fold of a dirty old terrycloth bathrobe, Old Horsemeat's basic garment. The kitten was intuitively certain of it and had proved it to himself as well as any Descartes or Aristotle. In a kitten-size tuck of that ancient bathrobe the atoms of his body had gathered and quickened into life. His earliest memories were of snoozing wrapped in terrycloth, warmed by Old Horsemeat's heat. Old Horsemeat and Kitty-Come-Here were his true parents. The other theory of his origin, the one he heard Old Horsemeat and Kitty-Come-Here recount from time to time—that he had been the only surviving kitten of a litter abandoned next door, that he had had the shakes from vitamin deficiency and lost the tip of his tail and the hair on his paws and had to be nursed back to life and health with warm yellowish milk-and-vitamins fed from an eyedropper—that other theory was just one of those rationalizations with which mysterious nature cloaks the birth of heroes, perhaps wisely veiling the truth from minds unable to bear it, a rationalization as false as Kitty-Come-Here and Old Horsemeat's touching belief that Sissy and Baby were their children rather than the cubs of Ashurbanipal and Cleopatra.

The day that Gummitch had discovered by pure intuition the secret of his birth he had been filled with a wild instant excitement. He had only kept it from tearing him to pieces by rushing out to the kitchen and striking and devouring a fried scallop, torturing it fiendishly first for twenty minutes.

And the secret of his birth was only the beginning. His intellectual faculties aroused, Gummitch had two days later intuited a further and greater secret: since he was the child of humans he would, upon reaching this maturation date of which Old Horsemeat had spoken, turn not into a sullen tom but into a godlike human youth with reddish golden hair the color of his present fur. He would be poured coffee; and he would instantly be able to talk, probably in all languages. While Sissy (how clear it was now!) would at approximately the same time shrink and fur out into a sharp-clawed and vicious she-cat dark as her hair, sex and self-love her only concerns, fit harem-mate for Cleopatra, concubine to Ashurbanipal.

Exactly the same was true, Gummitch realized at once, for all kittens and babies, all humans and cats, wherever they might dwell. Metamorphosis was as much a part of the fabric of their lives as it was of the insects'. It was also the basic fact underlying all legends of werewolves, vampires and witches' familiars.

If you just rid your mind of preconceived notions, Gummitch told himself, it was all very logical. Babies were stupid, fumbling, vindictive creatures without reason or speech. What could be more natural than that they should grow up into mute sullen selfish beasts bent only on rapine and reproduction? While kittens were quick, sensitive, subtle, supremely alive. What other destiny were they possibly fitted for except to become the deft, word-speaking, book-writing, music-making, meat-getting-and-dispensing masters of the world? To dwell on the physical differences, to point out that kittens and men, babies and cats, are rather unlike in appearance and size, would be to miss the forest for the trees—very much as if an entomologist should proclaim metamorphosis a myth because his microscope failed to discover the wings of a butterfly in a caterpillar's slime or a golden beetle in a grub.

Nevertheless it was such a mind-staggering truth, Gummitch realized at the same time, that it was easy to understand why humans, cats, babies and perhaps most kittens were quite unaware of it. How to safely explain to a butterfly that he was once a hairy crawler, or to a dull larva that he will one day be a walking jewel? No, in such situations the delicate minds of man- and feline-kind are guarded by a merciful mass amnesia, such as

Velikovsky has explained prevents us from recalling that in historical times the Earth was catastrophically bumped by the planet Venus operating in the manner of a comet before settling down (with a cosmic sigh of relief, surely!) into its present orbit.

This conclusion was confirmed when Gummitch in the first fever of illumination tried to communicate his great insight to others. He told it in cat patois, as well as that limited jargon permitted, to Ashurbanipal and Cleopatra and even, on the off chance, to Sissy and Baby. They showed no interest whatever, except that Sissy took advantage of his unguarded preoccupation to stab him with a fork.

Later, alone with Old Horsemeat, he projected the great new thoughts, staring with solemn yellow eyes at the old god, but the later grew markedly nervous and even showed signs of real fear, so Gummitch desisted. ("You'd have sworn he was trying to put across something as deep as the Einstein theory or the doctrine of original sin," Old Horsemeat later told Kitty-Come-Here.)

But Gummitch was a man now in all but form, the kitten reminded himself after these failures, and it was part of his destiny to shoulder secrets alone when necessary. He wondered if the general amnesia would affect him when he metamorphosed. There was no sure answer to this question, but he hoped not—and sometimes felt that there was reason for his hopes. Perhaps he would be the first true kitten-man, speaking from a wisdom that had no locked doors in it.

Once he was tempted to speed up the process by the use of drugs. Left alone in the kitchen, he sprang onto the table and started to lap up the black puddle in the bottom of Old Horsemeat's coffee cup. It tasted foul and poisonous and he withdrew with a little snarl, frightened as well as revolted. The dark beverage would not work its tongue-loosening magic, he realized, except at the proper time and with the proper ceremonies. Incantations might be necessary as well. Certainly unlawful tasting was highly dangerous.

The futility of expecting coffee to work any wonders

by itself was further demonstrated to Gummitch when Kitty-Come-Here, wordlessly badgered by Sissy, gave a few spoonfuls to the little girl, liberally lacing it first with milk and sugar. Of course Gummitch knew by now that Sissy was destined shortly to turn into a cat and that no amount of coffee would ever make her talk, but it was nevertheless instructive to see how she spat out the first mouthful, drooling a lot of saliva after it, and dashed the cup and its contents at the chest of Kitty-Come-Here.

Gummitch continued to feel a great deal of sympathy for his parents in their worries about Sissy and he longed for the day when he would metamorphose and be able as an acknowledged man-child truly to console them. It was heartbreaking to see how they each tried to coax the little girl to talk, always attempting it while the other was absent, how they seized on each accidentally wordlike note in the few sounds she uttered and repeated it back to her hopefully, how they were more and more possessed by fears not so much of her retarded (they thought) development as of her increasingly obvious maliciousness, which was directed chiefly at Baby . . . though the two cats and Gummitch bore their share. Once she had caught Baby alone in his crib and used the sharp corner of a block to dot Baby's large-doomed lightly downed head with triangular red marks. Kitty-Come-Here had discovered her doing it, but the woman's first action had been to rub Baby's head to obliterate the marks so that Old Horsemeat wouldn't see them. That was the night Kitty-Come-Here hid the abnormal psychology books.

Grummitch understood very well that Kitty-Come-Here and Old Horsemeat, honestly believing themselves to be Sissy's parents, felt just as deeply about her as if they actually were and he did what little he could under the present circumstances to help them. He had recently come to feel a quite independent affection for Baby—the miserable little proto-cat was so completely stupid and defenseless—and so he unofficially constituted himself the creature's guardian, taking his naps behind the door of the nursery and dashing about noisily whenever

Sissy showed up. In any case he realized that as a potentially adult member of a felino-human household he had his natural responsibilities.

Accepting responsibilities was as much a part of a kitten's life, Gummitch told himself, as shouldering unsharable intuitions and secrets, the number of which continued to grow from day to day.

There was, for instance, the Affair of the Squirrel Mirror.

Gummitch had early solved the mystery of ordinary mirrors and of the creatures that appeared in them. A little observation and sniffing and one attempt to get behind the heavy wall-job in the living room had convinced him that mirror beings were insubstantial or at least hermetically sealed into their other world, probably creatures of pure spirit, harmless imitative ghosts—including the silent Gummitch Double who touched paws with him so softly yet so coldly.

Just the same, Gummitch had let his imagination play with what would happen if one day, while looking into the mirror world, he should let loose his grip on his spirit and let it slip into the Gummitch Double while the other's spirit slipped into his body—if, in short, he should change places with the scentless ghost kitten. Being doomed to a life consisting wholly of imitation and completely lacking in opportunities to show initiative—except for behind-the-scenes judgment and speed needed in rushing from one mirror to another to keep up with the real Gummitch—would be sickeningly dull, Gummitch decided, and he resolved to keep a tight hold on his spirit at all times in the vicinity of mirrors.

But that isn't telling about the Squirrel Mirror. One morning Gummitch was peering out the front bedroom window that overlooked the roof of the porch. Gummitch had already classified windows as semi-mirrors having two kinds of space on the other side: the mirror world and that harsh region filled with mysterious and dangerously organized-sounding noises called the outer world, into which grownup humans reluctantly ventured at intervals, donning special garments for the purpose and shouting loud farewells that were meant to be reassuring but achieved just the opposite effect. The coexistence of two kinds of space presented no paradox to the kitten who carried in his mind the 27-chapter outline of *Space-Time for Springers*—indeed, it constituted one of the minor themes of the book.

This morning the bedroom was dark and the outer world was dull and sunless, so the mirror world was unusually difficult to see. Gummitch was just lifting his face toward it, nose twitching, his front paws on the sill, when what should rear up on the other side, exactly in the space that the Gummitch Double normally occupied, but a dirty brown, narrow-visaged image with savagely low forehead, dark evil walleyes, and a huge jaw filled with shovel-like teeth.

Gummitch was enormously startled and hideously frightened. He felt his grip on his spirit go limp, and without volition he teleported himself three yards to the rear, making use of that faculty for cutting corners in space-time, traveling by space-warp in fact, which was one of his powers that Kitty-Come-Here refused to believe in and that even Old Horsemeat accepted only on faith.

Then, not losing a moment, he picked himself up by his furry seat, swung himself around, dashed downstairs at top speed, sprang to the top of the sofa, and stared for several seconds at the Gummitch Double in the wall-mirror—not relaxing a muscle strand until he was completely convinced that he was still himself and had not been transformed into the nasty brown apparition that had confronted him in the bedroom window.

"Now what do you suppose brought that on?" Old Horsemeat asked Kitty-Come-Here.

Later Gummitch learned that what he had seen had been a squirrel, a savage, nut-hunting being belonging wholly to the outer world (except for forays into attics) and not at all to the mirror one. Nevertheless he kept a vivid memory of his profound momentary conviction that the squirrel had taken the Gummitch Double's place and been about to take his own. He shuddered to think what would have happened if the squirrel had been actively interested in trading spirits with him. Apparently mirrors and mirror-situations, just as he had always feared, were highly conducive to spirit transfers. He filed the information away in the memory cabinet reserved for dangerous, exciting and possibly useful information, such as plans for climbing straight up glass (diamond-tipped claws!) and flying higher than the trees.

These days his thought cabinets were beginning to feel filled to bursting and he could hardly wait for the moment when the true rich taste of coffee, lawfully drunk, would permit him to speak.

He pictured the scene in detail: the family gathered in conclave at the kitchen table, Ashurbanipal and Cleopatra respectfully watching from floor level, himself sitting erect on chair with paws (or would they be hands?) lightly touching his cup of thin china, while Old Horsemeat poured the thin black steaming stream. He knew the Great Transformation must be close at hand.

At the same time he knew that the other critical situation in the household was worsening swiftly. Sissy, he realized now, was far older than Baby and should long ago have undergone her own somewhat less glamorous though equally necessary transformation (the first tin of raw horsemeat could hardly be as exciting as the first cup of coffee). Her time was long overdue. Gummitch found increasing horror in this mute vampirish being inhabiting the body of a rapidly growing girl, though inwardly equipped to be nothing but a most blood-thirsty she-cat. How dreadful to think of Old Horsemeat and Kitty-Come-Here having to care all their lives for such a monster! Gummitch told himself that if any opportunity for alleviating his parents' misery should ever present itself to him, he would not hesitate for an instant.

Then one night, when the sense of Change was so burstingly strong in him that he knew tomorrow must be the Day, but when the house was also exceptionally unquiet with boards creaking and snapping, taps adrip, and curtains mysteriously rustling at closed windows (so that it was clear that the many spirit worlds including the mirror one must be pressing very close), the opportunity came to Gummitch.

Kitty-Come-Here and Old Horsemeat had fallen into especially sound, drugged sleeps, the former with a bad cold, the latter with one unhappy highball too many (Gummitch knew he had been brooding about Sissy). Baby slept too, though with uneasy whimperings and joggings—moonlight shone full on his crib past a window shade which had whirringly rolled itself up without human or feline agency. Gummitch kept vigil under the crib, with eyes closed but with wildly excited mind pressing outward to every boundary of the house and even stretching here and there into the outer world. On this night of all nights sleep was unthinkable.

Then suddenly he became aware of footsteps, footsteps so soft they must, he thought, be Cleopatra's.

No, softer than that, so soft they might be those of the Gummitch Double escaped from the mirror world at last and padding up toward him through the darkened halls. A ribbon of fur rose along his spine.

Then into the nursery Sissy came prowling. She looked slim as an Egyptian princess in her long thin yellow nightgown and as sure of herself, but the cat was very strong in her tonight, from the flat intent eyes to the dainty canine teeth slightly bared—one look at her now would have sent Kitty-Come-Here running for the telephone number she kept hidden, the telephone number of the special doctor—and Gummitch realized he was witnessing a monstrous suspension of natural law in that this being should be able to exist for a moment without growing fur and changing round pupils for slit eyes.

He retreated to the darkest corner of the room, suppressing a snarl.

Sissy approached the crib and leaned over Baby in the moonlight, keeping her shadow off him. For a while she gloated. Then she began softly to scratch his cheek with a long hatpin she carried, keeping away from his eye, but just barely. Baby awoke and saw her and Baby didn't cry.

Sissy continued to scratch, always a little more deeply. The moonlight glittered on the jeweled end of the pin.

Gummitch knew he faced a horror that could not be countered by running about or even spitting and screeching. Only magic could fight so obviously supernatural a manifestation. And this was also no time to think of consequences, no matter how clearly and bitterly etched they might appear to a mind intensely awake.

He sprang up onto the other side of the crib, not uttering a sound, and fixed his golden eyes on Sissy's in the moonlight. Then he moved forward straight at her evil face, stepping slowly, not swiftly, using his extraordinary knowledge of the properties of space *to walk straight through her hand and arm as they flailed the hatpin at him*. When his nose-tip finally paused a fraction of an inch from hers his eyes had not blinked once, and she could not look away. Then he unhesitatingly flung his spirit into her like a fistful of flaming arrows and he worked the Mirror Magic.

Sissy's moonlit face, feline and terrified, was in a sense the last thing that Gummitch, the real Gummitch-kitten, ever saw in this world. For the next instant he felt himself enfolded by the foul black blinding cloud of Sissy's spirit, which his own had displaced. At the same time he heard the little girl scream, very loudly but even more distinctly, "*Mommy!*"

That cry might have brought Kitty-Come-Here out of her grave, let alone from sleep merely deep or drugged. Within seconds she was in the nursery, closely followed by Old Horsemeat, and she had caught up Sissy in her arms and the little girl was articulating the wonderful word again and again, and miraculously following it with the command—there could be no doubt, Old Horsemeat heard it too—"Hold me tight!"

Then Baby finally dared to cry. The scratches on his cheek came to attention and Gummitch, as he had known must happen, was banished to the basement amid cries of horror and loathing chiefly from Kitty-Come-Here.

The little cat did not mind. No basement would be

one-tenth as dark as Sissy's spirit that now enshrouded him for always, hiding all the file drawers and the labels on all the folders, blotting out forever even the imagining of the scene of first coffee-drinking and first speech.

In a last intuition, before the animal blackness closed in utterly, Gummitch realized that the spirit, alas, is not the same thing as the consciousness and that one may lose—sacrifice—the first and still be burdened with the second.

Old Horsemeat had seen the hatpin (and hid it quickly from Kitty-Come-Here) and so he knew that the situation was not what it seemed and that Gummitch was at the very least being made into a sort of scapegoat. He was quite apologetic when he brought the tin pans of food to the basement during the period of the little cat's exile. It was a comfort to Gummitch, albeit a small one, Gummitch told himself, in his new black halting manner of thinking, that after all a cat's best friend is his man.

From that night Sissy never turned back in her development. Within two months she had made three years' progress in speaking. She became an outstandingly bright, light-footed, high-spirited little girl. Although she never told anyone this, the moonlit nursery and Gummitch's magnified face were her first memories. Everything before that was inky blackness. She was always very nice to Gummitch in a careful sort of way. She could never stand to play the game "Owl Eyes."

After a few weeks Kitty-Come-Here forgot her fears and Gummitch once again had the run of the house. But by then the transformation Old Horsemeat had always warned about had fully taken place. Gummitch was a kitten no longer but an almost burly tom. In him it took the psychological form not of sullenness or surliness but an extreme dignity. He seemed at times rather like an old pirate brooding on treasures he would never live to dig up, shores of adventure he would never reach. And sometimes when you looked into his yellow eyes you felt that he had in him all the materials for the book *Slit Eyes Look at Life*—three or four volumes at least—although he would never write it. And that was natural when you come to think of it, for as Gummitch knew very well, bitterly well indeed, his fate was to be the only kitten in the world that did not grow up to be a man.

The Tail

M.J. Engh

I blame the birds. I enjoy watching birds as a rule—the stimulation is very pleasant—but at times they are intolerable. It was one of those dry winter days that set the fur a-tingle, and the birds were maddening. They were hopping about on the bare branches just outside the window, bobbing their little heads and flirting their little tails at me, and all the while cheeping insultingly. I felt the fur rising along my spine, my tail twitching, and when one of the little beasts actually made a pass at the window, banking off at the last moment with that titillating motion of theirs, I sprang from the sill in a fury and raced up and down the apartment until I felt calmer. Sitting down again, I lashed my tail once or twice to get rid of the last tingles of rage.

Then, with a sudden spasm, it lashed itself.

I do not think you can understand. Perhaps if your right hand suddenly struck you in the face you would feel something of what I felt. But a hand cannot compare with a tail. At all times, a tail has its own character. It is not a *part*, like a hand or paw; it is a whole.

Now it lay curled on the floor beside me, and I stared at it. Could my own tail have (to put it so) seceded from me? Perhaps, after all, what had seemed like independent action had been only a violent twitch; certainly the birds had never been so infuriating. Tentatively, gently, I switched it.

Like a mouse in panic it leaped away, flinging itself out at full length. And, panicked too, I raced crazily through the rooms, as if I could escape by flight the second half of my backbone. I took refuge at last under the table where my humans sat at one of their interminable meals. There I lay flat, and beside me the tail lay twitching. It looked just as it always had—or did it? How often I had cleaned and sported with it, my familiar tabby tail; how often snuggled it neatly around my paws, and yet never (I saw now) truly observed it. Its tip was black. I knew that, of course, but exactly how many black rings should it have? I looked along the length of it, turning slowly to see if it was indeed attached to me. Attached, yes, but no longer mine; or mine, let us say, but not me. Faceless and footless it lay, like a blind furred serpent, and nervously twitched. And I realized that I had no sensation in that tail.

With caution, if not with prudence, I laid a paw upon it. At the first touch it grew perfectly still; then violently, it tried to jerk away. Instinctively I clutched it.

It was stronger than I had known. It plunged; it twisted; in frantic struggle we rolled and tumbled, knocking against the feet of the humans, and so burst out into the open again. It had escaped my grasp. We lay prone and watchful, as before.

I became aware that they were laughing at me. One does not expect much understanding from humans, but one all too easily grows fond of them. Hurt, mortified, I collected myself as best I could and stalked away to fight my strange battle in privacy. Behind me, the thing hung and followed stiffly. I shuddered as I walked.

In the hall, with the laughter of the humans still pursuing me, it struck. I felt an actual yank at the base of my spine, as if some rude child had tugged my tail sideways, and then another. It was lashing violently from side to side, thumping hard against my flanks. Like a spanked kitten, I scampered down the hall and bounded into the next room.

But I had had enough humiliation. I turned, at bay, and slashed at it. It was quick—as quick as I—and hard to hold. Round and round we plunged, one way and then another, in mutual flight and attack, a hideous parody of kittenhood tail-chases. And now, with fury it flung itself at me, whipping and pounding about my legs. With a lucky snatch I pinned it down and buried my teeth in its thick fur. But it tore convulsively away, lashed to the other side, fell lightly back, and lay twitching at full length.

Cautiously, I looked over my shoulder at it. A prickling shiver rose along my spine, and I began to feel my tail again. I turned slowly and patted it with my paw, and in paw and tail alike, I felt the touch. With some trepidation I flexed it. My tail—yes, it was mine, my own. Very thoughtfully I began to wash it.

And now I wait. And if sometimes I bite at it with a kind of tentative anger, if more often I lick it with a reluctant gentleness, if long I sit gazing or lie brooding upon it, I have my reasons, yes. You do not understand.

kitten, I scampered down the hall and bounced into the next room.

But I had had enough humiliation; I turned, at last, and slashed at it. It was quick—as quick as I—and hard to hold. Round and round we plunged, one way and then another, in mutual flight and attack, a hideous parody of kittenhood tail-chases. And now with fury it flung itself at me, whipping and pounding about my legs. With a lucky swoop I pinned it down and buried my teeth in its thick fur. But it tore completely away, lashed to the other side, fell lightly back, and lay twitching its full length.

Cautiously I looked over my shoulder at it. A prickling shiver rose along my spine, and I began to feel my tail again. I turned slowly and patted it with my paw, and in paw and tail alike I felt the touch. With some trepidation I licked it. My tail—yes, it was mine, my own. Very thoroughly I began to wash it.

And now I wear it. And if sometimes I [illegible] at it with a kind of tentative anger, if more often I lick it with a reluctant gentleness, if long I sit [illegible] at the [illegible] upon it I have my reasons, yes. You do not understand.

Well Worth the Money

Jody Lynn Nye

"We need volunteers," the video memo blaring in the I.A.T.A. employee cafeteria stated, "to crew an exciting but potentially hazardous and rewarding expedition featuring the latest in Drebian/Terran technology. If you are interested in being one of the few, the brave, call extension 6508."

That brief message had begun a dizzying odyssey for Balin Jurgenevski. He had been with the Intergalactic Assay and Trade Association on Fladium station for a mere five years, four months. His dream of becoming a trade ship captain had been heretofore laughed at, let alone unfulfilled. Men and women with four times his seniority were still without commands of their own. Everyone wanted to be a captain, sailing the stars in the command chair of a powerful vessel, or even one that had the training wheels off. Still, "potentially hazardous" didn't sound nearly as interesting as "rewarding." It wouldn't hurt to find out if their idea of rewarding matched his. He applied for the job.

As the personnel director explained it to him and the two other people who "made the cut" (Jurgenevski's suspicion was that they were the only ones who applied),

Humanity's newest ally and trading partner, the strange, bloblike Drebs, were seeking to pay their debt for goods and services tendered to them by the Terran government by offering it their space travel technology, which lay far beyond the Terrans' current reach. Naturally, every single company which had ever launched a charge into space was interested. The government threw open the rights at auction.

I.A.T.A. had been the winner of the sealed bid seeking to gain and manufacture the Drebian starship electronics. The Drebs duly signed, or rather smeared, their symbols on contracts, and the deal was done. All this had been beamed all over the news for months. At last, the first machinery off the line was finished and ready for testing. Jurgenevski's first command would be the double shakedown cruise of a newly refitted vessel, the *Pandora*.

Because the knowledge was irreplaceable and the ship wasn't, I.A.T.A. wanted three volunteers, chosen only from its rank of junior officers, for a quick mission to Argylenia, a textile supplicr orbiting a blue-white star in Leo Sector.

The flight to Argylenia was intended at first only to test the new superfast space drive, but I.A.T.A.'s board of directors had, at the last minute, decided to add the Drebs' interactive computer electronics system to the *Pandora*. This had not been leaked to the press, or as far as Jurgenevski could remember, throughout the rest of I.A.T.A.

So if it was potentially a one-way trip, why take it? Jurgenevski had to admit he knew the answers: the money and the prestige. There was trip pay to be earned, recording fees, specialist fees, and the big one: hazard pay. It was tough for anyone with less than ten years experience to pull down that much credit or accrue the instant seniority that they'd earn for bringing the *Pandora* back successfully. It might, it was hinted, get him at least exec officer status—if not a full command—if he, the crew, and the *Pandora* made it back in their several pieces.

"We have an emergency order for a shipment of

stauralinium 106 that has to get out to Argylenia as soon as possible to prevent the planetary computer system from melting down," the vice president of the company told him. "With a half-life of only 110 days, the sooner you get it out there, the better. With her new drives, the *Pandora* is the fastest ship we have, not to mention the only one ready to depart for a week. You're still going to the same destination. It's just more urgent that you get there quickly, even with an experimental ship. I'm prepared to offer you a bonus of 10% per day for every day you can knock off the transit time."

"I'm willing to try, sir," Jurgenevski promised.

Getting to know the ship with her reconstructed innards was a piece of cake. The controls were standard, and as for the new computer system, the Drebs made that effortless. The sky-blue-and-pink blob scientists guided them one by one into the fold-out booth that attached to the left side of the control unit.

"It reads your personality and intellect," the chief Dreb burbled through his translator, "thereby saving time between command and execution. This is particularly of use during a crisis."

As the newly promoted commander, Jurgenevski went first. At twenty-six, he was the youngest of the three crew members. The whole process consisted of a lot of lights flashing into his eyes, and probes poking into his ears and against his scalp, but beyond slightly disorienting him, it didn't feel like much. He shrugged to the other two as he came out. With a wary expression on her face, Diani Marius followed. She was the ship's helm and navigation officer. Okabe Thomas went last. Thomas, the old man of the crew at thirty-four, was known as a trade specialist and diplomat, aside from his talents as an engineer. None of them had been with the company more than seven years, and none had immediate family. I.A.T.A. was taking no chances with survivor benefits or suits for wrongful death.

All three of them acted with great solemnity during the departure ceremony, in which the Drebs and the Humans praised the spirit of cooperation and one another. Carrying the ship's cat, I.A.T.A's traditional mascot of good luck that went on every vessel it sent out, they filed on board with the floodlights of the media recorders following them into the *Pandora*'s hatch. They all waved goodbye to the press and their employers. Jurgenevski felt his heart sink. Fladium Base wasn't much, but it had been his home for years. He might never see it again. He felt a little uncomfortable being alone with the *Pandora*'s reconstructed innards for the first time.

Not everyone shared his anxiety. As soon as the white enameled doors sealed behind them, Okabe Thomas let out a whoop and slapped his hands together.

"Oh, friends, is this going to be a blast!" he cried, grabbing his shipmates in a three-and-a-half-way hug. Kelvin, a black-and-white female, mixed breed cat, protested and demanded to be put down.

Marius rescued Kelvin from the crush and put her on the deck. "What are you so thrilled about, Thomas? This thing could blow up on us. We could all die!"

"Not a chance, Helm. Ship?" Thomas said, addressing the air. "Or can I call you Pandora?"

"Working." The computer's pleasant, though burbly, voice responded.

"Crank this sucker up and let's get out of here."

"Destination?"

Marius dashed for her console and ran up the coordinates for Argylenia. "Twenty-seven degrees, fifty minutes, right ascendancy minus 15," she read off.

"Understood. On the command?"

Marius looked at Jurgenevski. "Given," he said, with some surprise.

Lights on the console shifted from red to green, and gradually up to white. The ship moved under their feet, but so gently that the crewmembers had no trouble getting to their assigned crash couches before the *Pandora* attained acceleration. Jurgenevski grabbed the cat and stuffed her into her crashbox under the console before he sat down. The huge screen, which took up the entire front of the pilo's compartment, warmed up to show the field of stars and those surrounding Fladium's sun.

"Destination will be reached within thirty-seven days," the *Pandora's* voice assured them, as they strapped in.

Jurgenevski grinned broadly at his crew and settled in with his hands tucked behind his head. "I think I'm going to like this ship. She's worth every credit they paid for her. *Twenty-five* days early. That means a 250% bonus on top of all our other pay."

"That's impossible," Marius protested. "It should take at least sixty-two, even at maxium acceleration."

Thomas winked. "She read our greedy little minds and knew we wanted to go fast. Pandora, honey, give the doubting member of our crew the details of the journey."

Unerringly, the red sensor lights of the Drebian personality monitor went on in front of Marius. Her personal screen filled with mathematical formulae and star maps, reflections of which shone on her face, her expression slowly gaining in enlightenment. "Hot damn, I didn't think a ship this size could do that." She looked up at the others. "Do you mean that's all I have to do? I love it!"

"Whee-hah!" Jurgenevski cheered. "I might be able to buy my own ship when we get home."

The galaxy on the big screen streaked into a shock of white, then all light vanished as the ship bounced into her first jump. When there was nothing more to look at, Jurgenevski cleared his throat.

"Um, well," he began. "Since we've got five weeks, I want us all to bone up on the features of this ship. We've got reports to send back at regular intervals, and I don't want them to catch us out on a single detail." He tapped the insignia on the shoulder of his dark blue coverall hopefully. "I want real ones of these when I get home."

"If we get home," Marius said, suddenly looking gloomy.

"What are you talking about?" Thomas asked, with his customary cheerful mien. "The *Pandora* will take good care of us. Won't you, sweetheart?" he said to the air.

"Working," the computer voice said. "Affirmative. Honeycakes."

Jurgenevski pointed toward one of the speakers. "Did you tell her to call you that?" he asked Thomas.

"Naw, but she's picking up on the things I usually say." Thomas thought about it a moment. "I don't think I've said 'honeycakes' yet, though. Not in the computer's presence. I guess the Drebs told the truth when they said that the box reads your mind."

"This is still an experimental vessel," Marius pointed out, resuming the previous argument.

"That's why I want us to know everything there is to know about the *Pandora*," Jurgenevski assented. "Engine capability, clearance under bridges, armaments . . ."

"Yes, why are we armed?" Thomas said. "We're only going to Argylenia. That's right through well-established, well-patrolled throughways."

"Not this time," Marius said, showing him her terminal. "*Pandora*'s redirected us. We go right through a corner of Smoot territory. Computer, put it on the big screen."

The diagrams appeared, greatly enlarged, with the ship's flight path indicated by a line of dashes in red. The Smoot were another bloblike race that Humanity had discovered, but had entirely failed to befriend. The Smoot seemed to be offended by the presence in the universe of a race of vertebrates, which they saw as an offense against their Creator, to be exterminated whenever possible. Thomas's smoky complexion drained to ash, and he swallowed.

"Can't we go around them?" the engineer asked.

"Two hundred-and-fifty percent bonus," Jurgenevski said, temptingly.

Thomas sighed heavily. "Maybe we won't meet any of them."

"Working," *Pandora* said. Thomas's own screen lit up suddenly with another array of formulae, this time referring to the schematics of two powerful, sidemounted laser cannon, and a nose-mounted plasma torpedo launcher. The screen blanked, only to fill again with a list of evasive maneuvers of which the *Pandora* was capable of executing, with diagrams, followed by a flashing cursor, and the legend, in block print, "YOUR CHOICE?"

"Whew!" Thomas whistled and patted the console. "You sure know how to make a fellow feel welcome, honey."

A querulous complaint erupted from underneath the control panel.

"You want to let the cat out, Thomas?" Marius asked.

So far as Jurgenevski could tell after only a week, the Drebs had done their work with the usual, expected degree of genius. The mind-reading capabilities of the computer were not only complete, but subtle. Every morning when he opened his eyes, a screen went on above his bunk, and beside his elbow, a door slid up to reveal a steaming cup of coffee. On the screen, the *Pandora* reported the ship's status, complete with a tiny diagram of how far they had traveled during his dark shift. Nothing was wrong or even remotely awry. Jurgenevski sighed and reached for the cup. The system was flawless. An eight-year-old could run the ship, play a video game, and do his homework all at the same time. Even the coffee was perfect. Never bitter, it always came out at exactly the temperature he liked to drink it, just under boiling, but cool enough that it didn't scorch his tongue. He drained his cup down to the melted sugar on the bottom. *Pandora* seemed to know that he didn't like his sugar mixed in, just dropped straight through, leaving a faint trail of sweetening in the top seven-eighths of the cup. It was absolutely uncanny what tiny details the computer picked up on and exploited. It scared him a little: what if the *Pandora* decided to take things into her own hands and run the show? He'd look an incredible fool back at I.A.T.A. headquarters.

A duty list popped up on the screen almost before the thought had finished forming. *Pandora* was asking permission to run scheduled system tests, send off personal mail, transmit the daily report to HQ, or do personal system maintenance. At the bottom was the flashing "YOUR CHOICE?"

Jurgenevski grinned as he set down the cup. "Thanks, honey. It's nice of you to let me think I'm in charge."

He met Marius and Thomas for breakfast in the small galley. He was deciding whether a hot, scrambled egg sandwich or blueberry pancakes would fill the gap in his belly and opted to let *Pandora* surprise him.

"Hi, gang," he said, sliding into the third chair. The hatch before him whisked open and a plate rose upward. Mmm, he thought, reaching for it. A baked pancake with blueberry filling—now that was a creative way to split the difference. He sent a mental thank you to the ship's computer. He was two or three forkfuls into the steaming cake when he noticed his two crewmembers weren't talking. They were staring into their cups of coffee with thoughtful expressions. "What's the matter?"

"Jurgy," Marius began, still staring at the cup between her fingers as if it troubled her. "Don't you feel kind of . . . useless?"

"No," he replied, surprised. He set down the fork. Were these the beginnings of mutiny? What had he done wrong? "I've hardly ever enjoyed a trip more in my life."

"Seriously, Jurgy, there's nothing for us to do."

"That's about it," Thomas said with a sigh. "Ship's too new to have loose bolts, and the blobs already dusted, oiled, and cleaned her up before we took her out. We're just watching her run. I thought it'd be fun, too, but even I'm getting bored."

"Yeah," Marius agreed. "All we do is send out reports and feed Kelvin."

Hearing her name, the cat walked over and rubbed her face against Marius's knee. The navigator reached down and scratched the top of the cat's head.

Jurgenevski nodded. "All right, we'll come up with something. Meantime, we've survived one whole week in the ship they all thought would blow up in drydock. What say we have us a party tonight to celebrate?"

Marius and Thomas perked up. "Now there's a fine concept," Thomas agreed.

The party started at the stroke of third shift. The three humans and the cat assembled in the control room for a round of special meals and entertainments. With all of her talents, the *Pandora*'s Drebian computer had one more heretofore undiscovered skill: she had in her memory banks every bartender's manual ever written.

"Honeycakes, make me up a . . . Viking's Elbow," Thomas commanded from his launch chair. He had staggered there for greater stability when, as he claimed, the deck started to spin.

"Are you still working your way through the alphabet?" Jurgenevski asked. He was bent raptly over a hand control for the video game *Pandora* had running on the screen. It was a commercial game that Jurgenevski had spent years learning to win. Tiny spaceships swirled in an attack pattern around a single red ship that dodged and evaded while it shot them down one by one. His running score was in the corner of the three-meter-high image. It was already in the millions, and Jurgenevski was still hot.

"No, man, I'm going through it again, only backwards this time," Thomas explained. The hatch next to his elbow disgorged a stylized noggin with a dragon-headed stirring rod in it. Thomas discarded the stick and took a deep drink from the mug.

"Have you tasted this banana mousse?" Marius asked, waving her spoon at the two men. "It's fabulous!"

Kelvin jumped up in her lap and demanded a taste. Marius gave her a fingerful.

"You know, it's too bad *Pandora* didn't whip up anything special for the cat," Thomas said, ordering up an Undertaker's Friend. "Hey, baby, make a treat for the cat, huh?"

"Working. Please clarify the command."

"The cat," Thomas repeated. "Give her a plate of tuna sushi, or whatever cats think is party food."

"Working. There is no record for 'Thecat' in these memory circuits."

"Kelvin's our ship's cat. She's right here." Thomas pointed to Kelvin, who was busily lapping up banana cream.

There was some puzzled whirring. The three crewmembers looked at one another, and Jurgenevski put down the game control and his glass of beer. He rose to his feet somewhat unsteadily. "It's not fair we should get everything we want when our little friend gets nothing but Fishy Nibbles," he pronounced. "Let's put her in the personality reader, and Pandora can figure out what she wants."

"Great idea," Marius applauded. Kelvin let out an offended yowl at being forced to leave a comfortable lap when Marius picked her up and carried her over to the expandable booth. Jurgenevski and Thomas pulled out the folding sides and set the corner braces. The helm officer set the cat inside and snapped the curtain shut before Kelvin, now confused and frightened, could escape.

"Working," *Pandora* said. The cat's ululations rose to angry growls, and then stopped abruptly. Through the transparent panel, they could see Kelvin sitting on the booth's bench with her pupils down to tiny slits and her ears, with the probes sticking out of them, laid flat along her skull. As soon as the lights ceased flashing and the probes retracted, Marius snatched the cat out of the booth and stroked her until the fighting ridge went down on the cat's back.

"There, there, kitty, sssshhaa," she said soothingly. The cat's fur smoothed out, and she emitted an interrogative trill. Marius hugged her. "What do you want? Some more mousse? That sounds a little like mouse."

For answer, a plate slid out of one of the service hatches at floor level, and Kelvin kicked out of Marius's arms to get to it.

"Tuna sushi," Jurgenevski nodded approvingly and went back to his game.

"Bartender," Thomas said, snapping his fingers above his head. "Make me a Tomato Surprise."

Thomas tried to grind the strata of sand out of his eyes long enough to find his morning cup of coffee. He didn't dare sit up lest his brain fall out of his ears before he could nail it in place with a bolt or two of caffeine. "I hope this is strong, baby," he pleaded the computer. "I was naughty last night."

It was strong enough to drag Thomas to his feet and halfway to the bathroom before he knew he'd moved. As he washed up, he realized he was starving. Probably not much of what he'd consumed the night before had significant food value.

"Aw, damn!" he smote himself on the forehead.

Pulling on a coverall, he hurried out into the galley, where Marius was sitting, sipping a cup of black coffee. She glanced up as he dashed in. He glanced past her at Kelvin, who was crouched close to the wall, munching from a bowl.

"Thanks for feeding the cat," he said. "I overslept."

"Didn't do it," Marius said, talking as if forming the words hurt her head. "Maybe Jurgy did."

Jurgenevski's eyes were red and half-closed as he slid into his chair and received a gigantic beaker of orange juice from the serving hatch. "Not me."

"Then, who?" They all looked at each other. "Did we do what I think I remember us doing last night?" Thomas asked, very carefully. The other two nodded slowly, the full reality of their actions returning to them through the mental haze.

As one, they turned to look at the cat, who had finished her meal and was washing her ear with a diligent paw.

From that day on, the human crew members watched as doors opened for the cat before she reached them. Kelvin never had to nag any of them for food, and sometimes got portions of the gourmet goodies that were supposed to be held aside for the individual humans who brought them aboard.

"Pandora," Jurgenevski complained, "that spicewurst was special! It took me years to get it."

"It was necessary to the well-being of Crewmember Kelvin," *Pandora* said without a trace of reproach or regret. The commander groaned.

"She got some of my Cornish butter, too," Marius reminded him.

"And the smoked turkey I got from my sister," said Thomas.

"That does it. Override the cat's program, will you, Pandora?" Jurgenevski asked. "Kelvin's not supposed to have things like that. It's probably bad for her."

"Working. Request formulae to judge difference between needs of one Terran crewmember and another."

"Darn those Drebs," Jurgenevski muttered. "We all look alike to them. How about job orientation? I'm a captain, this is the navigator, and this is the engineer. The cat's only a pet."

"There is no qualification on this ship's complement for a 'pet.' Identify this crewmember's position," *Pandora* instructed them.

Jurgenevski shrugged and looked at the others for inspiration. "She's the ship's cat."

"There is no entry in ship rosters for 'ship's cat.' "

Thomas's face lit up. "I guess you could call her Maintenance," he suggested. "She's supposed to handle pest control, even though this thing has never seen a mouse."

The commander could almost hear the mental clicking and whirring as the *Pandora* digested the information. "Working. As a Maintenance worker, Crewmember Kelvin is entitled to statutory three hundred-sixty credits per week, retroactive to the beginning of this flight, plus additions for trip pay, hazard pay . . ."

Jurgenevski smacked himself in the head and automatically regretted it. "Friends, I think we've just created a monster, but I'm afraid to try and change it again."

"Me, either," Thomas agreed. "One more slipup, and that cat'll end up an admiral."

"We'll have to straighten this out when we get back," Marius put in. "Anything else we do is going to make matters worse."

"I'm not looking forward to getting back to Fladium and explaining to them why the *cat* is drawing a salary." The brevet commander downed the last of his orange juice and put the empty glass on the serving hatch. It descended out of sight. "Goodbye, field promotion."

"Goodbye, instant seniority," Marius agreed.

"Farewell, smoked turkey," Thomas reminded them. "Still, I can live with it, if you two can."

A few days later, Jurgenevski awoke with a snort in the middle of the night and tried to cry out, but there was something over his mouth. He reached for the light. Marius was sitting on the edge of his bed with her hand plastered over his face to keep him from yelling. He nodded and she let him go.

"I heard some strange noises in the control room," she whispered.

"Something wrong?" he asked, sitting up.

"No. Come and see."

Curious, he followed her down the narrow, enameled corridor. She paused at the threshold of the main chamber, and gestured to him to look past her.

On the main computer screen, tiny, colorful objects shaped like mice scurried back and forth or lowered into view like spiders. As soon as one exited, more would appear. The cat, purring as loudly as a drive engine, was bounding all over the room, throwing herself at the screen, pounding the images with her paws. In the corner, the red numbers were mounting. *Pandora* must have been keeping score for her own amusement. The cat, focused on her myriad prey, was having a great time. She never acknowledged the humans in the hallway behind her.

Jurgenevski glanced at Marius, who was struggling to contain her laughter. "Why doesn't the computer do this kind of stuff for us?" he whispered. "It's terrific! Look at that, a custom video game!"

"Cats have more needs and they're not particularly ashamed to admit to them," Marius whispered. "I'm only happy that she's been fixed. Can you imagine having the ship decide we have to forego our urgent cargo stop to find a male cat in some other system? Going planet to planet in search of a tom?"

"The company isn't going to like that."

"Look, this is a shakedown cruise," Marius pointed out. "Like you said, when we get home, we can get the alien programmers to delete the cat's personality from the program. Right? How bad could it be for a couple more months?"

On the twentieth day, they entered Smoot-claimed space. Thomas was nervous throughout the first two jumps as the *Pandora* cut through a couple of barren systems to use the suns as bounce points. Neither were occupied, nor carrying so much as a system beacon. The crew were all keeping their fingers crossed against danger, but all went well.

In the third system, right in the heart of Smoot space, they had hardly exited the jump when the ship began to vibrate around them. Jurgenevski grabbed for his command chair.

"What's happening?" he shouted over the rattle of metal.

Thomas dashed across and leaned over his chair arm to his personal screen. "Smoot! We're in deep guano now."

"Is it a tractor beam?" Marius demanded, her inverted triangle of a face pale with fear.

"I don't know," Thomas started to say.

"Is it a weapon?" Jurgenevski asked. Then he realized his words had made no sense. Only a gutteral groan escaped his throat. He tried to speak again, but nothing at all came out. He was pondering the strangeness, when his knees and spine folded up, depositing him heavily onto the floor.

"What's happening to me?" he tried to scream. His body, out of his control, slumped against the side of the command chair. Thomas, his eyes wide with fear, collapsed over the arm of his chair like a curtain on a hanger. Jurgenevski was completely aware of everything that was happening to him, including how much his leg, which struck the side of the couch, was hurting. He suspected the shin was broken from striking the metal pedestal. He screamed at his muscles to move him, to obey his commands. The only voluntary muscles which responded were in his eye sockets. Out of the corner of his left eye, he saw Marius, slumped against the wall with her hands splayed out to either side of her, like a discarded rag doll. The vibration stopped. The *Pandora's* main viewscreen lit up to show a red-and-white painted vessel, long and sinuously flexible like a snake. It was a Smoot destroyer. Jurgenevski was terrified. Some insidious weapon in the Smoot arsenal prevented his brain's higher functions from interacting with the lower brain. He could *think* all he wanted, but he couldn't *do* a damned thing.

In a few moments, the Smoot would move in on them, take them aboard, and finish them off. There were legends told of the tortures the invertebrate monsters inflicted on Terran spacers, yanking the bones out of prisoners one at a time until they died in agony. He could see by the sweat breaking out on their faces that the others were thinking of those stories, too. All they could do was wait and hope it would be over quickly.

From behind him, out of his range of vision, came a tremendous hiss, modulating into a fearsome growl. Poor Kelvin, Jurgenevski thought. She's only a cat, and she's going to die, too.

Kelvin advanced into his peripheral vision. She was walking sideways, with her fur stuck up all along her spine in a fighting ridge, terminating in a tail fluffed like a bottle brush. He was struck by the heartbreaking futility of the tiny creature in her attempt to make herself look as large as possible so as to scare off a foe a thousand times her size.

"Eeeerrrrooooooooonnnngggghhhh," the cat growled, her voice advancing angrily up and down the scales. Her eyes fixed on the red, snakelike shape hanging in the center of the screen, and her enlarged tail switched back and forth.

A lot of good that would do, Jurgenevski thought, closing his eyes and letting them roll back in his head. He felt as if he could cry. In a minute, the Smoot would start blasting at the ship's system pods with lasers until nothing but life support remained. And then, the Smoot would have their fun with him. He willed his flaccid muscles to respond, to do anything at all. Drool ran out of a corner of his mouth onto his lap, and he realized his jaw was hanging open. What an undignified way to die.

The Smoot opened fire. Out of a turret on the top of the snake's head came a dot of fire, growing and growing in his field of vision until it smashed into the side of the *Pandora*. Thomas was thrown off his crash couch onto the floor and Jurgenevski's head bounced painfully against the frame of his chair.

Kelvin slid backwards along the floor. Her growl rose several decibels and she advanced on the screen with redoubled fury.

"Working," the computer's voice said suddenly. "Defense systems armed and ready." At the top of his range of vision, Jurgenevski's personal screen spread with the menu of defense diagrams and the blinking words, "YOUR CHOICE?"

Jurgenevski stared at the selections and tried to will the ship to maneuver and fire, but the safeties put in to prevent an accidental discharge of the weapons couldn't be overridden mentally. He wanted to scream, "We're incapacitated, you dumb computer! Do something yourself!"

Nothing happened. Nothing good. The Smoot ship moved closer.

Kelvin hunkered down before the screen, the very tip of her black and white tail twitching rapidly back and forth as she gathered herself to spring. To Jurgenevski, it was the very height of burlesque. They were about to die and the cat was chasing images on the computer as if it was a video game.

The Smoot snake shot out of its stationary pose and swung in a wide arc, choosing the next target with care. It had all the time in the universe on its side.

The movement set off the cat's springs like pulling a trigger. She bounded up at the screen and batted one-two punches at the head of the snake with either paw.

"Working," *Pandora* said.

The cat dropped to the floor and gathered on her haunches again. Astoundingly, where the cat had struck, two laser bolts lanced out of the *Pandora*'s own battery and smacked into the side of the Smoot ship, knocking it first one way, then the other. The view changed, dropping down below the ecliptic plane of the Smoot destroyer. Jurgenevski was dumbfounded. It had to be a fluke.

The Smoot shifted just as rapidly, diving toward the viewscreen. Those blobs must have been furious, thinking that their prey was already helpless and finding there was someone aboard who was still capable of fighting. They'd have gone crazy if they could see their opponent. Jurgenevski wished he could grin.

Kelvin was ready for it as soon as it turned, delivering a fierce roundhouse, and galloping backwards and to the right as soon as the blow struck, avoiding the burning light which made her pupils shrink to slits. *Pandora* followed her moves, pounding the Smoot's engine compartment with a full-strength bolt, then veering sideways. Good tactical maneuvering, Jurgenevski mentally complimented the cat.

He counted six laser emplacements on the snake's back. The *Pandora* was badly outgunned. Still, they had maneuverability on their side. If they could inflict enough small wounds, it might take all the fight out of the Smoot, allowing them a chance to get away.

Jurgenevski was overwhelmed with a wave of embarrassment. They weren't fighting this battle. Their lives depended on a five-kilo feline who liked to sharpen her claws on his pantleg. Still, it was a chance.

"Win this for us, kitty, and you can have every last scrap of my Sinosian spicewurst," Jurgenevski vowed, "and wash it down with Thomas's smoked turkey. I'll make it up to him."

To a slightly blurring eye, the Smoot ship did resemble a living creature. As it rounded on them, moving into position for its next shot, Jurgenevski could almost see it narrowing its eyes and twitching its pointed tail.

There *was* some movement in the rear section. It

attracted Kelvin, who pounced at it, smacking the tail with one paw and bounding immediately back to one-two the head as it turned toward them. Automatically, the *Pandora*'s battery fired three shots.

The Smoot fired back, but Kelvin dodged easily out of the way of the hot, yellow light of the fireball. Her next move surprised him. She jumped up on top of the console, trying to get above the Smoot. *Pandora* shifted upward along the z-axis and slid through space until the top of the snake was in view at the very bottom of the screen. Kelvin dove off the console onto the snake's back, pummeling and biting her intangible foe. The head and tail angled upward, guns firing at them, but Jurgenevski could see that the Smoot was suffering some internal distress. The first fireball knocked into the *Pandora*'s side, but the second missed by a million klicks. It was never followed by a third. Kelvin's attack must have hit squarely over the power plant. The snake blew into two pieces, each of which exploded silently, but magnificently, in the black, star-strewn sky.

Kelvin turned away from the screen, head and tail high, and walked majestically over to Thomas's crash couch. She bounded upward, settled herself with one leg over her head, and began to wash. The service hatch in the console opened up to disgorge a saucerful of rank-smelling fish. Jurgenevski couldn't possibly begrudge it to her.

It was hours before the paralysis of the Smoot ray wore off. As soon as their tongues and palates could move again, the three humans burst out talking about the unbelievable feat they had just witnessed. Damages to the ship were negligible, and Jurgenevski's leg proved to be bruised, not broken. The whole situation was the aftermath of a miracle. For the rest of the journey, every time the cat walked into a room, they petted and praised her. On Argylenia, the three of them took her into every gourmet shop in the main city, buying her a kilo of whatever seemed to interest her.

"This cat's a hero," Thomas explained to the dumbfounded shopkeepers, who were taken aback at selling their most prized delicacies to a ship's pet. "If I told you why, you'd never believe me. Just let her have what she wants."

The I.A.T.A. brass were waiting for the *Pandora* when she docked at Fladium Station with her hold full of textiles. Jurgenevski felt as if he could drop to the metal walkway and kiss it. Beyond the decontamination barrier, he could see dozens of reporters waiting. He exchanged glances with the other two crewmembers. Kelvin, curled up in Marius's arms, never bothered to look up.

"What are you going to say?" Thomas asked, nodding sideways at the cat.

"I don't know yet," he admitted.

"The brave crew returns!" The vice president who had seen them off came out of the V.I.P. waiting room with his arms outstretched. "Congratulations, one and all."

There was a clamor from the press, but the vice president whisked the crew into the lounge and locked the door. Following his gesture, the three sat down. Marius put the cat on the table between them.

"Well done," the executive said, nodding to them all. "We want to let the press in to talk to you in a little while, but not until we've cleared your story. For example, there are a few facets of your reports which we are finding hard to believe. And there's the matter of an item or two of expenditure which is even more difficult to justify. Are we to understand that we're paying a regular salary to a *cat*? Tell me why."

"She saved our lives," Jurgenevski explained, meeting the vice president's disbelieving scrutiny with a bland expression. "Everything in the reports I sent you is true. Review the ship's log if you want, but if you ask me, you won't question it."

"Kelvin here was a functioning member of the crew, and I think she deserves every minim," Marius added.

"Yes, but paying three hundred-sixty credits weekly to a *cat*? Plus hazard pay?" The vice president shook his head. Kelvin watched him without blinking, but her tail tip twitched.

"Look at it this way, sir," Thomas put in smoothly, and Jurgenevski remembered that he had had diplomatic training. Thomas leaned forward confidingly. "Notwithstanding the fact that Kelvin blew up a Smoot warship all by herself, could you ask for better publicity for the utility and easy operation of the Drebian system, if a mere cat can use it? Think of the numbers! The press'll love it!"

"As a matter of advertisement," the vice president mused, scrubbing his chin with the tips of his fingers, "I suppose it would be just about priceless."

"And what a spokesperson you could offer them, too," Jurgenevski said. Kelvin rolled over and presented her belly to the vice president to be scratched.

The man laughed and reached out to fluff the cat's fur. "I suppose we're getting off lightly. For a human model, I'd have to pay thousands. But what about the three of you? If we publicize that the cat ran the ship, won't you feel foolish?"

Jurgenevski gathered nods of approbation from the other two and drew a deep breath. "Not if it'll help the company, sir."

The vice president mused, staring at a wall as Kelvin squirmed happily under his fingertips. "Captain," he said at last, rising to his feet and gathering up the cat, "I like your loyalty. Come out with me to see the media. I'm sure you'd like to tell them the adventures the four of you had on your ship." The emphasis fell heavily on the last two words, and Jurgenevski caught his breath. Marius and Thomas looked hopeful. The vice president didn't miss their expressions.

"I presume you're happy with your crew complement as well?" he asked casually.

"Yes, *sir*," Jurgenevski said, with unconcealed joy. He gave the cat a quick and grateful scratch on the head. "I ordered another spicewurst for you this morning," he told Kelvin in a low murmur just before the door opened.

"What's that, captain?"

"Oh, nothing, sir. Nothing." Grasping Marius's and Thomas's hands in a triumphant squeeze, he followed the I.A.T.A. executive out of the lounge to the waiting press.

ALIEN CATS

Chanur's Homecoming
C.J. Cherryh

She was wobbling when she reached belowdecks, staggering with the weight of the gun; she ran face-on into the others as she came off the lift and into the corridor—regular crew, with Tully and Khym. "I sent orders," she said to them both. "*No*. Stay here."

"It's changed out there," Khym said, "Py, for godssakes—"

Panic set in, facing that obdurate desperation, that look in his eyes, which met hers and asked, O gods, with a desperate pleading for his own place. If she never got him back alive . . . if she lost him out here; if, if, and if. She saw all the crew in the same mind, all thin-furred and haunted-looking, ghosts of themselves, but with weapons in hand and ears pricked up and eyes alive though flesh was fading.

"We've got to hit fast," she said, and saw Chur come round the corner from crew quarters, leaning against the wall for support, Chur with a rifle slung at her side. "You—" she said, meaning Chur. "And *you*," meaning Tully, who was provocation to any hani xenophobe and a class one target. "You—"

"Tully and I hold the airlock and cover the rest of you,

right." Chur's voice was a hoarse whisper, befitting a ghost. "Got it, cap'n. Go on."

That was the way Chur worked, conspiracy and wit: Chur cheated at dice. So would Geran. For cause. Pyanfar drew a ragged breath, threw a desperate look at Geran Anify and got no help: silence again, now that Chur was back in business. "Then for godssakes keep Tully with you," she said, and jabbed Tully with a forefinger. "Stay on the ship. Help Chur. Take Chur's orders. Got?"

"Got." With that kind of Tully-look that meant he would argue to go with them if he thought he could. Language-barrier worked on her side this time. "Be careful."

"Gods-be sure. Come on," she said to the others, and shoved off the wall she was using to lean on for a moment, and trotted for the airlock.

Alert began to sound, *The Pride*'s crew call: not their business, though muscles tensed as if that alert were wired to Chanur nervous systems. There was the thunder of steps in the corridors, additional crew running to the lift behind them as they reached the airlock corridor. More footsteps behind. She looked back. Skkukuk appeared, coming from the other direction. "Orders!" she yelled at him, *"Get!"* and he vanished in the next blink of the eye. Then: *"Sirany!"* she yelled at the intercom pickup, her voice all hoarse, "open that lock—" because it was not Haral up there, Haral was beside her; and she had to depend on strangers to get their signals straight.

The airlock hatch opened. She threw the safety off the illegal AP, and inhaled the air as a wind whipped into their faces: *The Pride*'s pressurization was a shade off; and that wind out of Gaohn smelled of things forgotten. Of hani. Or cold and hazard, too, and the chill reek of space-chilled machinery. She jogged through the lock and into the passageway, yellow plastics of the access tube and steel jointed plating, and sucked up a second wide gulp of the air her physiology was born for. Something set into her like the stim: a second wind, a preternatural clarity of things in which the whole tumble of events began to go at an acceptable speed.

"These are hani," she said, drymouthed and panting as they ran along the tube, trusting her crew around her as she trusted her own reflexes, knowing where each would dispose themselves, that Chur was where she had said she would be, that she had Tully under control, that Tirun, hindmost with her lameness, would be watching everything they were too shortfocussed to see up front, that Haral was at her side like another right hand and Hilfy and Geran were with Khym in the middle, Khym being the worst shot in the lot, and not the fastest runner, but able to lay down barrage fire with any of them if it got to that. *Hani*, she reminded them as she came off that ramp and headed aside for cover of the gantry rig and the consoles. Down the row another crew was hitting the docks about as fast: that was Harun. And Sif Tauran arrived: Pyanfar spun around to stare at Sif in some confusion, saw Fiar coming at a dead run down the ramp. "We're offshift," Sif panted. "Captain says get out here and help."

"Come on," she said, seeing Fiar's youth, the grudging frown on Sif—sent along for Tauran's honor, then. Another Battle for Gaohn. Everyone wanted in on it.

Fool, Sirany, this is hani against hani, don't you see it? No glory here—

There were others arriving on the docks and running up the curved flooring toward them. Some of Shaurnurn, a trio each of Faha and Harun, not whole crews, but parts and pieces. That meant that those ships were still crewed, enough hands aboard to get them away if the kif came in; enough to make them a visual threat if nothing more. She had not ordered that. Perhaps Harun or Sifeny Tauran had. It was sane. It was prudent. She still wished she had the extra personnel on dockside, with their firepower. No other crew had the APs or even rifles: it was all legal stuff. Most of them that had run the long course from Meetpoint looked exhausted already; it showed in their faces, in the dullness of coats and the set of the ears. And Harun and the rest had only come from four jumps back.

But others were coming to join them, glossy of coat and in crisp blues; in vivid green; in skycolored silk: crews and captains of other ships from farther down the docks, ships which had run their own Long Course getting in, perhaps, but which were at least clear-eyed and fresh from their time on blockade. Banny Ayhar's contingents. The ships in from mahen space. Pyanfar drew a breath, blinked against dizziness and an insufficiency of blood and in a second hazed glance at that one in skyblue, recognized her own sister. Rhean Chanur, looking much as Rhean had looked two years ago; with a tall figure coming up behind Rhean amongst the girders and hoses and machinery of the dock, a male figure conspicuous amid that large crew of Chanur cousins and nieces. The man had too much gray on him to be her brother, but no, they were indisputably Kohan's features, it was Kohan's look about him, and he wore a gun at his hip, a pistol, which gods knew if he even knew how to use—

His Faha wife was with him, Huran, Hilfy's mother. So were others of his wives: Akify Llun was one, on his side and Chanur's and not with her own kin. "Pyanfar," Kohan said when they came to close range. They stared at one another a moment, before Kohan blinked in shock at what else he saw, the thin, scarred woman his favorite daughter had become, Hilfy Chanur *par* Faha, who came across to him and offered her left hand to touch, because she was carrying a black and illegal AP in the other. Hilfy Chanur touched his hand and her mother Huran Faha's, giving them and her Aunt Rhean and her cousins the nod of courtesy she might give any comrade-under-fire, with a quick word and an instant attention back to other of her surroundings, taking up guard with crewmates who shadowed her: she signed Geran one view toward the open docks and took another herself, all while everything was in motion, crews were taking positions of vantage, so there was no time to say anything, no time at all. Kohan looked stricken, Huran dismayed. Khym coughed, a nervous sound, somewhere behind her.

"We've got to get through to central," Pyanfar said. "Get Banny Ayhar out of there, get the Llun free—"

My gods, they don't know what to do, they're looking at me, at us to do something, as if none of them had fought here before this, as if they didn't know Gaohn station.

There was a time and a rhythm in leading the helpless and the morally confused; a moment to snatch up souls before they fell to wrangling or wondering or asking too keen questions.

"Come on," she yelled at them, at all the lunatic mass of hani spacers that was persistently trying to group round her like the most willing target in all the Compact; and yelled off instructions, corridors, crews, her voice cracking and her legs shaking under her as she started everyone into motion—in the next moment she could not remember what she had sent, where, when, as if her mind had wandered somewhere back into hyperspace and she had the overview of things but not the fine focus. . . .

. . . .battles fought at ports and in countrysides on a little blue pearl of a world where foolish hani thought to prevent a determined universe from encroaching on their business. . . .

. . . .Pyruun bundling Kohan onto a shuttle, smuggling him aloft to Rhean, gods knew how they had managed it or at what risk; but, then, mahendo'sat had once smuggled a human in a grain bin, right through a stsho warehouse. . . .

. . . .Banny Ayhar racing home with a message which proliferated itself across all of mahen space, sweeping up hani as she fled homeward: and alerting mahendo'sat as well, from Maing Tol to the mahen homeworld of Iji, so it could not then be taken by surprise by any kifish attack, try as Sikkukkut would. The incoming and outgoing ranges of solar systems would be mined: the mahendo'sat would have had time for that laborious action, especially up near Iji and Maing Tol, so nothing could have gotten in the back door. They *would* have done that, while hani ships were moving home like birds before the storm.

Mahendo'sat would have pulled every spare ship borderward in defense and offense, set in motion agreements with the tc'a, so that the elaborate timetable of mahen ship movements would have functioned as a spreading communications net, news streaking from jump to jump and spreading wide with every meeting of affected ships. . . .

. . . .even to hunter captains far removed from the inner reaches, captains like Goldtooth, no longer operating on their own discretion, but receiving information and reinforcements. . . .

. . . .Goldtooth had been vexed beyond measure when *Aja Jin* had violated the timetable by showing up at Kefk; *that* had been his anger, that, the reason of his fury at Jik, *that* the reason why Goldtooth had rushed away: his orders had dictated it. And what might he have told to Rhif Ehrran to send her kiting out of there with a message for homeworld? Look out, he must surely have told her: beware the consequences when the push *he* knew was coming rammed the kif right down hani throats. He had sent Ehrran where *The Pride* was supposed to be, and where Banny Ayhar was already headed, Jik would have told him, in a much slower ship but with a message he had given *her*, if she had lived to get to Maing Tol. Goldtooth's plan had worked till *The Pride* blew a vane coming out of Urtur and had to go in for repair, til Sikkukkut stole Hilfy and Tully and lured *The Pride* off to Mkks and then (Jik following his opportunity and a hani's desperation, and seeing only one way to make his schedule *and* keep his position on the inside of things) to Kefk, where things went even more grievously awry; where hani proved intractable and divided by bloodfeud, and Chur lay dying, preventing *The Pride* from making that critical dash homeward by the Kura route, to warn of disaster at Meetpoint. . . .

. . . .Goldtooth had given them that med equipment to make a long run possible, gave it to them the way mahendo'sat had spent millions upping *The Pride*'s running capacity, last-ditch try at sending updated information on to Anuurn and spacer hani. . . .

. . . .because no ship could get through the kifish blockade at Kita; and in the end they had to rely on the slim hope of Banny Ayhar's ship. Jik had failed to convince Ehrran to veer from her stshoward course and *The Pride* had involved itself deeper and deeper in the heart of Jik's schemes; Ehrran had not budged till Goldtooth confronted her with more truth than Jik had yet told any of them.

Pyanfar blinked, brought up against a brace and hung there while the dock spun in her vision. Her brain wanted to work for a change, and the white light and gray perspectives of the dock were chasing visions of dark and stars and tiny ships in wheeling succession. Her AP was in her fist. Steps thundered past her as others secured the other corner and the neighboring corridor turned up empty of everything but scattered paper and a closed windowed door that said DOCKSEAL in large letters. KEY ENTRY ONLY.

"Gods rot them all!" She fired. Thoughtlessly, because an AP was as good a key as any; and fired again through the smoke and the deafening thunder as shrapnel off her own shot peppered her hide. "Gods-be *fools*!"

The door was never armored to withstand that kind of blast. The window-seal went. She was not up to running, just walked behind the fleetfooted youngsters and the foolhardy who went racing up to step gingerly through the shattered pressure-seal window.

She stepped through: her own crew stayed about her, and Rhean's lot, as if it were a walk up a troubled dockside, back in the days when a winebottle was the most fearsome missile and an irate taverner the greatest hazard a hani crew on dockside had to deal with. She trod on something sharp, winced and flinched, walking into a corridor her followers had already taken possession of: Fiar and Sif jogged out to the fore.

"Slow down!" she yelled. "Rhean, hold it back!" —As the whole thing became a faster and faster rush forward; she could not keep up, had no wish to keep up there with the young and the energetic. They had to take the stairwells beyond this long corridor, they had to go up the hard way, not trusting the lifts that could be controlled from the main boards: Gaohn was too big to take quickly, except by overwhelming force. And time was on other sides. Time was, O gods, on the side of Sikkukkut. . . .

. . . .who arrived at Meetpoint to drive his kifish opposition against the anvil of mahen territory, knowing that there were limited routes Akkhtimakt could take: down the line into stsho territory was one, where there would be no resistance—but Goldtooth and the humans had sealed that route.

. . . .the second to methane-breather territory, but that was a deadly trap: *no* one wanted to contest the knnn.

. . . .the third course lay past Sikkukkut to Kefk, which would have put Akkhtimakt at psychological disadvantage, though ironically not a positional one: there was no worse place for a kif on the retreat to come, than into kifish territory, a wounded fish into an ocean of razor jaws. . . .

Think, Pyanfar, it's late to think. The enemy either has one choice more than you've thought of, or one fewer than they need.

Sikkukkut knew that some message had gone with Banny Ayhar—knew that someone would have carried it, and where mahen forces would come—he had used *the mahen push, anvil and hammer, but he never trusted the mahendo'sat, not Jik, manifestly not Goldtooth. He obviously didn't stop Ayhar.*

Or he didn't try because he wanted *it to happen.*

Gods, could Jik have told *him? No. No. He surely wouldn't. Not to someone that smart and that canny. They cooperated with limits. It was convenient for both sides. For separate reasons.*

But why did Sikkukkut value me *from the beginning? Why did he and the mahendo'sat both value me enough to keep us alive and set me here, with this much power?*

Is Sikkukkut a fool? He was never a fool. Neither is Jik. Nor Goldtooth.

If Sikkukkut lost too many ships fighting for power, my gods, he'd find some other kif gnawing up his leg the moment he looked weak. That's what the mahendo'sat are doing to him, whittling away at him. It's the kif's chief weakness, that aggressiveness of theirs. Does Sikkukkut know that? Can a species see its own deficiencies?

Look about us at ours, at this pitiful spectacle, hani against hani, spears and arrows flying in the sun, banners aflutter—

I see what keeps us from being what we might be.

Can he?

Can—?

"Look OUT!" someone yelled; and fire spattered from the end of the corridor.

"Any word?" Chur asked. She had left the rifle in lowerdecks. To carry the thing was more strength than she had, and there was no enemy aboard. She arrived on the bridge with Tully close behind her and clung to a seat at her regular post. It was a strange captain who turned a worried face toward her. "I'm taking orders," Chur breathed, to settle that, and clung to the chair with her claws, the whole scene wavering in and out of gray in her vision, her heart going like a motor on overload. "Any word on them?"

"Ehrran's threatening to back out of dock and blow us all. *Light*'s threatening to blow *Vigilance* where she sits. We're supposed to have a kifish ship in her picking up—that. Skkukuk. I've told him that's all we want to do." There was a fine-held edge to Sirany's voice, an experienced captain at the edge of her own limits. "Handle the kif."

"Aye," Chur said, and crawled into the vacant chair between scan and com and livened the aux com panel. With Tauran crew on either side of her. Tully sat one seat down. Other seats were vacant. Fiar's and Sif's.

Handle the kif. Indeed.

Skukkuk thought of himself as crew. He was loyal. Geran had said that much with a grimace. And Chur had gotten her own captain's instructions to the kif on open com. That and the encounter belowdecks was all she had to go on, while the kif waited below in lowerdeck ops, for transfer arrangements to be finalized. But she had been in the deep too long to panic over the unusual or the outré.

One of the black things skittered through the bridge and vanished like a persistent nightmare, long, furred, and moving like a streak.

On scan, one of the kifish ships nearest had just flared with vector shift.

Skkukuk's tight-beamed request for transport had had time to be heard and was evidently being honored.

"Tully," she said, leaning to look down the board where he had settled in. "We don't know when the humans come, right? You record message: *record*, understand? We send it to system edge, wide as we can, and constant—" She remembered in dismay she was not dealing with Pyanfar. "Your permission, cap'n."

"What?" the snapped answer came back. She had to explain it all again. In more detail. And: "Do it," Sirany said. "Just keep us advised *what* you do. You got whatever you want."

She drew a larger breath, activated com output and set about explanations, alternately to kif and to human and to *The Pride*'s interim captain. Then there was the matter of communicating with their mahen allies out there, whose disposition and intentions were another question: not many of the mahendo'sat ships had stayed insystem, but such as had were out there face-to-face with the kif, and nominally linked to the hani freighters who were also holding position out there in that standoff. So far they were letting the kifish ship move out where a kifish message with *The Pride*'s wrap on it had indicated it should go.

Blind acquiescence was asking a lot, of both mahendo'sat and hani. And even of the kif.

But things had to stay stable. More, they had to sort themselves out into some kind of defense, both internal and external. The next large group of ships to come in, at any given moment, could be Akkhtimakt's kif in a second strike, which would swing the whole kifish allegiance in the other direction; or it might be Sikkukkut, having disposed of Goldtooth; or Goldtooth and the humans. Or either without the other. Gods knew what else. Panicked stsho, for all they knew. Or tc'a.

Far better that whatever-it-was should meet an already existing wavefront of information designed to provoke discussion instead of indiscriminate fire.

Hande the kif, the woman said.

She sent it wide. In half a dozen languages and amplified via whatever ships would relay it, to all reaches of the system, continuously, since Gaohn station relays and apparently those of the second outsystem station and both buoys were not cooperating. She was talking to more than those insystem and those arriving; she was talking also to a certain mahen hunter, who had lost himself and gone invisible.

Chanur is taking Gaohn Station. This solar system is under control of Chanur and its allies and its subordinates. You are entering a controlled space. Identify yourselves.

"Hold fire!" Pyanfar yelled, turning, her back to the sidewall, the AP up in both hands where it bore on a flat-eared, white-round-the-eyes cluster of hani blackbreeches, Immunes, who were framed in the corridor opening and vulnerable as stsho in a hailstorm. A shot popped past her, high; one streaked back. *"Hold!"* Khym yelled, and: *"Hold it!"* Kohan Chanur echoed, two male voices that rumbled and rattled off the corridor walls in one frozen and terrible instant where slaughter looked likely.

But they were kids who had run up on them. Mere kids. Their ears were back in fright. None of them was armed except with tasers and they were staring down the barrels of APs that could take the deck out. They thought they were going to die there. It was in the look on their faces.

"Don't shoot!" one cried, with more presence of mind than the rest, and held her little pistol wide.

"Are you Ehrran?" Pyanfar yelled back at them, and one of them bolted and ran.

The others stayed still, eyes wide upon the leveled guns.

Prisoners we don't need.

Gods-be groundling fools.

"Get out of here!" she yelled at the rest of them. "*Out*, rot your hides!"

They ran, scrambling, colliding with each other as they cleared that hall, no shot fired.

She turned again, saw weary faces, bewildered faces, saw dread in Rhean Chanur and the rest, spacers who had come home to fight against kif and ended up fighting hani kids. That was the kind of resistance there was. That was what they had come down to, trying to take their station back from lunatics who threw beardless children at them.

"Gods save us," she said, and drew a ragged breath and shook her head and winced at the thump of explosion, which was Haral with their allies blasting their way through another pressure door that had been, with hani persistence, replaced with another windowed door after the *last* armed taking of Gaohn Station. Nothing bad would ever happen twice, of course. Not at civilized Gaohn. Not to hani, who had no wish to become involved in foreign affairs. Gaohn Station prized its staid ways, its internal peace, maintained by ceremonies of challenge and duel.

"Gods curse Naur," she said aloud. "Gods curse the *han*." And shocked her brother, and surely shocked *ker* Huran Faha, whose shoulder-scar was from downworld hunting, who knew little more of kif than she knew of hyperspace equations. Pyanfar shoved off from the wall and kept going, stepping through the ruined doorway.

"*Stop*," the intercom said from overhead. "*You are in violation of the law. Citizens are empowered to prevent you.*"

There were no citizens in sight. Everyone with sense had gotten out of the section. Those on Gaohn that were not spacers outright, excepting folk like Kohan and Huran, and red-maned Akify who had lived so long downworld with Chanur she had forgotten she was Llun, were all stationers, who knew the fragility of docksides, and knew there was a Chanur ship and a flock of kif and mahendo'sat looming over them. There was a way to slow station intruders down. Anyone in Central might have sealed and vented the whole area under attack, had they been prepared. Had Gaohn station ever been set up for such a defense. But no, the necessary modifications had been debated once, after the first taking of Gaohn, but never carried through: the Llun themselves had argued passionately against it.

There would never, of course, the Llun had thought, never in a thousand lifetimes come another invasion. The very thought of it disturbed hani tranquility, the acknowledgment of such a calamity was against hani principle: plan for an event and it might well create itself. To prepare Gaohn for defense might create a bellicose appearance that might cause it to need that defense. To provide Gaohn corridors with windowed pressure doors (which permitted visual communication between seal-zones in some contamination or fire emergency) was a safety measure and a moral statement: there would never come the day that the station would have to take extreme measures.

So it had fallen to Ehrran quite simply.

And the foreign forces that were coming in had never heard of such philosophy, and cared less. How could one even translate such a mindset to a kifish *hakkikt*?

How could a kif who planned across lightyears comprehend the Llun, let alone the groundling Naur, and the mind of the *han*, which decreed all on its own that hani would be let alone?

. . . .a kif who planned. . . .

. . . .a kif who let loose a mahen hunter ship and a hani force to accomplish a task for him which he—

—could not do himself?

—did a kif ever believe force insufficient?

Could a kif be so subtle?

Gods-rotted right a kif could be subtle. But not down any hani track. A kif wanted power, wanted adherents, wanted territory—

—Sikkukkut knew, by the gods, that Goldtooth was not done, and being capable of tricks like short-jumping himself, he knew what Goldtooth might have done at Meetpoint, a trick that *she* had only discovered when they pinned Jik down and wormed it out of him.

Knnn and gods-knew what had come in on Sikkukkut at Meetpoint, and what would Sikkukkut have done back there? Stayed to contest it? Run home to Kefk and Mkks, or Akkt?

One wished.

But that was not Sikkukkut's style. The wily bastard would have put more and more of the mahen puzzle together, the same as they, Jik's determined silence notwithstanding. Since Kefk, there was less and less left that Sikkukkut had to know.

That intrusion which had nearly run them over on their outbound course had been attack coming in again at Meetpoint, that was what it had to be, with the methane-breathers coming in the Out range as methane-breathers were crazy enough to do; and right before Sikkukkut launched his own pet hani toward Anuurn, he had been couriering messages right and left to other ships. . . .

. . . .Sikkukkut was planning something, and *he* had that babbling traitor Stle stles stlen aboard: the stsho would have told him anything and everything about Goldtooth he knew to tell.

Small black creatures stayed active during jump. They were from the kifish homeworld. So could the kif? Were they plotting and planning all the way, was that the secret to kifish daring and fierceness in their strikes, that they came out of hyperspace clearheaded and focused, revising plans such as hani and mahendo'sat and humans and anyone else would have to make well beforehand?

My gods, my gods.

She slogged along after the others, her own group lagging farther and farther back. Flesh had its limits. Even Hilfy flagged. Her pulse racketed in her ears like the laboring of some failing machine. There was that pain in her chest again, her eyes were blurred.

We may not have even this time. We shouldn't be here.

I should turn this back, get back to the ship, prepare to defend us—

—with what, fool? This vast armament you have?

—turn kif on kif? Can you lead such creatures as that, can you even keep a hold on Skkukuk if you can't get control of Gaohn?

Jik, gods rot you, where are you?

Another doorway. An AP shell took it out, just blew the window out, leaving jagged edges of plex. The youngsters and then the rest waded on through the wreckage that loomed in her vision like an insurmountable barrier, the gun weighing heavier and heavier in her hand. Kohan had gone ahead with Rhean. Khym was still with her. So were all her own crew. "Looks like we got rearguard," Haral gasped, a voice hardly recognizable. "Gods-be fools not watching their own backsides. Groundlings and kids."

"Yeah," she murmured, and got herself through the door, walked on and wobbled in her tracks. A big hand steadied her. Khym's.

The PA sputtered. "*Cease, go back to your ships immediately.* Vigilance *has armaments to enforce the decree of the* han. *It stands ready to use them. Do not endanger this station.*"

"*Ker* gods-be Rhif's safe on her ship," Geran said.

"Patience, we got the *Light* up there over her head, she's not going anywhere."

"We got a kifish ship coming into dock," Haral said. "*There's* trouble when it comes. Gods know what that fool Ehrran will do."

Another agonizing stretch of hallway. The first of them had gained the stairwell. There was much yelling of encouragement, inexperienced hani screwing up their courage before a long climb that meant head-on confrontation with an armed opposition.

They were out of range of the pocket-coms. Too much of the station's mass was between them and the ships at dock.

"M'gods." Footfalls came up at their backs, a thundering horde of runners. Pyanfar spun, on the same motion as the rest of the crew, on a straggle of hani in merchants' brights, with a crowd behind them all the way down the corridor, a crowd a lot of which was blackbreeches, strung out down the hall as they filtered through the obstacles of the shattered pressure doors. "*Over their heads!*" She popped off a shot into the overhead, and plastic panels near the shattered door disintegrated into flying bits and smoke and a thundering hail of ceiling panels that fell and bounced and paved the corridor in front of the onrush.

"Stop, stop!" the cry came back, with waving of hands, some of the merchants in full retreat coming up against the press behind, and a dogged few coming through, holding their hands in plain view. "Sfauryn!" one cried, naming her clan, which was a stationer clan: merchants, indeed, and nothing to do with Ehrran.

"We're Chanur!" Tirun yelled back at them, rifle leveled. "Stay put!"

The press had stalled behind, tide meeting tide in the hallway, those trying to advance through the broken doors and those in panic retreat. The few up front hesitated in the last doorway, facing the guns.

"Ehrran has Central!" the Sfauryn cried.

"You want to do something about it?" Pyanfar yelled back.

"We're trying to help! Gods, who're you aiming at? People all over the stations are trying to get in there!"

"Gods-be about time!" Her pulse hammered away, the blood hazed in gray and red through her vision. "If you can get the phones to work, get word to the other levels!"

"Llun's with us—Llun've got portable com, they got some rifles— It's Llun back there behind us, Chanur. They don't want to get shot by mistake!"

"Bring 'em on," she cried. Gods, what days they had come on, when Immune blacks meant target in a fight. She leaned on the wall and lowered the rifle. Blinked against the haze. Rest here awhile. Rest here till they had the reinforcements organized. Llun! Honest as sunrise and, thank the gods, self-starting. They had been doing something all the while, one could have depended on that.

But they could still get shot, coming up behind the spacers up front. Someone in spacer blues had to get up there and warn the others in the stairwell that what was coming on their tail was friendly. "Who of us has a run left in her?" she asked, and scanned a weary cluster of Chanur faces, ears flagged, fur standing in sweaty points and bloodied from the flying splinters.

"Me," Hilfy gasped, "me, I got it."

"Got your chance to be a gods-be fool. Go. Get. *Be careful!*"

To a departing back, flattened ears, a lithe young woman flying down that corridor while the shouting reinforcements got themselves organized and came on.

The tide oozed its way through the shattered door, over the rattling sheets of cream plastics that had been the ceiling. It swept on, past a bedraggled handful of heavy-armed hani that hugged the wall and waved them past.

"Time was," Pyanfar said, and hunkered down again as the last of them passed, the heavy gun between her knees, Haral and Geran and Khym already down, Tirun leaning heavily against the wall and slowly sliding down to her haunches, "time was, I'd've run that corridor."

"Hey," Khym said, tongue lolling. He licked his mouth and gasped. "With age comes smart, huh?"

"Yeah," Haral said, and cast a worried look down the corridor, the way Hilfy had gone. Hilfy with a ring in her ear and a gods-awful lot of scars, and a good deal more sense than the imp had ever had in her sheltered life. Hilfy the veteran of Kefk docks and *Harukk*'s bowels. Of Meetpoint and all the systems in between and the circle that led home.

"Kid'll handle it," Pyanfar said. "We hold this place awhile. Hold their backsides. Got to think. We got *Vigilance* out there. We got kif to worry about."

Station poured out a series of conflicting bulletins. Events were too chaotic for Ehrran to coordinate its lies. "They're still threatening to destroy the boards up there," Chur said. And: "Unnn," from Sirany Tauran. There was nothing for them to do about it. But there *was* a steady pickup of information from Llun scattered throughout the station, static-ridden, but decipherable. It gave out a name. "They've met up with the cap'n," Chur cried suddenly, on a wave of relief, and pressed the com-plug tighter into her ear to try to determine where that meeting was, but Llun was being cagey and giving out no positions. "They're saying they've linked up with Chanur and the rest and they're headed with that group."

There was a murmured cheer for that. ("Good?" Tully asked, leaning forward to catch Chur's eye. "Good?" "Gods-be good," Chur said back. "The captain's found help.") While Tauran crew stayed busy all about them, stations monitoring scan and outside movements, keeping Tully's recorded output and her own going out on as wide and rapid a sweep of the sphere as they and *Chanur's Light* could achieve in coordination, snugged against a rotating station, and sending with as much power as they could throw into the signal. Especially they kept an eye on *Vigilance* at its dock, *Vigilance*'s image relayed to them by *Light*, as a kifish ship headed for them, conspicuous now among all the others and coming the way a hunter-ship could, by the gods *fast*. While on a link all his own from belowdecks ops, and without a need to sweep the available sphere, Skkukuk maintained communications with his fellow kif.

"*Chanur-hakkikt skkutotik sotkku sothogkkt,*" his news bulletin went out, and Chur winced. "*Sfitktokku fikkrit koghkt hanurikktu makt.*" Other hani ships were picking that up, and there were spacers enough out there who knew main-kifish: *The Chanur* hakkikt *has subordinated other clans*. Something more about hani and a sea or tides or something the translator had fouled up. Skkukuk was being coded or poetic, was talking away down there, making his own kifish sense out of bulletins he got. She considered cutting him off. She thought of going down there and shooting him in lieu of ten thousand kif she could not get her hands on.

But the captain had given her orders. Pyanfar Chanur had asked it, and asked it with all sanity to the contrary, which meant it was one of the captain's dearly held notions, and *that* meant Pyanfar Chanur intended her crew to keep their hands off that kif and let him do what Pyanfar had said he should do.

This kif had saved the captain's life. Geran had told her so.

This kif was Pyanfar's kifish lieutenant. Pyanfar herself had told her so.

For Pyanfar's reasons. If they were to go down, as well be on the captain's orders, where they had lived forty years, onworld and off. If Pyanfar Chanur said jump the ship they jumped; if it was on course for the heart of a sun, they objected the fact once to be sure and then they jumped it.

It was a catching sickness. The Tauran captain was doing much the same, obeying orders she doubted.

While one of *The Pride*'s black, verminous inhabitants boldly sat on its haunches in the aisle by the start of the galley corridor and stared in wonder at the fools who ran the ship.

Up the stairs, up and up until the bones ached and the brain pounded for want of air. Hilfy Chanur had gotten herself up to the fore of the band, *after* dispersing parts of the Llun contingent down every available corridor as they ascended, to round up other stationers and get them moving down other corridors. There was one advantage to holding the heart of a city-sized space station, which was that one had all the controls to heat and light and air under one's hands.

The Ehrran had that.

But there was also an outstanding disadvantage to holding Central: that it was *one* small area, and that a city-sized space station had a lot of inhabitants, all of whom were converging on that point from all corridors, all passages, every clan on the station furiously determined to put the Llun *back* in control of systems the Llun understood and the Ehrran interlopers patently did not.

If there were Llun working systems up there at gunpoint, they were doing it all most unwillingly, and Ehrran had only the Llun's word for it just *what* they were doing with those controls.

Fools, aunt Pyanfar would say. A space station was a good deal different than a starship's controls; if there were even experienced spacers in the Ehrran contingent up there. Mostly it had to be groundling Ehrran, black-breeches whose primary job was trade offices and lick-footing to Naur and others of the Old Rich and the New.

Aunt Rhean was beside her as they climbed. Her father was just behind, grayed and older by the years *The Pride* had been away. And somewhere they had picked up two other men, young Llun, who had come in somewhere around level five and charged in among them in a camaraderie quite unlike men of the common clans—Immunes, free from challenge all their lives and having not a hope in the world of succeeding their own lord except by seniority, they came rushing in, stopped in a moment of recognition, likely neither one having known the other was coming, and surely daunted by Kohan's senior and downworld presence. Then: "Come ahead, rot you!" Kohan had yelled at them. And they had paired up with a great deal of shouting and bravado like two adolescents on a hunt. There were Llun women, armed and experienced in the last desperate battle for Gaohn. And it was all headed right into Ehrran's laps.

If the captive Llun up in control had been willing, they could at least have killed the lights and put the station reliant on the flashlights the Llun and the station merchants and some of the spacers had had the foresight to bring with them. They could have vented whole sections of the docks, with enormous loss of life. They could have fired the station stabilization jets and affected the gravity. They could have thrown the solar panels off their tracking and used some of the big mirrors to make it uncomfortable for *Chanur's Light*. Perhaps the Ehrran urged them to these things at gunpoint.

But none of them had happened.

The level twelve doorway was in front of them. Locked. Of course that was locked. One of the Ehrran had probably done that on manual. They surely held the corridors up here, between invaders and Central.

"Back," Hilfy yelled, and those in front of her cleared back and ducked down as best they could on the stairs, covering themselves. An AP threw things when it hit. And this door went like the others—the window was down, when she opened her eyes, her face and arms and body stung and bleeding with particles. The broken doorway let in a swirl of smoke, and a red barrage of laser fire lit the gray, exploding little holes off the stairwell wall up there.

For the first time panic hit her, real fear. This was the hero-stuff, being number one charging up the stairs into that mess. It was where her rashness and the possession of that illegal AP had put her.

"Hyyaaaah!" she yelled in raw terror, and rushed the stairs, because running screaming the other way was too humiliating. She fired one more time and got plastic-spatter all over her as the shell blew in the corridor and ceiling tiles hailed down in front of her. For a terrifying moment she was alone going through that doorway, and then she felt others at her back, blinked her burned eyes wider and saw blackbreeched hani lying in the corridor, some moving, some not; saw laser fire scatter in the smoke and aimed another shell that way.

There were screams. She flinched.

They were hani. They were downworlders. They had no experience of APs or what it was like to have a body blown apart or walls caving in with the percussion of shells. The survivors scrambled and fled and left guns lying in their disgrace, while outraged Llun charged after that lot, the two stationer-lads yelling as they went.

"Door," Rhean said, having arrived beside her, and she pointed to where the Llun were already headed.

"No problem," Hilfy gasped. She was cold all over. Her hand clenched about the grip of the gun as if it was welded there: she had lost all distinction between herself and the weapon, had lost a great deal of feeling all over her splinter-perforated skin. She cast a look back to see how many of their own had made it through, and it was a sea of their own forces in that corridor.

She walked now, over the littered floor, past the dead, where the others had run; and up to the sealed door their charge had secured, near where a shocked handful of Ehrran prisoners huddled under guard. It was the last door, the one that led into Central. "I'll blow it," she said. "You got to take it the hard way—" remembering only then that it was a senior captain she was telling how to do things. It was so simple a matter. It was hurtfully simple. Near Rhean Chanur, near her father, were hani who surely knew. There was Munur Faha, for one. And the Harun. They had to charge in there hand to hand against guns that might destroy fragile controls and kill fifty, sixty thousand helpless people.

Fools. She could have wept over the things she saw. *Poor fools. My people. Do you see now? Do you see what we've done to ourselves, what a plagued thing we've let in, because we tried to keep everything the old way?*

There was information coming in, finally, scattered reports booming out over the PA as Llun portable com began supplanting the reports out of Central: *"Ehrran is in violation of Immune law,"* one such repeated. *"Llun has appealed to all clans to enforce its lawful order for Ehrran withdrawal from station offices and enjoins Ehrran to signal its intent to comply."*

That announcement was becoming tiresome, dinning down from the overhead. Pyanfar wiped her bleeding face and flicked her ears and looked up at the wreckage of the speaker, which gave the advisories a rattling vibration and garbled the words.

"I'd like to shoot that thing," Geran muttered. Which was her own irritated thought.

"Gods-be little good we're doing here," Pyanfar said. "That's sure." Her throat was sore. Her limbs ached. She put effort into getting onto her feet. "Hilfy can take care of herself. Whole station's in on it. Better to get back to the ship, get Chur off her feet."

"Not putting her in any station hospital," Geran muttered. "Safer on the ship."

Which was what Geran thought of Gaohn's present chances, with kif incoming. Or Geran echoed Chur's wishes, if they all went to vacuum and there was no real difference.

"Yeah," she said, noncommittal, and pushed herself off the wall she had braced on. "Gods. What'd I do to stiffen the arm up?" The AP weighed like sin. The debris in the hall was an obstacle course, stuff that stuck in the feet, up in the sensitive arch of the toes. Broken plastics and bits of metal mingled indiscriminately on the deckplates. The mob that had come through had left bloody footprints, but they had seemed crazy enough not to feel it much. Pyanfar limped and winced her way over the stuff, the crew doing the same.

"We got that kif incoming," Tirun said.

"Gods, yes. Llun's not going to like that much." It was about the first thing the Llun partisans were going to learn when they got back into contact with whatever Llun personnel were keeping the station going under Ehrran guns. *Crazy Chanur's bringing kif in.* And Llun at that point had to wonder what side Chanur was on. So did the others, up there with Hilfy.

It was a fair question.

She caught her breath, wiped her nose, seeing a red smear across her thumb. No wonder she was snuffling. And how had *that* happened?

Down the corridor, past one and another of the shattered doorways, over debris of broken plastics, the stench of explosion and burned plastics still hanging in the air, cleaned somewhat by the fans: things were still working.

And Pyanfar was in a sudden fever, now she had begun, to get back to *The Pride* and get out to space again, to deal with the kif she had in hand before she suddenly had more kif than she could deal with.

They reached the corridor end, where the last shattered pressure door let out on the open dock. She stepped over the frame, swung the AP in a perfunctory and automatic sweep about the visible dock, right along with the glance of her eye, which had gotten to be habit.

An Ap thumped: her brain identified it as one of that category of dreadful sounds it knew; knew it intimately, right down to the precise sound an AP made when it was aimed dead on: and the twitch went right on to the muscles, which asked no questions. She sprawled and rolled as the world blew up around her; rolled all the way over and let off a shot with both her hands on the AP, in the maelstrom of her crew shouting and shots going off.

My gods, into the doorway, thing hit us dead center— O my gods!

Second shot, off into the cover of the girders.

"You all right?" she yelled back at her crew, at her husband. "You all right back there?"

"Get back here!" Khym's voice, deep and angry.

Third shot. *"Are you all right, gods rot it?"*

A shot came back, hit the wall. She made herself a part of the deck.

"Py!"

"Get out of the gods-be door!"

"Chanur!" a voice came over a loudhailer. *"Leave the weapons and come clear of there. You want your crew alive, we have you pinned! We have women coming down that corridor at your backs—"*

"Ehrran?" she yelled out, still belly-down. "Is that Ehrran?"

"This is Rhif Ehrran, Chanur. We have crew behind you. Give up!"

"She's the same gods-be fool she ever was." Haral's voice, somewhere behind her, something in the way of it. Door rim, Pyanfar earnestly hoped.

"You got to match her, Hal? F'godssakes, get out of that door!"

"Hey, she just told us we got company to the rear. You want us to go handle 'em, or you want help out there to fore, cap'n? She's a godsawful lousy shot."

"Chanur!"

"I'm thinking!" she shouted back. And to Haral: "Is everyone all right back there?"

"*Na* Khym caught a bit in the leg, not too bad. You want to back up, or you want us to come out there?"

She looked out toward that line-of-sight where structural supports gave cover. And up. Where a gantry joined that area, with its couplings and its huge hoses and cables. A grin rumpled her nose and bared her teeth. "It'll be for'ard." As Ehrran yelled again over the loudhailer. *"Chanurrr!"*

"You gods-be fool." She slipped up the sights, aimed, and sent the shell right into the center of the skein. That blew some of the huge hoses in two and blew the ligatures and dropped the whole ungainly snaking mass down behind Ehrran's position, hose thick as a hani's leg and long as a ship ramp dropping in from the exploded gantry skein, hitting, bouncing and snaking this way and that with perverse life of its own. Pumps screamed, air howled and safeties boomed; and blackbreeched figures scattered for very life, in every direction the bouncing hoses left open.

She scrambled up. "Come on," she yelled to her own crew, to get them clear in the confusion, out of that exposed position; and: "Captain!" Tirun yelled.

She whirled toward the targets, got off one shot toward the one figure who had stopped in the clear and lifted a gun. It was not the only shot. APs and rifles went off in a volley from the door behind her, and there was just not a hani at all where that figure had stood. The shock of it numbed her to the heart.

"Still a fool," Geran said, without a qualm in her voice.

And Haral: "Couldn't rightly say who hit her, cap'n, all this shooting going on."

"Move it!" she snarled then, and shoved the nearest shoulder, Geran's. The rest of them moved, covering as they went, Khym limping along and losing blood, but not overmuch of it. *The Pride* was a short run away, *Ehrran's Vigilance* out of sight around the station rim; it was *Harun's Industry* that might well have taken damage in that hit on the gantry lines, if its pumps had been on the draw. Still spaceworthy, gods knew, the pumps were a long way from a starship's heart. They ran across the edge of a spreading puddle of water and mixed volatiles: the toxics, thank gods, ran their skein separately, in the docking probe in space: *those* were not loose, or they would have been dead.

They could all still be dead if *Vigilance*'s second-in-command decided to rip her ship loose and start shooting. That little stretch of dock loomed like intergalactic distance, passed in a dizzy, nightmare effort, feet splashing across the deck in liquid that burned in cuts and stung the eyes to tears, that got into the lungs and set them all to coughing. Pumps had cut off. On both sides of the station wall. Gods hope no one set off a spark.

"Chur!" That was Geran's strangled voice, yelling at a pocketcom. "Chur, we're coming in, get that gods-be hatch open!"

They reached the ramp. She grabbed Khym's arm as he faltered, blood soaking his leg. She hauled at him and he at her as he struggled up the climb, into the safety of the gateway.

Then they could slow to a struggling upward jog, where at least no shot could reach them, and the hatch was in reach. She trusted Chur's experience, *The Pride*'s own adaptations: exterior camera and precautions meant no ambushes—

"We got that way clear?" Haral was asking on com.

"Clear," Chur's welcome voice came back. "You all right out there?"

All right. My gods!

"Yeah," Haral said. "Few cuts and scrapes."

A numbness insulated her mind. Even with eyes open on the ribbed yellow passage, even with the shock of space-chilled air to jolt the senses, there was this drifting sense of nowhere, as if right and wrong had gotten lost.

A hani that sold us out. A hani like that. A kif like that gods-be son Skkukuk. Which is worth more to the universe?

I shot her. We all did. Crew did it for me. *Why'd* I *do it?*

Hearth and blood, Ehrran.

For Chur. But that wasn't why.

For our lives, because we have to survive, because a fool can't be let loose in this. We have to do it, got to do something to stop this, play every gods-be throw we got and cheat into the bargain. Got to live. Long enough.

What will they say about us then?

That's nothing in the balances. That there's someone left to remember at all—that's what matters.

Duty Calls

Anne McCaffrey

With the sort of bad luck which has dogged the Alliance lately, escort and convoy came back into normal space in the midst of space debris.

We came from the queer blankness of FTL drive into the incredible starscape of that sector, so tightly packed with sun systems that we had had to re-enter far sooner than the Admiral liked, considering nearby Khalian positions. But we had no choice. We had to leave the obscurity of FTL in relatively "open" space. It would take nearly six weeks to reduce our re-entry velocity of 93%C to one slow enough to make an orbit over the beleaguered world of Persuasion, our eventual destination. We also were constrained to reduce that tremendous velocity before nearing the gravity wells of such a profusion of stars or the Fleet could be disrupted, or worse, scattered to be easily picked off by any roving Khalia. The Admiral had plotted a brilliant two-step braking progress through the gravity wells of nearer star systems to "lose" speed. So we emerged from FTL, nearly blinded by the blaze of brilliantly glowing stars which was, as suddenly, obscured. Then WOW! Every alert on the Dreadnought *Gormenghast* went spare.

Considering my position, attached to a landing pod, slightly forward of the main Bridge Section, I immediately went into action. Under the circumstances, the faster we could clear the junk the better, because 1) many of the supply pods towed by the freighters could be holed by some of the bigger tidbits flying around at the speeds they were moving and 2) we were awfuldam close to a colony the Khalia had overrun three galactic years ago. If they *had* set up any peripheral scanners, they'd catch the Cerenkov radiations from our plasma weapons. So everything that could blast a target throughout the length of the convoy was!

Me, I always enjoy target practice, if I'm not *it* (which in my line of work as pilot of the Admiral's gig is more frequently the case than the sane would wish). Against space debris I have no peer and I was happily potting the stuff with for'ard and port side cannon when I received an urgent signal from the Bridge.

"Hansing? Prepare to receive relevant charts and data for Area ASD 800/900. Are you flight ready?"

"Aye, aye, sir," I said, for an Admiral's gig is *always* ready or you're dropped onto garbage runs right smart. I recognized the voice as that of the Admiral's aide, Commander Het Lee Wing, a frequent passenger of mine and a canny battle strategist who enjoys the full confidence of Admiral Ban Corrie Eberhard. Commander Het has planned, and frequently participated in, some of the more successful forays against Khalian forces which have overrun Alliance planets. Het doesn't have much sense of humor; I don't think I would either if only half of me was human and the more useful parts no longer in working order. I think all his spare parts affected his brain. That's all that's left of me but I got spared an off-beat but workable humor. "Data received."

"Stand by, Bil," he said. I stifled a groan. When Het gets friendly, I get worried. "The Admiral!"

"Mr. Hansing." The Admiral's baritone voice was loud and clear, just a shade too jovial for my peace of mind. "I have a mission for you. Need a recon on the third planet of ASD 836/929: its settlers call it Bethesda. It's coming up below us in a half a light-year. The one the pirates got a couple of years back. Need to be sure the Khalia don't know we've passed by. Don't want them charging up our ass end. We've got to get the convoy, intact, to the colony. They're counting on us."

"Yes, sir!" I made me sound approving and willing.

"You'll have a brawn to make contact with our local agent who is, fortunately, still alive. The colony surrendered to the Khalia, you know. Hadn't equipped themselves with anything larger than handguns." The Admiral's voice registered impatient disapproval of people unable to protect themselves from invasion. But then, a lot of the earliest colonies had been sponsored by nonaggressives long before the Alliance encountered the Khalia. Or had they encountered us? I can never remember now, for the initial contact was several lifetimes ago, or so it seems to me, who has fought Khalia all my adult life. However, it had been SOP to recruit a few "observers" in every colonial contingent, and equip them with implanted receivers for just such an emergency as had overtaken Bethesda. "Het'll give you the agent's coordinates," the Admiral went on. "Had to patch this trip up, Bil, but you're the best one to handle it. Space dust! Hah!" I could appreciate his disgust at our bad luck. "You've got a special brawn partner for this, Bil. She'll brief you on the way."

I didn't like the sound of that. But time was of the essence if the Admiral had to prepare contingency plans to scramble this immense convoy to avoid a Khalian space attack. Somehow or other, despite modern technology, a fleet never managed to reassemble all the original convoy vessels and get them safely to their destination: some mothers got so lost or confused in the scramble they never did find themselves again. Much less their original destination. Merchantmen could be worse than sheep to round up, and often about as smart. Yeah, I remember what sheep are.

"Aye, aye, sir," I said crisply and with, I hoped, convincing enthusiasm for the job. I hate dealing with on-the-spots (o.t.s.): they're such a paranoid lot, terrified of exposure either to Khalian Overlords or to their planetary colleagues who could be jeopardized by the agent's very existence. Khalian reprisals are exceptionally vicious. I was glad that a brawn had to contact the o.t.s.

Even as I accepted the assignment, I was also accessing the data received from the *Gormenghast's* banks. The computers of an Ocelot Scout, even the Mark 18 which I drove, are programmed mainly for evasive tactics, maintenance, emergency repairs and stuff like that, with any memory limited to the immediate assignment. We don't *know* that the Khalia can break into our programs but there's no sense in handing them, free, gratis, green, the whole nine metres, is there? Even in the very unlikely chance that they *could* get their greasy paws on one of us.

The mortality and capture statistics for scouts like mine don't bear thinking about so I don't think about them. Leaves most of my brain cells able to cope with immediate problems. Brawns have an even lower survival rate: being personalities that thrive on danger, risk and uncertainty, and get large doses of all. I wondered what "she" was. What ancient poet said *The female of the species is more deadly than the male?* Well, he had it right by all I've seen, in space or on the surface.

"Good luck, Bil!"

"Thank you, sir."

Admiral Eberhard doesn't have to brief scout pilots like me but I appreciate his courtesy. Like I said, the mortality for small ships is high and that little extra personal touch makes a spaceman try that much harder to complete his mission successfully.

"Permission to come aboard." The voice, rather deeper than I'd expected, issued from the airlock com-unit.

I took a look and damned near blew a mess of circuits. "She" was a feline, an ironically suitable brawn for an Ocelot Scout like me, but she was the most amazing . . . colors, for her short thick fawn fur was splashed, dashed and dotted by a crazy random pattern of different shades of brown, fawn, black and a reddish tan. She was battle lean, too, with a few thin patches of fur on forearm and the deep ribcage, which might or might not be scars. At her feet was a rolled up mass of fabric, tightly tied with quick-release straps.

I'd seen Hrrubans before, of course: they're one of the few species in the Alliance who, like humans, are natural predators, consequently make very good combat fighters. I'm not poor-mouthing our Allies, but without naming types, some definitely have no fighting potential, though as battle support personnel they have no peer and, in their own specialties, are equally valuable in the Alliance war with the Khalia. *A shacking goo*, as the man said.

This representative of the Hrruban species was not very large: some of their troops are B I G mothers. I'd say that this Hrruban was young—they're allowed to fight at a much earlier age than humans—for even the adult females are of a size with the best of us. This one had the usual oddly scrunched shoulder conformation. As she stood upright, her arms dangled at what looked like an awkward angle. It would be for the human body. She held herself in that curious, straight-backed, half-forward crouch from her pelvis that Hrrubans affected: the way she stood, the weight on the balls of her furred feet, thighs forward, calves on the slant, the knee ahead of the toe, indicated that she stood erect right now, by choice, but was still effective on all fours. The Khalia had once been quadrupeds, too, but you rarely saw one drop to all fours, unless dying. And that was the only way I wanted to see Khalia.

"Permission. . . ," she began again patiently, one foot nudging the folded bundle of fabric beside her. I opened the airlock and let her in.

"Sorry, but I've never seen an Hrruban quite like you before . . ." I ended on an upward inflection, waiting for her to identify herself.

"B'ghra Hrrunalkharr," she said, "senior lieutenant, Combat Supply."

And if survival is low for brawns, it's even lower for Combat Supply personnel. If she had made a senior lieutenancy, she was *good*.

"Hi, I'm Bil Hansing," I replied cheerily. Ours might

be a brief association but I preferred to make it as pleasant as possible.

She flung a quick salute with her "hand" turned inward, for her wrist did not swivel for a proper Navy gesture. Then the corners of her very feline mouth lifted slightly, the lower jaw dropped in what I could readily identify as a smile.

"You can call me Ghra, easier than sputtering over the rest of it. Your lot can never get your tongues around *rs*."

"Wanna bet?" And I rolled off her name as easily as she had.

"Well, I am impressed," she said, giving the double *s* a sibilant emphasis. She had lugged her bundle aboard and looked around the tiny cabin of the Ocelot. "Where can I stow this, Bil?"

"Under the for'ard couch. We are short on space, we Ocelots!"

I could see her fangs now as she really smiled, and the tip of a delicate pink tongue. She quickly stowed the bundle and turned around to survey me.

"Yeah, and the fastest ships in the galaxy," she said with such a warm approval that my liking for her increased. "Mr. Hansing, please inform the Bridge of my arrival. I take it you've got the data. I'm to share the rest of my briefing when we're under way."

She was polite, but firm, about her eagerness to get on with what could only be a difficult assignment. And I liked that attitude in her. With an exceedingly graceful movement, she eased into the left-hand seat, and latched the safety harness, her amazing "hands" (they weren't really "paws"—Khalia have "paws"—for the "fingers" on her hands had evolved to digit status, with less webbing between them for better gripping) curving over the armrests. The end of her thickly furred tail twitched idly as the appendage jutted out beyond the back of the cushioned seat. I watched it in fascination. I'd never appreciated how eloquent such a tenable extremity could be.

Nevertheless, duty called and I alerted the Bridge to our readiness. We received an instant departure okay, and I released the pressure grapples of the airlock, gave the starboard repellers a little jolt and swung carefully away from the *Gormenghast*.

I enjoy piloting the Ocelot. She's a sweet ship, handles like a dream, can turn her thirty meters on her tail if she has to, and has, though not many believe me. I remind them that she's a Mark 18, the very latest off the Fleet's Research & Development Mother Ship. Well, five years galactic standard ago. But I oversee all maintenance myself and she's in prime condition, save for the normal space wear and tear and the tip of one fin caught by a Khalian bolt the second year I commanded her when Het and I ran a pirate blockade in FCD 122/785.

Of course, she's light on armament, can't waste maneuverability and speed on shielding, and I've only the four plasma cannons, bow and stern, and swivellers port and starboard. I'd rather rely on speed and zip: the ship's a fast minx and I'm a bloody good driver. I can say that because I've proved it. Five g.s. years in commission and still going.

I pumped us up to speed and the Fleet was fast disappearing into the blackness of space, only the slight halo of light where they were still firing to clear lanes through the damned dust and that quickly dispersed. Those telltale emissions which could prove very dangerous. That is, if the Khalia were looking our way. Space is big and the convoy was slowing to move cautiously through a congested globular ASD cluster to make our ultimate orbit about ASD 836/934. Everywhere in this young cluster there was dust which was a navigational hazard despite its small to minuscule size.

The reason the Fleet was convoying such an unwieldy number of ships through this sector of space, adjacent to that known to be controlled by Khalia, was to reinforce the sizeable and valuable mining colony on Persuasion 836/934: and strengthen the defenses of two nearby Alliance planets; the water world of Persepolis, whose oceans teemed with edible marine forms chockful of valuable protein for both humanoid and the weasellike Khalia, and the fabulous woods of Poinsettia which were more splendid and versatile in their uses than teak, mahogany or redwood. In the ASD Sector the Khalia had only three planets, none valuable except as stepping stones so that a takeover of the richer Alliance-held worlds had a high probability factor which the Alliance was determined to reduce by the reinforcement of troops and material in this convoy. Or, once again the great offensive strike planned for Target, the main Khalian base in Alliance space, would have to be set back.

As the tremendous entry speed was reduced, the convoy was, of course, vulnerable to any Khalian marauders during the six months that maneuver took. FTL is the fastest way to travel: it's the slowing down that takes so much time. (You got one, you got the other. You live with it.) So Alliance High Command had created a few diversions in Sectors BRE, BSF, attacks on two rather important Khalian-held planets and had thrown great Fleet strength into the repulsing maneuver at KSD: a strategy which was evidently working to judge by the lack of visible traces of Khalian force hereabouts. In FTL, you have obscurity—Alliance or Khalian. But in normal space, the emissions of your drive make ever-expanding "cones" which *are* detectable. The large number of ships included in our convoy increased the detection factor—to any spaceship crossing the "cone" trail. "Cones" were, fortunately, not detectable from a planetary source, but the plasma bursts were—that is, if Bethesda had the right equipment.

If we could be spared any further unforeseen incidents, the convoy had a good chance of relieving Persuasion and the other worlds before the piratic Weasels could summon strike elements to the ASD area.

I had never actually been near a Khalian. Maybe my decorative brawn had. I intended to ask her as soon as I had locked us on course. Ghra's tail tip continued to twitch, just slightly, as we reached the Ocelot's cruising speed. I had now programmed in the data needed to reach Bethesda, and to re-enter normal space at three planetary orbits away from it, on the dark side. I checked my calculations and then, warning Ghra, activated the FTL drive and we were off!

Ghra released the safety belt and stretched, her tail sticking straight out behind her. Good thing she couldn't see me gawping at it. Scoutships with a good pilot like me, and I'm not immodest to say so, could utilize the FTL drive between systems, where the Fleet, if it wanted to keep its many vessels together in some form of order, could not.

"If you'll put what is now the spaceport area of Bethesda on the screen, Bil, I'll brief you," she said, leaning forward to the terminal. I screened the relevant map. She extended one claw, using it to show me the landing site. "We're to go in north of the spaceport, low, where they won't be looking for anything. Just here, there're a lot of canyons and ravines. And a lot of volcanic debris, some of it bigger than your Ocelot. So you can pretend you're an old mountain fragment while I mosey into the settlement to see the o.t.s."

"And when the sun comes up and shines off my hull, it'll be bloody plain I'm no rock."

She gave a rippling chuckle, more like a happy growl. "Ah, but you'll be camouflaged by the time the sun rises," she said, pointing her left hand toward the couch under which her bundle was stored.

"Camouflaged?"

She chuckled again, and dropped her lower jaw in her Hrruban smile. "Just like me."

"Huh? You'd stand out a klick away."

"Not necessarily. D'you know why creatures evolved different exterior colors and patterns? Well, markings and colors help them become invisible to their natural enemies, or their equally natural victims. On your own home world, I'll cite the big felines as an excellent example." She twitched her dainty whisker hairs to indicate amusement, or was it condescension for us poorly endowed critters? "Tigers have stripes because they're jungle inhabitants; lions wear fur that blends into the veldt or grasslands; panthers are mottled black to hide on tree limbs and shadows. Their favorite prey is also colored to be less easily detected, to confuse the eye of the beholder, if they stand still.

"We've finally caught a few prisoners. A major breakthrough in Khalian biological research suggests that they are blind to certain colors and patterns." She indicated her sploshed flanks. "What I'm wearing should render me all but invisible to Khalia."

"Ah, come on, Ghra, I can't buy that!"

"Hear me out." She held her hand up, her lustrous big eyes sparkling with an expression that could be amusement, but certainly resulted in my obedience. "We've also determined that, while Khalian night vision is excellent, dawn and dusk produce a twilight myopia. My present camouflage is blended for use on this planet. I can move with impunity at dawn and dusk, and quite possibly remain unseen during daylight hours, even by Khalia passing right by me. Provided I choose my ground cover correctly. That's part of early Hrruban training, anyhow. And we Hrrubans also know how to lie perfectly still for long hours." She grinned at my skeptical snort.

"Add to that inherent ability the fact that the Khalia have lost much of the olfactory acuteness they originally had as they've relied more and more on high tech, and I doubt they'll notice me." Her own nostrils dilated slightly and her whiskers twitched in distaste. "I can smell a Khalian more than five klicks away. And a Khalian wouldn't detect, much less recognize my spoor. Stupid creatures. Ignored or lost most of their valuable natural assets. They can't even move as quadrapeds anymore. We had the wisdom to retain, and improve, on our inherited advantages. It could be something as simple and nontech as primitive ability that's going to tip the scale in this war. We've already proved that ancient ways make us valuable as fighters."

"You Hrrubans have a bloody good reputation," I agreed generously. "You've had combat experience?" I asked tactfully, for generally speaking, seasoned fighters don't spout off the way she was. As Ghra didn't seem to be a fully adult Hrruban, maybe she was indulging herself in a bit of psyching up for this mission.

"Frequent." The dry delivery of that single word assured me she was, indeed, a seasoned warrior. The "fingers" of her left hand clicked a rapid tattoo. "Khalia are indeed formidable opponents. Very." She spread her left hand, briefly exposing her lethal complement of claws. "Deadly in hand-to-hand with that stumpy size a strange advantage. A fully developed adult Khalian comes up to my chest: it's those short Khalian arms, incredibly powerful, that you've got to watch out for."

Some of the latest "short arm" jokes are grisly by any standards: real sick humor! And somehow, despite your disgust, you find yourself avidly repeating the newest one.

"The Khalia may prefer to use their technology against us in the air," Ghra continued, "but they're no slouches face to face. I've seen a Khalian grab a soldier by the knees, trip him up, and sever the hamstrings in three seconds. Sometimes they'll launch at the chest, compress the lungs in a fierce grip and bite through the jugular vein. However," Ghra added with understandable pride, "we've noticed a marked tendency in their troops to avoid Hrrubans. Fortunately we don't mind fighting in mixed companies."

I'd heard some incredible tales of the exploits of mixed companies and been rather proud that so many of the diverse species of the Alliance could forget minor differences for the main Objective. I'd also heard some horror tales of what the Khalia did to any prisoners of those mixed companies. (It had quickly become a general policy to dispatch any immobilized wounded.) Of course, such tales always permeate a fighting force. Sometimes, I think, not as much to encourage our own fighting men to fight that much more fiercely as to dull the edge of horror by the repetition of it.

"But it's not going to be brute force that'll overcome them: it'll be superior intelligence. We Hrrubans hope to be able to infiltrate their ground forces with our camouflages." She ran both hands down her lean and muscled thighs. "I'm going to prove we can."

"More power to you," I said, still skeptical if she was relying on body paint. While I was a space fighter pilot,

I knew enough about warfare strategies to recognize that it was only battles that were won in space: wars are won when the planets involved are secured against the invader. "There's just one thing. You may be able to fool those Weasels' eyes, but what about the humans and such on Bethesda? You're going to be mighty visible to them, you know."

Ghra chuckled. "The Khalia enforce a strict dusk-to-dawn curfew on their captive planets. You'll be setting us down in an unpopulated area. None of the captured folk would venture there and all the Khalian air patrols would see is the camouflage net."

I hoped so, not that I personally feared the Khalia in the air or on the ground. For one thing, an Ocelot is faster than any atmosphere planes they operate, or spacecraft. The Khalia prefer to fly small vehicles: as far as we know they don't have any longer than a cruiser. Which makes a certain amount of sense—with very short arms, and legs, they wouldn't have the reach to make effective use of a multiple function board. Their control rooms must be crowded. Unless the Khalia had prehensile use of their toes?

"Yeah, but you have to contact the o.t.s. and he lives in the human cantonment. How're you going to keep invisible there?"

She shrugged her narrow shoulders. "By being cautious. After all, no humans will be expecting an Hrruban on Bethesda, will they?" She dropped her jaw again, and this time I knew it was amusement that brought a sparkle to those great brown eyes. "People, especially captive people, tend to see only what they expect to see. And they don't want to see the unusual or the incredible. If they should spot me, they won't believe it nor are they likely to run off and tattle to the Khalia."

Then Ghra stretched, sinews and joints popping audibly. "How long before re-entry, Bil? Time enough for me to get a short nap?" Her jaw dropped in an Hrruban grin as she opened the lid of the deepsleep capsule.

"Depends on how long you want to sleep? One week, two?" Scoutships are fast but they also must obey the laws of FTL physics. I had to slow down just as the convoy had to, only I could waste my speed faster by braking a lot of it in the gravity well of Bethesda's sun.

"Get us into the system. We'll have plenty of time to swap jokes without boring each other," she said as she took two steps to the long cabinet that held the deepsleep tank.

She pulled it out and observed while I set the mechanism to time and calibrated the gas dose. Nodding her approval, she lay down on the couch, attached the life-support cups suitable for her species with the ease of long practice. With a final wink, she closed the canopy and then her eyes, her lean camouflaged frame relaxing instantly as the gas flooded the compartment.

Ghra was perceptive about the inevitable grating of two personalities cooped up in necessarily cramped conditions, for too long a time with too little activity. We brain ships are accustomed to being by ourselves, though I'm the first to tell new members of our Elite Corps that the first few months ain't easy. There are benefits. We are conditioned to the encapsulation long before we're placed in any kind of large, dangerous equipment. The good thing about being human is our adaptability. Or maybe it's sheer necessity. If you'd rather not be dead, there is an alternative: and if we, who have had bodies and have known that kind of lifestyle, are not as completely the ship we drive as shell people are, we have our uses. I have come to like this new life, too.

The Ocelot plunged on down toward the unseen planet and its mission. I set external alarms and went into recall trance.

As the Ocelot neared my target, a mild enough looking space marble, dark blues and greens with thin cloud cover, it roused both Ghra and me. She came alert right smart, just as a well-trained fighter should. Grabbing a container of the approved post-sleep fortified drink, she resumed her seat and we both read the Ocelot's auto-reports.

The detectors identified only the usual stuff—comsats, mining transfer gear, solar heater units, but nothing in orbit around Bethesda that could detect the convoy. The only way to be dead sure, or dead, was to check down below as well. Ghra agreed. Dawn was coming up over one of the water masses that punctuated the planet. The shoreline was marked by a series of half circles. They looked more like crater holes than natural subsidences, but there had once been a lot of volcanic activity on Bethesda.

"How're we going to make it in, Bil? Even with what the settlers put up, the Khalians could spot us."

"No, I've lined the Ocelot up with the same trajectory as a convenient trail of meteoritic debris. You can see the planet is pocked with craters. Perfect for our purpose. Even if they have gear sensitive enough to track the Ocelot's faint trail, they'd more than likely figure it was just more of the debris that's already come in."

"I had a look at Het's data on the planet," Ghra said. "Bethesda's spaceport facility had been ample enough to take the big colonial transport jobs. Last recorded flights in before the Khalian capture were for commercial freight lighters, but the port could take the biggest Khalian cruisers and destroyers, not just those pursuit fighters."

"What did Het say about Khalian update on the invasion?"

Ghra shrugged. "That is unknown. We'll find out." She grinned when I made one of those disgruntled noises I'm rather good at. "Well, they could be busy elsewhere. You know how the Khalia are, mad keen on one thing one moment, and then forget about it for a decade."

"Let's hope the decade doesn't end while we're in this sector. Well, we've got a day or so before we go in, did you hear the one about . . ."

Ghra knew some even *I* hadn't heard by the time I was ready to activate the trajectory I'd plotted. I matched speed with a group of pebbles while Ghra did a geology game with me. I thought I'd never see the last of the fregmekking marbles, or win the game, even though we were getting down at a fair clip. Ghra was betting the pebbles would hit the northern wasteland before we flattened out for the last segment of our run. Whose side was she on?

Ducking under the light cloud cover, I made a low altitude run over the night side toward the spaceport and the small town that serviced it. The Khalia had enslaved the planet's small resident human population in their inimitable fashion, but there might just be some sort of a night patrol.

"Here's our objective, Ghra," I told her as we closed in on our landing site, and screened the picture.

She narrowed her eyes, mumbling or purring as she memorized landscape. The town had been built along the coastline and there looked to be wharfs and piers but no sign of sea traffic or boats. Just beyond the town, on a plateau that had been badly resculptured to accommodate large craft landings, was the respectably sized spaceport, with towers, com-disks, quarters and what looked like repair hangars. Infra scan showed two cooling earthern circles but that didn't tell us enough. I got a quick glimpse of the snouts and fins of a few ships, none of them warm enough to have been flown in the past twenty-four hours, but I didn't have time to verify type and number before we were behind the coastal hill. I dropped the meteor ruse just in time to switch on the gravity drive and keep us from planting a new crater.

"And there," I put an arrow on the screen, "is where I make like a rock. You'll be only about five klicks from town."

"Good," and she managed to make the g into a growl, narrowing her eyes as she regarded the picture. Her tail gave three sharp swings. "May I have a replay of the spaceport facility?" I complied, screening the footage at a slower rate.

"Nothing fast enough to catch me, Ghra, either in the atmosphere or in space," I replied nonchalantly. I made the usual copies of the tapes of our inbound trip for the Mayday capsule. Commander Het collects updates like water rations. "Strap in, Ghra, I'm cutting the engines. Het found me a straight run through that gorge and I'm using it."

That's another thing about the Ocelot, she'll glide. Mind you, I was ready to cut in the repellers at any moment but Het had done me proud in choosing the site. We glided in, with due regard for the Ocelot's skin for we'd be slotted in among a lot of volcanic debris. Some of that was, as Ghra had promised, as large as the scout. No sooner had we landed than Ghra retrieved her bundle and hefted it to the airlock, which I opened for her. Locked in my sealed chamber, I couldn't be of any assistance in spreading the camouflage net but she was quick, deft and very strong.

"Have you got a com button, Bil?" she asked when she had returned, her breath only a little faster than normal. She walked past the console into the little galley and drew a ration of water. "Good, then you'll get the gen one way or another." She took a deep draught of the water. "Good stuff. Import it?"

"Yeah, neither Het nor the Admiral likes it recycled," and I chuckled. "Rank has some privileges, you know."

Shamelessly, she took a second cupful. "I need to stock up if I have to lie still all day. It's summer here." She ran a claw tip down the selection dial of the supply cupboard and finally pressed a button, wrinkling her nose. "I hate field rations but they do stay with you." She had ordered up several bars of compressed high protein/high carbohydrate mix. I watched as she stored them in what I had thought to be muscle but were carefully camouflaged inner forearm pockets.

"What else are you hiding?" Surprise overwhelmed tact.

She gave that inimitable chuckle of hers. "A few useful weapons." She picked up the button I had placed on the console. "Neat! What's the range?"

"Fifteen klicks."

"I can easy stay in that range, Bil." She fastened the little nodule to the skull side of her left ear, its metallic surface invisible in the tufty fur. "Thanks. How long till dawn?"

I gave her the times for false and real dawn. With a cheery salute she left the Ocelot. I listened to the soft slip of her feet as long as the exterior sensors could pick up the noise before I closed the airlock. She had been moving on all fours. Remembering old teaching clips about ancient Earth felines, I could see her lithe body bounding across the uneven terrain. For a brief moment, I envied her. Then I began worrying instead.

I had known Ghra longer than I knew most of my random passengers, and we hadn't bored each other after I roused her. In her quiet, wryly humorous way, her company had been quite a treat for me. If she'd been more humanoid, and I'd been more like my former self . . . ah well! That's one of the drawbacks for a gig like me; we do see the very best, but generally all too briefly.

Ghra had sounded real confident about this camouflage scheme of hers. Not talk-herself-into-believing-it confident, but sure-there'd-be-no-problem confident. Me, I'd prefer something more substantial than paint as protection. But then, I'm definitely the product of a high tech civilization, while Ghra had faith in natural advantages and instinctive talents. Well, it was going to take every asset the Alliance had to counter the Khalian pirates!

Shortly before Bethesda's primary rose in the east, Ghra reported.

"I'm in place, Bil. I'll keep the com button on so you'll know all I do. Our contact's asleep. I'm stretched out on the branch of a fairly substantial kind of a broad-leafed tree outside his window. He's not awake yet. I'll hope he isn't the nervous type."

An hour and a half later, we both discovered that he was not the believing type either. But then, who would have expected to be contacted by what at first appeared to be a disembodied smile among the broad leaves shading your side window. It certainly wasn't what Fildin Escobat had anticipated when his implant had given him the warning zing of impending visitation.

"What are you?" he demanded after Ghra had pronounced the meeting code words.

"An Hrruban," Ghra replied in a well-projected whisper. I could hear a rustle as she moved briefly.

"Arghle!"

There was a silence, broken by a few more throaty garglings.

"What's Hrruban?"

"Alliance felinoids."

"Cat people?" Fildin had some basic civic's education.

"I'm camouflaged."

"Damned sure."

"So I'm patently not Khalian . . ."

"Anyone can say they're Alliance. You could be Khalian, disguised."

"Have you ever seen a Khalian going about on all fours? The size of me? With a face and teeth like mine? Or a tail?"

"No . . ." This was a reluctant admission.

"Speaking Galactic?"

"That's true enough," Fildin replied sourly, for all captive species were forced to learn the spitting, hissing, Khalian language. Khalian nerve prods and acid whips effectively encouraged both understanding and vocabulary. "So now what?"

"You tell me what I need to know."

"I don't know anything. They keep it that way." There was an unmistakable anger in the man's voice, which he lowered as he realized that he might be overheard.

"What were you before the invasion?"

"A mining engineer." I could almost see the man draw himself up with remembered pride.

"Now?"

"Effing road sweeper. And I'm lucky to have that, so I don't see what good I can do you or the Alliance."

"Probably more than you think," was Ghra's soothing response. "You have eyes and ears."

"I intend keeping 'em."

"You will. Can you move freely about the town?"

"The town, yes."

"Near the spaceport, too?"

"Yeah." Now Fildin's tone became suspicious and anxious.

"So you'd know if there had been any scrambles of their fighter craft."

"Haven't been any."

"None?"

"I tol' you. Though I did hear there's supposed to be s'more landing soon."

"How soon?"

"I dunno. Didn't want to know." Fildin was resigned.

"Do you work today?"

"We work everyday, all day, for those fregmekking rodents."

"Can you get near the spaceport? And do a count of what kind of space vehicle and how many of each are presently on the ground?"

"I could, but what good does that do you if more are coming in?"

"Do you know that for sure?"

"Nobody knows anything for sure. Why? Are we going to be under attack? Is that what you need to know all this for?" Fildin was clearly dubious about the merits of helping a counterattack.

"The Alliance has no immediate plans for your planet."

"No?" Fildin now sounded affronted. "What's wrong? Aren't we important enough?"

"You certainly are, Fildin." Ghra's voice was purringly smooth and reassuring. "And if you can get that information for me, it'll be of major importance in our all-out effort to free your planet without any further bloodshed and unpleasantness."

He gave a snort. "I don't see how knowing what's on the ground now will help."

"Neither do I," Ghra said, allowing a tinge of resentment creep into her silken tone. "That's for my superiors to decide. But it is the information that is required, which I have risked my life to obtain, so it must be very important. Will you help the Alliance remove the yoke of the oppressor, help you return to your former prestige and comfort?"

There was a long pause during which I could almost hear the man's brain working.

"I just need to tell you what's on the ground now?"

"That's all, but I need to know the types of craft, scout,

destroyer, whatever, and how many of each. And would you know if there have been battlecruisers here?"

"No cruisers," he said in a tone of disgust. "They can't land."

If colonial transports could land on Bethesda so could Khalian battlecruisers, but he didn't need to know that. What Ghra had to ascertain from him was if there were cruisers or destroyers that could be launched in pursuit of our convoy. Even a scout could blow the whistle on us and get enough of a head start to go FTL right back to Target and fetch in some real trouble. Only the fighters and cruisers escorting the convoy would be able to maneuver adequately to meet a Khalian attack. They would not be able to defend all the slowing bulky transports and most of the supply pods and drones that composed a large portion of the total. And if the supply pods bought it, the convoy could fail. Slowing takes a lot of fuel.

I took it as a small sliver of good luck that Fildin reported no recent activity. Perhaps this backwater hadn't been armed by its Khalian invaders.

"Cruisers, destroyers and scouts," Ghra repeated. "How many of each, Fildin, and you will be giving us tremendously vital information."

"When'll we be freed?"

"Soon. You won't have long to wait if all goes well."

"If what goes well?"

"The less you know the better for you, Fildin."

"Don't I get paid for risking my hide? Those nerve prods and acid whips ain't a bit funny, you know."

"What is your monetary exchange element?"

"A lot of good that would do me," Fildin said disgustedly.

"What would constitute an adequate recompense for your risks?"

"Meat. Red meat. They keep us on short rations, and I'd love a decent meal of meat once in a while." I could almost see him salivating. Well, there's no accounting for some tastes. *A shacking goo.*

"I think something can be arranged," Ghra said purringly. "I shall meet you here at dusk, good Fildin."

"Don't let anyone see you come! Or go."

"No one shall, I can assure you."

"Hey, where . . . What the eff? Where did it go?"

I heard Fildin's astonished queries taper off. I also heard Ghra's sharply expelled breath and then a more even, but quickened respiration. Then some thudding, as if she had landed on a hard surface. I heard the shushing of her feet on a soft surface and then, suddenly, nothing.

"Ghra?" I spoke her name more as an extended *gr* sound than an audible word.

"Later," was her cryptic response.

With that I had to be content that whole day long. Occasionally I could hear her slow breathing. For a spate there in the heat of the afternoon, I could have sworn her breathing had slowed to a sleep rhythm.

Suddenly, as the sun went down completely, the comunit erupted with a flurry of activity, bleatings, sounds of chase and struggle, a fierce crump and click as, quite likely, her teeth met in whatever she had been chasing. I heard dragging sounds, an explosive grunt from her and then, for an unnervingly long period, only the slip-slid of her quiet feet as she returned to Fildin Escobat's dwelling.

"Fardles! How'd you get that? Where did you get that? Oh, fardles, let me grab it before someone sees the effing thing."

"You asked for red meat, did you not?" Ghra's voice was smooth.

"Not a whole fardling beast. Where can I hide it?"

"I thought you wanted to eat it."

"I can't eat a whole one."

"Then I'll help!"

"NO!" Fildin's desperate reply ended in a gasp as he realized that he had inadvertently raised his voice above the hoarse whisper in which most of his conversation had been conducted. "We'll be heard by the neighbors. Can't we talk somewhere else?"

"After curfew? Stand back from the window."

"No, no, no, ohhh," and the difference in the sound I now received told me that Ghra had probably jumped through the window, right into his quarters.

"Don't put it down. It'll bloody the floor. What am I going to do with all this meat." There was both pleasure and dismay at such largesse.

"Cook what you need then." Ghra was indifferent to his problem, having rendered the requested payment. "Now, what can you report?"

"Huh? Oh, well," and this had patently been an easier task than accepting his reward, and he rolled off the quantities and types of spacecraft he had seen. I started taping his report at that juncture.

"No further indication of when the new craft are due in?" Ghra asked.

"No. Nothing. I did ask. Carefully, you know. I know a couple of guys who're menials in the port but all they knew was that something was due in."

"Supply ships?"

"Nah! Don't you know that the Khalia make their subject planets support 'em? They live well here, those fregmekking Weasels. And we get sweetdamall."

"You'll eat well tonight and for a time, Friend Fildin. And there's no chance that it's troop carriers?"

"How'd I know? There're already more Khalia on this planet than people."

Bethesda was a large, virtually unpopulated planet and Alliance High Command had never figured out why the Khalia had suddenly invaded it. Their assault on Bethesda had been as unexpected as it had been quick. Then no more Khalian activity in the area, though there were several habitable but unoccupied planets in nearby systems. High Command was certain that the Khalia intended to increase their dominance in the ASD Sector, eventually invading the three richly endowed Alliance planets; Persuasion for its supplies of copper, vanadium and the now precious, germanium; Persepolis for its inexhaustible marine protein (the Khalia consumed astonishing quantities of sea creatures, preferably raw, a fact which had made their invasion of Bethesda, a relatively "dry" world, all the more unexpected.)

To send a convoy of this size was unusual in every respect. High Command hoped that the Khalia would not believe the Alliance capable of risking so many ships, matériel and personnel. Admiral Eberhard was staking his career on taking that risk, plus the very clever use of the gravity wells of the nearby star ASD 836/932 and Persuasion to reduce velocity, cutting down the time in "normal space" when the convoy's "light ripple cone" was so detectable.

Those fregmekking Khalia had been enjoying such a run of good luck! It'd better start going our way soon. Maybe Bethesda would come up on our side of the ledger.

I had screened Het's sector map, trying to figure out from which direction the Khalia might be sending in reinforcements of whatever. If they came through the ASD grid, they'd bisect the emission trail. That was all too likely as they controlled a good portion of the space beyond. But I didn't have more charts, nor any updated information on Khalian movements. The *Gormenghast* would. It was now imperative for the Admiral to know about those incoming spacecraft. Ghra was as quick.

"It would be good to know where those ships were coming from," Ghra told Fildin. "Or why they were landing here at all. There seem to be enough ships on hand for immediate defense, and surveillance."

"How the fardles would I know? And effing sure I can't find out, not a lowly sweeper like me. I done what I said I'd do, exactly what you asked. I can't do more."

"No, I quite perceive that, Fildin Escobat, but you've been more than helpful. Enjoy your meat!"

"Hey, come back . . ."

Fildin's voice dropped away from the com button although I heard no sounds of Ghra's physical exertion. I waited until she would be out of hearing.

"Ghra? Can you safely talk?"

"Yes," she replied, and then I could hear the slight noise of her feet and knew she was loping along.

"What're you up to?"

"What makes you think I'm up to anything?"

"Let's call it an educated guess."

"Then guess." Amusement rippled through her suggestion.

"To the spaceport to see if you can find out where those spaceships are coming from."

"Got it in one."

"Ghra? That's dangerous, foolhardy and quite likely it's putting your life on the line."

"One life is nothing if it saves the convoy."

"Heroic of you, but it could also blow the game."

"I don't think so. There's been a program of infiltrations on any Khalian base we could penetrate. Why make Bethesda an exception? Don't worry, Bil. It'll be simple if I can get into place now in the bad light."

"Good theory but impractical," I replied sourly. "No trees, bushes or vegetation around that spaceport."

"But rather a lot of old craters . . ."

"You are not crater-colored . . ."

"Enticing mounds of supplies, and some unused repair hangars."

"Or," I began in a reasonable tone, "we can get out of here, go into a lunar orbit and keep our eyes peeled. All I'd need is enough time to send a squeal and the Admiral will know."

"Now who's heroic? And not very practical. We're not supposed to be sighted. And we're to try and keep the convoy from being discovered. I think I know how. Besides, Bil, this mission has several facets. One of them is proving that camouflaged Hrrubans can infiltrate Khalian positions and obtain valuable information without detection."

"Ghra, get back here!"

"No!"

There wouldn't be much point of arguing with that particular, pleasant but unalterable brand of obstinacy, so I didn't try. Nor did I bother to threaten. Pulling rank on a free spirit like Ghra would be useless and a tactic I could scarcely support. Also, if she could find out whence came the expected flight, that would be vital information for the Admiral. Crucial for the convoy's safety!

At least we were now reasonably sure that the Bethesda-based Khalia had not detected those plasma blasts to clear the debris. Now, if only we could also neutralize the threat posed by incoming craft crossing the "light cone!" We needed some Luck!

"Where are you now, Ghra? Keep talking as long as it's safe and detail everything. Can you analyze what facilities the port has?"

"From what I can see, Bil, nothing more than the colonists brought with them." Having won her point, Ghra did not sound smug. I hoped that she had as much caution as camouflage.

Dutifully she described her silent prowl around the perimeter of the space facility, which I taped. Finally she reached the far side of the immense plateau, where some of the foothills had been crudely gouged deep enough to extend the landing grid for the huge colony transports. She had paused once to indulge herself in a long drink, murmuring briefly that the water on the Ocelot was much nicer.

"Ah," she said suddenly and exhaled in a snort of disgust. "Sensor rigs which the colonists certainly did not bring with them."

"You can't go through them without detection. Even if you could jump that high."

"I know that!" She rumbled as she considered.

"Ghra. Come on. Pack it in and get back to me. We can still do a lunar watch. Under the circumstances, I'd even try a solar hide." Which was one of the trickiest things a scout, even an Ocelot, could attempt. And the situation was just critical enough to make me try. Jockeying to keep just inside a sun's gravity well is a real challenge.

"You're a brave brain, Bil, but I think I've figured out how to get past the sensors. The natural way."

"What?"

"They've even supplied me with the raw materials."

"What are you talking about, Ghra? Explain!"

"I'm standing on an undercut ridge of dirt and stone, with some rather respectable boulders. Now if this mass suddenly descended thru the sensor rigs, it'd break the contact."

"And bring every Khalian from the base, but not before they'd sprayed the area with whatever they have handy, plus launch that scout squadron they've got on the pads."

"But when they see it is only sticks and stones . . ."

"Which could break your bones, and how're you going to start it all rolling?"

"Judiciously, because they really didn't shore this stuff up properly."

I could hear her exerting herself now and felt obliged to remind her of her risks even though I could well visualize what she was trying to do. But if the Khalia entertained even the remotest thought of tampering by unnatural agencies, they'd fling out a search net . . . and catch us both. Full dark was settling, so the time of their twilight myopia was nearly past. If she counted on only that to prevent them seeing her . . .

I heard the roll, her grunt and then the beginning of a mild roar.

"Rrrrrow," came from Ghra and she was running, running away from the sound. "There! Told you so!"

I could also hear the whine of Khalian alert sirens and my external monitors reflected the sudden burst of light on the skyline.

"Ghra!"

"I'm okay, okay, Bil. I'm a large rock beside two smaller ones and I shan't move a muscle all night."

I have spent the occasional fretful night now and again but this would be one of the more memorable ones. Just as I had predicted, the Khalia mounted an intensive air and land search. I willingly admit that the camouflage over me was effective. The Ocelot was overflown eight or nine times—those Khalia are nothing if not tenacious when threatened. It was nearly dawn before the search was called off and the brilliant spaceport lights were switched off.

"Ghra?" I kept my voice low.

A deep yawn preceded her response. "Bil? You're there, too. Good."

"Are you still a rock?"

"Yessss," and the slight sibilance warned me.

"But not the same rock. Right?"

"Got me in one."

"Where are you, Ghra?"

"Part of the foundation of their command post."

"Their command post?"

"Speak one decibel louder, Bil, and their audios will pick you up. It's dawn and I'm not saying anything else all day. Catch you at sunset."

I didn't have to wait all day for her next words, but it felt like a bloody Jovian year, and at that, I didn't realize that she was whispering to me for the first nano-seconds.

"They're coming in from the 700 quadrant, Bil. Straight from Target. As if they'd *planned* to intercept. And they'll be crossing the 800s by noon tomorrow. By all that's holy, there'll be no way they'd miss the ripple cone. You've got to warn the Admiral to scatter the convoy. Now. Get off now." She gave a little chuckle. "Keeping 'em up half the night was a good idea. Most of 'em are asleep. They won't see a thing if you keep it low and easy."

"Are you daft, Ghra? I can't go now. You can't move until dusk."

"Don't argue, Bil. There's no time. Even if they detect you, they can't catch you. Go now. You go FTL as soon as you're out of the gravity well and warn the Fleet. Just think of the Admiral's face when he gets a chance to go up Khalian asses for a change. You warn him in time, he can disperse the convoy and call for whatever fighters Persuasion has left. They can refuel from the convoy's pods. What a battle that will be. The Admiral's career is made! And ours. Don't worry about me. After all, I was supposed to subject the camouflage to a real test, wasn't I."

Her low voice rippled slightly with droll amusement.

"But . . ."

"Go!" Her imperative was firm, almost angry. "Or it's all over for that convoy. Go. Now. While they're sleeping."

She was right. I knew it, but no brain ship leaves a brawn in an exposed and dangerous situation. The convoy was also in an exposed and dangerous situation. The greater duty called. The lives of many superceded the life of one, one who had willingly sacrificed herself.

I lifted slowly, using the minimum of power the Ocelot needed. She was good like that, you could almost lift her on a feather, and that was all I intended to use. I kept at ground level, which, considering the terrain, meant some tricky piloting, but I also didn't want to go so fast that I lost that camouflage net. If I had to set down suddenly, it might save my skin.

I'm not used to dawdling, neither is the Ocelot and it needed finesse to do it, and every vestige of skill I possessed. I went back through the gap, over the water, heading toward the oncoming dusk. I'd use sunset to cover my upward thrust because I'd have to use power then. But I'd be far enough away from the big sensors at the spaceport to risk it. Maybe they'd still be snoozing. I willed those weaselly faces to have closed eyes and dulled senses and, as I tilted my nose up to the clear dark night of deep space, the camouflage net rippled down, spread briefly on the water and sank.

On my onward trajectory, I used Bethesda's two smaller moons as shields, boosting my speed out of the sun's gravity well before I turned on the FTL drive.

From the moment o.t.s. had mentioned the possibility of an incoming squadron of Khalia I had been computing a variety of courses from Target through the 700 quadrant to Bethesda's system. There was no way the Khalia would miss the convoy's emission trail entering from the 700s, and then they'd climb the tailpipes of the helpless, decelerating ships. I ran some calculations on the eta at the first gravity well maneuver the Admiral had planned and they were almost there. I had to buy them just a bit more time. This Ocelot was going to have to pretend it was advance scout for ships from another direction entirely.

So I planned to re-enter normal space on a course perpendicular to the logical one that the Khalia would take for Bethesda when they exited FTL space. Their ships would have sensors sensitive enough to pick up my "light cone" and I'd come in well in advance of any traces which the convoy had left. If I handled it right, they'd come after me. It's rare that the Admiral's gig gets such an opportunity as this, to anticipate the enemy, to trigger a naval action which could have a tremendous effect on this everlasting war. It was too good to work out. It had to work out.

I did have several advantages to this mad scheme. The Fleet was out of FTL: the enemy not yet. I needed only a moment to send my message off to the Admiral. The rest of it was up to him. The disadvantage was that I might not have the joy of seeing the Fleet running up Khalian asses.

Once in FTL, I continued to check my calculations. Even if I came out right in the midst of the approaching Khalia I could manage. I only needed two nano-seconds to launch the message and even Khalia need more than that to react.

They had to come out *somewhere* near my re-entry window. They were great ones for using gravity wells to reduce speed, and there were two suns lined up almost perfectly with Bethesda for that sort of maneuver, just far enough away to slow them down for the Bethesda landing. My risk was worth the gamble and my confidence was bolstered by the courage of a camouflaged Hrruban.

I had the message torp set and ready to launch at the *Gormenghast* as I entered normal space. I toggled it off just as the Khalian pirate ships emerged, a couple thousand klicks off my port bow, an emergence that made my brain reel. What luck!

I was spatially above them and should be quite visible on their sensors. I flipped the Ocelot, ostensibly heading back the way I had come. I sent an open Mayday in the old code, adding some jibber I had once whipped up by recording old Earth Thai backward, and sent a panic shot from the stern plasma cannon, just in case their detectors had not spotted me. I made as much "light" as I could, wallowing my tail to broaden it, trying to pretend there were three of me. Well, trying is it.

The Ocelot is a speedy beast, speedier than I let them believe, hoping they'd mistake us for one of the larger, fully manned scouts to make it worth their while to track and destroy me. The closer they got the faster they would be able to make a proper identification. I sent MAYDAY in several Alliance languages and again my Thai-jibber. Until they sent three of their real fast ones after me. It took them two days before their plasma bursts got close. I let them come in near enough for me to do some damage. I think I got one direct hit and a good cripple before I knew I was in their range. I hit the jettison moments before their cannon blew the Ocelot apart.

"Well, now, Mr. Hansing, how does that feel?" The solicitous voice was preternaturally loud through my audio circuits as consciousness returned.

"Loud and clear," I replied with considerable relief and adjusted the volume.

I'd made it after all. Sometimes we do. After all, the Fleet would have engaged the pirates, and someone was sure to search the wreckage for the vital titanium capsule that contained Mayday tapes and what was left of Lieutenant Senior Grade Bil Hansing. Brains have been known to drift a considerable time before being retrieved with no harm done.

"What've I got this time?" I asked, flicking on visual monitors.

As I half suspected, I was in the capacious maintenance bay of the Fleet's Mother, surrounded by other vehicles being repaired and reserviced. And camouflaged with paint. I made a startled sound.

"The very latest thing, Lieutenant."

I focused my visuals on the angular figure of Commander Davi Orbrinn, an officer well known to me. He still sported a trim black beard. His crews had put me back into commission half a dozen times. "An Ocelot

Mark 19, new, improved and . . ." Commander Orbrinn sighed deeply. "Camouflaged. But really, Mr. Hansing, can you not manage to get a shade more wear out of this one?"

"Did the convoy get in all right? Did the Admiral destroy the Khalia? Did anyone rescue Ghra? How long have I been out of service?"

The Commander might turn up stiff but he's an affable soul.

"Yes, yes, no and six months. The Admiral insisted that you have the best. You're due back on the *Gormenghast* at 0600."

"That's cutting it fine, Davi, but thanks for all you've done for me."

He gave a pleased grunt and waggled an admonishing finger at me. "Commander Het says they've saved something special for you for your recommission flight. Consider yourself checked out and ready to go. Duty calls!"

"What else?" I replied in a buoyant tone, happy to be able to answer, and rather hopeful that duty would send me to retrieve a certain camouflaged Hrruban.

And that was exactly what Duty called for.

Black Destroyer

A.E. Van Vogt

On and on Coeurl prowled! The black, moonless, almost starless night yielded reluctantly before a grim reddish dawn that crept up from his left. A vague, dull light, it was, that gave no sense of approaching warmth, no comfort, nothing but a cold, diffuse lightness, slowly revealing a nightmare landscape.

Black, jagged rock and black, unliving plain took form around him, as a pale-red sun peered at last above the grotesque horizon. It was then Coeurl recognized suddenly that he was on familiar ground.

He stopped short. Tenseness flamed along his nerves. His muscles pressed with sudden, unrelenting strength against his bones. His great forelegs—twice as long as his hindlegs—twitched with a shuddering movement that arched every razor-sharp claw. The thick tentacles that sprouted from his shoulders ceased their weaving undulation, and grew taut with anxious alertness.

Utterly appalled, he twisted his great cat head from side to side, while the little hairlike tendrils that formed each ear vibrated frantically, testing every vagrant breeze, every throb in the ether.

But there was no response, no swift tingling along his

intricate nervous system, not the faintest suggestion anywhere of the presence of the all-necessary id. Hopelessly, Coeurl crouched, an enormous catlike figure silhouetted against the dim reddish skyline, like a distorted etching of a black tiger resting on a black rock in a shadow world.

He had known this day would come. Through all the centuries of restless search, this day had loomed ever nearer, blacker, more frightening—this inevitable hour when he must return to the point where he began his systematic hunt in a world almost depleted of id-creatures.

The truth struck in waves like an endless, rhythmic ache at the seat of his ego. When he had started, there had been a few id-creatures in every hundred square miles, to be mercilessly rooted out. Only too well Coeurl knew in this ultimate hour that he had missed none. There were no id-creatures left to eat. In all the hundreds of thousands of square miles that he had made his own by right of ruthless conquest—until no neighboring coeurl dared to question his sovereignty—there was no id to feed the otherwise immortal engine that was his body.

Square foot by square foot he had gone over it. And now—he recognized the knoll of rock just ahead, and the black rock bridge that formed a queer, curling tunnel to his right. It was in that tunnel he had lain for days, waiting for the simple-minded, snakelike id-creature to come forth from its hole in the rock to bask in the sun—his first kill after he had realized the absolute necessity of organized extermination.

He licked his lips in brief gloating memory of the moment his slavering jaws tore the victim into precious tooth-some hits. But the dark fear of an idless universe swept the sweet remembrance from his consciousness, leaving only certainty of death.

He snarled audibly, a defiant, devilish sound that quavered on the air, echoed and re-echoed among the rocks, and shuddered back along his nerves—instinctive and hellish expression of his will to live.

And then—abruptly—it came.

* * *

He saw it emerge out of the distance on a long downward slant, a tiny glowing spot that grew enormously into a metal ball. The great shining globe hissed by above Coeurl, slowing visibly in quick deceleration. It sped over a blank line of hills to the right, hovered almost motionless for a second, then sank down out of sight.

Coeurl exploded from his startled immobility. With tiger speed, he flowed down among the rocks. His round, black eyes burned with the horrible desire that was an agony within him. His ear tendrils vibrated a message of id in such tremendous quantities that his body felt sick with the pangs of his abnormal hunger.

The little red sun was a crimson ball in the purple-black heavens when he crept up from behind a mass of rock and gazed from its shadows at the crumbling, gigantic ruins of the city that sprawled below him. The silvery globe, in spite of its great size, looked strangely inconspicuous against that vast, fairy-like reach of ruins. Yet about it was a leashed aliveness, a dynamic quiescence that, after a moment, made it stand out, dominating the foreground. A massive, rock-crushing thing of metal, it rested on a cradle made by its own weight in the harsh, resisting plain which began abruptly at the outskirts of the dead metropolis.

Coeurl gazed at the strange, two-legged creatures who stood in little groups near the brilliantly lighted opening that yawned at the base of the ship. His throat thickened with the immediacy of his need; and his brain grew dark with the first wild impulse to burst forth in furious charge and smash these flimsy, helpless-looking creatures whose bodies emitted the id-vibrations.

Mists of memory stopped that mad rush when it was still only electricity surging through his muscles. Memory that brought fear in an acid stream of weakness, pouring along his nerves, poisoning the reservoirs of his strength. He had time to see that the creatures wore things over their real bodies, shimmering transparent material that glittered in strange, burning flashes in the rays of the sun.

Other memories came suddenly. Of dim days when the city that spread below was the living, breathing heart of an age of glory that dissolved in a single century before flaming guns whose wielders knew only that for the survivors there would be an ever-narrowing supply of id.

It was the remembrance of those guns that held him there, cringing in a wave of terror that blurred his reason. He saw himself smashed by balls of metal and burned by searing flame.

Came cunning—understanding of the presence of these creatures. This, Coeurl reasoned for the first time, was a scientific expedition from another star. In the olden days, the coeurls had thought of space travel, but disaster came too swiftly for it ever to be more than a thought.

Scientists meant investigation, not destruction. Scientists in their way were fools. Bold with his knowledge, he emerged into the open. He saw the creatures become aware of him. They turned and stared. One, the smallest of the group, detached a shining metal rod from a sheath, and held it casually in one hand. Coeurl loped on, shaken to his core by the action; but it was too late to turn back.

Commander Hal Morton heard little Gregory Kent, the chemist, laugh with the embarrassed half gurgle with which he invariably announced inner uncertainty. He saw Kent fingering the spindly metalite weapon.

Kent said: "I'll take no chances with anything as big as that."

Commander Morton allowed his own deep chuckle to echo along the communicators. "That," he grunted finally, "is one of the reasons why you're on this expedition, Kent—because you never leave anything to chance."

His chuckle trailed off into silence. Instinctively, as he watched the monster approach them across that black rock plain, he moved forward until he stood a little in advance of the others, his huge form bulking the transparent metalite suit. The comments of the men pattered through the radio communicator into his ears:

"I'd hate to meet that baby on a dark night in an alley."

"Don't be silly. This is obviously an intelligent creature. Probably a member of the ruling race."

"It looks like nothing else than a big cat, if you forget those tentacles sticking out from its shoulders, and make allowances for those monster forelegs."

"Its physical development," said a voice, which Morton recognized as that of Siedel, the psychologist, "presupposes an animallike adaptation to surroundings, not an intellectual one. On the other hand, its coming to us like this is not the act of an animal but of a creature possessing a mental awareness of our possible identity. You will notice that its movements are stiff, denoting caution, which suggests fear and consciousness of our weapons. I'd like to get a good look at the end of its tentacles. If they taper into handlike appendages that can really grip objects, then the conclusion would be inescapable that it is a descendant of the inhabitants of this city. It would be a great help if we could establish communication with it, even though appearances indicate that it has degenerated into a historyless primitive."

Coeurl stopped when he was still ten feet from the foremost creature. The sense of id was so overwhelming that his brain drifted to the ultimate verge of chaos. He felt as if his limbs were bathed in molten liquid; his very vision was not quite clear, as the sheer sensuality of his desire thundered through his being.

The men—all except the little one with the shining metal rod in his fingers—came closer. Coeurl saw that they were frankly and curiously examining him. Their lips were moving, and their voices beat in a monotonous, meaningless rhythm on his ear tendrils. At the same time he had the sense of waves of a much higher frequency—his own communication level—only it was a machinelike clicking that jarred his brain. With a distinct effort to appear friendly, he broadcast his name from his ear tendrils, at the same time pointing at himself with one curving tentacle.

Gourlay, chief of communications, drawled: "I got a sort of static in my radio when he wiggled those hairs, Morton. Do you think—"

"Looks very much like it," the leader answered the unfinished question. "That means a job for you, Gourlay. If it speaks by means of radio waves, it might not be altogether impossible that you can create some sort of television picture of its vibrations, or teach him the Morse code."

"Ah," said Siedel. "I was right. The tentacles each develop into seven strong fingers. Provided the nervous system is complicated enough, those fingers could, with training, operate any machine."

Morton said: "I think we'd better go in and have some lunch. Afterward, we've got to get busy. The material men can set up their machines and start gathering data on the planet's metal possibilities, and so on. The others can do a little careful exploring. I'd like some notes on architecture and on the scientific development of this race, and particularly what happened to wreck the civilization. On Earth civilization after civilization crumbled, but always a new one sprang up in its dust. Why didn't that happen here? Any questions?"

"Yes. What about pussy? Look, he wants to come in with us."

Commander Morton frowned, an action that emphasized the deep-space pallor of his face. "I wish there was some way we could take it in with us, without forcibly capturing it. Kent, what do you think?"

"I think we should first decide whether it's an it or a him, and call it one or the other. I'm in favor of him. As for taking him in with us—" The little chemist shook his head decisively. "Impossible. This atmosphere is twenty-eight percent chlorine. Our oxygen would be pure dynamite to his lungs."

The commander chuckled. "He doesn't believe that, apparently." He watched the catlike monster follow the first two men through the great door. The men kept an anxious distance from him, then glanced at Morton questioningly. Morton waved his hand. "O.K. Open the second lock and let him get a whiff of the oxygen. That'll cure him."

A moment later, he cursed his amazement. "By Heaven, he doesn't even notice the difference! That means he hasn't any lungs, or else the chlorine is not what his lungs use. Let him in! You bet he can go in! Smith, here's a treasure house for a biologist—harmless enough if we're careful. We can always handle him. But what a metabolism!"

Smith, a tall, thin, bony chap with a long, mournful face, said in an oddly forceful voice: "In all our travels, we've found only two higher forms of life. Those dependent on chlorine, and those who need oxygen—the two elements that support combustion. I'm prepared to stake my reputation that no complicated organism could ever adapt itself to both gases in a natural way. At first thought I should say here is an extremely advanced form of life. This race long ago discovered truths of biology that we are just beginning to suspect. Morton, we mustn't let this creature get away if we can help it."

"If his anxiety to get inside is any criterion," Commander Morton laughed, "then our difficulty will be to get rid of him."

He moved into the lock with Coeurl and the two men. The automatic machinery hummed; and in a few minutes they were standing at the bottom of a series of elevators that led up to the living quarters.

"Does that go up?" One of the men flicked a thumb in the direction of the monsters.

"Better send him up alone, if he'll go in."

Coeurl offered no objection, until he heard the door slam behind him; and the closed cage shot upward. He whirled with a savage snarl, his reason swirling into chaos. With one leap, he pounced at the door. The metal bent under his plunge, and the desperate pain maddened him. Now, he was all trapped animal. He smashed at the metal with his paws, bending it like so much tin. He tore great bars loose with his thick tentacles. The machinery screeched; there were horrible jerks as the limitless power pulled the cage along in spite of projecting pieces of metal that scraped the outside walls. And then the cage stopped, and he snatched off the rest of the door and hurtled into the corridor.

He waited there until Morton and the men came up with drawn weapons. "We're fools," Morton said. "We should have shown him how it works. He thought we'd double-crossed him."

He motioned to the monster, and saw the savage glow fade from the coal-black eyes as he opened and closed the door with elaborate gestures to show the operation.

Coeurl ended the lesson by trotting into the large room to his right. He lay down on the rugged floor, and fought down the electric tautness of his nerves and muscles. A very fury of rage against himself for his fright consumed him. It seemed to his burning brain that he had lost the advantage of appearing a mild and harmless creature. His strength must have startled and dismayed them.

It meant greater danger in the task which he now knew he must accomplish: To kill everything in the ship, and take the machine back to their world in search of unlimited id.

With unwinking eyes, Coeurl lay and watched the two men clearing away the loose rubble from the metal doorway of the huge old building. His whole body ached with the hunger of his cells for id. The craving tore through his palpitant muscles, and throbbed like a living thing in his brain. His every nerve quivered to be off after the men who had wandered into the city. One of them, he knew, had gone—alone.

The dragging minutes fled; and still he restrained himself, still he lay there watching, aware that the men knew he watched. They floated a metal machine from the ship to the rock mass that blocked the great half-open door, under the direction of a third man. No flicker of their fingers escaped his fierce stare, and slowly, as the simplicity of the machinery became apparent to him, contempt grew upon him.

He knew what to expect finally, when the flame flared in incandescent violence and ate ravenously at the hard rock beneath. But in spite of his preknowledge, he deliberately jumped and snarled as if in fear, as that white heat burst forth. His ear tendrils caught the laughter of the men, their curious pleasure at his simulated dismay.

The door was released, and Morton came over and went inside with the third man. The latter shook his head.

"It's a shambles. You can catch the drift of the stuff. Obviously, they used atomic energy, but . . . but it's in wheel form. That's a peculiar development. In our science, atomic energy brought in the nonwheel machine. It's possible that here they've progressed *further* to a new type of wheel mechanics. I hope their libraries are better preserved than this, or we'll never know. What could have happened to a civilization to make it vanish like this?"

A third voice broke through the communicators: "This is Siedel. I heard your question, Pennons. Psychologically and sociologically speaking, the only reason why a territory becomes uninhabited is lack of food."

"But they're so advanced scientifically, why didn't they develop space flying and go elsewhere for their food?"

"Ask Gunlie Lester," interjected Morton. "I heard him expounding some theory even before we landed."

The astronomer answered the first call. "I've still got to verify all my facts, but this desolate world is the only planet revolving around that miserable red sun. There's nothing else. No moon, not even a planetoid. And the nearest star system is *nine hundred light-years* away.

"So tremendous would have been the problem of the ruling race of this world, that in one jump they would not only have had to solve interplanetary but interstellar space traveling. When you consider how slow our own development was—first the moon, then Venus—each success leading to the next, and after centuries to the nearest stars; and last of all to the anti-accelerators that permitted galactic travel. Considering all this, I maintain it would be impossible for any race to create such machines without practical experience. And, with the nearest star so far away, they had no incentive for the space adventuring that makes for experience."

* * *

Coeurl was trotting briskly over to another group. But now, in the driving appetite that consumed him, and in the frenzy of his high scorn, he paid no attention to what they were doing. Memories of past knowledge, jarred into activity by what he had seen, flowed into his consciousness in an ever developing and more vivid stream.

From group to group he sped, a nervous dynamo—jumpy, sick with his awful hunger. A little car rolled up, stopping in front of him, and a formidable camera whirred as it took a picture of him. Over on a mound of rock, a gigantic telescope was rearing up toward the sky. Nearby, a disintegrating machine drilled its searing fire into an ever-deepening hole, down and down, straight down.

Coeurl's mind became a blur of things he watched with half attention. And ever more imminent grew the moment when he knew he could no longer carry on the torture of acting. His brain strained with an irresistible impatience; his body burned with the fury of his eagerness to be off after the man who had gone alone into the city.

He could stand it no longer. A green foam misted his mouth, maddening him. He saw that, for the bare moment, nobody was looking.

Like a shot from a gun, he was off. He floated along in great, gliding leaps, a shadow among the shadows of the rocks. In a minute, the harsh terrain hid the spaceship and the two-legged beings.

Coeurl forgot the ship, forgot everything but his purpose, as if his brain had been wiped clear by a magic, memory-erasing brush. He circled widely, then raced into the city, along deserted streets, taking short cuts with the ease of familiarity, through gaping holes in time-weakened walls, through long corridors of moldering buildings. He slowed to a crouching lope as his ear tendrils caught the id vibrations.

Suddenly, he stopped and peered from a scatter of fallen rock. The man was standing at what must once have been a window, sending the glaring rays of his flashlight into the gloomy interior. The flashlight clicked off. The man, a heavy-set, powerful fellow, walked off with quick, alert steps. Coeurl didn't like that alertness. It presaged trouble, it meant lightning reaction to danger.

Coeurl waited till the human being had vanished around a corner, then he padded into the open. He was running now, tremendously faster than a man could walk, because his plan was clear in his brain. Like a wraith, he slipped down the next street, past a long block of buildings. He turned the first corner at top speed; and then, with dragging belly, crept into the half-darkness between the building and a huge chunk of debris. The street ahead was barred by a solid line of loose rubble that made it like a valley, ending in a narrow, bottlelike neck. The neck had its outlet just below Coeurl.

His ear tendrils caught the low-frequency waves of whistling. The sound throbbed through his being; and suddenly terror caught with icy fingers at his brain. The man would have a gun. Suppose he leveled one burst of atomic energy—*one burst*—before his own muscles could whip out in murder fury.

A little shower of rocks streamed past. And then the man was beneath him. Coeurl reached out and struck a single crushing blow at the shimmering transparent headpiece of the spacesuit. There was a tearing sound of metal and a gushing of blood. The man doubled up as if part of him had been telescoped. For a moment, his bones and legs and muscles combined miraculously to keep him standing. Then he crumpled with a metallic clank of his space armor.

Fear completely evaporated, Coeurl leaped out of hiding. With ravenous speed, he smashed the metal and the body within it to bits. Great chunks of metal, torn piecemeal from the suit, sprayed the ground. Bones cracked. Flesh crunched.

It was simple to tune in on the vibrations of the id, and to create the violent chemical disorganization that freed it from the crushed bone. The id was, Coeurl discovered, mostly in the bone.

He felt revived, almost reborn. Here was more food than he had had in the whole past year.

Three minutes, and it was over, and Coeurl was off like a thing fleeing dire danger. Cautiously, he approached the glistening globe from the opposite side to that by which he had left. The men were all busy at their tasks. Gliding noiselessly, Coeurl slipped unnoticed up to a group of men.

Morton stared down at the horror of tattered flesh, metal and blood on the rock at his feet, and felt a tightening in his throat that prevented speech. He heard Kent say:

"He *would* go alone, damn him!" The little chemist's voice held a sob imprisoned; and Morton remembered that Kent and Jarvey had chummed together for years in the way only two men can.

"The worst part of it is," shuddered one of the men, "it looks like a senseless murder. His body is spread out like little lumps of flattened jelly, but it seems to be all there. I'd almost wager that if we weighed everything here, there'd still be one hundred and seventy-five pounds by earth gravity. That'd be about one hundred and seventy pounds here."

Smith broke in, his mournful face lined with gloom: "The killer attacked Jarvey, and then discovered his flesh was alien—uneatable. Just like our big cat. Wouldn't eat anything we set before him—" His words died out in sudden, queer silence. Then he said slowly: "Say, what about that creature? He's big enough and strong enough to have done this with his own little paws."

Morton frowned. "It's a thought. After all, he's the only living thing we've seen. We can't just execute him on suspicion, of course—"

"Besides," said one of the men, "he was never out of my sight."

Before Morton could speak, Siedel, the psychologist, snapped, "Positive about that?"

The man hesitated. "Maybe he was for a few minutes. He was wandering around so much, looking at everything."

"Exactly," said Siedel with satisfaction. He turned to Morton. "You see, commander, I, too, had the impression that he was always around; and yet, thinking back over it, I find gaps. There were moments—probably long minutes—when he was completely out of sight."

Morton's face was dark with thought, as Kent broke in fiercely: "I say, take no chances. Kill the brute on suspicion before he does any more damage."

Morton said slowly: "Korita, you've been wandering around with Cranessy and Van Horne. Do you think pussy is a descendant of the ruling class of this planet?"

The tall Japanese archeologist stared at the sky as if collecting his mind. "Commander Morton," he said finally, respectfully, "there is a mystery here. Take a look, all of you, at that majestic skyline. Notice the almost Gothic outline of the architecture. In spite of the megalopolis which they created, these people were close to the soil. The buildings are not simply ornamented. They are ornamental in themselves. Here is the equivalent of the Doric column, the Egyptian pyramid, the Gothic cathedral, growing out of the ground, earnest, big with destiny. If this lonely, desolate world can be regarded as a mother earth, then the land had a warm, a spiritual place in the hearts of the race.

"The effect is emphasized by the winding streets. Their machines prove they were mathematicians, but they were artists first; and so they did not create the geometrically designed cities of the ultra-sophisticated world metropolis. There is a genuine artistic abandon, a deep joyous emotion written in the curving and unmathematical arrangements of houses, buildings and avenues; a sense of intensity, of divine belief in an inner certainty. This is not a decadent, hoary-with-age civilization, but a young and vigorous culture, confident, strong with purpose.

"There it ended. Abruptly, as if at this point culture had its Battle of Tours, and began to collapse like the ancient Mohammedan civilization. Or as if in one leap it spanned the centuries and entered the period of contending states. In the Chinese civilization that period occupied 480-230 B.C., at the end of which the State of Tsin saw the beginning of the Chinese Empire. This phase Egypt experienced between 1780-1580 B.C. of which the last century was the 'Hyksos'—unmentionable—time. The classical experienced it from Chæronea—338—and, at the pitch of horror, from the Gracchi—133—to Actium—31 B.C. The West European Americans were devastated by it in the nineteenth and twentieth centuries, and modern historians agree that, nominally, we entered the same phase fifty years ago; though, of course, we have solved the problem.

"You may ask, commander, what has all this to do with your question? My answer is: there is no record of a culture entering abruptly into the period of contending states. It is always a slow development: and the first step is a merciless questioning of all that was once held sacred. Inner certainties cease to exist, are dissolved before the ruthless probings of scientific and analytic minds. The skeptic becomes the highest type of being.

"I say that this culture ended abruptly in its most flourishing age. The sociological effects of such a catastrophe would be a sudden vanishing of morals, a reversion to almost bestial criminality, unleavened by any sense of ideal, a callous indifference to death. If this . . . this pussy is a descendant of such a race, then he will be a cunning creature, a thief in the night, a cold-blooded murderer, who would cut his own brother's throat for gain."

"That's enough!" It was Kent's clipped voice. "Commander, I'm willing to act the role of executioner."

Smith interrupted sharply: "Listen, Morton, you're not going to kill that cat yet, even if he is guilty. He's a biological treasure house."

Kent and Smith were glaring angrily at each other. Morton frowned at them thoughtfully, then said: "Korita, I'm inclined to accept your theory as a working basis. But one question: Pussy comes from a period earlier than our own? That is, we are entering the highly civilized era of our culture, while he became suddenly historyless in the most vigorous period of his. *But* it is possible that his culture is a later one on this planet than ours is in the galactic-wide system we have civilized?"

"Exactly. His may be the middle of the tenth civilization of his world; while ours is the end of the eighth sprung from Earth, each of the ten, of course, having been builded on the ruins of the one before it."

"In that case, pussy would not know anything about the skepticism that made it possible for us to find him out so positively as a criminal and murderer?"

"No; it would be literally magic to him."

Morton was smiling grimly. "Then I think you'll get your wish, Smith. We'll let pussy live; and if there are any fatalities, now that we know him, it will be due to rank carelessness. There's just the chance, of course, that we're wrong. Like Siedel, I also have the impression that he was always around. But now—we can't leave poor Jarvey here like this. We'll put him in a coffin and bury him."

"No, we won't!" Kent barked. He flushed. "I beg your pardon, commander. I didn't mean it that way. I maintain pussy wanted something from that body. It looks to be all there, but something must be missing. I'm going to find out what, and pin this murder on him so that you'll have to believe it beyond the shadow of a doubt."

It was late night when Morton looked up from a book and saw Kent emerge through the door that led from the laboratories below.

Kent carried a large, flat bowl in his hands; his tired eyes flashed across at Morton, and he said in a weary, yet harsh, voice: "Now watch!"

He started toward Coeurl, who lay sprawled on the great rug, pretending to be asleep.

Morton stopped him. "Wait a minute, Kent. Any other time, I wouldn't question your actions, but you look ill; you're overwrought. What have you got there?"

Kent turned, and Morton saw that his first impression had been but a flashing glimpse of the truth. There were dark pouches under the little chemist's gray eyes—eyes that gazed feverishly from sunken cheeks in an ascetic face.

"I've found the missing element," Kent said. "It's phosphorus. There wasn't so much as a square millimeter of phosphorus left in Jarvey's bones. Every bit of it had been drained out—by what superchemistry I don't know. There are ways of getting phosphorus out of the human body. For instance, a quick way was what happened to the workman who helped build this ship. Remember, he fell into fifteen tons of molten metalite—at least, so his relatives claimed—but the company wouldn't pay compensation until the metalite, on analysis, was found to contain a high percentage of phosphorus—"

"What about the bowl of food?" somebody interrupted. Men were putting away magazines and books, looking up with interest.

"It's got organic phosphorus in it. He'll get the scent, or whatever it is that he uses instead of scent—"

"I think he gets the vibrations of things," Gourlay interjected lazily. "Sometimes, when he wiggles those tendrils, I get a distinct static on the radio. And then, again, there's no reaction, just as if he's moved higher or lower on the wave scale. He seems to control the vibrations at will."

Kent waited with obvious impatience until Gourlay's last word, then abruptly went on: "All right, then, when he gets the vibration of the phosphorus and reacts to it like an animal, then—well, we can decide what we've proved by his reaction. Can I go ahead, Morton?"

"There are three things wrong with your plan," Morton said. "In the first place, you seem to assume that he is only animal; you seem to have forgotten he may not be hungry after Jarvey; you seem to think that he will not be suspicious. But set the bowl down. His reaction may tell us something."

Coeurl stared with unblinking black eyes as the man set the bowl before him. His ear tendrils instantly caught the id-vibrations from the contents of the bowl—and he gave it not even a second glance.

He recognized this two-legged being as the one who

had held the weapon that morning. Danger! With a snarl, he floated to his feet. He caught the bowl with the fingerlike appendages at the end of one looping tentacle, and emptied its contents into the face of Kent, who shrank back with a yell.

Explosively, Coeurl flung the bowl aside and snapped a hawser-thick tentacle around the cursing man's waist. He didn't bother with the gun that hung from Kent's belt. It was only a vibration gun, he sensed—atomic powered, but not an atomic disintegrator. He tossed the kicking Kent onto the nearest couch—and realized with a hiss of dismay that he should have disarmed the man.

Not that the gun was dangerous—but, as the man furiously wiped the gruel from his face with one hand, he reached with the other for his weapon. Coeurl crouched back as the gun was raised slowly and a white beam of flame was discharged at his massive head.

His ear tendrils hummed as they canceled the efforts of the vibration gun. His round, black eyes narrowed as he caught the movement of men reaching for their metalite guns. Morton's voice lashed across the silence.

"Stop!"

Kent clicked off his weapon; and Coeurl crouched down, quivering with fury at this man who had forced him to reveal something of his power.

"Kent," said Morton coldly, "you're not the type to lose your head. You deliberately tried to kill pussy, knowing that the majority of us are in favor of keeping him alive. You know what our rule is: If anyone objects to my decision, he must say so *at the time*. If the majority object, my decisions are overruled. In this case, no one but you objected, and, therefore, your action in taking the law into your own hands is most reprehensible, and automatically debars you from voting for a year."

Kent stared grimly at the circle of faces. "Korita was right when he said ours was a highly civilized age. It's decadent." Passion flamed harshly in his voice. "My God, isn't there a man here who can see the horror of the situation? Jarvey dead only a few hours, and this creature, whom we all know to be guilty, lying there unchained, planning his next murder; and the victim is right here in this room. What kind of men are we—fools, cynics, ghouls—or is it that our civilization is so steeped in reason that we can contemplate a murderer sympathetically?"

He fixed brooding eyes on Coeurl. "You were right, Morton, that's no animal. That's a devil from the deepest hell of this forgotten planet, whirling its solitary way around a dying sun."

"Don't go melodramatic on us," Morton said. "Your analysis is all wrong, so far as I am concerned. We're not ghouls or cynics; we're simply scientists, and pussy here is going to be studied. Now that we suspect him, we doubt his ability to trap any of us. One against a hundred hasn't a chance." He glanced around. "Do I speak for all of us?"

"Not for me, commander!" It was Smith who spoke, and, as Morton stared in amazement, he continued: "In the excitement and momentary confusion, no one seems to have noticed that when Kent fired his vibration gun, the beam hit this creature squarely on his cat head and didn't hurt him."

Morton's amazed glance went from Smith to Coeurl, and back to Smith again. "Are you certain it hit him? As you say, it all happened so swiftly—when pussy wasn't hurt I simply assumed that Kent had missed him."

"He hit him in the face," Smith said positively. "A vibration gun, of course, can't even kill a man right away—but it can injure him. There's no sign of injury on pussy, though, not even a singed hair."

"Perhaps his skin is a good insulation against heat of any kind."

"Perhaps. But in view of our uncertainty, I think we should lock him up in the cage."

While Morton frowned darkly in thought, Kent spoke up. "Now you're talking sense, Smith."

Morton asked: "Then you would be satisfied, Kent, if we put him in the cage?"

Kent considered, finally: "Yes. If four inches of microsteel can't hold him, we'd better give him the ship."

* * *

Coeurl fooled the men as they went out into the corridor. He trotted docilely along as Morton unmistakably motioned him through a door he had not hitherto seen. He found himself in a square, solid metal room. The door clanged metallically behind him; he felt the flow of power as the electric lock clicked home.

His lips parted in a grimace of hate, as he realized the trap, but he gave no other outward reaction. It occurred to him that he had progressed a long way from the sunk-into-primitiveness creature who, a few hours before, had gone incoherent with fear in an elevator cage. Now, a thousand memories of his powers were reawakened in his brain; ten thousand cunnings were, after ages of disuse, once again part of his very being.

He sat quite still for a moment on the short, heavy haunches into which his body tapered, his ear tendrils examining his surroundings. Finally, he lay down, his eyes glowing with contemptuous fire. The fools! The poor fools!

It was about an hour later when he heard the man—Smith—fumbling overhead. Vibrations poured upon him, and for just an instant he was startled. He leaped to his feet in pure terror—and then realized that the vibrations *were* vibrations, not atomic explosions. Somebody was taking pictures of the inside of his body.

He crouched down again, but his ear tendrils vibrated, and he thought contemptuously: the silly fool would be surprised when he tried to develop those pictures.

After a while the man went away, and for a long time there were noises of men doing things far away. That, too, died away slowly.

Coeurl lay waiting, as he felt the silence creep over the ship. In the long ago, before the dawn of immortality, the coeurls, too, had slept at night; and the memory of it had been revived the day before when he saw some of the men dozing. At last, the vibration of two pairs of feet, pacing, pacing endlessly, was the only human-made frequency that throbbed on his ear tendrils.

Tensely, he listened to the two watchmen. The first

one walked slowly past the cage door. Then about thirty feet behind him came the second. Coeurl sensed the alertness of these men; knew that he could never surprise either while they walked separately. It meant—he must be doubly careful!

Fifteen minutes, and they came again. The moment they were past, he switched his senses from their vibrations to a vastly higher range. The pulsating violence of the atomic engines stammered its soft story to his brain. The electric dynamos hummed their muffled song of pure power. He felt the whisper of that flow through the wires in the walls of his cage, and through the electric lock of his door. He forced his quivering body into straining immobility, his senses seeking, searching, to tune in on that sibilant tempest of energy. Suddenly, his ear tendrils vibrated in harmony—he caught the surging change into shrillness of that rippling force wave.

There was a sharp click of metal on metal. With a gentle touch of one tentacle, Coeurl pushed open the door, and glided out into the dully gleaming corridor. For just a moment, he felt contempt, a glow of superiority, as he thought of the stupid creatures who dared to match their wit against a coeurl. And in that moment, he suddenly thought of other coeurls. A queer, exultant sense of race pounded through his being; the driving hate of centuries of ruthless competition yielded reluctantly before pride of kinship with the future rulers of all space.

Suddenly, he felt weighed down by his limitations, his need for other coeurls, his aloneness—one against a hundred, with the stake all eternity; the starry universe itself beckoned his rapacious, vaulting ambition. If he failed, there would never be a second chance—no time to revive long-rotted machinery, and attempt to solve the secret of space travel.

He padded along on tensed paws—through the salon—into the next corridor—and came to the first bedroom door. It stood half open. One swift flow of synchronized muscles, one swiftly lashing tentacle that caught the unresisting throat of the sleeping man, crushing it; and the lifeless head rolled crazily, the body twitched once.

Seven bedrooms; seven dead men. It was the seventh taste of murder that brought a sudden return of lust, a pure, unbounded desire to kill, return of a millennium-old habit of destroying everything containing the precious id.

As the twelfth man slipped convulsively into death, Coeurl emerged abruptly from the sensuous joy of the kill to the sound of footsteps.

They were not near—that was what brought wave after wave of fright swirling into the chaos that suddenly became his brain.

The watchmen were coming slowly along the corridor toward the door of the cage where he had been imprisoned. In a moment, the first man would see the open door—and sound the alarm.

Coeurl caught at the vanishing remnants of his reason. With frantic speed, careless now of accidental sounds, he raced—along the corridor with its bedroom doors—through the salon. He emerged into the next corridor, cringing in awful anticipation of the atomic flame he expected would stab into his face.

The two men were together, standing side by side. For one single instant, Coeurl could scarcely believe his tremendous good luck. Like a fool the second had come running when he saw the other stop before the open door. They looked up, paralyzed, before the nightmare of claws and tentacles, the ferocious cat head and hate-filled eyes.

The first man went for his gun, but the second, physically frozen before the doom he saw, uttered a shriek, a shrill cry of horror that floated along the corridors—and ended in a curious gurgle, as Coeurl flung the two corpses with one irresistible motion the full length of the corridor. He didn't want the dead bodies found near the cage. That was his one hope.

Shaking in every nerve and muscle, conscious of the terrible error he had made, unable to think coherently, he plunged into the cage. The door clicked softly shut behind him. Power flowed once more through the electric lock.

He crouched tensely, simulating sleep, as he heard the rush of many feet, caught the vibration of excited voices. He knew when somebody actuated the cage audioscope and looked in. A few moments now, and the other bodies would be discovered.

"Siedel gone!" Morton said numbly. "What are we going to do without Siedel? And Breckenridge! And Coulter and— Horrible!"

He covered his face with his hands, but only for an instant. He looked up grimly, his heavy chin outthrust as he stared into the stern faces that surrounded him. "If anybody's got so much as a germ of an idea, bring it out."

"Space madness!"

"I've thought of that. But there hasn't been a case of a man going mad for fifty years. Dr. Eggert will test everybody, of course, and right now he's looking at the bodies with that possibility in mind."

As he finished, he saw the doctor coming through the door. Men crowded aside to make way for him.

"I heard you, commander," Dr. Eggert said, "and I think I can say right now that the space-madness theory is out. The throats of these men have been squeezed to a jelly. No human being could have exerted such enormous strength without using a machine."

Morton saw that the doctor's eyes kept looking down the corridor, and he shook his head and groaned:

"It's no use suspecting pussy, doctor. He's in his cage, pacing up and down. Obviously heard the racket and— Man alive! You can't suspect him. That cage was built to hold literally *anything*—four inches of micro-steel—and there's not a scratch on the door. Kent, even you won't say, 'Kill him on suspicion,' because there can't be any suspicion, unless there's a new science here, beyond anything we can imagine—"

"On the contrary," said Smith flatly, "we have all the

evidence we need. I used the telefluor on him—you know the arrangement we have on top of the cage—and tried to take some pictures. They just blurred. Pussy jumped when the telefluor was turned on, as if he felt the vibrations.

"You all know what Gourlay said before? This beast can apparently receive and send vibrations of any lengths. The way he dominated the power of Kent's gun is final proof of his special ability to interfere with energy."

"What in the name of all the hells have we got here?" One of the men groaned. "Why, if he can control that power, and send it out in any vibrations, there's nothing to stop him killing all of us."

"Which proves," snapped Morton, "that he isn't invincible, or he would have done it long ago."

Very deliberately, he walked over to the mechanism that controlled the prison cage.

"You're not going to open the door!" Kent gasped, reaching for his gun.

"No, but if I pull this switch, electricity will flow through the floor, and electrocute whatever's inside. We've never had to use this before, so you had probably forgotten about it."

He jerked the switch hard over. Blue fire flashed from the metal, and a bank of fuses above his head exploded with a single bang.

Morton frowned. "That's funny. Those fuses shouldn't have blown! Well, we can't even look in, now. That wrecked the audios, too."

Smith said: "If he could interfere with the electric lock, enough to open the door, then he probably probed every possible danger and was ready to interfere when you threw that switch."

"At least, it proves he's vulnerable to our energies!" Morton smiled grimly. "Because he rendered them harmless. The important thing is, we've got him behind four inches of the toughest of metal. At the worst we can open the door and ray him to death. But first, I think we'll try to use the telefluor power cable—"

* * *

A commotion from inside the cage interrupted his words. A heavy body crashed against a wall, followed by a dull thump.

"He knows what we were trying to do!" Smith grunted to Morton. "And I'll bet it's a very sick pussy in there. What a fool he was to go back into that cage and does he realize it!"

The tension was relaxing; men were smiling nervously, and there was even a ripple of humorless laughter at the picture Smith drew of the monster's discomfiture.

"What I'd like to know," said Pennons, the engineer, "is, why did the telefluor meter dial jump and waver at full power when pussy made that noise? It's right under my nose here, and the dial jumped like a house afire!"

There was silence both without and within the cage, then Morton said: "It may mean he's coming out. Back, everybody, and keep your guns ready. Pussy was a fool to think he could conquer a hundred men, but he's by far the most formidable creature in the galactic system. He may come out of that door, rather than die like a rat in a trap. And he's just tough enough to take some of us with him—if we're not careful."

The men backed slowly in a solid body; and somebody said: "That's funny. I thought I heard the elevator."

"Elevator!" Morton echoed. "Are you sure, man?"

"Just for a moment I was!" The man, a member of the crew, hesitated. "We were all shuffling our feet—"

"Take somebody with you, and go look. Bring whoever dared to run off back here—"

There was a jar, a horrible jerk, as the whole gigantic body of the ship careened under them. Morton was flung to the floor with a violence that stunned him. He fought back to consciousness, aware of the other men lying all around him. He shouted: "Who the devil started those engines!"

The agonizing acceleration continued; his feet dragged with awful exertion, as he fumbled with the nearest audioscope, and punched the engine-room number. The picture that flooded onto the screen brought a deep bellow to his lips:

"It's pussy! He's in the engine room—and we're heading straight out into space."

The screen went black even as he spoke, and he could see no more.

It was Morton who first staggered across the salon floor to the supply room where the spacesuits were kept. After fumbling almost blindly into his own suit, he cut the effects of the body-torturing acceleration, and brought suits to the semiconscious men on the floor. In a few moments, other men were assisting him; and then it was only a matter of minutes before everybody was clad in metalite, with anti-acceleration motors running at half power.

It was Morton then who, after first looking into the cage, opened the door and stood, silent as the others crowded about him, to stare at the gaping hole in the real wall. The hole was a frightful thing of jagged edges and horribly bent metal, and it opened upon another corridor.

"I'll swear," whispered Pennons, "that it's impossible. The ten-ton hammer in the machine shops couldn't more than dent four inches of micro with one blow—and we only heard one. It would take at least a minute for an atomic disintegrator to do the job. Morton, this is a super-being."

Morton saw that Smith was examining the break in the wall. The biologist looked up. "If only Breckenridge weren't dead! We need a metallurgist to explain this. Look!"

He touched the broken edge of the metal. A piece crumbled in his finger and slithered away in a fine shower of dust to the floor. Morton noticed for the first time that there was a little pile of metallic debris and dust.

"You've hit it." Morton nodded. "No miracle of strength here. The monster merely used his special powers to interfere with the electronic tensions holding the metal together. That would account, too, for the drain on the telefluor power cable that Pennons noticed. The thing used the power with his body as a transforming medium, smashed through the wall, ran down the corridor to the elevator shaft, and so down to the engine room."

"In the meantime, commander," Kent said quietly, "we are faced with a super-being in control of the ship, completely dominating the engine room, and its almost unlimited power, and in possession of the best part of the machine shops."

Morton felt the silence, while the men pondered the chemist's words. Their anxiety was a tangible thing that lay heavily upon their faces; in every expression was the growing realization that here was the ultimate situation in their lives; their very existence was at stake, and perhaps much more. Morton voiced the thought in everybody's mind:

"Suppose he wins. He's utterly ruthless, and he probably sees galactic power within his grasp."

"Kent is wrong," barked the chief navigator. "The thing doesn't dominate the engine room. We've still got the control room, and that gives us *first* control of all the machines. You fellows may not know the mechanical set-up we have; but, though he can eventually disconnect us, we can cut off all the switches in the engine room *now*. Commander, why didn't you just shut off the power instead of putting us into spacesuits? At the very least you could have adjusted the ship to the acceleration."

"For two reasons," Morton answered. "Individually, we're safer within the force fields of our spacesuits. And we can't afford to give up our advantages in panicky moves."

"Advantages. What other advantages have we got?"

"We know things about him," Morton replied. "And right now, we're going to make a test. Pennons, detail five men to each of the four approaches to the engine room. Take atomic disintegrators to blast through the big doors. They're all shut, I noticed. He's locked himself in.

"Selenski, you go up to the control room and shut off everything except the drive engines. Gear them to the master switch, and shut them off all at once. One thing, though—leave the acceleration on full blast. No anti-acceleration must be applied to the ship. Understand?"

"Aye, sir!" The pilot saluted.

"And report to me through the communicators if any of the machines start to run again." He faced the men. "I'm going to lead the main approach. Kent, you take No. 2; Smith, No. 3, and Pennons, No. 4. We're going to find out right now if we're dealing with unlimited science, or a creature limited like the rest of us. I'll bet on the last possibility."

Morton had an empty sense of walking endlessly, as he moved, a giant of a man in his transparent space armor, along the glistening metal tube that was the main corridor of the engine-room floor. Reason told him the creature had already shown feet of clay, yet the feeling that here was an invincible being persisted.

He spoke into the communicator: "It's no use trying to sneak up on him. He can probably hear a pin drop. So just wheel up your units. He hasn't been in that engine room long enough to do anything.

"As I've said, this is largely a test attack. In the first place, we could never forgive ourselves if we didn't try to conquer him now, before he's had time to prepare against us. But, aside from the possibility that we can destroy him immediately, I have a theory.

"The idea goes something like this: Those doors are built to withstand accidental atomic explosions, and it will take fifteen minutes for the atomic disintegrators to smash them. During that period the monster will have no power. True, the drive will be on, but that's straight atomic explosion. My theory is, he can't touch stuff like that; and in a few minutes you'll see what I mean—I hope."

His voice was suddenly crisp: "Ready, Selenski?"

"Aye, ready."

"Then cut the master switch."

The corridor—the whole ship, Morton knew—was abruptly plunged into darkness. Morton clicked on the dazzling light of his spacesuit; the other men did the same, their faces pale and drawn.

"Blast!" Morton barked into his communicator.

The mobile units throbbed; and then pure atomic flame ravened out and poured upon the hard metal of the door. The first molten droplet rolled reluctantly, not down, but up the door. The second was more normal. It followed a shaky downward course. The third rolled sideways—for this was pure force, not subject to gravitation. Other drops followed until a dozen streams trickled sedately yet unevenly in every direction—streams of hellish, sparkling fire, bright as fairy gems, alive with the coruscating fury of atoms suddenly tortured, and running blindly, crazy with pain.

The minutes ate at time like a slow acid. At last Morton asked huskily:

"Selenski?"

"Nothing yet, commander."

Morton half whispered: "But he must be doing something. He can't be just waiting in there like a cornered rat. Selenski?"

"Nothing, commander."

Seven minutes, eight minutes, then twelve.

"Commander!" It was Selenski's voice, taut. "He's got the electric dynamo running."

Morton drew a deep breath, and heard one of his men say:

"That's funny. We can't get any deeper. Boss, take a look at this."

Morton looked. The little scintilating streams had frozen rigid. The ferocity of the disintegrators vented in vain against metal grown suddenly invulnerable.

Morton sighed. "Our test is over. Leave two men guarding every corridor. The others come up to the control room."

He seated himself a few minutes later before the massive control keyboard. "So far as I'm concerned the test was a success. We know that of all the machines in the engine room, the most important to the monster was the electric dynamo. He must have worked in a frenzy of terror while we were at the doors."

"Of course, it's easy to see what he did," Pennons said. "Once he had the power he increased the electronic tensions of the door to their ultimate."

"The main thing is this," Smith chimed in. "He works with vibrations only so far as his special powers are concerned, and the energy must come from outside himself. Atomic energy in its pure form, not being vibration, he can't handle any differently than we can."

Kent said glumly: "The main point in my opinion is that he stopped us cold. What's the good of knowing that his control over vibrations did it? If we can't break through those doors with our atomic disintegrators, we're finished."

Morton shook his head. "Not finished—but we'll have to do some planning. First, though, I'll start these engines. It'll be harder for him to get control of them when they're running."

He pulled the master switch back into place with a jerk. There was a hum, as scores of machines leaped into violent life in the engine room a hundred feet below. The noises sank to a steady vibration of throbbing power.

Three hours later, Morton paced up and down before the men gathered in the salon. His dark hair was uncombed; the space pallor of his strong face emphasized rather than detracted from the outthrust aggressiveness of his jaw. When he spoke, his deep voice was crisp to the point of sharpness:

"To make sure that our plans are fully co-ordinated, I'm going to ask each expert in turn to outline his part in the overpowering of this creature. Pennons first!"

Pennons stood up briskly. He was not a big man, Morton thought, yet he looked big, perhaps because of his air of authority. This man knew engines, and the history of engines. Morton had heard him trace a machine through its evolution from a simple toy to the highly complicated modern instrument. He had studied machine development on a hundred planets; and there was literally nothing fundamental that he didn't know about mechanics. It was almost weird to hear Pennons, who could have spoken for a thousand hours and still only have touched upon his subject, say with absurd brevity:

"We've set up a relay in the control room to start and stop every engine rhythmically. The trip lever will work a hundred times a second, and the effect will be to create vibrations of every description. There is just a possibility that one or more of the machines will burst, on the principle of soldiers crossing a bridge in step—you've heard that old story, no doubt—but in my opinion there is no real danger of a break of that tough metal. The main purpose is simply to interfere with the interference of the creature, and smash through the doors."

"Gourlay next!" barked Morton.

Gourlay climbed lazily to his feet. He looked sleepy, as if he was somewhat bored by the whole proceedings, yet Morton knew he loved people to think him lazy, a good-for-nothing slouch, who spent his days in slumber and his nights catching forty winks. His title was chief communication engineer, but his knowledge extended to every vibration field; and he was probably, with the possible exception of Kent, the fastest thinker on the ship. His voice drawled out, and—Morton noted—the very deliberate assurance of it had a soothing effect on the men—anxious faces relaxed, bodies leaned back more restfully:

"Once inside," Gourlay said, "we've rigged up vibration screens of pure force that should stop nearly everything he's got on the ball. They work on the principle of reflection, so that everything he sends will be reflected back to him. In addition, we've got plenty of spare electric energy that we'll just feed him from mobile copper cups. There must be a limit to his capacity for handling power with those insulated nerves of his."

"Selenski!" called Morton.

The chief pilot was already standing, as if he had anticipated Morton's call. And that, Morton reflected, was the man. His nerves had that rocklike steadiness which is the first requirement of the master controller of a great ship's movements; yet that very steadiness seemed to rest on dynamite ready to explode at its owner's volition. He was not a man of great learning, but he "reacted" to stimuli so fast that he always seemed to be anticipating.

"The impression I've received of the plan is that it must be cumulative. Just when the creature thinks that he can't stand any more, another thing happens to add to his trouble and confusion. When the uproars's at its height, I'm supposed to cut in the anti-accelerators. The commander thinks with Gunlie Lester that these creatures will know nothing about anti-acceleration. It's a development, pure and simple, of the science of interstellar flight, and couldn't have been developed in any other way. We think when the creature feels the first effects of the anti-acceleration—you all remember the caved-in feeling you had the first month—it won't know what to think or do."

"Korita next."

"I can only offer you encouragement," said the archeologist, "on the basis of my theory that the monster has all the characteristics of a criminal of the early ages of any civilization, complicated by an apparent reversion to primitiveness. The suggestion has been made by Smith that his knowledge of science is puzzling, and could only mean that we are dealing with an actual inhabitant, not a descendant of the inhabitants of the dead city we visited. This would ascribe a virtual immortality to our enemy, a possibility which is borne out by his ability to breathe both oxygen and chlorine—or neither—but even that makes no difference. He comes from a certain age in his civilization; and he has sunk so low that his ideas are mostly memories of that age.

"In spite of all the powers of his body, he lost his head in the elevator the first morning, until he remembered. He placed himself in such a position that he was forced to reveal his special powers against vibrations. He bungled the mass murders a few hours ago. In fact, his whole record is one of the low cunning of the primitive, egotistical mind which has little or no conception of the vast organization with which it is confronted.

"He is like the ancient German soldier who felt superior to the elderly Roman scholar, yet the latter was part of a mighty civilization of which the Germans of that day stood in awe.

"You may suggest that the sack of Rome by the Germans in later years defeats my argument; however, modern historians agree that the 'sack' was an historical accident, and not history in the true sense of the word. The movement of the 'Sea-peoples' which set in against the Egyptian civilization from 1400 B.C. succeeded only as regards the Cretan island-realm—their mighty expeditions against the Libyan and Phœnician coasts, with the accompaniment of viking fleets, failed as those of the Huns failed against the Chinese Empire. Rome would have been abandoned in any event. Ancient, glorious Samarra was desolate by the tenth century; Pataliputra, Asoka's great capital, was an immense and completely uninhabited waste of houses when the Chinese traveler Hsinan-tang visited it about A.D. 635.

"We have, then, a primitive, and that primitive is now far out in space, completely outside of his natural habitat. I say, let's go in and win."

One of the men grumbled, as Korita finished: "You can talk about the sack of Rome being an accident, and about this fellow being a primitive, but the facts are facts. It looks to me as if Rome is about to fall again; and it won't be no primitive that did it, either. This guy's got plenty of what it takes."

Morton smiled grimly at the man, a member of the crew. "We'll see about that—right now!"

In the blazing brilliance of the gigantic machine shop, Coeurl slaved. The forty-foot, cigar-shaped spaceship was nearly finished. With a grunt of effort, he completed the laborious installation of the drive engines, and paused to survey his craft.

Its interior, visible through the one aperture in the outer wall, was pitifully small. There was literally room for nothing but the engines—and a narrow space for himself.

He plunged frantically back to work as he heard the approach of the men, and the sudden change in the tempest-like thunder of the engines—a rhythmical off-and-on hum, shriller in tone, sharper, more nerve-racking than the deep-throated, steady throb that had preceded it. Suddenly, there were the atomic disintegrators again at the massive outer doors.

He fought them off, but never wavered from his task. Every mighty muscle of his powerful body strained as he carried great loads of tools, machines and instruments, and dumped them into the bottom of his makeshift ship. There was no time to fit anything into place, no time for anything—no time—no time.

The thought pounded at his reason. He felt strangely weary for the first time in his long and vigorous existence. With a last, tortured heave, he jerked the gigantic sheet of metal into the gaping aperture of the ship—and stood there for a terrible minute, balancing it precariously.

He knew the doors were going down. Half a dozen disintegrators concentrating on one point were irresistibly, though slowly, eating away the remaining inches. With a gasp, he released his mind from the doors and concentrated every ounce of his mind on the yard-thick outer wall, toward which the blunt nose of his ship was pointing.

His body cringed from the surging power that flowed from the electric dynamo through his ear tendrils into that resisting wall. The whole inside of him felt on fire, and he knew that he was dangerously close to carrying his ultimate load.

And still he stood there, shuddering with the awful pain, holding the unfastened metal plate with hard-clenched tentacles. His massive head pointed as in dread fascination at that bitterly hard wall.

He heard one of the engine-room doors crash inward. Men shouted; disintegrators rolled forward, their raging power unchecked. Coeurl heard the floor of the engine room hiss in protest, as those beams of atomic energy tore everything in their path to bits. The machines rolled closer; cautious footsteps sounded behind them. In a minute they would be at the flimsy doors separating the engine room from the machine shop.

Suddenly, Coeurl was satisfied. With a snarl of hate, a vindictive glow of feral eyes, he ducked into his little craft, and pulled the metal plate down into place as if it was a hatchway.

His ear tendrils hummed, as he softened the edges of the surrounding metal. In an instant, the place was more than welded—it was part of his ship, a seamless, rivetless part of a whole that was solid opaque metal except for two transparent areas, one in the front, one in the rear.

His tentacle embraced the power drive with almost sensuous tenderness. There was a forward surge of his fragile machine, straight at the great outer wall of the machine shops. The nose of the forty-foot craft touched—and the wall dissolved in a glittering shower of dust.

Coeurl felt the barest retarding movement; and then he kicked the nose of the machine out into the cold of space, twisted it about, and headed back in the direction from which the big ship had been coming all these hours.

Men in space armor stood in the jagged hole that yawned in the lower reaches of the gigantic globe. The men and the great ship grew smaller. Then the men were gone; and there was only the ship with its blaze of a thousand blurring portholes. The ball shrank incredibly, too small now for individual portholes to be visible.

Almost straight ahead, Coeurl saw a tiny, dim, reddish ball—his own sun, he realized. He headed toward it at full speed. There were caves where he could hide and with other coeurls build secretly a spaceship in which they could reach other planets safely—now that he knew how.

His body ached from the agony of acceleration, yet he dared not let up for a single instant. He glanced back, half in terror. The globe was still there, a tiny dot of light in the immense blackness of space. Suddenly it twinkled and was gone.

For a brief moment, he had the empty, frightened impression that just before it disappeared, it moved. But he could see nothing. He could not escape the belief that they had shut off all their lights, and were sneaking up on him in the darkness. Worried and uncertain, he looked through the forward transparent plate.

A tremor of dismay shot through him. The dim red sun toward which he was heading was not growing larger. *It was becoming smaller* by the instant. And it grew visibly tinier during the next five minutes, became a pale-red dot in the sky—and vanished like the ship.

Fear came then, a blinding surge of it, that swept through his being and left him chilled with the sense of the unknown. For minutes, he stared frantically into the space ahead, searching for some landmark. But only the remote stars glimmered there, unwinking points against a velvet background of unfathomable distance.

Wait! One of the points was growing larger. With every muscle and nerve tensed, Coeurl watched the point becoming a dot, a round ball of light—red light. Bigger, bigger, it grew. Suddenly, the red light shimmered and turned white—and there, before him, was the great globe of the spaceship, lights glaring from every porthole, the very ship which a few minutes before he had watched vanish behind him.

Something happened to Coeurl in that moment. His brain was spinning like a flywheel, faster, faster, more incoherently. Suddenly, the wheel flew apart into a million aching fragments. His eyes almost started from their sockets as, like a maddened animal, he raged in his small quarters.

His tentacles clutched at precious instruments and flung them insensately; his paws smashed in fury at the very walls of his ship. Finally, in a brief flash of sanity, he knew that he couldn't face the inevitable fire of atomic disintegrators.

It was a simple thing to create the violent disorganization that freed every drop of id from his vital organs.

They found him lying dead in a little pool of phosphorus.

"Poor pussy," said Morton. "I wonder what he thought when he saw us appear ahead of him, after his own sun disappeared. Knowing nothing of anti-accelerators, he couldn't know that we could stop short in space, whereas it would take him more than three hours to decelerate; and in the meantime he'd be drawing farther and farther away from where he wanted to go. He couldn't know that by stopping, we flashed past him at millions of miles a second. Of course, he didn't have a chance once he left our ship. The whole world must have seemed topsy-turvy."

"Never mind the sympathy," he heard Kent say behind him. "We've got a job—to kill every cat in that miserable world."

Korita murmured softly: "That should be simple. They are but primitives; and we have merely to sit down, and they will come to us, cunningly expecting to delude us."

Smith snapped: "You fellows make me sick! Pussy was the toughest nut we ever had to crack. He had everything he needed to defeat us—"

Morton smiled as Korita interrupted blandly: "Exactly, my dear Smith, except that he reacted according to the biological impulses of his type. His defeat was already foreshadowed when we unerringly analyzed him as a criminal from a certain era of his civilization.

"It was history, honorable Mr. Smith, our knowledge of history that defeated him," said the Japanese archeologist, reverting to the ancient politeness of his race.

The Pride

Todd Hamilton and P.J. Beese

The blade flashed down, swift and hard, severing the umbilical. Captain Ki Lawwnum watched the small spurt of blood, then lifted the blade in salute to the new child. Taking a small square of silk, he wiped the blade carefully, then turned to the Empress. Her ladies were attempting to make her comfortable, so he did not approach. She was tired, tried to her limits. Even so, he thought she was the most regal human woman alive. It had not been an easy birth. Even Ki, Lionman of the Imperial Guard, was tired, the hours having taken their toll, and yet his only job had been to watch and wait. And still Elena Accalia, Empress Imperia of the Gran Imperium Alligantia, after her pain and exertion, retained all of her grandeur. A squall from the new infant drew Ki's attention. A nurse held the babe on an open blanket in outstretched arms for the Emperor's inspection.

Royal lips pursed in distaste, bringing the Emperor's full sensual mouth into a tight circle. His dark brows drew together over muddy brown eyes giving him the look of a hunting bird of prey.

"Unsatisfactory, Elena. Most unsatisfactory."

The dragons embroidered on his golden robe writhed

around each other as he swirled out of the sterile sea-foam green chamber.

Ki's hands, the right one natural, tawny as the rest of him, strong-nailed and fine-fingered, the left mechanical, grey metallic, automatically straightened his meticulous uniform.

"Your Majesty," he said, the sorrow he felt for the Emperor's reaction thickening his deep, rich voice.

Elena Accalia regarded this Lionman carefully. The distaste he felt for the Emperor's reaction did not escape her, even now in her extreme weariness. How long had he been with her? Ever since she had been sent from her own planet to the Homeworld to be the wife of the Emperor. He had been among those sent to escort her. His mane had been totally dark then. It seemed the years spent in this Emperor's court took their toll even on the long-lived Lionmen. The grey-white streaking his mane now was not unattractive, however, and Elena remembered the many kindnesses to her that had probably added to the streaks as she took his metallic hand in hers.

Ki "felt" the pressure of her touch, the softness of her skin, through his sensory receptors, but none of her warmth. That was not one of the hand's capabilities.

"Ki, the child is a girl. Firstborn, and a girl. Her life is in danger from her first breath." Elena took the square of silk and lifted it into his line of vision. "Her blood and mine are tied to your sword, Ki. Protect her. Love her. Stay with her as long as you can. Teach her the things she needs to know. Ki Lawwnum, I put her in your care." Elena tucked the silk into Ki's hand.

Ki bowed to his Empress, acknowledging her wishes, awed by the responsibility and the trust placed in him, and inserted the square of silk carefully into his sash. He felt unworthy in spite of his long association with the Empress. He gently withdrew his hand from her grasp, promised again with his eyes to do his best to obey her command, and backed respectfully out of the room to go to the royal nursery to stand guard over his newest charge until utter fatigue forced him to seek rest.

* * *

The door slid aside into its pocket and Aubin stepped back involuntarily, startled, as a rumbling war cry reverberated down the palace corridor. Looming over him, glowing menacingly in the bright yellow light from the hallway was a wild Nidean dressed in the deep desert robes of his people, untamed golden-brown mane free to the winds and stippled with braided-in beads. The warrior's face, with the ochre and scarlet tattoos that denoted his Pride, was a hardened mask of determination. The outstretched, gently curved hoj, the longer of the two blades Nideans traditionally wore, swept past Aubin's face. He shied as he felt the cold breath of air that followed it, too late, though, to have avoided the stroke had it been intended to be deadly.

Then, from behind the Nidean, Aubin caught a flash of blue-white skin, and he sank heavily against the wall of the wide palace hallway, shaking with warm relief.

"That's a damned puppet!" he exclaimed as his heart rate slowly began to recede to normal. "Ki Lawwnum, how could you do that to me?"

Lawwnum answered with his rumbling Nidean laugh, and dropped the massive puppet's head and built-in harness from its place on his wide, well-muscled shoulder. "I was a little homesick, and the 'General' here was helping me to practice my Pridecaft. Surely you remember 'General' Haarwaa?"

Aubin forced himself away from the wall and tugged at the royal blue skinsuit he was sporting on his stocky frame. "I'm afraid I don't," he said, with just a little acidity.

Ki grabbed the puppet's hair and raised the face so that it peered down into Aubin's. "Look again, my friend. He's been hanging on my living room wall ever since I took over these quarters."

Aubin studied the mask. Now that it was not animated, and therefore decidedly less vicious, he recalled. He nodded to Ki, then, drawn by this masterwork of the carver's craft, reached out to touch the heavily defined features with a tentative finger. He leaned in closer, and the distinctive odor of the wallumnar wood from which such puppets were traditionally carved reached him. It was an odor he loved, rich and clean, and it brought a smile to his world-weary face.

Ki gently pulled the puppet back. Aubin followed and Ki closed the door.

"You remember who Haarwaa was, don't you?" he asked Aubin.

Slightly embarrassed, the Lunar Envoy answered, "Sorry. I'm not up on such things."

Ki seated himself on one of the padded wooden benches that served as furniture in his spartan quarters and began to adjust the buckles that held the puppet's feet to his knees. "It was Haarwaa who united the Prides to keep the Imperium from overrunning Nide." Then he stood and raised the puppet's head so that it fitted with its harness over his left shoulder. He placed his hands into those of the puppet, and suddenly "General" Haarwaa lived again, a vicious, antique Nidean come to life out of dusty history.

"Please, sir," the "General" rumbled in full Nidean intonation. "Take a seat. There's a story to be told."

The hair on Aubin's arms raised, and he felt his skin prickle. The Nidean rumble, raspy and rash, always did that to him. He collapsed into the offered chair, afraid to speak, wanting very much to see the living history of Nide's oral tradition, something very few outsiders were ever permitted.

The "General" began to move, stalking an invisible quarry, eyes shifting, head turning, shoulders lifting, hands gesturing, all with the fluid grace of water over stone, and Ki no longer existed except as a white nimbus, a shadow, a ghost to match Haarwaa's movements.

Aubin forced himself to look away from the puppet and to his friend of some twenty years. Ki's leonine face with its broad, flat nose was only partially visible behind the cloud of Haarwaa's hair, but its fierce Lawwnum Pride tattoo of rose-colored swirls on the cheek and short, black downward strokes at the corners of the mouth were still impressive. Ki's mane, worn in the full style similar to that of the Lionmen of the Kabuki theatre of old Japan, floated like a blue-white halo behind the puppet's head. Then the "General" began the tale, and Ki once more faded from existence.

"When the Eighth Ozenscebo held the throne," rumbled Haarwaa, "he began the era of exploration. Many worlds were brought under his sway, and one was not. That one, *vateem*, friend, was Nide.

"When the Emperor's ships first filled our skies, we watched. When the soldiers landed, we killed them."

Aubin marvelled at the tidal fullness of the motions, the wholeness, the reality of what he was seeing. This was a wild Nidean, untamed by contact with the "civilized" worlds. Of course he knew Ki was still there, but he had diminished into insignificance. Aubin was amazed to realize that, at that moment, only the puppet was real.

"When more soldiers landed," the "General" continued, drawing his hoj, "we killed more!" This was accented with a broad arc of the sword.

"But we were a backward people," the "General" said sadly, "at least to those with technology. And the technology was defeating us. It killed us faster than we could kill in return."

Aubin's throat was suddenly constricted. How painful it must have been to those warlike creatures to lose! And how in blazes had that emotion been communicated? What a huge effort it must be to move the monstrous puppet with such grace and ease!

"But I knew we were fierce! I knew we were many! As Didentaar, Aashtraar, Lawwnum, Streestawwn, Gelshanaam, we could not win. But, as Nideans, we could not lose!"

Aubin's head bobbed as he nodded assent.

"We joined our people into one and we began to win, destroying the technology that had destroyed us."

There was a long dramatic pause and Aubin waited breathlessly for the "General" to continue.

"This Ozenscebo was not a fool. He saw us as fighters and recognized us as the best in the known worlds. He came to me, the Emperor Himself, and made this offer. We on Nide should have autonomy in perpetuity if we would swear fealty. But if we did not swear, our world would be destroyed." Haarwaa's head dropped in weariness. "It was a hard decision, and many preferred to fight on. But at last we swore."

Aubin wanted to cheer! They'd made the right choice.

The "General" turned his head quickly in Aubin's direction and caught some hint of the Envoy's emotion. His puppeteer was extremely attuned to the human audience, refining the motions to ones the human could comprehend, smelling his reactions, listening for the little clues such as indrawn breaths and subvocal sighs.

"But that is not the end of the tale, cub!" he hissed, menace spitting from voice and pointed finger.

Aubin quickly subsided, a slight shiver of fear stealing down his spine.

"This Emperor knew he needed fighters such as we, and he was . . . intrigued by our appearance, like the demons of their legend. And so we became his special soldiers, his Guardsmen, and he called us Lionmen in their honor."

The "General" faced Aubin squarely and, step by step, approached in a most menacing fashion. Aubin found himself retreating further and further into the cushions of the chair.

"And we still do not allow your kind on our world, human!"

"Then the "General" was gone, his head thrown to one side, Ki's hands slipping from those of his ancestor's. Aubin slumped in his chair, emotionally drained, surprised at his responses. And perhaps a bit embarrassed.

"Ki, that was marvelous!" Aubin said enthusiastically as he stood to pat his friend on his muscle-hard back. "I've never seen anything like it!"

"Nor will you, I hope. That was appallingly bad."

"Bad! It was wonderful. I felt it all! All the emotion! No wonder your people know their history so well!"

Ki shook his head in denial. "No, Aubin. It was not good. At my finest I was barely acceptable. I was never even in line to be puppetmaster. And now I'm grossly out of practice."

Aubin pouted. He did not like having his praise shunted aside. "I thought it was good."

"You are uneducated," Ki responded with typical candor.

Aubin's eyes opened wide in surprise. "Nobody's told me that for a long time. I thought I was rather worldly."

"Ah," Ki replied. "But which world?"

Aubin laughed, a rich and full sound that told anyone listening that here was one who enjoyed life. Then he shook his head. "Capitol Center and Luna, but obviously not Nide." He cocked his head and studied his friend.

Ki was dressed only in a fundoshi, a white loincloth that covered the minimum, and Aubin noticed that the pattern of the hair on the Nidean's body that covered a broad area across the chest and then ran in a narrow line down the hard, flat stomach to disappear into the cloth had indeed lost its youthful reddish-gold. But in spite of the labor of working the heavy and demanding puppet, there was not the smallest sign of exertion, not even a heavy breath. The finely honed, slim, lithe body worked to perfection, every motion as supple as Ki's blue-white skin. His legs were as powerful as ever, and longer than the norm.

Ki's nose twitched, and Aubin noticed, raising an eyebrow in question.

"Nothing. A scent from the garden."

Aubin nodded, and added to his inventory the fact that Ki's extraordinarily fine olfactory sense was as sharp as ever. But as Aubin's green-flecked brown eyes stayed locked with Ki's golden, slatted ones, he could not quite keep the humor out of them.

"I may be uneducated in the ways of Nide, but may I point out that you are hardly appropriately attired for an Imperial banquet at Capitol Center?"

Ki's lip curled back partially exposing semi-pointed teeth, and a snarl rumbled heavily in his throat. "I have no use for Imperial banquets where hangers-on and leechs guzzle the Emperor's roed until they're drowning in their own senses!"

Aubin nodded. He had no use for the drug either. He had seen many a fine mind lost to the siren song of the enhanced sensory input and long, long life that roedentritic quopapavaradine provided. Though it was supposedly non-habitforming, in fact many would suicide rather than do without their daily dose.

"Nonetheless," Aubin said, "you are the Commander of the Imperial Lionman Guard, and your presence is required."

Ki sneered, making a wonderfully exaggerated wild face. "I've never needed a human to tell me my duty," he rumbled.

"Perhaps not," Aubin returned as he flipped an item from an end table in Ki's direction, "but maybe you need a nanny to see you properly dressed."

Ki grabbed the missile out of the air with his left hand unerringly, though his eyes never left Aubin's. There was a soft "chink" as the metallic hand closed over it, and any humor that had been in Ki's face fled with the sound. "If you've damaged it, human . . ." rumbled threateningly from deep in his inflated chest.

Aubin winced. "I'm sorry, Ki," he said sincerely. "Check it."

Ki opened his hand. On it rested a beautifully crafted ring, an unusual affair that wrapped completely around the hand and was constructed of tarsh, a flexible silvery metal that, in the presence of body heat, moved as its wearer did. Set in it were two opals, one larger than the other, but each of excellent color and quality. It was intact and Ki nodded his acceptance of that fact.

Aubin let out a breath he hadn't realized he was holding. He really had no idea how Ki would have reacted to the destruction of the last gift he'd received from his now-dead wife. Relief that he wouldn't need to find out flooded over him.

"Aubin, will you always try my patience?" Ki asked with great exasperation.

With a silly smile that reflected his relief, Aubin answered, "Almost certainly."

Ki's nose was twitching. Something was wrong. All things have their peculiar scent, and a Lionman, born to use his senses to hunt, trained to use his senses for his own protection and the protection of those in his care, was keenly aware of the world about him. He changed his path from the one that led into the palace and followed instead the one that led off to the practice field. He was supposed to meet the Empress, but she would understand if he were delayed. She valued the men who served her.

He sniffed. It was there, among the dust and the sweat and the body-generated heat. One of the new recruits was bathed in arrogance. The odor of it was so strong it almost wiped away the traces of Nide that still clung to the new arrivals.

Ki walked to the edge of the field, then stopped in the dappled shade of the only tree and watched. The new recruits were all dressed alike in the jumpsuits that would constitute their uniforms until they won the right to wear the red Imperial tri-lozenge. Except for wide variations in coloring, they looked much the same. They were young, lithe, tall, and eager. The eagerness made Ki smile. He remembered his own well, and sometimes felt it still.

But the arrogance he was catching was a different and dangerous thing. The cub who gave in to that would think himself invincible, and Ki wore the case-hardened proof that no one was invulnerable. He rubbed his metallic left hand with his right, remembering, then dropped it to his side and pulled the digits across the palm in an unconscious motion, not really feeling the bumps and ridges of the hand as his "fingers" crossed them.

The arrogant one was not hard to find. He was showing off. While the rest of his group worked hard just to maintain the pace Lieutenant Mikal Lawwnum set for them during dueling practice, the arrogant one ran ahead, adding fillups and flourishes to passes that were intended to be clean and simple.

Ki rested his back against the rough bark of the tree and watched for a time, satisfying himself as to the quality of Mikal's leadership. His instructions were excellent. He judged the recruits well and gave them enough to challenge, but not so much as to discourage. The recruits were a good group, too, working hard, trying for perfection, taking instruction well. Except for one.

The Commander rumbled deep in his throat while musing, then nodded to himself. It was time for them to meet the boss. He clasped his hands behind his back and strode out onto the field.

Mikal had been aware of the Commander's attendance for some time. He had not been born into the same Pride and trained by the same men as Colonel Ki himself for nothing. But the Commander's presence brought with it something akin to panic. Mikal never understood why the Colonel's presence did that to him, bringing him to the edge of losing control. It was certainly nothing about Ki personally. But every time Colonel Ki looked in on Mikal, the same thought recurred. "Oh Mmumna! Don't let me mess up now!" He ran his eyes over the group, trying to assess them the way the Commander would. They were good, and they would become excellent. Except for one, there would be no difficulties. And he would be no difficulty either if his course could be changed from one of cocky display to one of quiet excellence.

Mikal turned as he heard the Commander's step behind him. "Awwmuum!" he called and was gratified that all activity came to an instant halt.

Though the men stood still at attention, there was a kind of ripple that passed through them as they recognized the Lionman who had joined the group.

Mikal asked politely as the Commander approached, "Would you like to see how this group is coming along, sir?"

Ki nodded once.

"Bakim!" Mikal barked, and the organized disorder of a swordsmanship practice resumed.

Ki walked among the men, slipping between the mock battles as if he were made of air. He knew he was being carefully and surreptitiously watched. He also knew his visual impression was a powerful one, his white face and hair floating over the black-fleck on black of his rank's mantle, demonic even, enhanced by the facial tattoos of his Pride, pale red slashes up across the eyes trailing down into an open swirl on each cheek. It was an unsettling appearance that Ki worked hard to maintain. He sneered a bit, squinting his eyes slightly, to enhance the fierceness of his appearance. A first impression of a ferocious Commander would be a deep and lasting one, one Ki chose to cultivate.

He stopped a little aside of the mock battle involving the braggert and watched for a time, aware always of the sounds and motions at his sides and back. It would not do to have the Commander sent sprawling by an errant blow from a raw recruit. He waited, making an effort to keep the dust from the hard-packed field from clogging his nostrils. When he was certain the attention of all the others was on their own forays, he turned to the new man.

"Your name?"

"Leenoww, sir!"

"You have been having some success with the sword, I see. Would you care to try me?"

Leenoww looked startled for a moment, but then a gleam of impious glee came into his eye. What a chance to show the Commander what he could do! With luck he might even best him!

Ki knew that look and understood perfectly what it meant. He also understood its foolishness. This recruit had to learn that there was always someone better near at hand.

"Strike at me, hard, whenever you feel you are ready," Ki ordered.

"But . . . But, sir . . . ," Leenoww stammered, disconcerted. The Commander had no boken, or practice sword.

"Strike!"

With a ragged smile, Leenoww raised the wooden weapon to strike and held onto the thought that he was the best in his group. Beating Commander Ki Lawwnum was not out of the question.

Almost before Leenoww knew he'd made the decision to strike, Ki saw the muscles of the man's shoulders begin to bunch under the form-fitting fatigues. The Colonel waited until he knew where the blow was aimed, then flashed his hands outward to where the sword would be in a microsecond. Clapping his hands together over the blade, he made a twisting motion with both wrists. The boken came out of Leenoww's hands as if it had the ability of motion in its own right. The recruit would have looked down at his empty hands, but Ki moved again, and before the man's eyes could follow his brain's direction, Ki had the boken at the recruit's throat.

"It would seem you have a thing or two to learn yet, cub," Ki said softly as he slid the boken along Leenoww's throat in what would have been a fatal stroke had the blade been steel. He held the blade there momentarily, then dropped the point.

"You have the makings of an excellent swordsman," Ki said heartily, not allowing any room for resentment to grow. "Just the kind I need under me." He returned the boken and brushed the dust from his hands. Dust in his artificial hand was most annoying, grating and rubbing and slowing its reaction time.

A look of incipient hero-worship washed across Leenoww's very young, brown face. "I must learn that move!"

Ki laughed. "That move is a dangerous one, cub." He held up his left hand. "And not always successful." He turned away.

Mikal regretted he was not close enough to hear what that conversation had been. He had seen the gesture of the raised hand and was eminently curious. He had never had the nerve to ask the Commander how he'd lost the hand. The question had always seemed extremely impertinent. And he wanted to know how the situation had been handled. Somehow, the Colonel always knew exactly the right words, a trick Mikal had never mastered.

"Is there something on your mind, Lieutenant?" Ki asked in response to the dissatisfied frown on Mikal's face. "You seem most thoughtful. Come, walk with me a way and we'll speak of it." Ki took Mikal by the arm and spun him toward the palace. "Are you displeased because I interrupted?"

"No, sir!" Mikal responded, shocked.

"I felt it was time I meet this group. I suppose the

story will make the rounds." Ki said it almost with a sigh, thinking of the next wave of unlicked cubs that would want to try the Commander.

"Yes, sir." Mikal hesitated, stopped, pulled himself to perfect attention. "Sir," Mikal began, choking on his own nerve, "did you tell that recruit how you came to lose your hand?" He cringed slightly now that he'd said it, wondering if he'd made the mistake of all time.

The Commander smiled a very wicked, mischievious smile. "Let's say that the story told at dinner will be an interesting fairy tale."

Mikal was swept with a mixture of relief that the Colonel was not angered by his question, and regret bordering on sheer frustration that he still did not know the truth. But his wildly raging hero-worship colored his face and he could not question further. "Thank you, Commander," he said, lowering his eyes.

Ki smiled indulgently and patiently began to explain something he thought Mikal had missed. "I think I have done myself a favor. That man will be good with a sword in time. Perhaps very good. That is the kind of man I want and need under me. After all, Mikal, I may find him at my side one day. And Mikal," he said, turning slightly so that he was facing the Lieutenant squarely, "I saw your awareness of Leenoww's problem. Though I tried my own solution, I'm certain yours would have been as effective. I have much confidence in you."

Mikal positively glowed under the praise, and he looked with unabashed pride at the Commander. His affection for Ki was great, and he could never understand the irrational nerves that struck every time the Commander came near. He had known Ki almost as long as he could remember, though time spent together had been necessarily brief. Ki's duties kept him off Nide most of the time, and when he had returned, his business had been with the adults. But there had usually been a moment for the cub who wanted to be in the Imperial Guard. Mikal had the right to call Ki "uncle" as they were of the same Pride and the same marital line, though Ki was not, in fact, his father's brother, and that had given Mikal some trouble as he'd come up through the ranks. As a result, Mikal worked twice as hard as any other man. And praise from his boyhood hero was twice as sweet.

Ki nodded as he watched the emotions flying over Mikal's face. "Return to your men now, Mikal. I think this is a good group. Work with them."

"Yes, sir!" Mikal saluted and turned back to the practice field.

Ki watched him for a moment, then continued on his way into the palace. The Empress would understand a brief delay, but she would not tolerate one moment wasted.

The training session had been an unexpected one. Ki took the lengthy walk back to his apartments and, for once, regretted that his quarters were not in the barracks with the rest of the Guard. He wiped his face and neck with his sleeve, thinking fondly of a hot tub, all the while realizing that it would have to wait while he prepared for his meeting. He put his hand to his privacy lock and opened the door, then stopped.

Just inside the door on the floor was a small parcel, no bigger than one could hold comfortably in one hand. But there had been no package when he'd left. That meant someone had been in his apartments. He dropped the towel and stooped down to get a good look at the box. Wrapped like a gift, it looked totally harmless, but with the situation being what it was in the Empire with a rebellion aborning, he was cautious. Certainly the death of the Commander of the famous Lionman Guard would be a welcome coup, and if this were indeed a bomb, it certainly was not the first ever to make its way into the palace in spite of all security precautions. It would, however, be the first directed at Ki.

He heard nothing from the package, so he leaned slightly closer to see if the could get a hint of an identifying odor of whoever had handled the package. He sniffed. He knew exactly who had left the package. There could be no mistake.

Reaching out, he pulled a cushion from his sofa. Gingerly, he settled the parcel on the pillow and lifted it.

Then he stood, slowly. Without tipping the box, he examined it from each side. It appeared quite ordinary. He held it closer to his face and breathed deeply, hoping to discover whatever was inside. Nothing came to him but the scent of the culprit. He paused, considering. Then he shrugged. He put another pillow over the top of the box, tore the paper and pulled off the lid. He half expected a very loud bang and discovered that he'd closed his eyes. When he peeked, he inhaled sharply.

For once, the Princess had not been playing games. Inside, resting on a small, brown velvet cushion, sat a nicely striated rock, alternating banks of black and white and greys that had been geologically folded at some point to form a fascinating swirl a little off-center. With some polish, it just might become a true thing of beauty. Also inside the box was a note in the Princess' own, not-quite-mature hand that said, "For your garden." He smiled, knowing exactly where he'd put it and padded softly out the double French doors that led onto the lawn, hoping the Empress would not miss him just yet.

In actuality, the garden was not his as several of the apartments in this wing opened onto it. In practice, however, it was his private place of refuge. One of the apartments was not occupied and the tenants of the others never entered, preferring the larger, more elaborate gardens that abounded, or to stay indoors entirely. And even though there was an entrance to the garden from a hallway, the place was so little known and in such a restricted section of the palace that strangers were an extreme rarity. Gradually, therefore, the garden had taken on the personality Ki chose for it. It was a mingling of the carefully tended and planned gardens of old Japan and the wild freedom of Nide. A small patch of lawn ran up to Ki's doors, across the way to another set of doors, then jumped the small stream that trickled through the garden to end in a riot of flowers that had once only grown on Ki's planet. The stream, though small, provided the sound of running water as it splashed down over a small waterfall of rocks and dropped away over the open wall at the end of the garden that overlooked the city of Osaka. As this palace stood on a promontory that once held a medieval castle, the view into the city was magnificent, and Ki frequently watched the sun rise over the small wall.

The weapons range was a busy place just now. The junior Lionmen were attempting to move up their ratings. The quiet "pffuft" of the weapons was coming repeatedly, as were the blinding flashes of harsh white light. Mikal Lawwnum, Ki's marital line nephew, long ago found that he no longer heard the sound, but the light still disturbed him, partly because it was so intense and partly because it always reminded him of the brilliance of Nide's sun. He continued to walk the line, stopping at each man, watching, correcting, checking, making certain that they would be ready for Captain Res's inspection. Most had improved markedly. The rest would probably never improve. But even at their current stage, they were better than you'd find anywhere else in the Empire. Of course, Mikal realized, that would not be good enough for the Commander. He would keep them at it till most of them would be able to hit their marks dead center 99 times out of 100, and then push them for the extra 1. And if Ki didn't, he, Mikal, would.

"Aallaard Lawwnum."

Mikal had been watching a young Nidean ready his weapon. He responded automatically with, "Det," then looked up, surprised at being addressed in Nidean.

"Aallaard Lawwnum, why do we practice with these . . . things," asked Private Leenoww very formally while he held the small box that was the energy weapon extended on the palm of his hand. "There is no honor bound to this thing. Only a sword has honor."

Mikal considered his answer carefully, wanting very much to say the right thing for once. "Private," he answered in common, "the sword is the more elegant weapon, and certainly the sword is more useful than that," he gestured disdainfully at the energy weapon, "in a ship where one shot with one of those can rupture the hull and kill all aboard. But you must understand that these can kill, too, and at long range. There will be times when you will be asked to use them. Certainly you must understand them. But I will never ask you to give them the respect that you give your blade."

The young private considered what the Lieutenant had said, then nodded sagely. "As you say, Lieutenant. It is good to practice."

Mikal was elated. This time, it seemed, he'd said exactly the right thing.

The Empress, dressed most delicately in a blue floor-length dress that sparkled when she moved, stood watching her husband's Lionmen from a balcony, guarded and accompanied only by Commander Ki. She frequently reviewed the men from this perch which was located on the rear side of the palace and ran in an "L" around two walls, one facing the weapons range, the other an enclosed drill field. It gave her the opportunity to be alone (except for the company of Commander Ki, of course, but he could be as talkative or as still as she wished) if she so desired. Today she was tired of everyone with whom she had regular contact, and worried, very worried. Too many things preyed on her mind, too many things happened much too quickly. She wanted very much to hear Ki's voice so full of quiet confidence. But instead of asking him to talk, to tell her of the goings on in the palace to which an Empress is never privy, she spoke.

"Take care of the Princess." The Silk was the very one Ki had used to wipe his sword at Natanha's birth. The blood of the Princess and the Empress still stained it.

Standing fully and correctly erect, Ki answered, "You know I have sworn to do so." Then he leaned down to put his elbow on the railing so that his face would be more on a level with Elena's, and so that she would know they were now speaking as friend to friend. "Afraid of rebels?"

Elena sighed heavily and grabbed the ornate, cast iron rail with both hands. She stood looking out over the firing range for some time without speaking. Then she shook a fold of her skirt and smoothed it. Finally, she turned to Ki. "We live in interesting times, my friend."

"Indeed." Ki noticed the deepening mauve circles under her eyes. They vaguely resembled the markings of the Didentaar, a Pride which had special attachments to the Lawwnum. Where Ki had found the markings beautiful on Nideans, they were wrong, even ugly, on Elena. And there were tiny lines around her mouth that told she had been frowning a great deal. He hoped she would say more, but she merely continued to stare out at the bright white flashes beneath her. Sensing that, more than anything, she wanted to be truly alone, he said, "I will leave you, Highness. Your guard will be outside the door. You know I am yours to command," and he withdrew.

Ki left Elena feeling very uneasy. It was obvious to any who cared to look that she was worried. It was in every aspect of her, her sleepy-looking eyes, her mouth, her very stance. And that had never been like Elena. Even when she had first come here, hardly more than a child, as soon as she saw that Ozenscebo did not see to his duties, she stepped in and worked at making things right. Had she stopped working? Stopped fighting? It was a question that plagued him as he walked down the hall on the way to the Emperor's audience chamber. Though it was time to find out what Ozenscebo was up to, it was Elena who worried him. He wished he knew what was going on.

"Is something troubling you?" Aubin's light voice rang in Ki's ear.

"Mmmmmm," Ki rumbled, and then laughed as the hair on Aubin's arm stood at attention. "Yes, I'm troubled, but not so much as you are by my speech."

"Ki, you do that to me on purpose, and you know it. And if you didn't already look down in the mouth, as if you could look anything else with those barbaric marks on your face, I would chew you out for it."

Ki halted mid-stride, snarled, "Barbaric!" before he realized that Aubin had baited him. Then he let it pass, and continued with Aubin down the hall. "Yes, I'm worried. I'm concerned about the Empress."

"Ahhh. Now there's a lady who lives in interesting times."

Ki sighed. "Again?" he asked of the wind, thinking of what the Empress had said just a few moments earlier.

"I beg your pardon?" asked Aubin, not understanding the reference.

"It's not important," Ki answered as they drew near the audience chamber. "You have business here today?"

"Unfortunately, yes. Ozenscebo has called several of the Envoys together to discuss, in the most disguised of terms, of course—we dare not even admit that rebels exist—how to deal with the rebels. I had hoped I wouldn't be found down in the recesses of the law library, but I didn't hide well enough."

Ki opened the door quietly, and the two stepped through. Several men and women were near the front of the room, packed as closely as they dared to get to the Emperor, hanging on his every word. One figure, however, stood in the very back of the hall. She was tall, taller even than Ki, with the broad nose and leonine features of his race. Her white hair was close cropped, however, and stranger still, she wore no facial markings except for the lines of great age. She was swathed in the deep-desert robes of her planet, wrapped as if to protect her from the cold, and she kept them pulled closely about her with her crossed arms. The only jewelry she wore was an amulet hanging from her belt that bore the Pride markings of the Didentaar. An unmarried woman, then, a person of no standing in her own Pride, and yet Nide's Ambassador to Homeworld.

Ki greeted her, "Learaa Maaeve, waarrsho nu Mmumna," in the traditional way, her name first, then "Mmumna hold you," the "in the circle of her claws" part being understood.

She nodded to Ki respectfully, totally ignored Aubin even though he was Luna's Envoy, and turned back to the proceedings at the front of the hall.

Aubin stared at her curiously. Though he had spent much time in the same room with her on numerous occasions, she was still a total stranger. She was odd, always at the back of things, never saying a word, always watching, listening, this woman who was the only Ambassador at the Emperor's court. Nide was an affiliate by choice, not a conquered world.

I'll bet she misses nothing, Aubin thought. *I imagine that her reports to Nide are fascinating. Probably more complete than anyone else's. I'll bet she has a better overall picture of what goes on in this empire than I do.* He tilted his head, considering her unmarked face. If he understood Ki correctly, that meant that she had never married. But it also meant that she was still a child, regarded as a non-person. She must be quite a woman to survive a total lack of status to become Ambassador.

But in spite of his open stare, Maaeve still did not acknowledge Aubin, so he made his way forward to listen, and Ki edged around the side of the group so that he might see the Emperor.

The usual gathering of servants scurried about like ants, carrying wine, or more likely *roed*, to the Emperor and his audience, passing between them with little sweetmeats, holding out fresh transcriber disks. But though it was usual, it was also unusual. Ki stiffened as he smelled it—fear, far and away more than the usual discomforture of servants that waited on an uneven master. Trouble. Somewhere in this room a very frightened human was contemplating trouble.

"We have to consolidate the Empire," Ozenscebo was saying. "We must find a way to bring the worlds closer together."

Ki edged closer to the group of Envoys. No. The fear scent did not rise from them. From the servants then. It had to be. He turned like a dancer, lightly, on the balls of his feet, ready to change direction with the smallest of notice. His head turned and he sniffed again. A nondescript servant approached the Emperor with a goblet. But there was already a goblet at Ozenscebo's hand, and the servant hid his face. There was a blur of motion that was Ki and a sliding, savage sword that moved into an eerie, dreamlike lack of sound, and the servant's head skipped down among the Envoys, spraying blood among them as it rolled. They stared at it like dumb cattle, the silence holding until some started to scream.

The Emperor looked away from the ball-shaped object that had been a head and directly at Ki. There was only mild surprise on his jaded face. "Amusing. But why?"

"I could not permit him to kill." Ki re-sheathed his

blade, blood and all, and stooped over the body. From somewhere inside the fashionably full gown that the Emperor had ordered as costume of the day for his servants, Ki removed a high-carbon plastic needle, strong, sharp, and totally invisible to metal detectors. He sniffed the end of the unlikely weapon. "It's been poisoned," he said over his shoulder to the Emperor. "It probably appeared as a stay on the security monitors."

The Emperor suddenly realized what his danger had been, and his face turned snow white, drained of all color. He looked pasty and sick at the thought of his own death. Ki, realizing that a sick Emperor is not a sight for everyone, took charge, dismissing the Envoys, who were only too happy to go, and calling for Lionmen to clear away the debris. The Emperor, still somewhat dazed, looked down at his irridescent green robes. They were spattered with blood. Ki expected an outburst of some sort, rage at the spoiled finery, and was repulsed and revolted by what he got instead.

"It's ruined, of course," mumbled Ozenscebo as he fumbled with a golden-green sleeve, "but the blood is such a lovely color. Rich. A lovely color."

Ki was grateful when the Emperor decided to leave as well. Seeing that everything was as he ordered, Ki wanted nothing so much as to leave the carnage behind. As he walked toward the back of the hall, he noticed that two people remained behind. One was Aubin, the other Ambassador Maaeve. As Ki approached, she bowed to him, deeply, and departed, never having said a word. Aubin stood and stared as if he were some sort of bumpkin who had never seen a Lionman before. Ki began to walk out the door, expecting Aubin to follow, but Aubin only turned his head and continued to stare, unable to absorb what he had seen. Ki retraced his steps, took Aubin by the arm and led him down the corridor until Aubin shook him loose. Aubin did not speak, either. Their course led in no particular direction, but they continued to walk at the pace Ki set.

At last Ki asked, "Why are you so quiet, my friend?"

Aubin stumbled slightly, awkward with emotion. "I've

walked half my life with you and I never suspected. The man who moved like that is not the man I know."

Ki sneered, somewhat offended. "You've always known what I am."

"Yes. But there's knowing and there's seeing."

"Do you find me distasteful?"

Though Ki's voice was cold and deadly even, Aubin was certain he heard sadness in the question.

"No," Aubin answered thoughtfully. "Merely interesting. Interesting times need interesting men."

"And yet again," Ki mumbled with a grimace.

They walked on a way in silence, each alone with his thoughts. But they had, by unspoken mutual consent, taken the turn toward Aubin's quarters.

"I'd like to examine that sword sometime," Aubin said quietly, with a hint of shyness. "It is apparently something I do not understand as well as I should."

"When it's clean."

They entered Aubin's apartment, two old friends standing now on shaky ground. Aubin headed for his liquor cabinet while Ki disappeared into the bathroom. While he waited, Aubin looked at himself carefully in the mirrored wall behind the bar. He was getting old. His shoulders were no longer so straight, and his hair, which had once been brown and rich and wavy, was no longer so full or so dark. His sleepy brown eyes reflected his deep weariness and his body sagged with a little excess weight. His hand shook slightly as he raised the glass, reaction to the fear fountaining inside him. This day had been too full. Ki was gone for some time, and Aubin was achingly certain he had lost his friend as well as his youth. The wait was a sad and long one for him, full of interior terrors, and yet he was startled when Ki at last reappeared.

"It's clean," Ki said of the naked blade he held. He extended it to Aubin, hilt first. "Don't touch the blade. The acid in your skin will etch it, and your fingerprints will become a permanent part of the edge. This hoj has been in my Pride for four generations. See? Each of these stones set here in the pommel represent a man who has kept the blade. Another shanshen will be added for me when the blade goes to Mikal. It was made by the master swordsmith Kaanshaar." He ran his long, thick, slightly pointed nail along the steel, and it hissed in response, sending a chill running down Aubin's human spine. "If you look at the pattern, you will see his handiwork. The wave and ruffle pattern of the folded metal is his signature."

Aubin was a jumble of emotion and still hesitated to take the proffered sword. He looked at the gleaming steel blue of the killing surface and the hilt covered with grey blue stuff like sharkskin. At last he took it in his hands, awed by the purpose for which it had been used such a short time ago, and found to his surprise that he quickly drifted deeper and deeper into a flow that followed the wave pattern on the edge.

Very quietly, Ki said, "Usually the only ones who are permitted a close inspection of a hoj are Pride members and those who feel its cutting edge. Please keep this to yourself."

Ki waited, watching Aubin lose himself in the pattern, seeing the beginnings of real understanding of what the blade meant to Ki dawning in Aubin's face. He flexed his left hand, feeling the lightness that meant the sword was not part of him at the moment. He waited what he felt was a reasonable time, longer than he wanted to, a small eternity, then extended his hand to take the blade back. Aubin released it slowly. In spite of its intended purpose, it was a thing of delicate luster and deep pattern, and Aubin found he was entranced.

Ki took the blade to himself like a lost lover. He held it quietly for a moment, then slid his thumb along the cutting edge hard enough to draw blood in order to satisfy the steel. It sighed as he replaced it in its scabbard.

It was very cool and the air was dead still and damp with dew. The trees in the garden and on the ground far below the palace walls sat perfectly still in true wooden fashion, as if carved, waiting for the breeze that would signal the beginning of the day. The dark had begun to fade, but barely. The stars still winked, but Ki could feel that very soon they would dim and disappear.

This was the only time of day when the entire palace was still. The men on guard were not stirring yet, restless to be relieved. The men who would do the relieving had not yet awakened. The serving staff was still abed as well. And the residents of this place, the cream of society, would not stir until well into the day.

Every morning without fail, duty permitting, rain, snow or sleet notwithstanding, Ki sat in his garden. He would rise very early and work out, hard, in the gym when he had the place totally to himself. Then he would shower. With his mane still wet, he would come to the garden to listen to it dry. He would get down on his knees, place his swords in front of him within easy reach, sit on his heels and rest his hands on his thighs. It was ritual with him, this time for reflection and peace. The only thing that would change from day to day was the position of his head. At times, if things were well within him, he would watch the sky as the stars died and the sun was born. If he needed to see inside Ki, he would lower his head till his chin touched his breast. Then there was nothing to see but himself.

This morning, though disturbed by the events of the day before, he watched the sun come up. His mind was too jumbled even to begin a logical process of thought. He would need time to sort through the events and the emotions they evoked in him. There had been the kill. Clean, swift, it should have been satisfying, but it was not. It left too many questions and too few answers. Then there was Aubin. He had seen the hoj, held it naked in his frail human hand, and he did not bear the tattoo of an adult Nidean male of the Lawwnum Pride. Did that mean that Ki, without Pride consent, had conferred member status on Aubin? The way he, Ki, interpreted the legend, it did. His mouth turned up at the corners, smiling at what Mikal would say to that. Then the smile broadened as he tried to picture Aubin wearing Pride tattoos. The smile fled. The Empress. She was tired, so tired that her fragile human beauty was beginning to fade. Her husband's excesses had finally begun to take their toll even on her. And those excesses had moved into the realm of murder. The corners of his mouth turned down all the way into a frown. Seven men died yesterday, only one with cause. They died because Ozenscebo needed revenge for the threat against him, and the perpetrator of the threat was already dead. So he had pointed at six of the servants, quite randomly, and had declared them traitors. Lionmen had executed them as ordered, but it had left a bad taste in everyone's mouth. More than that, it was a waste.

As the sky began to lighten, faint bands of pink appearing where the sun would soon be, Ki realized that he, too, was tired. He needed Nide and a good rest, something he had denied himself for too long. Perhaps he would invite Aubin to join him there, to instruct him, subtly, of course, in the ways of the Lionmen now that Aubin was an unofficial member of his Pride. It would not hurt that hedonist to toughen up a bit. Vaguely he wondered what the response of his people would be to a Nidean bringing a human home to a planet that did not have a single foreigner anywhere on it outside of the Emperor's embassy compound. Would they resent Aubin as ferociously as only a Nidean could? Would they harass him openly? It was conceivable that they would accept Aubin with open arms while rejecting Ki for enlisting him without Pride consent. He sighed. He needed to go home, with or without Aubin. If only he could talk to Ambassador Maaeve. Her reaction would reflect all the others' . . .

At last his thoughts drifted off, leaving him in quiet peace. Finally he could lose himself in the sound of the running water, broken only by his own breath. His heart beat loudly in his ears, a drum to accompany the beginning fluting of the birds.

He left his drifting in the split second it took to recognize the sound. Someone was at his door, the exterior door that joined his apartment to the public hallway. Though he did not appear to have moved, his muscles, which had been slack, were now tensed, ready for whatever came through his door.

It opened, then shut carefully, quietly. The steps were hesitant, furtive, the culprit obvious and loud in his caution. Ki's right hand edged down his thigh closer to his knee, that much closer to the swords that rested just in front of him. He attempted to catch the scent of the intruder and was frustrated by the ventilation system that kept the air constantly moving out of his quarters to be replenished with fresh. When he finally caught the scent, well known, the hand crept back to its original position. The sounds changed again. The maker was attempting to sneak up on him. The effort at stealth was clumsy at best, but Ki waited.

"Beautiful sunrise, is it not?" Ki asked the intruder.

About three feet behind him, the Princess stamped her foot in disgust. "How? I thought I'd caught you with your back to a door. How did you know it was me?"

"I heard you, I heard you, I smelled you, I heard you."

"I beg your pardon?" Natanha said as she came around to sit by his side. "I don't understand."

"I heard you at the door. Quite noisy. I heard you moving about the room, I suppose attempting to find out where I was. Then I caught your scent. You are quite distinct, you know, different even from your mother. Then I heard you again when you tried to sneak up on me. You are as quiet as a herd of imlowwn."

Natanha's balled fist hit her leg in a cute little gesture of frustration. "One of these days I'll catch you. One day you'll be dreaming, and I'll catch you."

He turned his head away from the sunrise and to Natanha for the first time. He studied her face, so much like her mother's, the determination there, and raised an eyebrow. It was the only response such a statement deserved.

She was about to insist, then changed her mind. "Where's the rock? Did you like it? Did you like it?"

Ki raised his left hand which caused a glint on the metal and pointed to the water.

"Where?" she demanded. "I don't see it."

"It's at the base of the waterfall. The water is polishing it. When the time is right, I'll take it out." Ki was suddenly intensely aware of the similarity of Natanha and her cherished bit of earth. She, too, would be ready for public viewing only after she'd been polished. He only hoped the process would not be too painful.

"No one can see it at the bottom of the waterfall," she pouted.

"I know it's there, as do you. Who else needs to?"

Natanha subsided, and found herself regarding the sun rising over her father's capital. In this light, delicate, fragile, none too sharp, the city was wonderful. The tall towers picked up the pinks and yellows of the dawn and threw them back at her. She could not see from here the hovels that had grown up at the edges of the city, filled with squatters who could not pay the land tax. From here it was golden, warm, exciting. She imagined the people beginning to get ready for the day, soon to fill the streets with writhing snakes made of people, patchy snakes with colors from all over the Empire. The low residential districts lost their bone whiteness in this light, becoming fragile pink roses almost lost in the high canes of the skyscrapers. Where the 'scrapers left their shadows, there were dark pools of blue, deep, deep, like the lake that filled Fuji's crater.

After a time, she found her voice and the courage to speak of what had brought her here.

"They tried to kill Daddy yesterday."

"Yes," Ki answered, aware of where this line of questioning was likely to go.

"Will they try to kill Mama, too?"

"Probably."

Natanha paused. This next was the heart of the matter. "Am I going to die?"

Ki was relieved that she had brought this question to him. He did not want another to answer it, to frighten her, or, worse yet, to lie to her. "Eventually. We all do."

She was frustrated. "YOU know! Are the rebels going to kill Mama and me?"

"No."

"How do you know?"

Ki opened his right hand, slowly turned it palm up, and extended it gracefully to Natanha. It was answer enough. He would never permit it. She put her small hand in his, feeling safe now, and returned to watching the sunrise.

"Scarlet and cadmium yellow going into violets contrast nicely with the oranges in the highlights in the blue shadows, right . . . ?" She was showing off for him.

He turned his face toward her, his eyes open wide, and this time raised both eyebrows. Softly, she withdrew her hand from his.

"Yes," she sighed. "Mama says I talk too much, too." And, as if Mama had reminded her, she smoothed her skirt in unconscious imitation. Then she looked at Ki. His back was straight, his hands on his thighs, relaxed, his face to the new morning. She shifted her weight, straightened her back, too, and placed her hands. Then she checked Ki again, to see that she'd done it correctly, and went back to watching her father's city come to life.

Ki smiled indulgently.

The Ballad of Lost C'mell

Cordwainer Smith

She got the which of the what-she-did,
Hid the bell with a blot, she did,
But she fell in love with a hominid.
Where is the which of the what-she-did?
from *The Ballad of Lost C'mell*

She was a girly girl and they were true men, the lords of creation, but she pitted her wits against them and she won. It had never happened before, and it is sure never to happen again, but she did win. She was not even of human extraction. She was cat-derived, though human in outward shape, which explains the C in front of her name. Her father's name was C'mackintosh and her name C'mell. She won her tricks against the lawful and assembled Lords of the Instrumentality.

It all happened at Earthport, greatest of buildings, smallest of cities, standing twenty-five kilometers high at the western edge of the Smaller Sea of Earth.

Jestocost had an office outside the fourth valve.

1

Jestocost liked the morning sunshine, while most of the other Lords of Instrumentality did not, so that he had no trouble in keeping the office and the apartments which he had selected. His main office was ninety meters deep, twenty meters high, twenty meters broad. Behind it was the "fourth valve," almost a thousand hectares in extent. It was shaped helically, like an enormous snail. Jestocost's apartment, big as it was, was merely one of the pigeonholes in the muffler on the rim of Earthport. Earthport stood like an enormous wineglass, reaching from the magma to the high atmosphere.

Earthport had been built during mankind's biggest mechanical splurge. Though men had had nuclear rockets since the beginning of consecutive history, they had used chemical rockets to load the interplanetary ion-drive and nuclear-drive vehicles or to assemble the photonic sailships for interstallar cruises. Impatient with the troubles of taking things bit by bit into the sky, they had worked out a billion-ton rocket, only to find that it ruined whatever countryside it touched in landing. The Daimoni-people of Earth extraction, who came back from somewhere beyond the stars—had helped men build it of weatherproof, rustproof, timeproof, stressproof material. Then they had gone away and had never come back.

Jestocost often looked around his apartment and wondered what it might have been like when white-hot gas, muted to a whisper, surged out of the valve into his own chamber and the sixty-three other chambers like it. Now he had a back wall of heavy timber, and the valve itself was a great hollow cave where a few wild things lived. Nobody needed that much space any more. The chambers were useful, but the valve did nothing. Planoforming ships whispered in from the stars; they landed at Earthport as a matter of legal convenience, but they made no noise and they certainly had no hot gases.

Jestocost looked at the high clouds far below him and talked to himself.

"Nice day. Good air. No trouble. Better eat."

Jestocost often talked like that to himself. He was an individual, almost an eccentric. One of the top council of mankind, he had problems, but they were not personal problems. He had a Rembrandt hanging above his bed—the only Rembrandt known in the world, just as he was possibly the only person who could appreciate a Rembrandt. He had the tapestries of a forgotten empire hanging from his back wall. Every morning the sun played a grand opera for him, muting and lighting and shifting the colors so that he could almost imagine that the old days of quarrel, murder and high drama had come back to Earth again. He had a copy of Shakespeare, a copy of Colegrove and two pages of the Book of Ecclesiastes in a locked box beside his bed. Only forty-two people in the universe could read Ancient English, and he was one of them. He drank wine, which he had made by his own robots in his own vineyards on the Sunset coast. He was a man, in short, who had arranged his own life to live comfortably, selfishly and well on the personal side, so that he could give generously and impartially of his talents on the official side.

When he awoke on this particular morning, he had no idea that a beautiful girl was about to fall hopelessly in love with him—that he would find, after a hundred years and more of experience in government, another government on Earth just as strong and almost as ancient as his own—that he would willingly fling himself into conspiracy and danger for a cause which he only half understood. All these things were mercifully hidden from him by time, so that his only question on arising was, should he or should he not have a small cup of white wine with his breakfast. On the 173rd day of each year, he always made a point of eating eggs. They were a rare treat, and he did not want to spoil himself by having too many, nor to deprive himself and forget a treat by having none at all. He puttered around the room, muttering, "White wine? White wine?"

C'mell was coming into his life, but he did not know it. She was fated to win; that part, she herself did not know.

Ever since mankind had gone through the Rediscovery of Man, bringing back governments, money, newspapers, national languages, sickness and occasional death, there had been the problem of the underpeople—people who were not human, but merely humanly shaped from the stock of Earth animals. They could speak, sing, read, write, work, love and die; but they were not covered by human law, which simply defined them as "homunculi" and gave them a legal status close to animals or robots. Real people from off-world were always called "hominids."

Most of the underpeople did their jobs and accepted their half-slave status without question. Some became famous—C'mackintosh had been the first earth-being to manage a fifty-meter broad-jump under normal gravity. His picture was seen in a thousand worlds. His daughter, C'mell, was a girly girl, earning her living by welcoming human beings and hominids from the outworlds and making them feel at home when they reached Earth. She had the privilege of working at Earthport, but she had the duty of working very hard for a living which did not pay well. Human beings and hominids had lived so long in an affluent society that they did not know what it meant to be poor. But the Lords of the Instrumentality had decreed that underpeople—derived from animal stock—should live under the economics of the Ancient World; they had to have their own kind of money to pay for their rooms, their food, their possessions and the education of their children. If they became bankrupt, they went to the Poorhouse, where they were killed painlessly by means of gas.

It was evident that humanity, having settled all of its own basic problems, was not quite ready to let Earth animals, no matter how much they might be changed, assume a full equality with man.

The Lord Jestocost, seventh of that name, opposed the policy. He was a man who had little love, no fear, freedom from ambition and a dedication to his job: but there are passions of government as deep and challenging as the emotions of love. Two hundred years of thinking himself right and of being outvoted had instilled in Jestocost a furious desire to get things done his own way.

Jestocost was one of the few true men who believed in the rights of the underpeople. He did not think that mankind would ever get around to correcting ancient wrongs unless the underpeople themselves had some of the tools of power—weapons, conspiracy, wealth and (above all) organization with which to challenge man. He was not afraid of revolt, but he thirsted for justice with an obsessive yearning which overrode all other considerations.

When the Lords of the Instrumentality heard that there was the rumor of a conspiracy among the underpeople, they left it to the robot police to ferret out.

Jestocost did not.

He set up his own police, using underpeople themselves for the purpose, hoping to recruit enemies who would realize that he was a friendly enemy and who would in course of time bring him into touch with the leaders of the underpeople.

If those leaders existed, they were clever. What sign did a girly girl like C'mell ever give that she was the spearhead of a crisscross of agents who had penetrated Earthport itself? They must, if they existed, be very, very careful. The telepathic monitors, both robotic and human, kept every thought-band under surveillance by random sampling. Even the computers showed nothing more significant than improbable amounts of happiness in minds which had no objective reason for being happy.

The death of her father, the most famous cat-athlete which the underpeople had ever produced, gave Jestocost his first definite clue.

He went to the funeral himself, where the body was packed in an ice-rocket to be shot into space. The mourners were thoroughly mixed with the curiosity-seekers. Sport is international, inter-race, inter-world, inter-species. Hominids were there: true men, 100% human, they looked weird and horrible because they or their ancestors had undergone bodily modifications to meet the life conditions of a thousand worlds.

Underpeople, the animal-derived "homunculi," were

there, most of them in their work clothes, and they looked more human than did the human beings from the outer worlds. None were allowed to grow up if they were less than half the size of man, or more than six times the size of man. They all had to have human features and acceptable human voices. The punishment for failure in their elementary schools was death. Jestocost looked over the crowd and wondered to himself, "We have set up the standards of the toughest kind of survival for these people and we give them the most terrible incentive, life itself, as the condition of absolute progress. What fools we are to think that they will not overtake us!" The true people in the group did not seem to think as he did. They tapped the underpeople peremptorily with their canes, even though this was an underperson's funeral, and the bear-men, bull-men, cat-men and others yielded immediately and with a babble of apology.

C'mell was close to her father's icy coffin.

Jestocost not only watched her; she was pretty to watch. He committed an act which was an indecency in an ordinary citizen but lawful for a Lord of the Instrumentality: he peeped her mind.

And then he found something which he did not expect.

As the coffin left, she cried, "Ee-telly-kelly, help me! Help me!"

She had thought phonetically, not in script, and he had only the raw sound on which to base a search.

Jestocost had not become a Lord of the Instrumentality without applying daring. His mind was quick, too quick to be deeply intelligent. He thought by gestalt, not by logic. He determined to force his friendship on the girl.

He decided to await a propitious occasion, and then changed his mind about the time.

As she went home from the funeral, he intruded upon the circle of her grimfaced friends, underpeople who were trying to shield her from the condolences of ill-mannered but well-meaning sports enthusiasts.

She recognized him, and showed him the proper respect.

"My Lord, I did not expect you here. You knew my father?"

He nodded gravely and addressed sonorous words of consolation and sorrow, words which brought a murmur of approval from humans and underpeople alike.

But with his left hand hanging slack at his side, he made the perpetual signal of *alarm! alarm!* used within the Earthport staff—a repeated tapping of the thumb against the third finger—when they had to set one another on guard without alerting the offworld transients.

She was so upset that she almost spoiled it all. While he was still doing his pious doubletalk, she cried in a loud clear voice:

"You mean *me*?"

And he went on with his condolences: ". . . and I do mean *you*, C'mell, to be the worthiest carrier of your father's name. *You* are the one to whom we turn in this time of common sorrow. *Who could I mean but you* if I say that C'mackintosh never did things by halves, and died young as a result of his own zealous conscience? Good-by, C'mell, I go back to my office."

She arrived forty minutes after he did.

2

He faced her straight away, studying her face.

"This is an important day in your life."

"Yes, my Lord, a sad one."

"I do not," he said, "mean your father's death and burial. I speak of the future to which we all must turn. Right now, it's you and me."

Her eyes widened. She had not thought that he was that kind of man at all. He was an official who moved freely around Earthport, often greeting important offworld visitors and keeping an eye on the bureau of ceremonies. She was a part of the reception team, when a girly girl was needed to calm down a frustrated arrival or to postpone a quarrel. Like the geisha of ancient Japan, she had an honorable profession; she was not a bad girl but a professionally flirtatious hostess. She stared at the Lord Jestocost. He did not *look* as though he meant anything improperly personal. But, thought she, you can never tell about men.

"You know men," he said, passing the initiative to her.

"I guess so," she said. Her face looked odd. She started to give him smile No. 3 (extremely adhesive) which she had learned in the girly-girl school. Realizing it was wrong, she tried to give him an ordinary smile. She felt she had made a face at him.

"Look at me," he said, "and see if you can trust me. I am going to take both our lives in my hands."

She looked at him. What imaginable subject could involve him, a Lord of the Instrumentality, with herself, an undergirl? They never had anything in common. They never would.

But she stared at him.

"I want to help the underpeople."

He made her blink. That was a crude approach, usually followed by a very raw kind of pass indeed. But his face was illuminated by seriousness. She waited.

"Your people do not have enough political power even to talk to us. I will not commit treason to the true-human race, but I am willing to give your side an advantage. If you bargain better with us, it will make all forms of life safer in the long run."

C'mell stared at the floor, her red hair soft as the fur of a Persian cat. It made her head seem bathed in flames. Her eyes looked human, except that they had the capacity of reflecting when light struck them; the irises were the rich green of the ancient cat. When she looked right at him, looking up from the floor, her glance had the impact of a blow. "What do you want from me?"

He stared right back. "Watch me. Look at my face. Are you sure, *sure* that I want nothing from you personally?"

She looked bewildered. "What else is there to want from me except personal things? I am a girly girl. I'm not a person of any importance at all, and I do not have much of an education. You know more, sir, than I will ever know."

"Possibly," he said, watching her.

She stopped feeling like a girly girl and felt like a citizen. It made her uncomfortable.

"Who," he said, in a voice of great solemnity, "is your own leader?"

"Commissioner Teadrinker, sir. He's in charge of all out-world visitors." She watched Jestocost carefully; he still did not look as if he were playing tricks.

He looked a little cross. "I don't mean him. He's part of my own staff. Who's your leader among the underpeople?"

"My father was, but he died."

Jestocost said. "Forgive me. Please have a seat. But I don't mean that."

She was so tired that she sat down into the chair with an innocent voluptuousness which would have disorganized any ordinary man's day. She wore girly-girl clothes, which were close enough to the everyday fashion to seem agreeably modish when she stood up. In line with her profession, her clothes were designed to be unexpectedly and provocatively revealing when she sat down—not revealing enough to shock the man with their brazenness, but so slit, tripped and cut that he got far more visual stimulation than he expected.

"I must ask you to pull your clothing together a little," said Jestocost in a clinical turn of voice. "I am a man, even if I am an official, and this interview is more important to you and to me than any distraction would be."

She was a little frightened by his tone. She had meant no challenge. With the funeral that day, she meant nothing at all; these clothes were the only kind she had.

He read all this in her face.

Relentlessly, he pursued the subject.

"Young lady, I asked about your leader. You name your boss and you name your father. I want your leader."

"I don't understand," she said, on the edge of a sob. "I don't understand."

Then, he thought to himself, I've got to take a gamble. He thrust the mental dagger home, almost drove his words like steel straight into her face. "Who . . . ," he said slowly and icily, "is . . . Ee . . . telly . . . kelly?"

The girl's face had been cream-colored, pale with sorrow. Now she went white. She twisted away from him. Her eyes glowed like twin fires.

Her eyes . . . like twin fires.

(No undergirl, thought Jestocost as he reeled, could hypnotize me.)

Her eyes . . . were like cold fires.

The room faded around him. The girl disappeared. Her eyes became a single white, cold fire.

Within this fire stood the figure of a man. His arms were wings, but he had human hands growing at the elbows of his wings. His face was clear, white, cold as the marble of an ancient statue; his eyes were opaque white. "I am the E-telekeli. You will believe in me. You may speak to my daughter C'mell."

The image faded.

Jestocost saw the girl staring as she sat awkwardly on the chair, looking blindly through him. He was on the edge of making a joke about her hypnotic capacity when he saw that she was still deeply hypnotized, even after he had been released. She had stiffened and again her clothing had fallen into its planned disarray. The effect was not stimulating; it was pathetic beyond words, as though an accident had happened to a pretty child. He spoke to her.

He spoke to her, not really expecting an answer.

"Who are you?" he said to her, testing her hypnosis.

"I am he whose name is never said aloud," said the girl in a sharp whisper. "I am he whose secret you have penetrated. I have printed my image and my name in your mind."

Jestocost did not quarrel with ghosts like this. He snapped out a decision. "If I open my mind, will you search it while I watch you? Are you good enough to do that?"

"I am very good," hissed the voice in the girl's mouth.

C'mell arose and put her two hands on his shoulders. She looked into his eyes. He looked back. A strong telepath himself, Jestocost was not prepared for the enormous thought-voltage which poured out of her.

Look in my mind, he commanded, for the subject of *underpeople* only.

I see it, thought the mind behind C'mell.

Do you see what I mean to do for the underpeople?

Jestocost heard the girl breathing hard as her mind served as a relay to his. He tried to remain calm so that he could see which part of his mind was being searched. Very good so far, he thought to himself. An intelligence like that of Earth itself, he thought—and we of the Lords not knowing it!

The girl hacked out a dry little laugh.

Jestocost thought at the mind, Sorry. Go ahead.

This plan of yours—thought the strange mind—may I see more of it?

That's all there is.

Oh, said the strange mind, you want me to think for you. Can you give me the keys in the Bank and Bell which pertain to destroying underpeople?

You can have the information keys if I can ever get them, thought Jestocost, but not the control keys and not the master switch of the Bell.

Fair enough, thought the other mind, and what do I pay for them?

You support me in my policies before the Instrumentality. You keep the underpeople reasonable, if you can, when the time comes to negotiate. You maintain honor and good faith in all subsequent agreements. But how can I get the keys? It would take me a year to figure them out myself.

Let the girl look once, thought the strange mind, and I will be behind her. Fair?

Fair, thought Jestocost.

Break? thought the mind.

How do we re-connect? thought Jestocost back.

As before. Through the girl. Never say my name. Don't think it if you can help it. Break?

Break! thought Jestocost.

The girl, who had been holding his shoulders, drew

his face down and kissed him firmly and warmly. He had never touched an underperson before, and it never had occurred to him that he might kiss one. It was pleasant, but he took her arms away from his neck, half-turned her around, and let her lean against him.

"Daddy!" she sighed happily.

Suddenly she stiffened, looked at his face, and sprang for the door. "Jestocost!" she cried. "Lord Jestocost! What am I doing here?"

"Your duty is done, my girl. You may go."

She staggered back into the room. "I'm going to be sick," she said. She vomited on his floor.

He pushed a button for a cleaning robot and slapped his desk-top for coffee.

She relaxed and talked about his hopes for the underpeople. She stayed an hour. By the time she left they had a plan. Neither of them had mentioned E-telekeli, neither had put purposes in the open. If the monitors had been listening, they would have found no single sentence or paragraph which was suspicious.

When she had gone, Jestocost looked out of his window. He saw the clouds far below and he knew the world below him was in twilight. He had planned to help the underpeople, and he had met powers of which organized mankind had no conception or perception. He was righter than he had thought. He had to go on through.

But as partner—C'mell herself!

Was there ever an odder diplomat in the history of worlds?

3

In less than a week they had decided what to do. It was the Council of the Lords of the Instrumentality at which they would work—the brain center itself. The risk was high, but the entire job could be done in a few minutes if it were done at the Bell itself.

This is the sort of thing which interested Jestocost.

He did not know that C'mell watched him with two

different facets of her mind. One side of her was alertly and wholeheartedly his fellow-conspirator, utterly in sympathy with the revolutionary aims to which they were both committed. The other side of her—was feminine.

She had a womanliness which was truer than that of any hominid woman. She knew the value of her trained smile, her splendid kept red hair with its unimaginably soft texture, her lithe young figure with firm breasts and persuasive hips. She knew down to the last millimeter the effect which her legs had on hominid men. True humans kept few secrets from her. The men betrayed themselves by their unfulfillable desires, the women by their irrepressible jealousies. But she knew people best of all by not being one herself. She had to learn by imitation, and imitation is conscious. A thousand little things which ordinary women took for granted, or thought about just once in a whole lifetime, were subjects of acute and intelligent study to her. She was a girl by profession; she was a human by assimilation; she was an inquisitive cat in her genetic nature. Now she was falling in love with Jestocost, and she knew it.

Even she did not realize that the romance would sometime leak out into rumor, be magnified into legend, distilled into romance. She had no idea of the ballad about herself that would open with the lines which became famous much later:

She got the which of the what-she-did,
Hid the bell with a blot, she did,
But she fell in love with a hominid.
Where is the which of the what-she-did?

All this lay in the future, and she did not know it.

She knew her own past.

She remembered the off-Earth prince who had rested his head in her lap and had said, sipping his glass of motl by way of farewell:

"Funny, C'mell, you're not even a person and you're the most intelligent human being I've met in this place. Do you know it made my planet poor to send me here?

And what did I get out of them? Nothing, nothing, and a thousand times nothing. But you, now. If you'd been running the government of Earth, I'd have gotten what my people need, and this world would be richer too. Manhome, they call it. Manhome, my eye! The only smart person on it is a female cat."

He ran his fingers around her ankle. She did not stir. That was part of hospitality, and she had her own ways of making sure that hospitality did not go too far. Earth police were watching her; to them, she was a convenience maintained for outworld people, something like a soft chair in the Earthport lobbies or a drinking fountain with acid-tasting water for strangers who could not tolerate the insipid water of Earth. She was not expected to have feelings or to get involved. If she had ever caused an incident, they would have punished her fiercely, as they often punished animals or underpeople, or else (after a short formal hearing with no appeal) they would have destroyed her, as the law allowed and custom encouraged.

She had kissed a thousand men, maybe fifteen hundred. She had made them feel welcome and she had gotten their complaints or their secrets out of them as they left. It was a living, emotionally tiring but intellectually very stimulating. Sometimes it made her laugh to look at human women with their pointed-up noses and their proud airs, and to realize that she knew more about the men who belonged to the human women than the human women themselves ever did.

Once a policewoman had had to read over the record of two pioneers from New Mars. C'mell had been given the job of keeping in very close touch with them. When the policewoman got through reading the report she looked at C'mell and her face was distorted with jealousy and prudish rage.

"Cat, you call yourself. Cat! You're a pig, you're a dog, you're an animal. You may be working for Earth but don't ever get the idea that you're as good as a person. I think it's a crime that the Instrumentality lets monsters like you greet real human beings from outside! I can't stop it. But may the Bell help you, girl, if you ever touch a real Earth man! If you ever get near one! If you ever try tricks here! Do you understand me?"

"Yes, ma'am," C'mell had said. To herself she thought, "That poor thing doesn't know how to select her own clothes or how to do her own hair. No wonder she resents somebody who manages to be pretty."

Perhaps the policewoman thought that raw hatred would be shocking to C'mell. It wasn't. Underpeople were used to hatred, and it was not any worse raw than it was when cooked with politeness and served like poison. They had to live with it.

But now, it was all changed.

She had fallen in love with Jestocost.

Did he love her?

Impossible. No, not impossible. Unlawful, unlikely, indecent—yes, all these, but not impossible. Surely he felt something of her love.

If he did, he gave no sign of it.

People and underpeople had fallen in love many times before. The underpeople were always destroyed and the real people brainwashed. There were laws against that kind of thing. The scientists among people had created the underpeople, had given them capacities which real people did not have (the fifty-meter jump, the telepath two miles underground, the turtle-man waiting a thousand years next to an emergency door, the cow-man guarding a gate without reward), and the scientists had also given many of the underpeople the human shape. It was handier that way. The human eye, the five-fingered hand, the human size—these were convenient for engineering reasons. By making underpeople the same size and shape as people, more or less, the scientists eliminated the need for two or three or a dozen different sets of furniture. The human form was good enough for all of them.

But they had forgotten the human heart.

And now she, C'mell had fallen in love with a man, a true man old enough to have been her own father's grandfather.

But she didn't feel daughterly about him at all. She remembered that with her own father there was an easy comradeship, an innocent and forthcoming affection, which masked the fact that he was considerably more cat-like than she was. Between them there was an aching void of forever-unspoken words—things that couldn't quite be said by either of them, perhaps things that couldn't be said at all. They were so close to each other that they could get no closer. This created enormous distance, which was heart-breaking but unutterable. Her father had died, and now this true man was here, with all the kindness—

"That's it," she whispered to herself, "with all the kindness that none of these passing men have ever really shown. With all the depth which my poor underpeople can never get. Not that it's not in them. But they're born like dirt, treated like dirt, put away like dirt when they die. How can any of my own men develop real kindness? There's a special sort of majesty to kindness. It's the best part there is to being people. And he has whole oceans of it in him. And it's strange, strange, strange that he's never given his real love to any human woman."

She stopped, cold.

Then she consoled herself and whispered on, "Or if he did, it's so long ago that it doesn't matter now. He's got *me*. Does he know it?"

4

The Lord Jestocost did know, and yet he didn't. He was used to getting loyalty from people, because he offered loyalty and honor in his daily work. He was even familiar with loyalty becoming obsessive and seeking physical form, particularly from women, children and underpeople. He had always coped with it before. He was gambling on the fact that C'mell was a wonderfully intelligent person, and that as a girly girl, working on the hospitality staff of the Earthport police, she must have learned to control her personal feelings.

"We're born in the wrong age," he thought, "when I meet the most intelligent and beautiful female I've ever met, and then have to put business first. But this stuff about people and underpeople is sticky. Sticky. We've got to keep personalities out of it."

So he thought. Perhaps he was right.

If the nameless one, whom he did not dare to remember, commanded an attack on the Bell itself, that was worth their lives. Their emotions could not come into it. The Bell mattered: justice mattered: the perpetual return of mankind to progress mattered. He did not matter, because he had already done most of his work. C'mell did not matter, because their failure would leave her with mere underpeople forever. The Bell did count.

The price of what he proposed to do was high, but the entire job could be done in a few minutes if it were done at the Bell itself.

The Bell, of course, was not a Bell. It was a three-dimensional situation table, three times the height of a man. It was set one story below the meeting room, and shaped roughly like an ancient bell. The meeting table of the Lords of the Instrumentality had a circle cut out of it, so that the Lords could look down into the Bell at whatever situation one of them called up either manually or telepathically. The Bank below it, hidden by the floor, was the key memory-bank of the entire system. Duplicates existed at thirty-odd other places on Earth. Two duplicates lay hidden in interstellar space, one of them beside the ninety-million-mile gold-colored ship left over from the War against Raumsog and the other masked as an asteroid.

Most of the Lords were offworld on the business of the Instrumentality.

Only three besides Jestocost were present—the Lady Johanna Gnade, the Lord Issan Olascoaga and the Lord William Not-from-here. (The Not-from-heres were a great Norstrilian family which had migrated back to Earth many generations before.)

The E-telekeli told Jestocost the rudiments of a plan.

He was to bring C'mell into the chambers on a summons.

The summons was to be serious.

They should avoid her summary death by automatic justice, if the relays began to trip.

C'mell would go into partial trance in the chamber.

He was then to call the items in the Bell which E-telekeli wanted traced. A single call would be enough. E-telekeli would take the responsibility for tracing them. The other Lords would be distracted by him, E-telekeli.

It was simple in appearance.

The complication came in action.

The plan seemed flimsy, but there was nothing which Jestocost could do at this time. He began to curse himself for letting his passion for policy involve him in the intrigue. It was too late to back out with honor; besides, he had given his word; besides, he liked C'mell—as a being, not as a girly girl—and he would hate to see her marked with disappointment for life. He knew how the underpeople cherished their identities and their status.

With heavy heart but quick mind he went to the council chamber. A dog-girl, one of the routine messengers whom he had seen many months outside the door, gave him the minutes.

He wondered how C'mell or E-telekeli would reach him, once he was inside the chamber with its tight net of telepathic intercepts.

He sat wearily at the table—

And almost jumped out of his chair.

The conspirators had forged the minutes themselves, and the top item was: "C'mell daughter to C'mackintosh, cat-stock (pure) lot 1138, confession of. Subject: conspiracy to export homuncular material. Reference: planet De Prinsensmacht."

The Lady Johanna Gnade had already pushed the buttons for the planet concerned. The people there, Earth by origin, were enormously strong but they had gone to great pains to maintain the original Earth appearance. One of their first-men was at the moment on Earth. He bore the title of the Twilight Prince (Prins van de

Schemering) and he was on a mixed diplomatic and trading mission.

Since Jestocost was a little late, C'mell was being brought into the room as he glanced over the minutes.

The Lord Not-from-here asked Jestocost if he would preside.

"I beg you, sir and scholar," he said, "to join me in asking the Lord Issan to preside this time."

The presidency was a formality. Jestocost could watch the Bell and Bank better if he did not have to chair the meeting too.

C'mell wore the clothing of a prisoner. On her it looked good. He had never seen her wearing anything but girly-girl clothes before. The pale-blue prison tunic made her look very young, very human, very tender and very frightened. The cat family showed only in the fiery cascade of her hair and the lithe power of her body as she sat, demure and erect.

Lord Issan asked her: "You have confessed. Confess again."

"This man," and she pointed at a picture of the Twilight Prince, "wanted to go to the place where they torment human children for a show."

"What!" cried three of the Lords together.

"What place?" said the Lady Johanna, who was bitterly in favor of kindness.

"It's run by a man who looks like this gentleman here," said C'mell, pointing at Jestocost. Quickly, so that nobody could stop her, but modestly, so that none of them thought to doubt her, she circled the room and touched Jestocost's shoulder. He felt a thrill of contact-telepathy and heard bird-cackle in her brain. Then he knew that the E-telekeli was in touch with her.

"The man who has the place," said C'mell, "is five pounds lighter than this gentleman, two inches shorter, and he has red hair. His place is at the Cold Sunset corner of Earthport, down the boulevard and under the boulevard. Under people, some of them with bad reputations, live in that neighborhood."

The Bell went milky, flashing through hundreds of

combinations of bad underpeople in that part of the city. Jestocost felt himself staring at the casual milkiness with unwanted concentration.

The Bell cleared.

It showed the vague image of a room in which children were playing Hallowe'en tricks.

The Lady Johanna laughed. "Those aren't people. They're robots. It's just a dull old play."

"Then," added C'mell, "he wanted a dollar and a shilling to take home. Real ones. There was a robot who had found some."

"What are those?" said Lord Issan.

"Ancient money—the real money of old America and old Australia," cried Lord William. "I have copies, but there are no originals outside the state museum." He was an ardent, passionate collector of coins.

"The robot found them in an old hiding place right under Earthport."

Lord William almost shouted at the Bell. "Run through every hiding place and get me that money."

The Bell clouded. In finding the bad neighborhoods it had flashed every police point in the Northwest sector of the tower. Now it scanned all the police points under the tower, and ran dizzily through thousands of combinations before it settled on an old toolroom. A robot was polishing circular pieces of metal.

When Lord William saw the polishing, he was furious. "Get that here," he shouted. "I want to buy those myself!"

"All right," said Lord Issan. "It's a little irregular, but all right."

The machine showed the key search devices and brought the robot to the escalator.

The Lord Issan said, "This isn't much of a case."

C'mell sniveled. She was a good actress. "Then he wanted me to get a homunculus egg. One of the E-type, derived from birds, for him to take home."

Issan put on the search device.

"Maybe," said C'mell, "somebody has already put it in the disposal series."

The Bell and the Bank ran through all the disposal devices at high speed. Jestocost felt his nerves go on edge. No human being could have memorized these thousands of patterns as they flashed across the Bell too fast for human eyes, but the brain reading the Bell through his eyes was not human. It might even be locked into a computer of its own. It was, thought Jestocost, an indignity for a Lord of the Instrumentality to be used as a human spy-glass.

The machine blotted up.

"You're a fraud," cried the Lord Issan. "There's no evidence."

"Maybe the offworlder tried," said the Lady Johanna.

"Shadow him," said Lord William. "If he would steal ancient coins he would steal anything."

The Lady Johanna turned to C'mell. "You're a silly thing. You have wasted our time and you have kept us from serious inter-world business."

"It *is* inter-world business," wept C'mell. She let her hand slip from Jestocost's shoulder, where it had rested all the time. The body-to-body relay broke and the telepathic link broke with it.

"We should judge that," said Lord Issan.

"You might have been punished," said Lady Johanna.

The Lord Jestocost had said nothing, but there was a glow of happiness in him. If the E-telekeli was half as good as he seemed, the underpeople had a list of checkpoints and escape routes which would make it easier to hide from the capricious sentence of painless death which human authorities meted out.

5

There was singing in the corridors that night.

Underpeople burst into happiness for no visible reason.

C'mell danced a wild cat dance for the next customer who came in from outworld stations, that very evening. When she got home to bed, she knelt before the picture of her father C'mackintosh and thanked the E-telekeli for what Jestocost had done.

But the story became known a few generations later, when the Lord Jestocost had won acclaim for being the champion of the underpeople and when the authorities, still unaware of E-telekeli, accepted the elected representatives of the underpeople as negotiators for better terms of life; and C'mell had died long since.

She had first had a long, good life.

She became a female chef when she was too old to be a girly girl. Her food was famous. Jestocost once visited her. At the end of the meal he had asked, "There's a silly rhyme among the underpeople. No human beings know it except me."

"I don't care about rhymes," she said.

"This is called 'The what-she-did.' "

C'mell blushed all the way down to the neckline of her capacious blouse. She had filled out a lot in middle age. Running the restaurant had helped.

"Oh, that rhyme!" she said. "It's silly."

"It says you were in love with a hominid."

"No," she said. "I wasn't." Her green eyes, as beautiful as ever, stared deeply into his. Jestocost felt uncomfortable. This was getting personal. He liked political relationships; personal things made him uncomfortable.

The light in the room shifted and her cat eyes blazed at him, she looked like the magical fire-haired girl he had known.

"I wasn't in love. You couldn't call it that. . . ."

Her heart cried out, *It was you, it was you, it was you*.

"But the rhyme," insisted Jestocost, "says it was a hominid. It wasn't that Prins van de Schemering?"

"Who was he?" C'mell asked the question quietly, but her emotions cried out, *Darling, will you never, never know?*

"The strong man."

"Oh, him. I've forgotten him."

Jestocost rose from the table. "You've had a good life, C'mell. You've been a citizen, a committeewoman, a leader. And do you even know how many children you have had?"

"Seventy-three," she snapped at him. "Just because they're multiple doesn't mean we don't know them."

His playfulness left him. His face was grave, his voice kindly. "I meant no harm, C'mell."

He never knew that when he left she went back to the kitchen and cried for a while. It was Jestocost whom she had vainly loved ever since they had been comrades, many long years ago.

Even after she died, at the full age of five-score and three, he kept seeing her about the corridors and shafts of Earthport. Many of her great-granddaughters looked just like her and several of them practiced the girly-girl business with huge success.

They were not half-slaves. They were citizens (reserved grade) and they had photopasses which protected their property, their identity and their rights. Jestocost was the godfather to them all; and he was often embarrassed when the most voluptuous creatures in the universe threw playful kisses at him. All he asked was fulfillment of his political passions, not his personal ones. He had always been in love, madly in love—

With justice itself.

At last, his own time came, and he knew that he was dying, and he was not sorry. He had had a wife, hundreds of years ago, and had loved her well; their children had passed into the generations of man.

In the ending, he wanted to know something, and he called to a nameless one (or to his successor) far beneath the ground. He called with his mind till it was a scream.

I have helped your people.

"Yes," came back the faintest of faraway whispers, inside his head.

I am dying. I must know. Did she love me?

"She went on without you, so much did she love you. She let you go, for your sake, not for hers. She really loved you. More than death. More than life. More than time. You will never be apart."

Never apart?

"Not, not in the memory of man," said the voice, and was then still.

Jestocost lay back on his pillow and waited for the day to end.

The Man Who Would Be Kzin

Greg Bear and S.M. Stirling

"I am become overlord of a fleet of transports, supply ships, and wrecks!" Kfraksha-Admiral said. "No wonder the First Fleet did not return; our Intelligence reports claimed these *humans* were leaf-eaters without a weapon to their name, and they have destroyed a fourth of our combat strength!"

He turned his face down to the holographic display before him; it was set for exterior-visual, and showed only bright unwinking points of light and the schematics that indicated the hundreds of vessels of the Second Fleet. Here beyond the orbit of Neptune the humans' sun was just another star . . . *we will eat you yet*, he vowed silently. A spacer's eye could identify those suns whose worlds obeyed the Patriarch. More that did not, unvisited, or unconquered yet like the Pierin holdouts on Zeta Reticuli. *Yes, you and all like you!* So many suns, so many . . .

The kzin commander's tail was not lashing; he was beyond that, and the naked pink length of that organ now stood out rigid as he paced the command deck of the *Sons Contend With Bloody Fangs*. The orange fur around his blunt muzzle bristled, and the reddish washcloth of his tongue kept sweeping up to moisten his black nostrils. The other kzinti on the bridge stayed prudently silent, forcing their batwing ears not to fold into the fur of their heads at the spicy scent of high-status anger. The lower-ranked bent above the consoles and readouts of their duty stations, taking refuge in work; the immediate staff prostrated themselves around the central display tank, laying their facial fur flat. Aide-to-Commanders covered his nose with his hands in an excess of servility; irritated, Kfraksha kicked him in the ribs as he went by. There was no satisfaction to the gesture, since they were all in space-combat armor save for the unhinged helmets, but the subordinate went spinning a meter or so across the deck.

"Well? Advise me," the kzin admiral spat. "Surely *something* can be learned from the loss of a squadron of *Gut Tearer*–class cruisers?"

Reawii-Intelligence-Analyst raised tufted eyebrows and fluttered his lips against his fangs.

"Frrrr. The . . . rrrr, humans have devoted great resources to the defense of the gas-giant moons, whose resources are crucial."

As Kfraksha-Admiral bared teeth, the Intelligence officer hurried on. Reawii's Homeworld accent irritated Kfraksha-Admiral at the best of times. His birth was better than his status, and it would not do to anger the supreme commander, who had risen from the ranks and was proud of it. He hurried beyond the obvious.

"Their laser cannon opened fire with uncanny accuracy. We were unprepared for weapons of this type because such large fixed installations are seldom tactically worthwhile; also, our preliminary surveys did not indicate space defenses of any type. It is worth the risk to further fleet units to recover any possible Intelligence data from wreckage or survivors on appropriate trajectories."

Kfraksha-Admiral's facial pelt rippled in patterns equivalent to a human nod.

"Prepare summaries of projected operations for data and survivors," he said. Then he paused; now his tail did lash, sign of deep worry or concentration. "Hrrr. It is time we stopped being surprised by the Earth-monkeys and started springing unseen from the long grass ourselves. Bring me a transcript of all astronomical anomalies in this system."

The staff officers rose and left at his gesture, and Kfraksha-Admiral remained staring into the display tank; he keyed it to a close-in view of the animal planet. Blue and white, more ocean than Homeworld, slightly lighter gravity. A rich world. A soft world, or so the telepaths said, no weapons, a species that was so without shame that it deliberately shunned the honorable path of war. Thousands of thousands squared of the animals. Unconsciously, he licked his lips. *All the more for the feeding.*

The game was wary, though. He must throttle his leap, though it was like squeezing his own throat in his claws.

"I must *know* before I fight," he muttered.

He was the perfect spy.

He could also be the perfect saboteur.

Lawrence Halloran was a strong projecting telepath.

He could read the minds of most people with ease. The remaining select few he could invade, with steady concentration, within a week or two. Using what he found in those minds, Halloran could appear to be anybody or anything.

He could also make suggestions, convincing his subjects—or victims—that they were undergoing some physical experience. In this, he relied in large measure on auto-suggestion; sometimes it was enough to plant a subliminal hint and have the victims convince themselves that they actually experienced something. The problem was that the Earth of the twenty-third century had little use for spies or saboteurs. Earth had been at peace for two hundred years. Everyone was prosperous; many were rich. The planet was a little crowded, but those who strongly disliked that could leave. Psychists and autodocs saw that nobody was violent or angry or unhappy for long. Most people were only vaguely aware that things had ever been very different, and the ARM, the UN technological police, kept it that way, ensuring that no revolutionary changes upset the comfortable status quo.

Lawrence Halloran had an unusual ability that seemed to be completely useless. He had first used his talents in a most undignified way, appearing as the headmaster of his private Pacific Grove secondary school, *sans* apparel, in the middle of the quad during an exercise break. The headmaster had come within a hair's breadth of being relieved of duty; an airtight alibi, that he had in fact been in conference with five teachers across the campus, had saved his job and reputation. Halloran's secret had not been revealed. But Halloran had learned an important object lesson—foolish use of his talents could have grave consequences. He had been raised to feel strong guilt at any hint of aggression. Children who scuffled in the schoolyard were sick and needed treatment.

Human society was not so very different from an ant's nest, at the end of the Long Peace; a stick, inserted from an unexpected direction, could raise hell. And woe to the wielder if he stayed around long enough to let the ants crawl up the stick.

That Halloran had not manifested his ability as an infant—not until his sixteenth year, in fact—was something of a miracle. The talent had undoubtedly existed in some form, but had kept itself hidden until five years after Halloran's first twinges of pubescence.

At first, such a wild talent had been exhilarating. After the headmaster fiasco, and several weirder if less immediately foolish manifestations (a dinosaur on a slidewalk at night, Christ in a sacristy), and string of romantic successes everyone else found bewildering, he had undergone what amounted to a religious conversion. Halloran came to realize that he could not use his talent without destroying himself, and those around him. The only thing it was good for was deception and domination.

He buried it. Studied music. Specialized in Haydn.

In his dreams, he became Haydn. It beat being himself.

When awake, he was merely Lawrence Halloran Jr., perpetual student: slightly raucous, highly intuitive (he could not keep his subconscious from exercising certain small forays) and generally regarded by his peers as someone to avoid. His only real friend was his cat. He knew that his cat loved him, because he fed her. Cats were neither altruists nor hypocrites, and nobody expected them to be noble. If he could not be Haydn, he would rather have been a cat.

Halloran resented his social standing. *If only they knew how noble I am.* He had a talent he could use to enslave people, and by sublimating it he became an irritating son of a bitch; that, he thought, was highly commendable self-sacrifice.

And they hate me for it, he realized. *I don't much love them either. Lucky for them I'm an altruist.*

Then the war had come; invaders from beyond human space. The kzinti: catlike aliens, carnivores, aggressive imperialists. Human society was turned upside down once again, although the process was swift only from a historical perspective. With the war eight years along, Halloran had grown sick of this masquerade. Against his better judgment, he had made himself available to the UN Space Navy; UNSN, for short. Almost immediately, he had been sequestered and prepared for just such an eventuality as the capture of a kzinti vessel. In the second kzin attack on the Sol system, a cruiser named *War Loot* was chopped into several pieces by converted launch lasers and fell into human hands.

In this, Earth's most desperate hour, neither Halloran nor any of his commanding officers considered his life to be worth much in and of itself. Nobility of purpose . . .

And if Halloran's subconscious thought differently—

Halloran knew himself to be in control. Had he not sublimated the worst of his talent? Had he not let girls pour drinks on his head?

Halloran's job was to study the kzin. Then to *become* one, well enough to fool another kzin. After all, if he could convince humans he was a dinosaur—which was obviously an impossibility—why not fool aliens into seeing what they expected?

The first test of Halloran-Kzin was brief and simple.

Halloran entered the laboratory where doctors struggled to keep two mangled kzin from the *War Loot* alive. In the cool ice-blue maximum isolation ward, he approached the flotation bed with its forest of pipes and wires and tubing. Huddled beneath the apparatus, the kzin known to its fellows as Telepath dreamed away his final hours on drugs custom-designed for his physiology.

Telepaths were the most despised and yet valued of kzinti, something of an analogue to Halloran—a mind reader. To kzinti, any kind of addiction was an unbearably shameful thing—a weakness of discipline and concentration, a giving in to the body whose territorial impulses established so much of the rigid Kzinti social ritual. To be addicted was to be less self-controlled than a kzin already was, and that was pushing things very close to the edge. And yet addiction to a drug was what produced kzinti telepaths.

This kzin would not have looked very good in the best of times, despite his two hundred and twenty centimeters of height and bull-gorilla bulk; now he was shrunken and pitiful, his ribs showing through matted fur, his limbs reduced to lumpy bone, lips pulled back from yellow teeth and stinking gums. Telepath had been without his fix for weeks. How much this lack, and the presence of anesthetics, had dulled his talents nobody could say, but his kind offered the greatest risk to the success of Halloran's mission. The kzin had been wearing a supply of the telepath drug on a leather belt when captured. Administered to him now, it would allow him to reach into the mind of another, with considerable effort . . .

Halloran-Kzin had to pass this test.

He signaled the doctors with a nod, and from behind their one-way glass they began altering the concentration of drugs in Telepath's blood. They added some of the kzinti drug. A monitor wheeped softly, pitifully, indicating that their kzin would soon be awake and that he would be in pain.

The kzin opened his eyes, rolled his head, and stared in surprise at Halloran-Kzin. The dying Telepath concealed his pain well.

"I have been returned?" he said, in the hiss-spit-snarl of what his race called the Hero's Tongue.

"You have been returned," Halloran-Kzin replied.

"And am I too valuable to terminate?" the kzin asked sadly.

"You will die soon," Halloran-Kzin said, sensing that this would comfort him.

"Animals . . . eaters of plants. I have had nightmares, dreams of being pursued by herbivores. The shame. And no meat, or only cold rotten meat . . ."

"Are you still capable?" Halloran-Kzin asked. He had learned enough about kzinti social structure from the relatively undamaged prisoner designated Fixer-of-Weapons to understand that Telepath would have no position if he was not telepathic. Fixer was the persona he would assume. "Show me you are still capable."

The Kzin had shielded himself against stray sensations from human minds. But now he closed his eyes and knotted his black, leathery hands into fists. With an intense effort, he reached out and tapped Halloran's thoughts. Telepath's eyes widened until the rheumy circles around the wide pupils were clearly visible. His ears contracted into tight knots beneath the fur. Then he emitted a horrifying scream, like a jaguar in pain. Against all his restraints, he thrashed and twisted until he had torn loose the internal connections that kept him alive. Orange-red blood pooled around the flotation bed and the monitor began a steady, funereal tone.

Halloran left the ward. Colonel Buford Early waited for him outside; as usual, his case officer exuded an air of massive, unwilling patience.

"Just a minor problem," Halloran said, shaken more than he wished the other man to know.

"Minor?"

"Telepath is dead. He saw my thoughts."

"He thought you were a kzin?"

"Yes. He wouldn't have tried reading me if he thought I was human."

"What happened?"

"I drove him crazy," Halloran said. "He was close to the edge anyway . . . I pushed him over."

"How could you do that?" Colonel Early asked, brow lowered incredulously.

"I had a salad for lunch," Halloran replied.

Halloran knew better than to wake a kzin in the middle of a nightmare. Fixer-of-Weapons had not rested peacefully the last four sleeps, and no wonder, with Halloran testing so many hypotheses, hour by hour, on the captive.

The chamber in which the kzin slept was roomy enough, five meters on a side and three meters high, the walls colored a soothing mottled green. The air was warm and dry; Halloran had chapped lips from spending hours and days in the hapless kzin's company.

Thinking of a kzin as hapless was difficult. Fixer-of-Weapons had been Chief Weapons Engineer and Alien Technologies Officer aboard the invasion cruiser *War Loot*, a position demanding great strength and stamina even with the wartime dueling restrictions, for many other kzinti coveted such a billet.

War Loot had been on a mission to probe human defenses within the ecliptic; to that extent, the kzinti mission had succeeded. The cruiser had been disabled within the outer limits of the asteroid belt by converted propulsion beam lasers three weeks before, and against all odds, Fixer-of-Weapons and two other kzin had been captured. The others had been severely injured, one almost cut in half by a shorn and warped bulkhead. The same bulkhead had sealed Fixer-of-Weapons in a cabin corner, equipped with a functional vent giving access to seven hours of trapped air. At the end of six and a half hours, Fixer-of-Weapons had passed out. Human investigators had cut him free . . .

And brought him to Ceres, largest of the asteroids, to be put in a cage with Halloran.

To Fixer-of-Weapons, in his more lucid moments, Halloran looked like a particularly clumsy and socially inept kzin. But Halloran was a California boy, born and bred, a graduate of UCLA's revered school of music. Halloran did not look like a kzin unless he wanted to.

Four years past, to prove to himself that his life was not a complete waste, he had spent his time learning to differentiate one Haydn piano sonata or string quartet from another, not a terribly exciting task, but peaceful and rewarding. He had developed a great respect for Haydn, coming to love the richness and subtle invention of the eighteenth century composer's music.

To Earth-bound flatlanders, the war at the top of the solar system's gravity well, with fleets maneuvering over periods of months and years, was a distant and dimly perceived threat. Halloran had hardly known how to feel about his own existence, much less the survival of the human race. Haydn suited him to a tee. Glory did not seem important. Nobody would appreciate him anyway.

Halloran's parents, and their fathers and mothers before them for two and a half centuries, had known an Earth of peace and relative prosperity. If any of them had desired glory and excitement, they could have volunteered for a decades-long journey by slowboat to new colonies. None had.

It was a Halloran tradition; careful study, avoidance of risk, lifetimes of productive peace. The tradition had gained his grandfather a long and productive life—one hundred and fifty years of it, and at least a century more to come. His father, Lawrence Halloran Sr., had made his fortune streamlining commodities distribution; a brilliant move into a neglected field, less crowded than information shunting. Lawrence Halloran Jr., after the death of his mother in an earthquake in Alaska, had bounced from school to school, promising to be a perpetual student, gadding from one subject to another, trying to lose himself . . .

And then peace had ended. The kzinti—not the first visitors from beyond the Solar System, but certainly the most aggressive—had made their presence known. Presence, to a kzin, was tantamount to conquest. For hundreds of thousands of kzin warriors, serving their Patriarchy, Earth and the other human worlds represented advancement; many females, higher status and lifetime sinecures, without competition.

Humans had been drawn into the war with no weapons as such. To defend themselves, all they had were the massive planet- and asteroid-mounted propulsion lasers and fusion drives that powered their starships. These technologies, some of them now converted to thoroughgoing weapons by Belters and UN engineers, provided what little hope humans had . . .

And there was the bare likelihood—unconfirmed as yet—that humans were innately more clever than kzinti, or at least more measured and restrained. Human fusion drives were certainly more efficient—but then, the kzinti had gravity polarizers, not unlike that found on the Pak ship piloted by Jack Brennan, and never understood. The Brennan polarizer still worked, but nobody knew how to control it—or build another like it. Gradually, scientists and UNSN commanders were realizing that capture of kzinti vessels, rather than complete destruction, could provide invaluable knowledge about such advanced technology.

Gravity polarizers gave kzin ships the ability to travel at eight-tenths the speed of light, with rapid acceleration and artificial gravitation . . . The Kzinti did not *need* super-efficient fusion drives.

Halloran waited patiently for the Fixer-of-Weapons to awaken. An hour passed. He rehearsed the personality he was constructing, and toned the image he presented for the kzin. He also studied, for the hundredth time, the black markings of fur in the kzin's face and along his back, contrasting with the brownish-red undercoat. The kzin's ears were ornately tattooed in patterns Halloran had learned symbolized the intermeshed bones of kzinti enemies. This was how the Kzinti recognized each other, beyond scent and gross physical features; failure to know and project such facial fur patterns and ear tattoos would mean discovery and death. The kzinti's own mind would supply the scent, given the visual clues; their noses were less sensitive than a dog's, much more so than a human's.

Another hour, and Halloran felt a touch of impatience. Kzinti were supposed to be light and short-term sleepers.

Fixer-of-Weapons seemed to have joined his warrior ancestors; he barely breathed.

At last, the captive stirred and opened his eyes, glazed nictitating membranes pulling back to reveal the large, gorgeous purple-rimmed golden eyes with their surprisingly humanlike round irises. Fixer-of-Weapons's wedge-shaped, blunt-muzzled face froze into a blank mask, as it always did when he confronted Halloran-Kzin, who stood on the opposite side of the containment room, tapping his elbow with one finger. Distance from the captive was imperative, even when he was "restrained" by imaginary bonds suggested by Halloran. A kzin did not give warning when he was about to attack, and Fixer-of-Weapons was being driven to emotional extremes.

The kzin laid back his ears in furious misery. "I have done nothing to deserve such treatment," he growled. He believed he was being detained on a kzinti fleet flagship. Halloran, had he truly been a kzin, would have preferred human capture to kzinti detention. *I can't say I like the ratcat,* he thought, with a twinge of guilt, quickly suppressed. *But you've got to admit he's about as tough as he thinks he is.*

"That is for your superiors to decide," Halloran-Kzin said. "You behaved with suspected cowardice, you allowed an invasion cruiser to be disabled and captured—"

"I was not Kufcha-Captain! I cannot be responsible for the incompetence of my commander." Fixer-of-Weapons rose to his full two hundred and twenty centimeters, short for a kzin, and flexed against the imaginary bonds. The muscles beneath the smooth-furred limbs and barrel chest were awesome, despite weight loss under weeks of captivity. "This is a travesty! Why are you doing this to me?"

"You will tell us exactly what happened, step by step, and how you allowed animals—plant-eaters—to capture *War Loot.*"

Fixer-of-Weapons slumped in abject despair. "I have told, again and again."

Halloran-Kzin showed no signs of relenting. Fixer-of-Weapons lashed his long pink rat-tail, sitting in a tight ball on the floor, swallowed hard and began his tale again, and again Halloran used the familiar litany as a cover to probe the kzin's inner thoughts.

If Halloran was going to be a kzin, and think like one for days on end, then he had to have everything exactly right. His deception would be of the utmost delicacy. The smallest flaw could get him killed immediately.

Kzinti, unlike the UN Space Navy, did not take prisoners except for Intelligence and culinary purposes.

Fixer-of-Weapons finished his story. Halloran pulled back from the kzin's mind.

"If I have disgraced myself, then at least allow me to die," Fixer-of-Weapons said softly.

That's one wish you can be granted, Halloran thought. One way or another, the kzin would be dead soon; his species did not survive in captivity.

Halloran exited the cell and faced three men and two women in the antechamber. Two of the men wore the new uniform—barely ten years old—of the UN Space Navy. The third man was a Belter cultural scientist, the only one in the group actually native to Ceres, dressed in bright lab spotter orange. The two women Halloran had never seen before; they were also Belters, though their Belter tans had faded. All three wore the broad Belter Mohawk. The taller of the two offered Halloran her hand and introduced herself.

"I'm Kelly Ysyvry," she said. "Don't bother trying to spell it."

"Y-S-Y-V-R-Y," Halloran said, displaying the show-off mentality that had made his social life so difficult at times.

"Right," Ysyvry said, unflappable. "This," she nodded at her female companion, "is Henrietta Olsen."

Colonel Buford Early, the shortest and most muscular of the three men, nodded impatiently at the introductions; he was an Earther, coal-black and much older than he looked, something Ultra Secret in the ARM before the war. Early had recruited Halloran four years ago, trained him meticulously, and shown remarkable patience toward his peculiarities.

"When are you going to be ready?" he asked Halloran.

"Ready for what?" Halloran asked.

"Insertion."

Halloran, fully understanding the Colonel's meaning, inspected the women roguishly.

"I'm confused," he said, smiling.

"What he means," Ysyvry said, "is that we're all impatient, and you've been the stumbling block throughout this mission."

"What is she?" Halloran asked Early.

"We are the plunger of your syringe," Henrietta Olsen answered. "We're Belter pilots. We've been getting special training in the kzinti hulk."

"Pleased to meet you," Halloran said. He glanced back at the hatch to the cell airlock. "Fixer-of-Weapons will be dead within a week. I can't learn any more from him. So . . . I'm ready for a test."

Early stared at him. Halloran knew the Colonel was restraining an urge to ask him, *Are you sure?*, after having displayed such impatience.

"How do you know Fixer-of-Weapons will die?" the black man said.

Halloran's smile stiffened. He disliked being challenged. "Because if I were him, and part of me is, I would have reached my limit."

"It hasn't been an easy assignment," the cultural scientist commented.

"Easier for us than Fixer-of-Weapons," Halloran said, smirking inwardly as the scientist winced.

There would be many problems, of course. Halloran would never be as strong as a kzin, and if there were any sort of combat, he would quickly lose . . .

Halloran, among the kzinti, thinking himself a kzin, would have to carefully preprogram himself to avoid such dangerous situations, to keep a low profile concomitant with his status, whatever that might be. That would be difficult. A high-status kzin had retainers, sons, flunkies, to handle status-challenges; many of the retainers picked carefully for a combination of dim wits and excellent reflexes. An officer with recognized rank could not be challenged while on a warship; punishments for trying included blinding, castration and execution of all descendants—all more terrible than mere death to a kzin. Nameless ratings could duel as they pleased, provided they had a senior's permission . . . and Halloran-Kzin would be outside the rank structure, with no protector.

Fixer-Halloran, when he returned to the kzinti fleet, would likely find all suitable billets on other vessels filled. To regain his position and keep face among his fellows, he could not simply "fit in" and be docile. But there were more ways than open combat to gain social status.

The kzinti social structure was delicately tuned, though how delicately perhaps not even the kzinti understood. Halloran could wreak his own kind of havoc and none would suspect him of anything but overweening ambition.

All of this, he knew, would have to be accomplished in less than three hundred hours: just twelve days. His body would be worn out by that time. Bad diet—all meat, and raw at that, though digestible, with little chance for supplements of the vitamins a human needed and the life of a kzin did not produce; mental strain; luck running out.

He did not expect to return.

Halloran's hope was that his death would come in the capture or destruction of one or more kzinti ships.

The chance for such a victory, however negligible it might be in the overall strategy of the war, was easily worth one's life, certainly his own life.

The truth was, Halloran thought he was a thorough shit, not of much use to anyone in the long run, a petty dilettante with an unlikely ability, more a handicap than an asset.

Self-sacrifice would give him a peculiar satisfaction: *See, I'm not so bad.*

Nobility of purpose.

And something deeper: *to actually be a kzin.* A kzin could be all the things Halloran had trained himself not to be, and not feel guilty about it. Dominant. Vicious. Competitive.

Kzinti were allowed to have fun.

* * *

The short broadcast good-byes to his friends and relatives on Earth, as yet unassailed by Kzinti:

His father, now one hundred and twenty, he was able to say farewell to; but his grandfather, a Struldbrug and still one of the foremost collectors of Norman Rockwell art and memorabilia, was unavailable.

He disliked his father, yet respected him, and loved his grandfather, but felt a kind of contempt for the man's sentimental passion.

His grandfather's answering service did not know where the oldest living Halloran was. That brought on a sharp tinge of disappointment, against which he quickly raised a shield of aloofness. For a moment, a very young Lawrence—Larry—had surfaced, wanting, desperately needing to see Grandpa. And there was no room for such active sub-personalities, not with Fixer-of-Weapons filling much of his cranium. Or so he told himself, drowning the disappointment as an old farmer might have discarded a sack of unwanted kittens.

Halloran met his father on the family estate at the cap of Arcosanti Two in Arizona. The man barely looked fifty and was with his fifth wife, who was older than Halloran but only by five or ten years. The sky was gorgeous robin's egg at the horizon and lapis overhead and the green desert spread for ten kilometers around in a network of canals and recreational sluices. Arcosanti Two prided itself on its ecological balance, but in fact the city had taken a wide tract of Arizona desert and made it into something else entirely, something in which bobbing lizards and roadrunners would soon go crazy or die. Halloran felt just as much out of place on the broad open-air portico at two kilometers above sea level. Infrared heaters kept the high autumn chill away.

"I'm volunteering for a slowboat," Halloran told his father.

"I thought they'd been suspended," said Rose Petal, the new wife, a very attractive natural blond with oriental features. "I mean, all that expense, and we're bound to lose them to the, mmm, outsiders. . . ." She looked slightly embarrassed; even after nearly a decade, the words *war* and *enemy* still carried a strong flavor of obscenity to most Earthers.

"There's one going out in a few weeks, a private venture. No announcements. Tacit government support; if we survive, they send more."

"That does not sound like my son," Halloran Sr. ventured.

When I tried to assert myself, you told me it was wrong. When I didn't, you despised me. Thanks, Dad.

"I think it is wonderful," Rose Petal said. "Whether characteristic or not."

"It's a way out from under family," Halloran Jr. said with a little smile.

"*That* sounds like my son. Though I'd be much more impressed if you were doing something to help your own people . . ."

"Colonization," Halloran Jr. interjected, leaving the word to stand on its own.

"More directly," Halloran Sr. finished.

"Can't keep all our eggs in one basket," his son continued, amused by arguing a case denied by his own actions. *So tell him.*

But that wasn't possible. Halloran Jr. knew his father too well; a fine entrepreneur, but no keeper of secrets. In truth, his father, despite the aggressive attitude, was even more unsuited to a world of war and discipline than his son.

"That's not what you're doing," Halloran Sr. said. Rose Petal stood by, wisely keeping out from this point on.

"That's what I'm saying I'm doing."

His father gave him a peculiar look then, and Halloran Jr. felt a brief moment of camaraderie and shared secrets. *He has a little bit of the touch too, doesn't he? He knows. Not consciously, but . . .*

He's proud.

Against his own expectations for the meeting and farewell, Halloran left Arcosanti II, his father, and Rose Petal, feeling he might have more to lose than he had guessed, and more to learn about things very close to him. He left feeling good.

He hadn't parted from his father with positive feelings in at least ten years.

There were no longer lovers or good friends to take leave of. He had stripped himself of these social accoutrements over the last five years. It was difficult to have friends who couldn't lie to you, and he always felt guilty with women. How could he know he hadn't influenced them subconsciously? Knowing this, as he returned to the port and took a shuttle to orbit, brought back the necessary feeling of isolation. He would not be human much longer. Things would be easier if he had very little to regret losing.

Insertion. The hulk of the kzin cruiser, its gravity polarizer destroyed by the kzin crew to keep it out of human hands, was propelled by a NEO mass-driver down the solar gravity well to graze the orbital path of Venus, piloted by the two Belter women to the diffuse outer reaches of the asteroids, there set adrift with the bodies of Telepath and the other unknown kzin restored to the places where they would have died. The Belters would take a small cargo craft back home. Halloran would ride an even smaller lifeboat from *War Loot* toward the Kzin fleet. He might or might not be picked up, depending on how hungry the kzin strategists were for information about the loss.

The fleet might or might not be in a good position; it might be mounting another year-long attack against Saturn's moons, on the opposite side of the sun; it might be moving inward for a massive blow against Earth. With the gravity polarizers, the kzin vessels were faster and far more maneuverable than any human ships.

And there could be more than one fleet.

The confined interior of the cargo vessel gave none of its three occupants much privacy. To compensate, they seldom spoke to each other. At the end of a week, Halloran began to get depressed, and it took him another week to express himself to his companions.

While Henrietta Olsen buried herself in reading, when

she wasn't tending the computers, Kelly Ysyvry spent much of her time apparently doing nothing. Eyes open, blinking every few seconds, she would stare at a bulkhead for hours at a stretch. This depressed Halloran further. Were all Belters so inner-directed? If they were, then what just God would place him in the company of Belters during his last few weeks as a human being?

He finally approached Olsen with something more than polite words to punctuate the silence. *A kzin wouldn't have to put up with this*, he thought. Kzinti females were subsapient, morons incapable of speech. *That would have its advantages*, Halloran thought half-jokingly.

Women frightened him. He knew too much about what they thought of him.

"I suppose lack of conversation is one way of staying sane," he said.

Olsen looked up from her page projector and blinked. "Flatlanders talk all the time?"

"No," Halloran admitted. "But they talk."

"We talk," Olsen said, returning to her reading. "When we want to, or need to."

"I need to talk," Halloran said.

Olsen put her book down. Perversely guilty, Halloran asked what she had been reading.

"Montagu, *The Man Who Never Was*," she replied.

"What's it about?"

"It's ancient history," she said. "Forbidden stuff. Twentieth century. During the Second World War—remember that?"

"I'm educated," he said. As much as such obscene subjects had been taught in school. Pacific Grove had been progressive.

"The Allies dressed up a corpse in one of their uniforms and gave him a courier's bag with false information. Then they dumped him where he could be picked up by the Axis."

Halloran gawped for a moment. "Sounds grim."

"I doubt the corpse minded."

"And I'm the corpse?"

Olsen grinned. "You don't fit the profile at all. You're

not *The Man Who Never Was*. You're one of those soldiers trained to speak the enemy's language and dropped behind the lines in the enemy's uniforms to wreak havoc."

"Why are you so interested in World War Two?"

"Fits our times. This stuff used to be pornography—or whatever the equivalent is for literature about violence and destruction, and they'd send you to the psychist if they caught you with it. Now it's available anywhere. Psychological refitting. Still, the thought of . . ." She shook her head. "Killing. Even thinking like one of *them*—so ready to kill . . ."

Ysyvry broke her meditation by blinking three times in quick succession and turned pointedly to face Halloran.

"To the normal person of a few years ago, what you've become would be unspeakably disgusting."

"And what about now?"

"It's necessity," Ysyvry said. That word again. "We're no better than you. We're all soldiers now. Killers."

"So we're too ashamed to speak to each other?"

"We didn't know you wanted to talk," Olsen said.

Throughout his life, even as insensitive as he had tried to become, he had been amazed at how others, especially women, could be so ignorant of their fellows. "I'll probably be dead in a month," he said.

"So you want sympathy?" Olsen said, wide-eyed. "The Man Who Would be Kzin wants sympathy? Such bad technique . . ."

"Forget it," Halloran said, feeling his stomach twist.

"We learned a lot about you," Ysyvry continued. "What you might do in a moment of weakness, how you had once been a troublemaker, using your abilities to fool people . . . Belters value ingenuity and independence, but we also value respect. Simple politeness."

Halloran felt a deep void open up beneath him. "I was young when I did those things." His eyes filled with tears. "Tanjit, I'm sacrificing myself for my people, and you treat me as if I'm a bleeping dog turd!"

"Yeah," Olsen said, turning away. "We don't like flatlanders, anyway, and . . . I suppose we're not used to this whole war thing. We've had friends die. We'd just as soon it all went away. Even you."

"So," Ysyvry said, taking a deep breath. "Tell us about yourself. You studied music?"

The turnabout startled him. He wiped his eyes with his sleeve. "Yes. Concentrating on Josef Haydn."

"Play us something," Olsen suggested, reaching into a hidden corner slot to pull out a portable music keyboard he hadn't known the ship carried. "Haydn, Glenn Miller, Sting, anything classical."

For the merest instant, he had the impulse to become Halloran-Kzin. Instead, he took the keyboard and stared at the black and white arrangement. Then he played the first movement of Sonata Number 40 in E Flat, a familiar piece for him. Ysyvry and Olsen listened intently.

As he lightly completed the last few bars, Halloran closed his eyes and imagined the portraits of Haydn, powdered wig and all. He glanced at the Belter pilots from the corners of his eyes.

Ysyvry flinched and Olsen released a small squeak of surprise. He lifted his fingers from the keyboard and rotated to face them.

"Stop that," Olsen requested, obviously impressed.

Halloran dropped the illusion.

"That was beautiful," Ysyvry said.

"I'm human after all, even if I am a flatlander, no?"

"We'll give you that much," Olsen said. "You can look like anything you want to?"

"I'd rather talk about the music," Halloran said, adjusting tones on the musicomp to mimic harpsichord.

"We've never seen a kzin up close, for real," Ysyvry said. The expression on their faces was grimly anticipatory: Come on, scare us.

"I'm not a freak."

"So we've already established that much," Olsen said. "But you're a bit of a show-off, aren't you?" "And a mind-reader," Ysyvry said.

He had deliberately avoided looking into their thoughts. Nobility of purpose.

"Perfect companion for a long voyage," Olsen added.

"You can be whatever, whomever you want to be." Their expressions had become almost salacious. Now Halloran was sorry he had ever initiated conversation. How much of this was teasing, how much—actual cruelty?

Or were they simply testing his stability before insertion?

"You'd like to see a Kzin?" he asked quietly.

"We'd like to see Fixer-of-Weapons," Ysyvry affirmed. "We were told you'd need to test the illusion before we release the hulk and your lifeship."

"It's a bit early—we still have two hundred hours."

"All the more time to turn back if you don't convince us," Olsen said.

"It's not just a hat I can put on and take off." He glanced between them, finding little apparent sympathy. Belters were polite, individualistic, but not the most socially adept of people. No wonder their mainstay on long voyages was silence. "I won't wear Fixer-of-Weapons unless I become him."

"You won't consciously know you're human?"

Halloran shook his head. "I'd rather not have the dichotomy to deal with. I'll be too busy with other activities."

"So the Kzinti will think you're one of them, and . . . will *you*?"

"I will be Fixer-of-Weapons, or as close as I can become," Halloran said.

"Then you're worse than the fake soldiers in World War II," Olsen commented dryly.

"Show us," Ysyvry said, over her companion's words.

Halloran tapped his fingers on the edge of the keyboard for a few seconds. He could show them Halloran-Kzin—the generic Kzin he had manufactured from Fixer-of-Weapons's memories. That would not be difficult.

"No," he said. "You've implied that there's something wrong, somehow, in what I'm going to do. And you're right. I only volunteered to do this sort of thing because we're desperate. But it's not a game. I'm no freak, and I'm not going to provide a sideshow for a couple of bored and crass Belters."

He tapped out the serenade from Haydn's string quartet Opus 3 number 5.

Ysyvry smiled: "All right, Mr. Halloran. Looks like the UNSN made a good choice—not that they had much choice."

"I don't need your respect, either," Halloran said, a little surprised at how deeply he had been hurt. *I thought I was way beyond that.*

"What she's saying," Olsen elaborated, "is that we were asked to isolate you, and harass you a little. See if you're as much of a show-off as your records indicate you might be."

"Fine," Halloran said. "Now it's back to the silence?"

"No," Ysyvry said. "The music is beautiful. We'd appreciate your playing more for us."

Halloran swore under his breath and shook his head.

"Nobody said it would be easy, being a hero . . . did they?" Ysyvry asked.

"I'm no hero," Halloran said.

"I think you have the makings for one," Olsen told him, regarding him steadily with her clear green eyes. "Whatever kind of bastard you were on Earth. Really."

Will a flatlander ever understand Belters? They were so mercurial, strong, and more than a little arrogant. Perhaps that was because space left so little room for niceties.

"If you accept it," Ysyvry said, "we've decided we'll make you an honorary Belter."

Halloran stopped playing.

"Please accept," Olsen said, not wheedling or even trying to placate; a simple, polite request.

"Okay," Halloran said.

"Good," Ysyvry said. "I think you'll like the ceremony."

He did, though it made him realize even more deeply how much he had to lose . . .

And why do I have to die before people start treating me decently?

The Belter pilots dropped the hulk a hundred and three hours after his induction into the ranks. They cut loose the kzin lifeship, with Halloran inside, five hours later, and then turned a shielded ion drive against their orbital path to drop inward and lose themselves in the Belt.

There were beacons on the lifeship, but no sensors. In the kzinti fleet, rescue of survivors was strictly at the discretion of the commanding officers. Halloran entered the digitized odor-signature and serial number of Fixer-of-Weapons into the beacon's transmitter and sat back to wait.

The lifeship had a month's supplies for an individual kzin. What few supplements he dared to carry, all consumable, would be gone in a week, and his time would start running out from that moment.

Still, Halloran half hoped he would not be found. He almost preferred the thought of failure to the prospect of carrying out his mission. It would be an ordeal. The worst thing that had ever happened to him. His greatest challenge in a relatively peaceful lifetime.

For a few days, he nursed dark thoughts about manifest destiny, the possibility that the Kzinti really were the destined rulers of interstellar space, and that he was simply blowing against a hurricane.

Then came a signal from the Kzinti fleet. Fixer-of-Weapons was still of some value. He was going to be rescued.

"Bullshit," Halloran said, grinning and hugging his arms tightly around himself. "Bullshit, bullshit, bullshit."

Now he was *really* afraid.

Wherever you are, whether in the crowded asteroid belt or beyond the furthest reaches of Pluto, space appears the same. Facing away from the sun—negligible anyway past the Belt—the same vista of indecipherable immensity presents itself. You say, yes, I know those are stars, and those are galaxies, and nebulae; I know there is life out there, and strangeness, and incident and death and change. But to the eye, and the animal mind, the universe is a flat tapestry sprinkled with meaningless points of fire. Nothing meaningful can emerge from such a tapestry.

The approach of a ship from the beautiful flat darkness and cold is itself a miracle of high order. The animal mind asks, *Where did it come from?*

Halloran, essentially two beings in one body, watched the kzinti dreadnought with two reactions. As Fixer-of-Weapons, now seating himself in the center of Halloran's mind, the ship—a rough-textured spire with an X cross at the "bow"—was both rescue and challenge. Fixer-of-Weapons had lost his status. He would have to struggle to regain his position, perhaps wheedle permission to challenge and supplant a Chief Weapons Officer and Alien Technologies Officer. He hoped—and Halloran prayed—that the positions on the rescue ship were held by one kzin, not two.

The battleship would pick up his lifeship within an hour. In that time, Halloran adjusted the personality that would mask his own.

Halloran would exist in a preprogrammed slumber, to emerge only at certain key points of his plan. Fixer-of-Weapons would project continuously, aware and active, but with limitations; he would not challenge another kzin to physical combat, and he would flee at an opportune moment (if any came) if so challenged.

Halloran did not have a kzin's shining black claws or vicious fangs. He could project images of these to other kzinti, but they had only a limited effectiveness in action. For a moment, a kzin might think himself slashed by Fixer-of-Weapons's claws (although Halloran did not know how strong the stigmata effect was with kzinti), but that moment would pass. Halloran did not think he could convince a kzin to die. . . .

He had never done such a thing with people. Exploring those aspects of his abilities had been too horrifying to contemplate. If he was pushed to such a test, and succeeded, he would destroy himself rather than return to Earth. Or so he thought, now. . . .

Foolishness, Fixer-of-Weapons's persona grumbled. *A weapon is a weapon.*

Halloran shuddered.

The battleship communicated with the lifeship; first difficulty. The coughing growl and silky dissonance of the Hero's Tongue could not be readily mimicked, and Halloran could not project his illusion beyond a few miles; he did not respond by voice, but by coded signal. The signal was not challenged.

The kzinti could not conceive of an interloper invading their fold.

"Madness," he said as the ships closed. Humming the Haydn serenade, Lawrence Halloran Jr. slipped behind the scenes, and Fixer-of-Weapons came on center stage.

The interior of the *Sons Contend With Bloody Fangs*—or any kzinti vessel, for that matter—smelled of death. It aroused in a human the deepest and most primordial fears. Imagine a neolithic hunter, trapped in a tiger's cave, surrounded by the stench of big cats and dead, decaying prey—and that was how the behind-the-scenes Halloran felt.

Fixer-of-Weapons salivated at the smells of food, but trembled at the same time.

"You are not well?" the escorting Aide-to-Commanders asked hopefully; Fixer's presence on the battleship could mean much disruption. The kzin's thoughts were quite clear to Fixer: *Why did Kfraksha-Admiral allow this one aboard? He smells of confinement . . . and . . .*

Fixer did not worry about these insights, which might be expected of a pitiful telepath; he would use whatever information was available to re-establish his rank and position. He lifted his lip at the subordinate, lowest of ranks aboard the battleship, a *servant* and licker-of-others'-fur. Aide-to-Commanders shrank back, spreading his ears and curling his thick, unscarred pink tail to signify non-aggression.

"Do not forget yourself," Fixer reminded him. "Kfraksha-Admiral is my ally. He chose to rescue me."

"So it is," Aide-to-Commanders acknowledged. He led Fixer down a steep corridor, with no corners for hiding would-be assailants, and straightened before the hatch to Kfraksha-Admiral's quarters. "I obey the instructions of the Dominant One."

That the commander did not allow Fixer to groom or eat before debriefing signified in how little regard he was held. Any survivor of a warship lost to animals carried much if not all the disgrace that would adhere to a surviving commander.

Kfraksha-Admiral bade him enter and growled to Aide-to-Commanders that they would be alone. This was how the kzin commander maintained his position without losing respect, by never exhibiting weakness or fear. Loss of respect could mean constant challenge, once they were out of a combat zone with its restrictions. As a kzin without rank, Fixer might be especially volatile; perhaps deranged by long confinement in a tiny lifeship, he might attack the commander in a foolish effort to regain and then better his status with one combat. But Kfraksha-Admiral apparently ignored all this, spider inviting spider into a very attractive parlor.

"Is your shame bearable?" Kfraksha-Admiral asked, a rhetorical question since Fixer was here, and not immediately contemplating suicide.

"I am not responsible for the actions of the commander of *War Loot*, Dominant One," Fixer replied.

"Yes, but you advised Kufcha-Captain of alien technologies, did you not?"

"I now advise you. Your advantage that I am here, and able to tell you what the animals can do."

Kfraksha-Admiral regarded Fixer with undisguised contempt and mild interest. "Animals destroyed your home. How did this happen?"

This is why I am aboard, Fixer thought. *Kfraksha-Admiral overcomes his disgust to learn things that will give him an edge.*

"They did not engage *War Loot* or any of our sortie. There is still no evidence that they have armed their worlds, no signs of an industry preparing for manufacture of offensive weapons—"

"They defeated you without weapons?"

"They have laser-propulsion systems of enormous strength. You recall, in our first meetings, the animals used their fusion drives against our vessels—"

"And allowed us to track their spoor back to their home worlds. The Patriarchy is grateful for such uneven exchanges. How might we balance this loss?"

Fixer puzzled over his reluctance to tell Kfraksha-Admiral everything. Then: *My knowledge is my life.*

"I am of no use to the fleet," Fixer said, with the slightest undertone of menace. He was gratified to feel—but not see—Kfraksha-Admiral tense his muscles. Fixer could measure the commander's resolve with ease.

"I do not believe that," Kfraksha-Admiral said. "But it is true that if you are no use to me, you are of no use to anybody . . . and not welcome."

Fixer pretended to think this over, and then showed signs of submission. "I am without position," he said sadly. "I might as well be dead."

"You have position as long as you are useful to me," Kfraksha-Admiral said. "I will allow you to groom and feed . . . if you can demonstrate how useful you might be."

Fixer cocked his fan-shaped ears forward in reluctant obeisance. These maneuvers were delicate—he could not concede too much, or Kfraksha-Admiral would come to believe he had no knowledge. "The humans must be skipping industrialization for offensive weapons. They are converting peaceful—"

Kfraksha-Admiral showed irritation at that word, not commonly used by kzinti.

"—propulsion systems into defensive weapons."

"This contradicts reports of their weakness," Kfraksha-Admiral said. "Our telepaths have reported the animals are reluctant to fight."

"They are adaptable," Fixer said.

"So much can be deduced. Is this all that you know?"

"I learned the positions from which two of the propulsion beams were fired. It should be easy to calculate their present locations. . . ."

Kfraksha-Admiral spread his fingers before him,

unsheathing long, black and highly polished claws. Now it was Fixer's turn to tense.

"You are my subordinate," the commander said. "You will pass these facts on to me alone."

"What is my position?" Fixer asked.

"Fleet records of your accomplishments have been relayed to me. Your fitness for position is acceptable." The days when mere prowess in personal combat decided rank were long gone, of course; qualifications had to be met before challenges could be made. "You will replace the Alien Technologies Officer on this ship."

"By combat?" A commander could grant permission . . . which was tantamount to an order to fight. Another means of intimidating subordinates.

"By my command. There will be no combat. Your presence here will not be disruptive, so do not become *too* ambitious, or you will face me . . . on unequal terms."

"And the present officer?"

"I have a new position he will not be unhappy with. That is not your concern. Now stand and receive my mark."

Halloran-Fixer could not anticipate what the commander intended quickly enough to respond with anything more than compliance. Kfraksha-Admiral lifted his powerful leg and swiftly, humiliatingly, peed on Halloran-Fixer, distinctly marking him as the commander's charge. Then Kfraksha-Admiral sat on a broad curving bench and regarded him coldly.

Deeply ashamed but docile—what else could he be?—Fixer studied the commander intently. It would not be so difficult to . . . what?

That thought was swept away even before it took shape.

Fixer-of-Weapons had no physical post as such aboard the flagship. He carried a reader the size of a kzin hand slung over his shoulder—with some difficulty, which did not immediately concern him—and went from point to point on the ship to complete his tasks, which were many, and unusually tiring.

The interior spaces of the *Sons Contend With Bloody Fangs* were strangely unfamiliar to him. Halloran had not had time (nor the capacity) to absorb all of his kzin subject's memories. He did not consciously realize he was giving himself a primary education in kzinti technology and naval architecture. His disorientation would have been an infuriating and goading sign of weakness to any inferior seeking his status, but he was marked by Kfraksha-Admiral—physically marked with the commander's odor, like female or a litter—and that warned aggressive subordinates away. They would have to combat Kfraksha-Admiral, not just Fixer.

And Fixer was proving himself useful to Kfraksha-Admiral. This aspect of Halloran's mission had been carefully thought out by Colonel Early and the Intelligence Staff—what could humans afford to have Kzinti know about their technology? What would Fixer logically have deduced from his experience aboard the *War Loot*?

Kfraksha-Admiral, luckily, expected Fixer to draw out his revelations for maximum advantage. The small lumps of information deemed reasonable and safe—past locations of two Belter laser projectors that had since burned out their mirrors and lasing field coils, now abandoned and useless except as scrap—could be meted out parsimoniously.

Fixer could limp and cavil, and nobody would find it strange. He had, after all, been defeated by animals and lost all status. His current status was bound to be temporary. Kfraksha-Admiral would coax the important facts from him, and then—

So Fixer was not harassed. He studied his library, with some difficulty deciphering the enigmatic commas-and-dots script and mathematical symbologies. Unconsciously, he tapped the understanding of his fellows to buttress his knowledge.

And that was how he attracted the attention of somebody far more valuable than he, and of even lower status—Kfraksha-Admiral's personal telepath.

Kzinti preferred to eat alone, unless they had killed a large animal by common endeavor. The sight of another eating was likely to arouse deep-seated jealousies not conducive to good digestion; the quality of one's food aboard the flagship was often raised with rank, and rank was a smoothly ascending scale. Thus, the officers could not eat together safely, because there were no officers at the same level, and if there was no difference in the food, differences could be imagined. No. It was simply better to eat alone.

This suited Fixer. He had little satisfaction from his meals. He received his chunks of reconstituted meat-substitute heated to blood temperature—common low-status battle rations from the commissary officer, and retired to his quarters with the sealed container to open it and feed. His head hurt after eating the apparent raw slabs of gristle, bone and meager muscle; he preferred the simulated vegetable intestinal contents and soft organs, which were the kzinti equivalent of dessert. A kzin could bolt chunks the size of paired fists. . . . But none of it actually pleased him. What he did not eat, he disposed of rapidly: pitiful, barely chewed-fragments it would have shamed a kzin to leave behind. Fixer did not notice the few pills he took afterwards, from a pouch seemingly beneath his chest muscles.

After receiving a foil-wrapped meal, he traversed the broad central hall of the dining area and encountered the worst-looking kzin he had ever seen. Fur matted, tail actually *kinked* in two places, expression sickly-sycophantic, ears recoiled as if permanently afraid of being attacked. Telepath scrambled from Fixer's path, as might be expected, and then—

Addressed him from behind.

"We are alike, in some respects—are we not?"

Fixer spun around and snarled furiously. One did not address a superior, or even an equal, from behind.

"No anger necessary," Telepath said, curling obeisantly, hands extended to show all claws sheathed. "There is an odd sound about you . . . it makes me curious. I have not permission to read you, but you are strong. You send. You *leak*."

Halloran-Fixer felt his fury redouble, for reasons

besides the obvious impertinence. "You will stand clear of me and not address me, *Addict*," he spat.

"Not offending, but the sound is interesting, whatever it is. Does it come from time spent in solitude?"

Fixer quelled his rage and bounded down the Hall—or so it appeared to Telepath. The mind reader dropped his chin to his neck and resumed his half-hearted attempts to exercise and groom, his thoughts obviously lingering on his next session with the drug that gave him his abilities.

Fixer could easily tell what the commander and crew were up to, if not what they actually thought at any given moment. But Telepath was a blank slate. Nothing "leaked."

He returned to his private space, near the commander's quarters, and settled in for more sessions in the library. There was something that puzzled him greatly, and might be very important—something called a ghost star. The few mentions in the library files were unrevealing; whatever it was, it appeared to be somewhere about ten system radii outside the planetary orbits. It seemed that a ghost star was nothing surprising, and therefore not clearly explicated; this worried Fixer, for he did not know what a ghost star was.

Kzinti aboard spaceships underwent constant training, self-imposed and otherwise. There were no recreation areas as such aboard the flagship; there were four exercise and mock-combat rooms, however, for the four rough gradations of rank from executive officers to servants. When kzinti entered a mock-combat room, they doffed all markings of rank, wearing masks to disguise their facial characteristics and strong mesh gloves over their claws to prevent unsheathing and lethal damage. Few kzinti were actually killed in mock-combat exercise, but severe injury was not uncommon. The ship's autodocs could take care of most of it, and Kzinti considered scars ornamental. Anonymity also prevented ordinary sparring from affecting rank; even if the combatants *knew* the other's identity, it could be ignored through social fiction.

Fixer, in his unusual position of commander's charge, did not receive the challenges to mock-combat common among officers. But there was nothing in the rules, written or otherwise, that prevented subordinates from challenging each other, unless their officers interfered. Such combats were rare because most crewkzin knew their relative strengths, and who would be clearly outmatched.

Telepath, the lowest-ranked and most despised kzin aboard the flagship, challenged Fixer to mock-combat four day-cycles after his arrival. Fixer could not refuse; not even the commander's protection would have prevented his complete ostracization had he done so. His existence would have been an insult to the whole kzinti species. A simple command not to fight would have spared him—but the commander did not imagine that even the despised Fixer would face much of a fight from Telepath. And Fixer could not afford to be shunned; ostensibly, he had his position to regain.

So it was that Halloran faced a kzin in mock-combat. Fixer—the kzin persona—did not fall by the wayside, because Fixer could more easily handle the notion of combat. But Halloran did not remain completely in the background. For while Fixer was "fighting" Telepath, Halloran had to convince any observers—including Telepath—that he was winning.

Fixer's advantages were several. First, both combatants could emerge unharmed from the fray without raising undue suspicions. Second, there would be no remote observers—no broadcasts of the fight.

The major disadvantage was that of all the kzinti, a telepath should be most aware of having psychic tricks played on him.

The exercise chambers were cylindrical, gravitation oriented along one flat surface at kzin normal, or higher for more strenuous regimens. The walls were sand-colored and a constant hot dry wind blew through hidden vents, conditions deemed comfortable in the culture that had dominated kzin when the species achieved spaceflight.

The floor was sprinkled with a flaked fluid-absorbing material. Kzinti rules for combat were few, and did not include prohibitions against surprise targeting of eye-stinging urine. The flakes were more generally soaked with blood, however. The rooms were foul with the odors of fear and exertion and injury.

Telepath was puny for a kzin. He weighed only a hundred and fifty kilograms and stood only two hundred and five centimeters from crown to toes, reduced somewhat by a compliant stoop. He was not in good shape, but he had little difficulty bending the smallest of the ten steel bars adjacent to his assigned half of the combat area—a little gesture legally mandated to give a referee some idea how the combatants were matched in sheer strength. This smallest bar was two centimeters in diameter.

Halloran-Fixer made as if to bend the next bar up, and then ostentatiously re-bent it straight, hoping nobody would examine it closely and find the metal completely unmarked. Probably nobody would; kzinti were less given to idle curiosity than humans.

Telepath screamed and leaped, arms spread wide. The image of Fixer was a bare ten centimeters to one side of his true position, and that allowed one of the kzin's feet to pass a hairsbreadth to one side of Halloran's head. Halloran convinced Telepath he had received a glancing blow across one arm. Telepath recovered somewhat sloppily, for a kzin, and sized up the situation.

There were only the mandated two observers in the antechamber. This fight was regarded as little more than comedy, and comedy, to kzinti, was shameful and demeaning. The observers' attentions were not sharply focused. Halloran-Fixer took advantage of that to dull their perceptions further. This allowed him to concentrate on Telepath.

Fixer did not crouch or make any overt signs of impending attack. He hardly breathed. Telepath circled at the outside of the combat area, nonchalant, apparently faintly amused.

Halloran had little experience with fighting. Fortunately, Fixer-of-Weapons had been an old hand at all kinds of combat, including the mortal kind that had quickly moved him up in rank while the fleet was in base, and much of that information had become lodged in the Fixer persona. Halloran waited for Telepath to make another energy-wasting move.

Kzinti combat was a matter of slight advantages. Possibly Telepath knew this, and sensed something not right about Fixer. Something weak . . .

But Telepath could not read Fixer's thoughts in any concentrated fashion; that required a great effort for the kzin, and debilitating physical weakness afterward. Halloran's powers were much more efficient and much less draining.

Fixer snarled and feigned a jump. Telepath leaped to one side, but Fixer had not completed his attack. He stood with tail twitching furiously several meters from the kzin, needle teeth bared in a hideous grin.

Telepath had good reason to be puzzled. It was rare for a threatened attack to be aborted, from a kzin so much larger and stronger than his opponent. Now the miserable kzin was truly angry, and afraid. Several times he rushed Fixer, but Fixer was never quite where he appeared to be. Several times, Halloran came near to having his head crushed by a passing swipe of the weak kzin's gloved hand, but managed to avoid the blow by centimeters. Something was goading Telepath beyond the usual emotions aroused by mock combat.

"Fight, you sexless female!" Telepath shrieked. A deeply obscene curse, and the observers did some of their own growling now. Telepath had done nothing to increase their esteem.

Fixer used the Kzin's anger to his own advantage. The fight would have to end quickly—he was tiring rapidly, far faster than his puny opponent. Fixer seemed to run to a curved wall, leaping and rebounding, crossing the chamber in a flash—and bypassing Telepath without a blow. Telepath screamed with rage and tried to remove his gloves, but they were locked, and only the observers had the keys.

While Telepath was yowling fury and frustration,

Fixer-Halloran delivered a bolt of suggestion that staggered the kzin, sending him to all fours with an apparent cuff to the jaw. The position was not as dangerous for a kzin—they could run more quickly on fours than erect—but Halloran-Kzin's image loomed over the stunned Telepath and kicked downward. The observers did not see the maneuver precisely, and Telepath was on the floor writhing in pain, his ear and the side of his head swelling with auto-suggestion injury.

Fixer offered his gloves to the observers and they were unlocked. He had not harmed Telepath, and had not received so much as a scratch himself. Fixer had acquitted himself; he still wore Kfraksha-Admiral's stink, but he was not the lowest of the Kzinti on *Sons Contend With Bloody Fangs*.

"The humans obviously have a way of tracking our ships, yet they do not have the gravity polarizer. . . ." Kfraksha-Admiral sat on his curved bench, legs raised, black-leather fingers clasped behind his thick neck, seeming quite casual and relaxed. "What is our weakness, that they spy on us and can aim their miserable adapted weapons upon us?"

Fixer's turmoil was not apparent. He knew the answer—but of course he could not give it. He had to maneuver this conversation to determine if the commander was asking a rhetorical question, or testing him in some way.

"By our drives," he suggested.

"Yes, of course, but not by spectral signatures or flare temperatures, for in fact we do not use our fusion drives when we enter the system. And without polarizer technology, gravitational gradient warps cannot be detected . . . short of system wide detectors, which these animals do not have, correct?"

Fixer rippled his fur in agreement.

"No. They detect not the effects of our drives, but the power sources themselves. It is obvious they have discovered magnetic monopoles. I have suspected as much for years, but now plans are taking shape. . . ."

Fixer-Halloran was relieved, and horrified, at once.

This was indeed how kzinti ships were tracked; in fact, it was a little slow of the enemy not to have thought of it before. The cultural scientists back on Ceres had been puzzled as well; the kzinti had a science and technology more advanced than the human, but they seemed curiously inept at pure research. Almost as if the knowledge had been pasted onto a prescientific culture. . . .

Every Belter prospector had monopole detection equipment; mining the super-massive particles was a major source of income for individual Belters, and for huge Belt corporations. Known monopole storage centers and power stations were automatically compensated for in even the cheapest detector. In an emergency, a detector could be used to determine position in the Belt—or anywhere else in the solar system—by triangulation from those known sources. An unknown—or kzinti—monopole source set detectors off throughout the solar system. And the newly converted propulsion lasers could then be locked onto their targets. . . .

"This much is now obvious. It explains our losses. Do you concur?"

"This is a fact," Fixer said.

"And how do you know it is a fact?" Kfraksha-Admiral challenged.

"The lifeship from *War Loot* is not powered by monopoles. I survived. Animals would not distinguish monopole sources by the size of the vessel—they would attack all sources."

Kfraksha-Admiral pressed his lips tight together and twitched whiskers with satisfaction. "Precisely so. We must have patience in our strategies, then. We cannot enter the system using our monopole-powered gravity polarizers. But there is the ghost star . . . if we enter the system without monopoles, and without approaching the gas-giant planets, where we might be expected . . . We can enter from an apparently empty region of space, unexpectedly, and destroy the animal populations of many worlds and asteroids. This plan's success is my sinecure. Many females, much territory—glory. We are moving outward now to pass around the ghost star and gain momentum."

Fixer-Halloran again felt a chill. Truly, without the monopoles, the kzinti ships would be difficult to detect.

Fixer pressed his hands together before his chest, a sign of deep respect. Kfraksha-Admiral nodded in condescending fashion.

"You have proven valuable, in your own reluctant, rankless way," he acknowledged, staring at him with irises reduced to pinpoints in the wide golden eyes. "You have endured humiliation with surprising fortitude. Some, our more enlightened and patient warriors, might call it courage." The commander drew a rag soaked in some pale liquid from a bucket behind his bench. He threw it at Fixer, who caught it.

The rag had been soaked in diluted acetic acid—vinegar. "You may remove my mark," Kfraksha-Admiral said. "Henceforth, you have the status of full officer, on my formal staff, and you will be in charge of interpreting the alien technologies we capture. Your combat with Telepath . . . has been reported to me. It was not strictly honorable, but your forbearance was remarkable. In part, this earns you a position."

Fixer now had status. He could not relax his vigilance, for he would no longer be under the commander's protection, but he could assume the armor of a true billet; separate quarters, specific duties, a place in the ritual of the kzinti flagship. Presumably the commander would not grant permission for many challenges, and as a direct subordinate he would count as one of the commander's faction, who would retaliate for any unprovoked attack.

The *Sons Contend With Bloody Fangs* had pulled its way out of the sun's gravity well at a prodigious four-tenths of the speed of light, faster than was safe within a planetary system, and was racing for the ghost star a hundred billion kilometers from the sun. Sol was now an anonymous point of light in the vastness of the Sagittarius arm of the galaxy; the outer limits of the solar system were almost as far behind.

The commander's plans for the whiplash trip around the ghost star were secret to all but a few. Fixer was still not even certain what the ghost star was—it was not listed under that name in the libraries, and there was obviously a concept he was not connecting with. But it was fairly easy to calculate that to accomplish the orbital maneuvers the commander proposed, the ghost star would have to be of at least one-half solar mass. Nothing that size had ever been detected from Earth; it was therefore dark and absolutely cold. There would be no perturbed orbits to give it away; its distance was too great.

So for the time being, Fixer assumed they were approaching a rendezvous with either a dark, dead hulk of a star, or perhaps a black hole.

A hundred billion kilometers was still close to the solar neighborhood, as far as interstellar distances were concerned. That kzinti knew more about these regions than humans worried the sublimated Halloran. What other advantages would they gain?

The time had come for Halloran to examine what he had found. With his personality split in half, and locked into a Kzin mentality, he might easily overlook something crucial to his mission.

In his quarters, with the door securely bolted, Halloran came to the surface. Seven days in the Kzinti flagship had taken a terrible toll on him; in a small mirror, he saw himself almost cadaverous, his face deeply lined. Kzinti did not use water to groom themselves, and there were no taps in his private quarters—the aliens were descended from a pack-hunting desert carnivore, and had efficient metabolisms—so his skin and clothing would remain dirty. He took a medicinal towelette, used to treat minor scratches received during combats, and wiped as much of his face and hands clean as he could. The astringent solution in the towelette served to sharpen his wits. After so long in Fixer's charge, there seemed little brilliance and fire left in Halloran himself.

And Fixer is just not very bright, he thought sourly. *Think, monkey, think!*

He looked *old.*

"Bleep that," he murmured, and picked up the library pack. As Fixer, he had subliminally marked interesting passages in the Kzinti records. Now he set out to learn what the ghost star was, and what he might expect in the next few hours, as they approached and parabolically orbited. A half-hour of inquiry, his eyes reddening under the strain of reading the kzinti script without Fixer's intercession, brought no substantial progress.

"Ghost," he muttered. "Specter. Spirit. Ancestors. A star known to ancestors? Not likely—they would have come on into the solar system and destroyed or enslaved us centuries ago . . . what the tanj *is* a ghost star?"

He queried the library on all concepts incorporating the words ghost, specter, ancestor, and other synonyms in the Hero's Tongue. Another half-hour of concentrated and fruitless study, and he was ready to give up, when the projector displayed an entry. *Specter Mass.*

He cued the entry. A flagged warning came up; the symbol for shame-and-disgrace, a Patriarchal equivalent of Most Secret.

Fixer recoiled; Halloran had to intervene instantly to stop his hand before it halted the search. Curiosity was not a powerful drive for a kzin, and shame was a *very* effective deterrent.

A basic definition flashed up. "*That mass created during the first instants of the universe, separated from kzinti space-time and detectable only by weak gravitational interaction. No light or other communication possible between the domain of specter mass and kzinti space-time.*"

Halloran grinned for the first time in seven days. Now he had it—he could *feel* the solution coming. He cued more detail.

"*Stellar masses of specter matter have been detected, but are rare. None has been found in living memory. These masses, in the specter domain, must be enormous, on the order of hundreds of masses of the sun*"—the star of Kzin, more massive and a little cooler than Sol—"*for their gravitational influence is on the order of .6 [base 8] Kzin suns. The physics of the specter domain must differ widely from our own. Legends warn against searching for ghost stars, though details are lost or forbidden by the Patriarchy."*

Not a black hole or a dark star, but a star in a counter-universe. Human physicists had discovered the possible existence of *shadow mass* in the late twentieth century—Halloran remembered that much from his physics classes. The enormously powerful superstring theory of particles implied *shadow mass* pretty much as the Kzinti entry described it. None had been detected. . . .

Who would have thought the Earth was so near to a ghost star?

And now, Kfraksha-Admiral was recommending what the kzinti had heretofore forbidden—close approach to a ghost star to gain a gravitational advantage. The kzinti ships would appear, to human monopole detectors, to be leaving the system—retreating, although slowly. Then the fleet would decelerate and discard its monopoles, sending them on the same outward course, and swing around the ghost star, gaining speed from the star's angular momentum. No fusion drives would be used, so as not to alarm human sentries. Slowly, the fleet would swing back into the solar system, and within a kzinti year, attack the worlds of men. Undetected, unsuspected, the kzinti fleet could end the war then and there. The monopoles would be within retrieval distance.

And all it would require was a little kzinti patience, a rare virtue indeed.

Someone scratched softly at the ID plate on his hatch. Halloran did not assume the Fixer persona, but projected the Fixer image, before answering. The hatch opened a safe crack, and Halloran saw the baleful, rheumy eye of Telepath peering in.

"I have bested you already," the Fixer image growled. "You wish to challenge for a shameful rematch?" Not something Fixer need grant in any case, now that his status was established.

"I have a problem which I must soon bring to the attention of Kfraksha-Admiral," Telepath said, with the edge of a despicable whimper.

"Why come to me?"

"You are the problem. I hear sounds from you. I *remember* things from you. And I have dreams in which you appear, but not as you are now . . . sometimes I am you. I am the lowest, but I am important to this fleet, especially with the death of *War Loot*'s Telepath. I am the last Telepath in the fleet. My health is important—"

"Yes, yes! What do you want?"

"Have you been taking the telepath drug?"

"No."

"I can tell . . . you speak truth, yet you hide something."

The kzin could not now deeply read Halloran without making an effort, but Halloran was "leaking." Just as he had never been able to quell his "intuition," he could not stop this basic hemorrhage of mental contents. The kzin's drug-weakened mind was there to receive, perhaps more vulnerable because the subconscious trickle of sensation and memory was alien to it.

"I hide nothing. Go away," the Fixer-image demanded harshly.

"Questions first. What is an 'Esterhazy'? What are these sounds I hear, and what is a 'Haydn'? Why do I feel emotions which have no names?"

The kzin's pronunciation was not precise, but it was close enough. "I do not know. Go away."

Halloran began to close the door, but Telepath wailed and stuck his leathery digits into the crack. Halloran instinctively stopped the hatch to prevent damage. A kzin would not have. . . .

"I cannot see Kfraksha-Admiral. I am the lowest . . . but I feel danger! We are approaching very great danger. My shields are weakening and my sensitivity increases even with lower doses of the drug. . . . Do you know where we are going? I can feel this danger deep, in a place my addiction has only lightly touched. . . . Others feel it too. There is restlessness. I must report what I feel! Tell the commander—"

Cringing, Halloran pressed the lever and the door continued to close. Telepath screamed and pulled out his digits in time to avoid loosing more than a tip and one sheathed claw.

That did it. Halloran began to shake uncontrollably. Sobbing, he buried his face in his hands. Death seemed very immediate, and pain, and brutality. He had stepped into the lion's den. The lions were closing in, and he was weakening. He had never faced anything so horrible before. The kzinti were insane. They had no softer feelings, nothing but war and destruction and conquest. . . .

And yet, within him there were fragments of Fixer-of-Weapons to tell him differently. There was courage, incredible strength, great vitality.

"Not enough," he whispered, removing his face from his hands. Not enough to redeem them, certainly, and not enough to make him feel any less revulsion. If he could, he would wipe all kzinti out of existence. If he could just expand his mind enough, reach out across time and space to the distant homeworld of kzin, touch them with a deadliness . . .

The main problem with a talent like Halloran's was hubris. Aspiring to god-like ascendancy over others, even kzinti. That way lay more certain madness.

A kzin wouldn't think that way, Halloran knew. *A kzin would scream and leap upon a tool of power like that.* "Kzin have it easier," he muttered.

Time to marshal his resources. How long could he stay alive on the kzinti flagship?

If he assumed the Fixer persona, no more than three days. They would still be rounding the ghost star. . . .

If he somehow managed to take control of the ship, and could be Halloran all the time, he might last much longer. And to what end?

To bring the *Sons Contend With Bloody Fangs* back to human space? That would be useful, but not terribly important—the kzinti would have discarded their gravity polarizers. Human engineers had already studied the hulk of *War Loot*, not substantially different from *Sons Contend.*

But he wanted to *survive*. On that Halloran and Fixer-Halloran were agreed. He could feel survival as a clean, metallic necessity, cutting him off from all other considerations. The Belter pilots and their initiation . . . Coming to an understanding of sorts with his father. Early's wish-list. What he knew about kzinti . . .

That could be transmitted back. He did not need to survive to deliver that. But such a transmission would take time, a debriefing of weeks would be invaluable.

Survival.

Simple life.

To *win*.

Thorough shit or not, Halloran valued his miserable life.

Perhaps I'm weak, like Telepath. Sympathetic. Particularly towards myself.

But the summing up was clear and unavoidable. The best thing he could do would be to find some way to inactivate at least this ship, and perhaps the whole kzinti fleet. Grandiose scheme. At the very top of Early's wish-list. All else by the wayside.

And he could not do it by going on a rampage. He had to be smarter than the kzinti; he had to show how humans, with all their love of life and self-sympathy, could beat the self-confident, savage invaders.

No more being Fixer. Time to use Fixer as a front, and be a complete, fully aware Halloran.

Telepath whimpered in his sleep. There was no one near to hear him in this corridor; disgust could be as effective as status and fear in securing privacy.

Hands were lifting him. *Huge* hands, tearing him away from Mother's side. His own hands were tiny, so tiny as he clung with all four limbs to Mother's fur.

She was growling, screaming at the males with the Y-shaped poles who pinned her to the wicker mats, lashing out at them as they laughed and dodged. Hate and fury stank through the dark air of the hut.

"Maaaa!" he screamed. "Maaaa!"

The hands bore him up, crushed him against a muscular side that smelled of leather and metal and *kzintosh*, male kzin.

They will eat me, they will eat me! cried instinct. He lashed out with needle-sharp baby claws, and the booming voice above him laughed and swore, holding the wriggling bundle out at arm's length.

"*This one has spirit,*" the Voice said.

"*Puny,*" another replied dismissively. "*I will not rear it. Send it to the creche.*"

They carried him out into the bright sunlight, and he blinked against the pain of it. Fangs loomed above him, and he hissed and spat; a hand pushed meat into his mouth. It was good, warm and bloody; he tore loose chunks and bolted them, ears still folded down. From the other enclosures came the growls and screams of females frightened by the scent of loss, and behind him his mother gave one howl of grief after another.

Telepath half-woke, grunting and starting, pink bat-ears flaring wide as he took in the familiar subliminal noises of pumps and ventilators.

He was laughing, walking across the quadrangle. Faces turned toward him

—*naked faces?*—

Mouths turning to round O shapes of shock.

—*Flat mouths? Flat teeth?*—

Students and teachers were turning toward him, and he knew they saw the headmaster, buck-naked and piriapically erect. He laughed and waved again, thinking how Old Man Velasquez would explain *this*—

Telepath struggled. Something struck him on the nose and he started upright, pink tongue reflexively washing at the source of the welcome, welcome pain. The horror of the nightmare slipped away, too alien to comprehend with the waking mind.

"Silence, *sthondat*-sucker!" Third Gunner snarled, aiming a kick that thudded drumlike on Telepath's ribs. Another harness-buckle was in one hand, ready to throw. "Stop screaming in your sleep!"

Telepath widened his ears and flattened his fur in propitiation as he crouched; Third Gunner was not a great intellect, but he was enormous and touchy even for a young kzin. After a moment the hulking shape turned and padded off down the corridor to his own doss, grumbling and twitching his whiskers. The smaller kzin sank down again to his thin pallet, curling into a fetal ball and covering his nose with his hands, wrapping his tail around the whole bundle of misery. He quivered, his matted fur wrinkling in odd patterns, and forced his eyes to close.

I must sleep, he thought. His fingers twitched toward the pouch with his drug, but that only made things worse. *I must sleep; my health is important to the fleet.* Unless he was rested he could not read minds on command. Without that, he was useless and therefore dead, and Telepath did not want to die.

But if he slept, he dreamed. For the last four sleeps the dreams of his kittenhood had been almost welcome. Eerie combinations of sound plucked at the corners of his mind as he dozed, as precise as mathematics but carrying overtones of feelings that were not *his*—

He jerked awake again. *Mother*, he thought, through a haze of fatigue. *I want my mother.*

The alienness of the dreams no longer frightened him so much.

What was really terrifying was the feeling he was beginning to *understand* them. . . .

Halloran flexed and raised his hands, crouching and growling. Technician's-Assistant stepped aside at the junction of the two corridors, but Fire-Control-Technician retracted his ears and snarled, dropping his lower jaw toward his chest. Aide-to-Commanders had gone down on his belly, crawling aside. Beside the disguised human Chief-Operations-Officer bulked out his fur and responded in kind.

Sure looks different without Fixer, Halloran thought as he sidled around the confrontation.

The kzinti were almost muzzle-to-muzzle, roaring at each other in tones that set the metal around them to vibrating in sympathy; thin black lips curled back from wet half-inch fangs, and the ruffled fur turned their bodies into bristling sausage shapes. The black-leather shapes of their four-fingered hands were almost skeletal, the long claws shining like curves of liquid jet. Dim orange-red light made Halloran squint and peer. The walls here in this section of officer country were covered with holographic murals; a necessity, since kzinti were very vulnerable to sensory deprivation. Twisted thorny orange vegetation crawled across shattered rock under a lowering sky the color of powdered brickdust, and in the foreground two kzinti had overturned something that looked like a giant spiked turtle with a bone club for a tail. They were burying their muzzles in its belly, ripping out long stretches of intestine.

Abruptly, the two high-ranking kzin stepped back and let their fur fall into normal position, walking past each other as if nothing had happened.

Nothing did, a ghost of Fixer said at the back of Halloran's head; the thin psychic voice was mildly puzzled. *Normal courtesy*. Passing by without playing at challenge would be an insult, showing contempt for one not worthy of interest. Real challenge would be against regulations, now.

Chief-Operations-Officer scratched at the ID plate on the commander's door, releasing Kfraksha-Admiral's coded scent. A muffled growl answered.

Kfraksha-Admiral was seated at his desk, worrying the flesh off a heavy bone held down with his hands. A long shred of tendon came off as he snapped his head back and forth, and his jaws made a wet *clop* sound as he bolted it.

"Is all proceeding according to plan?" he asked.

"Yes, Dominant One," Chief-Operations-Officer said humbly.

"*Then why are you taking up my valuable time?*" Kfraksha-Admiral screamed, extending his claws.

"Abasement," Chief-Operations-Officer said. He flattened to the floor in formal mode; the others joined him. "The jettisoning of the monopoles and gravity polarizer components has proceeded according to your plans. There are problems."

"Describe them."

"A much higher than normal rate of replacement for

all solid-state electronic components, Kfraksha-Admiral," the engineer said. "Computers and control systems particularly. Increasing as a function of our approach to the ghost star. Also personnel problems."

Kfraksha-Admiral's whiskers and fur moved in patterns that meant lively curiosity; discipline was the problem any kzin commander would anticipate, although perhaps not so soon.

"Mutiny?" he said almost eagerly.

"No. Increased rates of impromptu dueling, sometimes against regulations. Allegations of murderous intent unsupported by evidence. Superstitions. Several cases of catatonia and insanity leading to liquidation by superiors. Suicides. Also rumors."

"*Hrrrr!*" Kfraksha-Admiral said. Suicide was an admission of cowardice, and very rare.

Time to fish or be *bait*, Halloran decided.

Gently, he probed at the consciousness of the kzin, feeling the three-things-at-once sensation of indecision. Kfraksha-Admiral knew something of why the Patriarchy forbade mention of phenomenon; because the Conservors of the Ancestral Past couldn't figure out what was involved. Inexplicable and repeated bad luck, usually; the kzin was feeling his fur try to bristle. Kzinti *believed* in luck, as firmly as they believed in games theory. Eternal shame for Kfraksha-Admiral if he turned back now. His cunning suggested aborting the mission; an unwary male would never have become a fleet commander. Gut feeling warred with it; even for a kzin, Kfraksha-Admiral was aggressive; otherwise he could never have achieved or held his position.

Shame, Halloran whispered, ever so gently. It was not difficult. Easier than it had ever been before, and now he felt *justified*.

Eternal disgrace for retreating, his mind intruded softly. *Two years of futility already. Defeat by plant-eaters*. Sickening images of unpointed grinding teeth chewing roots. *Endless challenges*. A commander turned cautious had a line of potential rivals light-years long, waiting for stand-down from Active Status. Kzin were extremely territorial; modern kzin had transferred the instinct from physical position to rank.

Glory if we win. More glory for great dangers overcome. Conquest Hero Kfraksha-Admiral—no, Kfraksha-Tchee, a full name, unimaginable wealth, planetary systems of slaves with a fully industrialized society. Many sons. Generations to worship my memory.

The commander's ears unfolded as he relaxed, decisions made. "This is a perilous course. Notify *Flashing Claws*"—a Swift Hunter–class courier, lightly armed but lavishly equipped with drive and fuel—"to stand by on constant datalink." The Patriarchy would know what happened. "The fleet will proceed as planned. Slingshot formation, with *Sons Contend With Bloody Fangs* occupying the innermost trajectory."

That would put the flagship at the point of the roughly conical formation the fleet was to assume; the troopships with their loads of infantry would be at the rear. "Redouble training schedules. Increase rations." Well-fed Kzin were more amenable to discipline. And—"Rumors of what?"

"That we approach the Darkstar of Ill-Omen, Dominant One."

Kfraksha-Admiral leaned forward, his claws prickling at the files of printout on his desk. "*That was confidential information!*" He glared steadily at Chief-Operations-Officer, extreme discourtesy among carnivores. The subordinate extended hands and ears, with an aura of sullenness.

"I have told no one of the nature of the object we approach," he said. Few kzinti would trouble to prod and poke for information not immediately useful, either. "The ship and squadron commanders have been informed; so have the senior staff."

"Hrrr. Chirrru. You—" a jerk of the tail towards Aide-to-Commanders. "Fetch me Telepath."

Halloran slumped down on the mat in his quarters, head cradled in his hands, fighting to control his nausea. *Murphy, don't tell me I'm developing an alergy to kzin,* he thought, holding his shaking hands out before him. The mottled spots were probably some deficiency disease, or his immune system might be giving up under the strain of ingesting all these not-quite-earthlike proteins. He belched acid, swallowed past a painfully dry throat, remembering his last meeting with his father. A kzin ship was like the *real* Arizona desert, and it was sucking the moisture out of his tissues, no matter how much he drank. A dry cold, though. It held down the soupy smell of dried rancid sweat that surrounded him; that had nearly given him away half a dozen times.

A sharp pain thrilled up one finger. Halloran looked down and found he had been absently stropping nonexistent claws on the panel of corklike material set next to the pallet. A broken fingernail was bent back halfway. He prodded it back into place, shuddering, tied one of the antiseptic pads around it and secured it with a strip of cloth before he lowered himself with painful slowness to his back. Slow salt-heavy tears filled the corners of his eyes and ran painfully down the chapped skin of his face.

It was easier to be Fixer. Fixer did not hurt. Fixer was not lonely. Fixer did not feel guilt; shame, perhaps, but never guilt.

Fixer doesn't exist. I am Lawrence Halloran Jr. He closed his eyes and tried to let his breathing sink into a regular rhythm. It was difficult for more reasons than the pain; every time he began to drop off, he would jerk awake again with unreasoning dread. Not of the nightmares, just dread of *something*.

Intuition. Halloran had always believed in intuition. Or maybe just the trickle of fear from the crew, but he should not be *that* sensitive, even with fatigue and weakness wearing down his shields. His talent should be weaker, not stronger.

Enough. "My status is that of a complete shit, but my health is important to the mission," he mumbled sardonically to himself. Sleep was like falling—

—and the others were chasing him again, through the corridors of the creche. Pain shot in under his ribs as he bounded along four-footed, and his tongue lolled dry and grainy. They were all bigger than him, and there were a double handful of them! Bright light stabbed at his eyes as he ran out into the exercise yard, up the tumbled rocks of the pile in the center, gritty ocher sandstone under his hands and feet. Nowhere to run but the highest . . .

Fear cut through his fatigue as he came erect on the central spire. He was above them! The high-status kits would think he was challenging them!

Squalls of rage confirmed it as the orange-and-spotted tide boiled out of the doorway and into the vast quadrangle of scrub and sand. Tails went rigid, claws raked toward him; he stood and screamed back, but he could hear the quaver in it, and the impulse to grovel and spread his ears was almost irresistible. Hate flowed over him with the scent of burning ginger, varied only by the individual smells of the other children. Rocks flew around him as they poured up the miniature crags; something struck him over one eye. Vision blurred as the nictitating membranes swept down, and blood poured over one. The smell of it was like death, but the others screeched louder as they caught the waft.

Hands and feet gripped him as he slumped down on the hard rock, clawing and yanking hair and lifting, and then he was flying. Instinct rotated his head down, but he was already too stunned to get his hands and feet well under him; he landed sprawling across an edge of sandstone and felt ribs crack. Then the others were on him, mauling, and he curled into a protective ball but two of them had his tail, they were stretching it out and raising rocks in their free hands and *crack* and *crack*—

Halloran woke, shuddering and wincing at pain in an organ he did not possess. Several corridors away, Telepath screamed until the ratings dossed near him lost all patience and broke open an arms locker to get a stunner.

"Dreams? Explain yourself, *kshat*," Kfraksha-Admiral growled.

Telepath ventured a nervous lick of his nose, eyes

darting around, too genuinely terrified to resent being called the kzin equivalent of a rabbit.

"Nothing. I said nothing of dreams," he said, then shrieked as the commander's claws raked along the side of his muzzle.

"You dare to contradict me?"

"I abase mysel—"

"Silence! You distinctly said 'dreams' when I asked you to determine the leakage of secret information."

"Leaks. First Fixer-of-Weapons was leaking. He is strong. He *leaks*. I run from him but I cannot hide in sleep. Such shame. Now *more* are leaking. The officers dream of the Ghost Star. Ancestors who died without honor haunt it . . . their hands reach up to drag us down to nameless rot. One feels it. All feel it—"

"Silence! Silence!" Kfraksha-Admiral roared, striking open-handed. Even then he retained enough control not to use his claws; this thing *was* the last Telepath in the fleet, after all, even if insanity was reducing its usefulness.

And even such a sorry excuse for a kzin shouldn't be much harmed by being beaten unconscious.

"You find time to groom?" Kfraksha-Admiral asked sullenly.

Finagle, Halloran swore inwardly, drawing the Fixer persona more tightly around him. The last sleep-cycle had seen a drastic deterioration in *everyone's* grooming, except his memorized projection. The commander's pelt was not quite matted; it would be a long time before he looked as miserable as Telepath—Finagle alone knew what Telepath looked like now, he seemed to have vanished—but he was definitely scruffy. The entire bridge crew looked peaked, and several were absent, their places taken by younger, less-scarred understudies. Some of those understudies had new bandages, evidence that their superiors' usefulness had deteriorated to the point where the commander would allow self-promotion. The human's talent told him the dark cavern of the command deck smelled of fear and throttled rage and bewilderment; the skin crawled down his spine as he sensed it.

Kzinti did not respond well to frustration. They also did not expect answers to rhetorical questions.

Kfraksha-Admiral turned to Chrung-Fleet-Communications Officer. "Summarize."

"*Hero's Lair* still does not report," that kzin said dully.

That was the first of the troop-transports, going in on a trajectory that would leave them "behind" the cruisers, dreadnoughts, and stingship carriers when the fleet finally made its out-of-elliptic slingshot approach to Earth. Kfraksha-Admiral had calculated that Earth was probably the softest major human target, and less likely to be alert. Go in undetected, take out major defenses and space-industrial centers, land the surface-troops; the witless hordes of humankind's fifteen billions would be hostages against counterattack.

If things go well, Halloran thought, easing a delicate tendril into the commander's consciousness. *Murphy rules the kzin, as well as humans.* Wearily: *When do things ever go well?*

—and the long silky grass blew in the dry cool wind, that was infinitely clean and empty. His Sire and the other grown males were grouped around the carcass, replete, lapping at drinks in shallow, beautifully fashioned silver cups. He and the other kits were round-stomached and content, play-sparring lazily, and he lay on his back batting at the bright-winged insect that hovered over his nose, until Sire put a hand on his chest and leaned over to rasp a roughly loving tongue across his ears—

"It is well, it is well," Kfraksha-Admiral crooned softly, almost inaudibly. Then he came to himself with a start, looking around as heads turned toward him.

Finagle, I set him off on a memory-fugue! Halloran thought, feeling the kzin's panic and rising anger, the tinge of suspicion beneath that.

"All must admire Kfraksha-Admiral's strategic sense," Halloran-Fixer said hastily. "Light losses, for a strategic gain of the size this operation promises."

Kfraksha-Admiral signed curt assent, turning his attention from the worthless sycophant. Behind Fixer's mask, Halloran's human face contorted in a savage grin. Manipulating Kfraksha-Admiral's subconscious was more fun than haunting the other kzin. *Even for a ratcat, he's a son-of-a . . . pussy, I suppose. Singleminded, too.* Relatively easy to keep from wondering what was causing all this—*I wish I knew*—and tightly, tightly focus on getting through the next few hours. Closest approach soon.

And it was all so *easy*. He was *unstoppable*. . . .

Scabs broke and he tasted the salt of blood. *I'm not going to make it.* He ground his jaws and felt the loosening teeth wobble in their sockets. Death was a bitterness, no glory in it, only this foul decay. *Maybe I shouldn't make it. I'm too dangerous.* His face had been pockmarked with open sores, the last time he looked. Maybe that was how he looked inside.

So easy, sucking the kzinti crews down into a cycle of waking nightmare. As if they were doing it to themselves. Fixer howled laughter from within his soul.

"I have the information by the throat, but I still do not understand," Physicist said, staring around wildly. He was making the *chiruu-chiruu* sounds of kzinti distress. *Dealer-With-Very-Small-and-Large* was a better translation of his name/title. "I do not understand!"

Most of the bridge equipment was closed down. Ventilation still functioned, internal fields, all based on simple feedback systems. Computers, weapons, communications, all had grown too erratic to trust. A few lasers still linked the functioning units of the fleet.

Outside, the stars shone with jeering brightness. Of the Ghost Star there was no trace; no visible light, no occlusion of the background . . . and instruments more sophisticated had given out hours ago. Many of the bridge crew still stayed at their posts, but their scent had soured; the steel *wtsai* knives at their belts attracted fingers like unconscious lures.

"Explain," Kfraksha-Admiral rasped.

"The values, the records just say that physical law in the shadow-matter realm is unlike kzinti timespace . . . and there is crossover this close! The effect increases exponentially as we approach the center of mass; we must be within the radius the object occupies in the other continuum. The cosmological constants are varying. Quantum effects. The U/R threshold of quantum probability functions itself is increasing, that is why all electronic equipment becomes unreliable—probability cascades are approaching the macrocosmic level."

Kfraksha-Admiral's tail was quivering-rigid, and he panted until thin threads of spittle drooled down from the corners of his mouth.

"Then we shall win! We are nearly at point of closest approach. Our course is purely ballistic. Systems will regain their integrity as we recede from the area of singularity."

Murphy wins again, Halloran thought wearily, slumping back against the metal wall. His body was shaking, and he felt a warm trickle down one leg. *He's right.* The irony of it was enough to make him laugh, except that that would have hurt too much. Halloran had done the *noble* thing. He had put everything into controlling Kfraksha-Admiral, blinding him to the voices of prudence. . . .

And the bleeping ratcat was right *after all.*

His shields frayed as the human despaired. Frayed more strongly than he had ever felt, even drunk or coming, until he felt/was Kfraksha-Admiral's ferocious triumph, Physicist's jumble of shifting equations, Telepath's hand pressing the ampule of his last drug capsule against his throat in massive overdose, *why have the kzinti disintegrated like this—*

Halloran would never have understood it. He lacked the knowledge of physics—the ARM had spent centuries discouraging that—but Physicist was next to him, and the datalink was strong. No kzinti could have understood it; they were simply not introspective enough. Halloran-Fixer *knew*, with the whole-argument suddenness of revelation; knew as a composite creature that had experienced the inwardness of Kzin and Man together.

The conscious brain is a computer, but one of a very special kind. Not anything like a digital system; that was one reason why true Artificial Intelligence had taken so long to achieve, and had proven so worthless once found.

Consciousness does not operate on mathematical algorithms, with their prefixed structures. It is a quantum process, indeterminate in the most literal sense. Thoughts became conscious—decision was taken, will exercised—when the nervous system amplified them past the one-graviton threshold level. So was insight, a direct contact with the paramathematical frame of reality.

They couldn't know, Halloran realized. Kzinti physics was excellent but their biological sciences primitive by human standards.

And I *know what's driving them crazy*, he realized. Telepathy was another threshold effect. Any conscious creature possessed *some* ability. The Ghost Star was amplifying it to a terrifying level, even as it disabled the computers by turning their off/on synapses to off *and* on. Humans might be able to endure it; Man is a gregarious species.

Not the kzinti. Not those hard, stoic, isolated killer souls. Forever guarded, forever wary, disgusted by the very thought of such an involuntary sharing . . . whose only glimpse of telepathy was creatures like Telepath. Utter horror, to feel the boundaries of their personalities fraying, merging, becoming *not-self*.

Halloran knew what he had to do. *It's the right thing.* Fixer-of-Weapons stirred exultantly in his tomb of flesh. *Die like a Hero!* he battle-screeched.

Letting go was like thinning out, like dying, like being free for the first time in all his life. Halloran's awareness flared out, free of the constraints of distance, touching lightly at the raw newly forged connections between thousands of minds in the Ghost Sun's grip. *I get to be omnipotent just before the end*, he thought in some distant corner. To his involuntary audience: *MEET EACH OTHER.*

The shock of the steel was almost irrelevant, the reflex that wrenched him around to face Telepath automatic. Undeceived at last, the kzin's drug-dilated eyes met the human's. Halloran slumped forward, opening his mouth, but there was no sound or breath as

—he—

"Get out of my dreams!"

—the human—

—fell—

—released—

"Shit," Halloran murmured. His heels drummed on the deck. *Mom.*

The roar from Colonel Buford Early's office was enough to bring his aide-de-camp's head through the door. One glance at his Earther superior was enough to send it back through the hatch.

Early swore again, more quietly but with a scatological invention that showed both his inventiveness and his age; it had been *many* generations since some of those Anglo-Saxon monosyllables had been in common use.

Then he played the audio again; without correction, but listening carefully for the rhythm of the phrasing under the accent imposed by a vocal system and palate very unlike that of *Homo sapiens sapiens*:

"—so you see"—it sounded more like *zo uru t'zee*—"it's not really relevant whether I'm Halloran or whether he's dead and I'm a kzinti with delusions. Halloran's . . . memories were more used to having an alien in his head than Telepath's were, poor bleeping bastard. The Fleet won't be giving you any trouble, the few that are still alive will be pretty thoroughly insane.

"On the other hand," the harsh nonhuman voice continued, "remembering what happened to Fixer I really don't think it would be all that advisable to come back. And you know what? I've decided that I really don't owe any of you that much. Died for the cause already, haven't I?"

A rasping sound, something between a growl and a purr: kzinti laughter. "I'm seeing a lot of things more clearly now. Amazing what a different set of nerves and hormones can do. My talent's almost as strong now as it was . . . before, and I've got a *lot* less in the way of inhibitions. It's the Patriarchy that ought to be worried, but of course they'll never know."

Then a hesitation: "Tell my Sire . . . tell Dad I died a Hero, would you, Colonel?"

Epilogue

The kzin finished grooming his pelt to a lustrous shine before he followed Medical-Technician to the deepsleep chamber of the Swift Hunter courier *Flashing Claws*. His face was expressionless as the cover lowered above him, and then his ears wrinkled with glee; there would be nobody to see until they arrived in the Alpha Centauri system a decade from now.

The Patriarchy had never had a Telepath who earned a full name before.

Too risky! Telepath wailed.

Kshat, Fixer thought with contempt.

Shut up both of you, Halloran replied. *Or I'll start thinking about salads again.* All of them understood the grin that showed his/their fangs.

The Patriarchy had never had one like Halloran before, either.